Books should be returned or renewed by the last
date above. Renew by phone **03000 41 31 31** or
online *www.kent.gov.uk/libs*

AVAILABLE FROM T.M.E. WALSH

For All Our Sins

The Principle of Evil

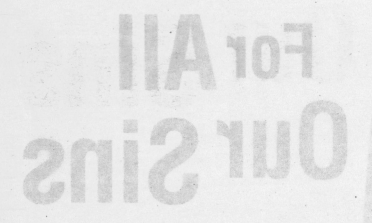

For All Our Sins

CARINA

Carina UK
An imprint of HarperCollins*Publishers*
1 London Bridge Street
London SE1 9GF
www.carinauk.com

This paperback edition 2016
1
First published in Great Britain by
Carina an imprint of HarperCollins*Publishers* 2016

ISBN: 978-0-263-92739-9

Set by CPI - Group(UK) Limited,
Printed and bound by CPI Group (UK) Ltd, Croydon, CR0 4YY

Tania (T. M. E.) Walsh began writing full time after becoming a casualty to the recession in late 2008. She successfully self-published the first two novels in the DCI Claire Winters series in 2013, and both appeared in the various best-selling Amazon Kindle charts before being picked up by Carina UK in 2015. In 2011 Tania was the winner of the Wannabe a Writer competition sponsored by Writing Magazine and judged by Matt Bates, the Fiction buyer for WHSmith Travel.

Although writing now takes up most of her time, Tania has previously produced digital artwork that was published on a DVD-ROM for ImagineFX magazine's FXPosé section twice in the early and latter part of 2007, which has been published worldwide. Tania is currently working on a new standalone novel and a third book in the DCI Claire Winters series. She lives in Hertfordshire with her husband and young daughter. You can follow her at tmewalsh.com, facebook.com/tmewalsh or @tmewalsh.

For Daniel and Eden

The room smelled of blood, so thick that she could almost taste it...

CHAPTER 1

'Bless me, Father, for I have sinned.'

Amelia scarcely heard the words escape her mouth as she crossed herself and clasped the rosary tighter in her hands.

The little dark-red wooden beads didn't give her the strength they once did. As she stared at the silver cross that dangled between her fingers, she knew her traditional faith in God had died a long time ago and part of her felt like a fraud.

From inside the confessional, Father Malcolm Wainwright shifted his weight awkwardly, but never broke his concentration. He continued to remain silent, awaiting the inevitable confession.

But the confession never came.

The silence felt as though it would swallow him whole. He turned his head slightly, peering through the ornate carvings of the wooden partition, but could see little in the darkness.

His eyes were not what they used to be but he could just make out the outline of her face, and where the light crept through the small cracks in the wood, he saw the most beautiful shade of red hair. Like fire, it seemed to reflect in his eyes, flecks of light dancing across his iris.

'Take your time, my child. Trust in God.'

Amelia closed her eyes, squeezed her rosary, but remained silent.

Then she turned to face him, her hands placed flat
against the partition, her fingertips poking through the
spaces in the wood.

The cross on the rosary was swaying back and forth
against the wood, like a crude attempt at Morse code.

Wainwright saw her eyes for the first time as a stray
beam of light caught the brightest shades of green, the
colour of a turquoise sea.

Her eyes started to mist as she brought her face closer,
her breathing heavy, her lips just inches from his face.

'Do you remember the girl, Father?' Her voice rasped
from within her throat as her demeanour changed.

Wainwright frowned as Amelia contorted her body, until
she was pressed against the wooden partition.

'You remember, Father? She tried to tell, to cry for help.'
Her voice began to rise. 'There were times you could've
stopped it. All the pain she suffered… You had the chance
to set her soul free, but instead you did nothing.'

Wainwright felt the air in the room change, and for the
first time in all his years in the ministry, he felt what could
only be described as fear.

What could I have done?

Amelia saw the recognition flicker across his eyes. Her
mouth pulled into a grin, her eyes knowing. 'There's blood on
your hands, Father. Can't you smell it, feel it on your skin?'

Wainwright snapped.

'You've mistaken me for someone else,' he said, trying
to control his voice. 'I want you to leave immediately
and…' He trailed off as he heard someone approach the
curtain to his compartment.

The last thing Wainwright saw was the flash of light
against the steel of a slim blade as the curtain was pulled
aside, just seconds before the knife tore through his robes
and sliced through his withered skin.

Pain ripped through every muscle in his body. As blood soaked through his garments, he swore he could feel his soul screaming for release.

Looking up to see his attacker he saw only the woman, now standing in front of him. Her hair was like fire with the glow of sunlight cascading through the stained-glass windows behind her.

She grasped his hair, slammed his head back against the confessional, and brought her face closer to his. Despite the pain in his body, he could smell her sweet perfume so vividly.

'You remember this face, Father.' Her lips were just inches away from his. 'Do you remember these eyes? My voice?'

Wainwright tried to scream but blood pooled in his throat, a thick taste of copper.

He knew her. And he silently damned her to Hell.

His eyelids fluttered involuntary as the energy began to drain from his body.

'What does it feel like to hurt, Father? The pain you feel is nothing compared to the years of torment you let be inflicted on the innocent. Too many years you've kept that secret that stops you from sleeping at night.' She shook her head. 'There's blood on your hands, priest…you shouldn't have helped him that day.'

Tears pricked Wainwright's eyes. *How does she know? There were only three there that day…and the other.*

Amelia took the cross hanging from her rosary and pressed it hard against his dry lips.

Wainwright's eyes widened, begging in silent prayer for forgiveness.

'For all the years you've preached your poison, and for the tormented souls who will never be free from your idea of faith, I shall unite you with God, and *He* will decide the punishment for your soul.'

Wainwright tried to fight her off as she forced the cross past his lips and into his throat. Much stronger than she appeared, Amelia pushed his jaw up hard, and pulled on the rosary beads until they broke free.

They scattered to the floor, dancing over the flagstones, as he began to choke.

His lungs felt like they were on fire, desperate for air. He fell to his knees, his hands reaching up and clutching at Amelia's clothes.

She stepped back and watched him crawl after her, one hand at his throat and the other reaching out, silently begging.

Amelia's face was resolute as he wheezed and spluttered, his face turning vivid shades of blue and purple. He collapsed face down, his forehead hitting the flagstones hard. His eyes felt heavy. He let them close, as his breath slowed to a whisper.

Wainwright's last thoughts were not of his childhood or a fond trip down memory lane. They were of a moment in a not so distant part of history.

Yes, Wainwright remembered her.

He also remembered a large oak staircase bathed in blood and a door closing, containing the screams within. Even now he knew it was too late to repent and change the fate of his soul.

He recalled a quote he'd read once. Something that had stayed with him all this time, scratching away in the back of his mind: *The dead cannot cry out for justice. It is a duty of the living to do so for them.*

Subconsciously, Wainwright had always known that one day his past would come back to haunt him.

Now the time had come, he welcomed it with open arms.

CHAPTER 2

Ice-blue irises pulled tight leaving the pupils the size of a pin prick as she stared skyward, hand raised to her brow, useless against the might of the sun's rays.

Detective Chief Inspector Claire Winters felt a shiver shoot up her spine, like icy skeletal fingers scraping against her skin, despite the heat of the day. It was early morning, but the temperature on the dash of her car had said it was close to twenty-four degrees already.

Her shirt was sticking to her back underneath her suit jacket like a second skin. The air was muggy, close, pulling at each breath she took, yet despite this she still felt like ice, right down to her bones.

A feeling of dread pulled at her inside as she lowered the sunglasses from the top of her head back down on her face.

She stared at the door ahead, the entrance to the looming tower block opposite her. A place she'd just left. A place she hated. A place that had become more somewhere to call home than her house several miles out of Haverbridge.

Claire's mind drifted to dark thoughts. They came thick and fast lately. Like a nightmare that didn't end after she woke each morning. It continued long through the days. Sometimes it threatened to swallow her whole.

Sometimes Claire wondered if perhaps that'd be easier.

Just let all the fight be torn out of her and scattered to the wind, until all that remained was an empty shell.

Wouldn't that be too easy?

She felt her BlackBerry vibrating inside her trouser pocket. She'd turned the ringer off whilst she'd been inside the building, inside that wretched flat that housed someone she'd long since come to loathe and love in equal measure.

She glanced at the screen; her grip tightened on the phone resting in her palm. Her finger hovered over the *Answer* button.

How easy it would be to just throw it away, forget her job, forget this life. Forget everything that'd passed and start again.

This is not you, she told herself. *He does not define who you are, what you do, what comes next.* She glanced up at the tower block again as she answered the call.

Take back the control.

'DCI Winters,' she said. Her lips were dry, cracked, sore. She touched her fingers on her free hand to her bottom lip, pulled them away. Tiny dots of blood were on her fingertips.

'Guv?' said Detective Constable Gabriel Harper at the other end of the phone.

Claire snapped back to the here and now. She'd detected something in his voice that was different. Whatever he was going to say, wasn't going to be good.

'What is it, Gabe?'

There was a drawn-out pause. Claire could hear his breathing. It was far from normal. A new sensation gripped at her insides. She bit down on her bottom lip, made herself turn away from the tower block.

'What's wrong, Harper?' she said as she crossed the road towards where she'd parked her car earlier, a steely edge returning to her voice.

She heard Harper's sharp intake of breath. 'Guv, this isn't something I can explain over the phone.' He paused. 'We need you back now, something's happened at one of the local churches. Reports are coming in about a woman collapsing outside St Mary's, completely covered in blood…someone else's, not her own.'

CHAPTER 3

The coffee was like lava over his tongue, scorching the roof of his mouth, but for Detective Sergeant Michael Diego there were worse things in life than bad coffee.

With his unwashed hair and two-day-old stubble, he was still a handsome man, but the insomnia suffered last night through to the early hours of this morning was taking its toll before the clock had struck nine this morning.

He'd been out of the office for a few hours, and now that he was back in time for lunch, he didn't feel like working.

Haverbridge had that effect on him. Nestled in the county of Hertfordshire, the large town was fast becoming a magnet for outsiders and, despite the recession, a construction haven.

Just thirty miles north of London, Haverbridge was attracting people from all walks of life and, being somewhat averse to change, Michael barely raised a smile at the prospect of more investment in his home town, despite the prosperity it could bring.

He hated what was overflowing from the London boroughs. He liked the old, hated the new.

Modernisation was something he was reluctant to adapt to. Like Haverbridge Police Station's CID room, situated on the second floor in a modern part of the building.

It was a recent extension to the original building that'd been updated and refurbished despite impending government cuts, and, although it was fairly spacious, Michael always felt claustrophobic in it.

He knew it was something that came from an experience rooted deep in his past.

Something he didn't like to dwell on. He tried to push it from his thoughts.

He turned to glance around the room, and sipped his coffee.

The walls were lined with maps, photographs and notes for ongoing inquiries, including several pictures from the case he was investigating. He saw the photograph of the suspect involved, whose eyes looked like they would burn holes in Michael's flesh and carve his name on his soul.

Pushing the thoughts from his head, his eyes swept over the room again. There were groups of desks broken up in sections for detective constables, sergeants and inspectors, and behind floor-to-ceiling glass wall partitions was Detective Chief Inspector Claire Winters's office.

Her lair.

There she could keep an eye on him, watch his every move.

But not today. Not so far anyway. In fact he didn't know where half the people were right now for that matter. Harper had been rushing off to his car when Michael had reached the station, something too urgent to wait.

It wasn't Harper that bothered him anyway. It was Claire.

He hadn't even caught a glimpse of her, which, whilst it was unnerving, pleased him somewhat. He conceded that he was just too tired to fight with her today, although part of him still enjoyed the banter.

He walked back to his desk and slumped down in his chair. He flicked the switch on the old desk fan beside him. It blew warm air at his face but it was better than nothing.

He grinned to himself. All the money that'd been spent on this new office, with air con, and it chooses one of the hottest days in August to break down. Change wasn't always for the better.

He pressed the plastic cup to his lips, drinking the rest of his coffee in one go. He crushed the cup in his palm and, aiming it at the wastepaper basket, he threw it. The crushed cup hit the rim then fell on the floor.

Shit.

He needed sleep. *Quality* sleep, not just a few captured hours while working a case in the early hours of the morning, while living off a diet of caffeine and cigarettes.

Michael looked at his reflection in the window next to him, which overlooked the station's car park.

He looked terrible, even by his own standards.

Dark circles created the illusion of crescent moons under his brown eyes, and the corners of his mouth were turned down in a fixed sorrowful pout.

He returned his gaze to his desk, which was cluttered and stacked high with paper and files. There were dirty coffee-ring marks on the wood and month-old dust congregating around his computer monitor and keyboard.

Michael hated computers.

Computers were for the ones who were no more than a number on the payroll system. Michael was more than that and he knew it, and he had no time for modesty. Not in this job.

He was disturbed from his thoughts by the vibrating of his mobile phone in his pocket.

He glanced at the caller ID.

Claire Winters. So much for not locking horns with her today.

He sighed and tried to ignore it. After the call failed to divert to his voicemail, he decided to answer it.

'Where have you been, Diego?'

In a bad mood, as per-fucking-usual...

'Sorry, Guv, I've been out of the office for a bit and I've been ignoring my phone, trying to catch up on work.'

'Well you'd better pull your finger out your arse and get down here. I'm on Ryder Way, St Mary's church.'

Michael paused, rubbing his eyes hard as a headache began to emerge, crossing over his forehead. The blood in his ears began to pound. 'What's going on?'

'We found a body.'

'Claire, I'm working on the Hargreaves case, do I really need to be down there?' He heard her sharp intake of breath and cursed himself in his head.

That was not the attitude to show the Guv right now, or ever.

She could bust your balls just by giving you one icy look from her emotionless blue eyes. He awaited the inevitable lashing of her tongue.

'Look,' she said, 'I've had a rough morning. Don't be another pain in my arse.'

Michael paused. 'Where *have* you been anyway?'

'It's...it's personal.'

'Something wrong? You can tell me.'

She paused, part of her wanting to offload her frustrations of the morning, but then her resolve hardened. 'What are you, my therapist? Just drop what you're doing and get down here.'

He bristled at her words, his shoulders locking up. He lowered his voice so the next words out of his mouth came in a forceful hiss. 'I can't just drop everything. I've been working flat out and I'm *this* close,' he said, miming a small distance between his thumb and finger, despite knowing she couldn't see, 'from getting the lead we've been after. The Hargreaves case needs—'

'*Fuck* the Hargreaves case,' she cut in, her patience waning. 'I'll reassign it to Matthews.'

Michael was silent, his face twisted. His eyes wandered back to the picture on the wall he'd studied earlier.

Gavin Hargreaves was a local thug, dealer and complete thorn in his side.

He was a man who'd been in and out of police custody for years, served a prison sentence for a drug-related offence, but this hadn't deterred him. He carried on with his little enterprise, controlling Haverbridge's seedy underbelly, and he'd just been accused of a serious assault.

Trouble was there were no witnesses and little evidence of Hargreaves's involvement. If they wanted Hargreaves away for a long time, they had to gather more evidence than they had already but it was a shitty investigation.

No one would put the finger on Hargreaves, such was his power and the fear he exerted over those in his pocket. Even local gangs feared him.

Michael had been working the Hargreaves case for two months now and had no intention of letting it go to anyone, especially not DI David Matthews.

Claire sensed his anger in the silence. She let him stew a few more moments before she gave a half smile.

'Trust me, Diego, you'll want to take this one. Right up your street.'

'You've lost me,' he said, beginning to lose patience.

'When was the last time you went to church?'

'Why?'

She paused then said, 'The deceased was a priest.'

CHAPTER 4

Michael had left the station as soon as he'd ended the phone call with Claire. The roads had been unusually empty for that time of day but the closer he'd driven towards the crime scene at St Mary's, the heavier the traffic had become.

The hacks and ghouls are already out in full force, he thought as he flashed his warrant card at officers who waved him past the police tape.

A Beds and Herts Scientific Services Unit van came into view and Michael saw a SOCO clad in a white hooded bodysuit, police evidence bag in hand, standing next to it.

Michael exchanged a nod with him as he approached and entered the church.

He found Claire was waiting for him in the entrance.

Her ice-blue eyes studied him from head to toe with no subtlety, as she held out a sealed Tyvek paper suit for him, with overshoes and a face mask.

'Have you eaten today?' Claire said.

Michael stopped changing and eyed her suspiciously. Her own face mask was hanging below her chin, the hood of her suit covering her hair. Her face was serious.

He half laughed. 'I didn't know you cared.'

'Don't flatter yourself. I just don't want you spewing up and contaminating my crime scene.'

Michael zipped up the bodysuit. 'Nothing I've ever seen in this job has ever made me sick. Not even close.'

Claire's mouth twitched and she gestured over her shoulder. 'We'll see… You've never seen anything like this before.'

She raised her hand for him to walk with her before he could ask what she'd meant.

'The deceased is sixty-two-year-old Father Malcolm Wainwright. The pathologist thinks the time of death occurred within the last two hours. Photography and videoing have been done and the SOCOs finished twenty minutes ago with not a lot to show for it. I've got officers on a house-to-house as we speak and the press crawling up my arse.' She paused. 'Fucking parasites.'

Michael stared ahead over the tops of the pews.

There were four large lamps illuminating the area near the altar and he knew that was where the body lay.

As he drew closer he caught the glimpse of blood spatters on the flagstone floor, just before they turned into the aisle. He glanced back at Claire.

'We think that's the deceased's. It's possible these drops of blood fell from the murder weapon, which,' she said, before he could speak, 'we haven't recovered yet.'

'What was the cause of death?'

Claire stopped in her tracks. 'That's anybody's guess right now, given the state of the body.'

'What do you mean?'

Claire paused, and then gestured with her hand. 'See for yourself.'

His eyes narrowed at her in frustration but he kept his mouth shut. He walked ahead, careful to keep to the plastic walkway created to avoid contamination, and headed up the aisle.

As the body came into view primal instinct caught him.

Clasping a hand to his mouth he forced himself to swallow the lump of bile that had risen up his throat. His eyes watered at the acidic taste against his tongue.

His eyes darted around Wainwright's naked and desecrated body, seeing glimpses of red, and pink, then spots of stark white bone.

He looked back over his shoulder at Claire.

She raised her eyebrows. *Told you so.*

She walked around the large pool of blood, her bodysuit rustling with each step. She crouched down at a distance and observed the body.

'Whoever did this must have a strong stomach,' she said as she pulled her mask back up. Michael pulled his own up over his nose and mouth to block out the smell.

Claire glanced up at him.

Michael couldn't determine whether or not it was with pity or embarrassment; either way he knew he had to pull himself together.

He squatted down next to her. She glanced at him, her eyes narrowed as if to ask him if he was OK. He held her gaze.

'Don't spew.'

'I'm fine.'

She gave him a slight nod, unsure whether to believe him or not, and Michael guessed she probably didn't care how he was coping. She just wanted to wrap this up and return to the station.

'We'll know more when we get the pathologist's report, but Wainwright may have died from asphyxiation.' Claire let her words sink in for a moment.

'I thought it was anybody's guess?'

'It's our *best* guess so far, taking the discoloration of his face into account, although there're no ligature marks on the neck.'

Michael stared at the wound to Wainwright's abdomen. The tear was clean and deep. 'What about the stab wound?'

'It appears to have been inflicted first.'

The voice came from behind Michael and he quickly swivelled around and got to his feet.

A tall man in his mid-forties and dressed in an identical body suit stared back at him with curious eyes.

'DS Michael Diego, this is Principal SOCO Jason Meadows,' Claire said as she got to her feet.

Meadows gave Michael a faint smile. 'Sergeant.' Michael managed a small nod.

Claire now stood beside them both. 'Why don't you fill DS Diego in on what we know so far?'

Meadows smiled and pointed towards the long curtain of the confessional box to their right.

'He was attacked in there. The blood spatter pattern on the curtain and the interior of the confessional would indicate a quick thrusting motion to the body.'

Meadows walked around patches of dried blood leading from the confession box towards the altar. 'He must have crawled by himself towards the altar.'

'He could've been dragged,' Michael said.

'Not likely, because of the spatter pattern,' Meadows said. 'If he was dragged you'd expect the blood to be smeared across the flagstones. The pattern here doesn't indicate anything consistent with that.'

Michael shot a look towards Claire. 'And the chest?'

'This desecration of the chest, I'm relieved to say, happened after death,' she said.

Leaning forward for a closer look, Michael controlled his composure.

Wainwright's skin had been cut and pulled back carefully, exposing his chest cavity, slick with blood.

Michael stared hard, fascinated by the fusion of blood and muscle partially covering Wainwright's ribcage. 'And the instrument?'

'Probably a scalpel or a knife similar in shape. Whatever was used had to be very sharp,' Meadows explained. 'Look at the clean lines. It would've cut through the skin and muscle like butter.'

Michael looked closer at Wainwright's mouth, which appeared to be clenched awkwardly. His eyes squinted and he looked at Meadows.

'Has anyone looked inside his mouth yet?'

'Not yet. That'll be the job for the pathologist at the PM.'

Michael then locked eyes with Claire, amazed no one else had seemed to notice the unnatural shape of the mouth. Claire pulled a blank expression before realising Michael's intention.

'You're not doing it, Diego.'

'The mouth looks unnatural.'

'Does anything about this crime scene look *natural* to you?' she said.

'I'll do it,' Meadows said. He crouched down, careful to avoid touching the blood with his plastic overshoes.

A female SOCO approached and handed Meadows a long thin black torch. He flicked the switch, illuminating Wainwright's face, then set the torch aside.

Placing the fingertips of his left hand on the top of Wainwright's head, he carefully pulled apart the jaw with his right. The skin felt cool beneath his touch, despite the barrier of his gloves.

He gently pulled and Wainwright's mouth began to open.

His lips, which had been glued together with his own blood, started to part, leaving strands of dried blood over the pale, almost translucent skin.

Meadows resisted the urge to gag as the smell of death wafted up through the dead man's throat and into his face.

Just as he went to aim the torch light inside Wainwright's mouth, Claire's BlackBerry rang, the shrill ringtone making everyone in the church jump as the tense silence broke.

Meadows lost his grip on Wainwright's face and it slumped back to one side, causing two of Meadows's fingers to slide into the cold mouth.

Cursing under his breath, he shot Claire a hard stare as she reached inside her bodysuit and pulled the phone from her pocket.

She glanced at the caller ID, held up her hand as if to apologise, before yanking the mask over her head and rushing towards the entrance to the church. She answered the phone before she had even walked halfway from the body.

'Winters,' she barked.

Returning his attention to Wainwright, Michael watched Meadows take hold of the man's head and resume his inspection, pulling open the mouth once again.

He lowered the torch and peered inside.

White teeth gleamed back, with only a few shiny metal fillings towards the back of the mouth to taint a fairly perfect set of teeth. There were a few cuts on the bloated tongue but something caught Meadows's eye further down the back of the throat.

Michael heard Claire's feet shuffle over the flagstones towards him.

'Nothing wrong, I hope. Nothing that will get in the way of business, I mean,' he asked, cocking his eyebrow in her direction. 'Rough morning, as you put it.'

'Piss off, Diego. Is there anything in there or are you just wasting our time?'

Meadows held out his hand in the direction of the female SOCO. 'Tweezers please, Charlotte.'

She handed him a set.

Pushing the tongue out of the way, Meadows lowered the tweezers inside the throat until the metal lightly brushed against something solid. 'There *is* something in there. Here, hold the light.'

Michael took it, holding it closer just as Meadows pulled out a silver object, with a couple of small wooden beads still attached to it. The light from the torch danced over the metal.

Claire leaned in closer as Meadows held it aloft. 'It's a cross,' he said, as Charlotte held open a clear evidence bag. He dropped it inside. 'I'm no expert but it looks like it's from a rosary. That'll explain what those other beads were that we found on the floor.'

'Great,' Claire sighed. 'This changes the whole game.'

Michael stared at her, confused. 'What do you mean, this changes the game?'

Claire stared at him and shook her head in frustration. She looked back at Meadows. 'I think we're done here. I'm going to need the Scene of Crime Report ASAP.'

'Yes, Chief Inspector.'

Claire walked towards the entrance to the church and started to remove her bodysuit.

There was an uncomfortable silence between Michael and Meadows.

'I think that's your indication to follow her.'

Michael shot Meadows a dark look. 'Yeah, thanks for that.'

***

After removing his own bodysuit, Michael followed Claire out into the street, where extra police had been drafted in to make sure no one in the massing crowd tried to breach the police cordon.

It had started to spit with rain, despite the heat, and Claire pulled out a packet of cigarettes. She offered Michael the pack, but he pushed her hand away.

'What the hell was that about? I've told you before, don't show me up like that. Respect. That's all I want.'

Claire exhaled smoke towards Michael's face, her eyes narrowing slightly. She plucked the cigarette from her mouth.

'Do you really need me to spell it out for you, Diego?'

'If it helps me understand why you felt like trying to make me look stupid, then yeah.'

Claire scoffed. 'You make yourself look stupid, Diego, you don't need my help.'

She took another drag on her cigarette.

'We find a man – not just any man but a priest – murdered in his church with his chest cut open. Then to top that off, we find a cross inserted inside his throat. The beads attached to it suggest the pendant was snapped off while it lodged inside blocking his airways.'

She let the statement hang in the air a moment. 'Why not leave it at the stab wound? The pathologist said that cut would've been enough for Wainwright to bleed to death. He would've been in excruciating pain, but that wasn't enough for the killer.'

Claire pointed at Michael, cigarette firmly wedged between her fingers. 'That's anger in there, that's what that is. We're not dealing with just *any* murderer, not like we've faced before.'

She gestured towards the church. 'Somebody wanted to send one big message, and not just to those who knew the victim. There's a message especially for us.'

Michael nodded. 'The cross is symbolic and more than just its association with the fact Wainwright was a priest.'

Claire expelled another plume of smoke. 'And now you're starting to think like someone who holds your rank.'

He avoided her eyes.

Claire had always been a hard case. With her natural bright blonde hair and tall 'average' figure, right down to her cold blue eyes that could rival the most ravaging of winter days, she could control any situation.

The well-known saying 'It's a Man's World' didn't apply to her.

She'd worked her way up the ladder, fast-tracked to a DCI, taking down any man or woman who stood in her way. If you ever crossed her in some way, you'd better be watching your back, because you never knew when you just might need her help.

She was far from malicious but there was a darker side. Something anyone with half a brain knew not to tap into. Michael knew there were other things, something in her past that made her the way she was. He could sympathise if she'd let him; after all, he had similar demons from his past too. He just never got close enough to her to find out what hers was.

He sensed her childhood hadn't been great, but he also knew it hadn't been anything like the awful things you read about. Whatever it was, though, it was still affecting her now. That call she took in the church, the disappearing act all morning – the effects of it were clearly visible to him, despite the mask she tried hard to wear.

A person's flaws can be someone else's idea of beauty.

She had some steel in her, he'd give her that.

Claire's ambition had got her this far and would bring her years of success, but it would also be the reason for her demise later in life if she wasn't careful. He knew all too well.

He'd seen people fall from grace before.

For some reason it was this that had attracted him to her in the first place and he wasn't ashamed to admit it.

***

Michael arrived back at Haverbridge station before Claire so he lit himself a cigarette and leaned back against his car. He undid the top button of his shirt, arched his neck, and wiped the sweat from his brow.

Minutes later, he saw Claire's silver Mazda enter the car park.

He met her gaze as she parked in the bay next to his. He watched her pulling her hands through her hair, securing it back into a ponytail with an elastic band.

He pulled open her car door. 'It's too hot today, huh?'

She shrugged off her suit jacket and tossed it over to the back seat. 'Well, it is August.'

Michael muttered under his breath and shook his head. Claire gave him a sideways glance. 'You don't like me very much, do you, Diego?'

He looked at her briefly before returning his attention to his cigarette.

'Why wouldn't I like you?' he said, as he tapped ash to the floor. 'I mean you're a fucking peach to work for, what with your take-no-prisoners attitude, bluntness and, let's not forget my personal favourite, plain arrogance.'

She stared at him until he made eye contact with her. He shrugged. 'Well, at least we know where we stand with each other,' she said at length. 'I don't like you, you don't like me, that much is clear, and it's all out in the open… That's quite a good basis for a working relationship. There's no bullshit in-between, just black and white and straight down the middle.'

Michael dropped his cigarette to the floor, crushing it under his foot. 'You're anything but black and white.' He saw her bristle. 'You made it like this, Claire, not me.'

'As I remember, *you* called wanting to end *it*.'

She swung her legs out of the car, pulled her bag onto her lap and began to rummage inside.

Michael looked at her as she leaned forward.

She was wearing a fitted light-pink sleeveless blouse. It clung to her body where she'd been sweating with the heat of the day in her suit jacket. A few of the top buttons had worked themselves undone and he could see the top of her bra.

He could remember how good she'd looked naked.

Claire found her BlackBerry and stood up to face him. She began checking her emails. She glanced at him. 'You seemed eager to get rid of me anyway.'

'You were too much of a control freak, Claire, let's face it, and not to mention a married woman.'

'*Was* a married woman. We're talking past tense here and besides, we were never meant for anything other than a quick shag now and again when we had a break in the schedule.'

Michael held her stare. 'Why do I get the feeling this hurt you a lot more than it hurt me?'

She broke eye contact and shook her head. 'Don't worry about me, Diego…you weren't that good.'

There was a long pause.

He thought it best to let her have this one. He hated arguing about who did what to who and when.

They'd had a brief affair six months ago and it was over after two months. Although it'd got very intense towards the end, they had to be realistic.

Claire had been married to another policeman based in Welwyn Garden City, some eight miles from Haverbridge. It would have been devastating for them both if they were found out.

It was Claire who finally broke the silence, tapping furiously on the buttons on the BlackBerry. 'I think we have a lead already with the murdered priest.' She slung the phone back into her bag.

'What lead?'

'We have the name and address of the last person believed to see Wainwright alive. Mark Jenkins, fifty-eight years old and a Religious Studies teacher at St Catherine's secondary school.'

Michael exchanged glances with her and half laughed. He ran his right hand roughly back through his hair, and shook his head.

'You want me to check him out, don't you?'

'I have other cases that need solving, Diego, and I have to see Matthews about you handing over the Hargreaves case to him this week.'

Michael shuddered at the mention of Matthews's name. Like fingernails on a blackboard, the name cut through him to the bare bone.

'It's not that I don't think you're up to the case, Diego,' Claire continued, studying his face. 'I just need someone who can give this new investigation some insight. You told me once – fleetingly, I might add – that you had a religious upbringing. Your knowledge could prove crucial.'

He shook his head. 'I haven't attended church since I was a kid. I hated it. My mother forced me to memorise scripture to the point where I would have gladly torn my own eyes out if it meant I never had to read any of it again. I've erased it from my memory.'

'Well, you'd better *un*-erase it.'

'We always said that what happened wouldn't affect us working together.'

Claire sighed. 'Seriously, please don't turn this into some…*Diego-drama*. I've got too much on my plate right now.' Her BlackBerry rang again. She removed it from her bag and he caught the look on her face when she saw the caller ID.

'Haven't we all? We all have shit to deal with, Claire,' he said, edging closer towards her. She pulled the BlackBerry from his line of vision, but made no attempt to answer the call. 'Is this,' he said, gesturing towards the phone, 'the reason you were AWOL this morning?'

She avoided his eyes, glanced at the screen again and killed the call. A few seconds later, a voicemail alert broke the awkward silence between them.

'Fuck's sake…' she said, gripping the phone tighter in a sweaty palm.

Michael leaned in too close for comfort. Claire pushed past him, BlackBerry now at her ear as she listened to the message. He watched her, mouth parting when he saw her getting back into her car.

'Where are you going now?'

Claire squinted at the sun and reached for her shades. She started the engine and snapped her seatbelt in place, as Michael banged his hand on the window. 'Claire!'

She wound down the passenger-side window, but didn't speak.

'Where are you going?' he said.

'I've got to run a quick errand.'

'Bullshit.'

'I'll be back in half an hour.' She paused, then said, 'Hour, tops.'

He moved back from the car as she began to reverse. He shouted after her. 'What's wrong?'

The car stopped reversing, and her face looked pained. 'What's wrong?' she muttered. 'The thorn in my side.'

CHAPTER 5

Haverbridge town centre was teeming with Wednesday afternoon shoppers enjoying the glorious sunshine. The Costa coffee shop was doing a roaring trade, with not a seat to be found at the metal tables and chairs scattered about outside.

Inside felt like a blazing inferno; the hot pastries and lattes combined with the heat of the day had many of its employees congregating behind the shop in the shade, just to find some form of relief.

A young male employee with *Dean* emblazoned across his name badge stooped to wipe down a vacant table. As he began to wipe the crumbs to the floor and remove the circle of coffee-ring stains, he glanced up, catching the flash of red in his peripheral vision.

Then he saw her, her red hair almost glowing in the sunlight like hellfire. She was small and slender, with very pale skin which was like porcelain.

Dean's eyes followed after her, looking at her from the top of her head, past her light-green top, to tight low-slung jeans, to her simple black open-backed flats. She casually slung her large leather bag higher on her shoulder before disappearing in the crowd.

Mesmerised, Dean walked away from the table. He tried to keep her in his sights, but soon the fiery hair was lost in a sea of ordinary faces.

***

Amelia had known he was looking.

Why wouldn't he? Most men did, and from past experience, so did women on occasion.

She smiled to herself as she opened her bag and caught sight of the red stain running the length of her thumb, smudged and flaky.

Blood really did get everywhere. She knew what happened could have been so different, less violence, less mess, less frenzied.

But then it would have been *less* enjoyable. *Less* fitting.

She raised her hand to her lips, and licked the blood from her thumb. Then she searched for her keys. She raised her security fob to the sensor on the heavy door and awaited the red glow from the panel before pushing the door and entering the communal halls.

She walked to the lift, which always smelt of urine and was decorated with some form of new graffiti each day.

Living above shops in the centre of town, sharing the area with drug dealers and users alike, was as good as it got. When she reached the doors to the lift she saw a large piece of white paper sellotaped roughly across the stainless steel and remembered the lift was out of order still.

She sighed, heading towards the door leading to the stairwells. As she pushed the glass door open she remembered the day she first came here to view the flat.

It had been another hot day not unlike this one, and she'd deliberately worn a low-cut top and a short low-slung skirt to distract the estate agent when they discussed the monthly rent.

As planned, he'd taken the bait.

All men are weak...

He would tell the landlord she accepted the monthly rent but he would 'fix the books', as he put it, and she would pay less.

'It will be our little secret of course,' he'd said.

'I can't thank you enough, Mr Brown,' Amelia had replied in her sweetest of voices.

He'd extended his hand once again, eyes narrowed. 'Call me Adrian, I insist.'

Amelia had almost reached the top of the stairs and she shuddered, recalling the events that had taken place that afternoon.

She turned to face another door leading to the second floor of flats, and pushed it half-heartedly, the hinges squeaking.

The once brightly painted wood, now a grimy shade of brown, had been vandalised again. The frosted glass window had been smashed for the second time in two weeks and there was additional coloured graffiti climbing the length of the door frame.

Amelia wandered further along the corridor, hearing a dog bark from behind the door of flat fifteen, not unlike any other day, but it made her jump nonetheless.

Although keeping animals in the flats was prohibited, she knew that tenant had probably struck a deal with Adrian to keep him sweet.

Besides, considering what she'd seen, no one with any common sense would confront the tenant about the noise level from the dog. Most people draw the line at suicide.

After walking past a few more doors, Amelia rested her head against her own, not wanting to enter. After a few moments of staring at the heavily soiled brown carpet beneath her feet, she forced her key into the lock and quickly turned it.

She pushed the door open and kicked off her shoes before dumping her bag down on the kitchen table. She pulled a chair out from under the table, went to the fridge, retrieved a bottle of wine and poured herself a glass, before returning to the table and taking a seat. She took a long drink from the large glass and stared around at her tiny living area.

The walls were painted a neutral colour throughout the flat, with plain light-coloured carpets. She had a small red two-seat sofa in the corner facing a small portable television set. Her battered coffee table had seen better days, but it'd been a bargain purchase from a charity shop in the centre of town.

Her thoughts were broken by the thudding of a stereo above her head, which seemed to shake the ceiling to a continuous beat.

Sighing, she opened her bag, her breathing suddenly rapid as she zipped apart the soft leather. She found the blister pack of small white pills, popped one out and swallowed it dry.

The stereo above her head pounded harder and Amelia checked her watch. Soon she would welcome the distraction of the music above; it would give her something to focus on and forget where she was and what she was doing.

During her life, Amelia had learnt how to detach herself from her body and imagine she was somewhere else.

Today would be no different.

Glancing at her watch again, she headed towards the bedroom. She began to remove her clothes, folded them neatly and placed them on the cream-coloured duvet in front of her. She drew the dark-red curtains, blocking most of the light from the room, which now cast black-red shadows across her face.

She hoped it would be in the dark this time, and then she wouldn't have to keep her eyes open and pretend she wanted to be there.

As was routine, she pulled back the duvet and slid between the sheets. She shivered at the coolness of the fabric against her skin. As the bed began to warm with the heat of her body, it offered little comfort while she waited.

Then she heard a key turn in the front door.

The hinges whined as the door swung open then closed softly. She heard shoes being removed and slung carelessly, thudding on the floor. She heard the heavy footsteps approaching the bedroom door, hesitating before the door was pushed open.

A shaft of light broke the shadows in the room and she closed her eyes tight, pretending to be asleep. The door shut and someone moved closer to the bed and Amelia tried to sneak a look beneath her thick eyelashes.

She saw a tall shadow move around the foot of the bed and peek through the curtains.

He is so afraid of being caught…and I wish he would be.

The figure at the curtain pulled the material shut and then wandered back around the bed towards the light switch.

Amelia winced at the sudden break in the darkness, her eyes trying to adjust as she slowly opened them, seeing him looking at her.

'I told you I want the lights on. That was the agreement,' said Adrian.

'*Your* agreement. Not mine,' she spat as she rolled over to face towards the window.

Adrian smiled as he removed his navy suit jacket, placing it over the back of a chair. He unbuttoned his light-blue shirt.

Amelia glanced over her shoulder towards him. She could tell he'd recently visited the tanning salon, judging by his golden tan. His hair looked freshly styled too, glued into place with expensive hair gel. His fingernails were also well groomed and his fingers set off with expensive rings.

Amelia hated what money could do to people. She hated the way Adrian paraded himself around with his expensive suits and fast cars. She hated the way he could talk his way into people's heads and convince them to part with vast amounts of money for a new home. He would even take extra money from people and keep it for himself, despite his high pay grade and commission perks. She hated this and she hated *him*.

Her thoughts were broken when she saw him remove his underwear, and then approach the bed.

'I haven't got long today. I have a viewing to do at three,' he whispered as his hand clasped her shoulder.

Amelia lay back and detached herself from the moment.

Robotically she spent the next twenty minutes making the right moves and noises in the right places before he finished, dressed, then left as quickly as he'd arrived.

***

After Amelia had scrubbed herself so hard her skin almost bled, she had towelled off and sat on the bed staring at her phone in one hand and Adrian's business card in the other.

After she'd put in a call to Adrian's office and hung up, she drafted a text message to send to the name listed only as '*G*' in the contacts list.

Made the call. Will let you know when it's done... A

She hit send.

Amelia knew the plan set for her and knew she'd have no trouble executing it to its full exquisite potential. She only hoped that when it came down to it, she had enough self-control not to cut too deep.

CHAPTER 6

The light from the sun beating down on her head flashed across the black plastic of her sunglasses as she tilted her head towards the sky.

Drawing the last pull on the cigarette pinched tightly between her fingers, Claire exhaled a stream of smoke from between parched lips, and felt as if her very being was becoming more withered with each step she took.

She glanced down at the butt of the cigarette, stopped in her tracks and flicked it to the ground. She watched it roll into the gutter, joining the rest that had been discarded near the entrance of Gladstone Court.

Claire cocked her head skyward once again.

Her second visit here today in such a short space of time. Someone's idea of a sick joke. Was this all her life was meant to be from now on?

The old council block loomed above, the dull redbrick cutting an ominous shape through the bright blue sky.

To Claire, coming here meant putting on a brave face. It meant trying to cast aside the memories of the past, if only temporarily. It meant casting away the pain she had tried to bury for all these years.

She fumbled in her bag for the separate keyring she deliberately kept away from her main set. It was an attempt, symbolically at least, to keep *this* part of her life, the one inside the building, from clashing with the other.

Her fingers felt like ice as she clasped the fob and pulled it from her bag. She swiped it over the sensor on the wall beside her and the front door to the building gave an audible click and a green light flashed on the panel.

Grasping the handle, Claire yanked it and went inside.

As usual the lift was out of order, so she took a slow walk up the stairs to the fourth floor. The air on this level was stale. The large windows on this floor, at this time in the afternoon, allowed direct sunlight through the thin single-glazing glass. The heat generated was relentless and Claire popped open another button of her shirt.

There were two flats on this side of the building, and Claire now stood in front of the second one and steeled herself inside.

She pushed her spare key into the lock…

CHAPTER 7

Another viewing with a client had gone well and Adrian had negotiated an unfair price on behalf of another greedy landlord taking full advantage of the housing crisis for another shitty little studio flat.

Another successful day for some.

Adrian sauntered through the office leaving his usual sense of arrogance and pride wafting in invisible lines behind him.

He made himself a coffee before heading back to his office. He unlocked his PC screen, taking a sip of his coffee while he checked his diary for the afternoon. He scrolled down the page in front of him, and then paused, his gut tightening.

He glanced at his watch.

It was after 3:30pm and Amelia Williams would be there in ten minutes according to his diary. Confused, Adrian shouted to his PA through the closed door rather than ring her using the internal phone.

'Mary!'

He could hear her rushing up from her seat. Mary slid her head around the door, her long brown curly hair falling around her face, which always reminded Adrian of a poodle crossed with a King Charles spaniel. Her big blank brown eyes stared back at him.

'Yes, Adrian?'

He pointed to the screen. She glanced at it and pulled a face.

'Why is she booked to come and see me in ten minutes? This appointment wasn't in my diary this morning.'

Mary flushed. 'Sorry, Adrian. She called up this afternoon and said she needed to talk to you. I tried to speak with you but you were busy on a conference call.' She paused and looked upset. 'She was very forceful. I just booked her in. I meant to tell you but…I guess I forgot. I'm sorry.'

Adrian cursed under his breath. He turned and waved her away and she scurried out of the room.

Before Adrian had a chance to think, his phone rang. It was the main reception calling and Adrian pulled a face as he picked up the receiver.

'Adrian Brown…OK…I'll send Mary.' He hung up and rested his forehead in his hands. He was dreading what might come next.

He asked Mary to prepare some coffee after she had seen Amelia to his office and asked that she not disturb them. Mary soon returned carrying two steaming cups. She watched bright green eyes follow her as she placed a coffee cup in front of Amelia on Adrian's desk, before passing her a sideways glance of disapproval.

This amused Amelia.

Clearly the buck hadn't stopped with her and who knew how many women Adrian had cheated.

She glanced up towards Adrian and his eyes met hers, studying her face intensely. Amelia waited until Mary closed the door to his office before smiling at him. She reached for her coffee and took a sip.

'You may want to keep that one. She makes quite good coffee.'

He shook his head. 'Why are you here? We're not supposed to meet like this.'

'There're lots of things we shouldn't be doing but that hasn't stopped you.'

Adrian's lips pulled upright into a grin. His eyes wandered from her face towards her shoulders, noting the thin white camisole top that hugged her delicate body. Her hair fell roughly tousled around her face, with tendrils touching the tops of her bare arms.

'Still, we shouldn't be meeting here at the office like this. You draw too much attention and unwanted questions. I don't make it a habit to meet tenants privately in my office.'

'Just screw them, then?'

'Only you.'

Adrian watched her eyes, which seemed to him to be a darker shade of green today. It made him uneasy and restless.

'Why are you here? You saw me a few hours ago. Why not say something then?'

Amelia lowered her cup back onto his desk, her eyes never leaving his. 'You were rather pre-occupied at the time.'

'I'm a busy man. Spit it out, I don't have time for games.'

'But you play them so well.' She leaned forward, her hair framing her pretty face in a wild red glow.

Adrian cursed under his breath but still he stared longingly at her.

At length, Amelia got up from her chair and walked around the desk to stand behind his chair.

Her hands pressed down hard on top of his shoulders.

Her fingers curled, clawing him in her grasp.

Adrian felt her nails dig into his flesh.

CHAPTER 8

By the time Claire had driven back to the office, she tried to look as if the last forty minutes hadn't happened.

She sat in her car in the station car park, pulled her sunglasses off, and tossed them on the dash. She peered into the rear-view mirror. She dabbed around her eyes with her fingertips, removing any smears of make-up before heading into the station.

As she walked into CID, DI David Matthews was on her as soon as she was through the door.

'Guv,' he said, too loudly, in her ear, enough for her to glance across the room to where Michael was sitting, watching them closely.

'Guv, can I have a word?'

She gave a curt nod, and he followed her through to her office, shutting the door behind him. As Claire sat down in her chair, she risked another glance at Michael. She had a perfect line of sight to his desk through the glass partition walls of her office.

He was rifling paperwork on his desk, and then peering at his computer screen, pretending to be busy.

Claire knew he was watching them, watching *her*.

Every single move.

'Have a seat, Matthews,' she said as she booted up her computer. He sat in one of the chairs opposite her desk and just smiled. Claire raised her eyes to meet his. 'Why are you grinning at me like a Cheshire cat?'

Matthews leaned forward, clasping his hands together and rested them on her desk. 'The Hargreaves case?' he said. 'I got your email. Thought now would be a good time to go through everything.'

Claire glanced towards Michael's desk again. He wasn't there. She felt herself relax a little.

She found herself smiling back at Matthews, her ice-blue eyes glowing in amusement. 'I thought you'd be pleased. You wanted to work the Hargreaves case and now I'm making you SIO, we'll discuss the details tomorrow, with Diego.'

She paused and considered her next words carefully.

'And before you ask, Diego didn't take it too well – about Hargreaves – so do me a favour and don't rub his bloody nose in it. I'm working the Wainwright murder with him. The last thing I need is him resenting me any more than he does already.'

Matthews was beaming. His dark-brown eyes looked out of Claire's office, across the incident room to the work station he shared with the other underdogs – mainly the DCs in his eyes. He shouldn't even be sitting *near* them. He was meant for better things.

He wanted Claire's crown and this was his big foothold on the ladder.

He leaned forward, his floppy brown hair falling around his eyes. He brushed it back with his left hand and offered his other to Claire. 'I can't thank you enough.'

Claire stared at his hand then reluctantly shook it. 'Just don't let me down… Don't make me regret this.'

Business and pleasure didn't mix, Claire knew that, and she'd learnt the hard way. The last thing she needed was people talking about her and Matthews and she couldn't afford to be showing any favouritism.

'I need results on the Hargreaves case. I've got DSI Donahue breathing down my neck and the press aren't exactly painting a pretty picture about us at the moment,' she said, her eyes lowered. 'They're calling the whole investigation a farce. No justice for the families…the usual.'

Her eyes met his.

He nodded. 'Not a problem, Guv. I won't let you down.'

Claire gestured for him to leave. 'I'll be holding you to that.'

After Matthews had left, Claire's BlackBerry rang.

She saw the screen. Chose to ignore it. When the call diverted to voicemail, she switched the phone off.

                                  ***

Michael headed outside the main building, lit himself a cigarette and walked towards the designated smoking area. He leaned up against the wall and exhaled a stream of smoke.

He closed his eyes.

'You look like shit.'

Michael opened his eyes and saw the familiar grin of DC Gabriel Harper standing a few feet from him.

Michael allowed himself a small smile. 'Love you too, Gabe.'

'It's just an observation, mate,' he said, now standing beside him. 'Got one to spare?' he said, nodding towards Michael's cigarette.

Michael offered him the pack and lighter from his pocket. Harper lit one, and gave Michael a prod in the arm as he handed it back.

'What's been going on with you?'

Michael shrugged. 'The Hargreaves case. I've worked my arse off on it, and it's drained me.'

Harper squinted, the sun hurting his eyes. 'And now Matthews is taking it on.'

Michael shot him a look. 'I wasn't aware that was common knowledge yet.'

'It wasn't until, like, five minutes ago, when he waltzed out the Guv's office, smug grin on his face, and made a big show of collecting the Hargreaves files.' He gave him a sympathetic look. 'Wasn't very subtle, mate.' He paused. 'I'm gutted for you, if I'm honest. The one chance we had to get Hargreaves once and for all and you could've nailed him. Now, I'm not so sure…'

Michael plucked the half-smoked cigarette from between his lips and chucked it to the ground.

'You'd better keep that to yourself, Gabe,' he said, brushing past him on his way back into the building.

CHAPTER 9

Amelia turned the key and let herself into her flat. She reached for her mobile phone which she'd left on the kitchen worktop and dialled the number she knew off by heart.

Calling G flashed across the screen before she put it to her ear. It seemed an eternity but finally her call was answered.

'Is it done?' the voice said.

'It is. He won't be bothering me any time soon, but I get the feeling it won't be the last time we'll be dealing with him.'

'What did you do?'

'I used my…persuasive charms.'

There was a long pause.

'You didn't hurt him, did you?'

'Just a scratch… Did I do wrong?'

'No, but we must focus on our goal.'

'He'll keep up the rent side of the deal. He won't get my body in return, if that's what's bothering you.'

The quietness on the line told Amelia this was pleasing news.

'When can I see you?' she said.

'Soon.' There was another long pause. All Amelia could hear was soft breathing on the line.

'I loved you, since the moment you first came into my life. Remember that.'

Amelia bit her bottom lip hard. Every time she heard those words it all but stopped her heart right there and then. 'I know,' she said at length.

The phone clicked before going dead.

Amelia placed her phone back on the counter top and took the flick knife from her pocket, pulled back the blade and smiled.

***

Adrian Brown looked down at his blood-soaked shirt sleeve.

Bile began to rise in his throat, but he suppressed the urge to vomit. He applied pressure to the wound, fighting back the urge to scream.

He doubled over in pain, and blood seeped through his fingers.

He remembered the look on Amelia's face as she'd plunged the knife into his upper arm, and how her other hand had pressed firmly over his mouth as he had screamed.

He'd felt like he would pass out but he had fought against it when they had heard Mary approach the office. Under duress he'd told her through the door that he was fine.

He'd waited with bated breath until he'd heard footsteps leading away, Mary's curiosity shot down in an instant.

He'd sighed and shut his eyes.

When he had looked back at Amelia, her attention was on the blood seeping through his shirt. His gaze had followed down to her right hand, fingers gripping the handle of the knife firmly, her knuckles white. In that moment he had tried to think back to where it had all started to fall apart.

Then she had wrenched the blade from his arm.

Her eyes had never left his as she wiped the knife clean with a tissue. The perks he'd got from their financial agreement were over. She'd made that crystal clear.

He waited until she'd left his office before removing his tie and securing it tightly around his shoulder, pulling it tight. He then put his suit jacket on. He would wait half an hour before risking going to A&E.

He waved Mary away when she tried to enter his office. She looked hurt but he didn't care.

Amelia had been a worthwhile distraction at the time but now she was a threat, an inconvenience.

She had to be dealt with as quickly and discreetly as possible.

CHAPTER 10

It was just after nine the next morning and Michael sighed at the No Smoking sign on the door in front of him. He dropped the remainder of his cigarette on the floor, crushing it under his foot. He exhaled the last dreg of smoke from his dry lips, pushed open the main door and entered the reception area of St Catherine's.

He felt the eyes of the middle-aged receptionist burning into his body as he approached the glass window at the front of the reception booth.

Looking behind her he could see other workstations and a main office at the back with a sign on it.

'Can I help you?' she said, brushing an imaginary strand of hair behind her ear. Michael noticed how, although her face was lined and her hair was showing signs of grey, she was not an unattractive lady. He forced a smile and maintained direct eye contact with her.

'Detective Sergeant Michael Diego,' he said, showing her his warrant card.

He saw her stiffen.

He was used to that response as soon as people found out what he was. 'I need to speak with the Head, if he's around.'

'*He* is a *she*, and rather busy this morning. You should have made an appointment.'

He'd been anticipating this response. 'Tell her it's important. Tell her it's in relation to a murder inquiry.'

The woman froze.

'I'll wait right here until she's ready to see me,' he said, taking a seat in one of the chairs in the waiting area. 'Oh, and I take my coffee black, one sugar, thanks.'

The receptionist bristled but headed towards the office behind her. After five minutes she reappeared with a mug of coffee and handed it over, handle facing away from him deliberately. He smiled, wincing inwardly at the heat burning his fingers.

The receptionist forced a smile. 'Miss Wallis will be with you soon. Until then, please wait here. We don't allow visitors to wander around the school unescorted.'

***

Miss Wallis was a mature lady, Michael noticed, as she approached him twenty minutes later. She had grey hair which was immaculately kept at shoulder length. She wore a long black skirt with a matching suit jacket. Her glasses sat low on her nose, and she pushed them higher before extending her hand to him.

'Sergeant Diego? I'm Linda Wallis, what can I do for you?'

Michael rose from his chair and took her hand, noticing how firm her handshake was. He smiled at her but was met with a cold hard stare, her eyes studying him with caution.

Michael released her hand and slid his own back into his trouser pocket.

He grew aware of the receptionist's eyes on them both.

'Perhaps we should speak in your office, Mrs Wallis.'

'It's *Miss*.' Linda paused before extending her arm towards her office. 'This way, please, Sergeant.'

Linda's office was small and static. Everything was formal and had its place: a small bookcase filled with educational books, a rather dull-looking print of something Michael recognised as by Henri Matisse, and a very bare-looking desk with only a few essential pieces of stationery.

Linda sat behind her desk but Michael waited until she motioned him to one of the two large blue upholstered chairs in front of her desk.

'Forgive me if we skip the pleasantries, Sergeant, but I have a school to run, and I don't take too kindly to people who demand to see me without making an appointment first.'

Linda let the statement rest in the air for a few moments, making Michael stir in his chair before continuing. 'I'm sure you can appreciate that I'm a very busy woman.'

She pulled her lips into a forced smile. Michael could tell she was the kind of employer to defend her colleagues to the end. In his experience, closing ranks was typical of teachers and quite frankly, he didn't have a lot of time for them.

'Miss Wallis, I must apologise for not making an appointment first but this is an urgent...*delicate* matter. I'm investigating a murder that took place yesterday in St Mary's church.'

Linda stared at him, her face hardening. 'I heard about that... I fail to see how I can help you.'

'It's not you I've come to see. I must speak with one of your teachers, a Mr Jenkins. I believe he teaches RS here.'

'I'm well aware of his credentials, Sergeant Diego. What concerns me is why you would wish to speak to him.'

Michael knew this wouldn't be a walk in the park.

'He's believed to have been the last person to see the deceased alive.'

'What's that got to do with anything?'

Michael's eyes narrowed slightly. *This bitch is stalling...*

'He may be able to offer some crucial information, clues to the identity and whereabouts of the killer.' He gave her a few moments to take in his words. 'I need to speak with him now.'

'Impossible. He's teaching. I will not interrupt and have the students gossiping about why an officer came into their classroom to question their teacher. Surely you must understand the sensitivity of the situation?'

Michael had anticipated this, but he wasn't taking no for an answer. He smiled at her. 'I understand, but nevertheless I must speak with him. Here in your office will do just fine.'

Linda knew arguing would get her nowhere, but had every intention of showing her reluctance. 'This is unheard of. You could've waited until the end of the school day,' she said before rising from her desk. 'Follow me.'

***

Michael walked at a reasonable distance behind Linda, looking around at his surroundings, taking note of everything before dismissing it again in a blink of an eye.

He followed her down a corridor, then climbed two flights of stairs, before she turned to him just outside a classroom. Michael saw the small glass window in the classroom door and guessed her intention.

'Please stay away from the door, Sergeant.'

He tipped his head. 'Absolutely.'

A deep crease furrowed in the middle of Linda's brow. She turned and peered into the classroom.

Mark Jenkins stood at the front of the class, reading from a textbook, occasionally looking around the class, picking on anyone who didn't appear to be paying attention.

Michael stole a quick glance through the window, and guessed the pupils were about fourteen to fifteen years old. A few of them in the front rows caught his gaze.

They stared at him. He then heard Jenkins's voice rise in anger. The students flinched and returned to their textbooks. Jenkins's face suddenly turned towards the door and Linda motioned to him.

Michael didn't miss the hard frown on Jenkins's face. He turned to the class and barked a command. The students began rummaging in their bags, pulling out notepads. Jenkins waited a moment, making sure they were progressing with his task before heading towards the door.

Once he'd shut the door behind him, he eyed Michael with suspicion. His cold light-green eyes reminded Michael of a fish he'd caught once while fishing.

Mark Jenkins was a man of average height, with thinning light-brown hair. He was dressed in a slightly eccentric suit, the colour made up of different chequered shades of brown, complete with tie and waistcoat. He looked ridiculous and Michael could picture the kids ripping the piss behind his back.

Jenkins turned to Linda, his face confused. 'Who is this?'

Linda looked uncomfortable, trying to find the right words.

'I'm Detective Sergeant Diego, Haverbridge CID,' Michael said, cutting in, showing his warrant card. 'I need to speak with you regarding the murder of Father Malcolm Wainwright at St Mary's church yesterday afternoon.' His voice sounded almost robotic, as if the words had been rehearsed a thousand times before.

Jenkins looked stunned. He mouth opened and a small voice from somewhere within him tried to escape.

Michael's face dropped. 'You didn't know?'

Jenkins shook his head in disbelief. 'I don't understand. I just spoke to him only yesterday.'

Michael looked apologetic. 'I'm sorry you've had to find out like this.' Jenkins's eyes were on his but seemed to be looking through him. 'As painful as this is, I need to speak with you. You're believed to be the last person to see him alive.'

Jenkins felt his voice catch in his throat. He raised a tightly curled fist to his mouth and bit it, fighting back tears. 'Tell me this is a mistake. How can he be dead?'

Linda reached out her hand and placed it on Jenkins's shoulder. 'Come, Mark, let us go back to my office and talk.'

She turned to glare at Michael, her eyes narrowed into slits.

***

Jenkins looked like he'd aged ten years in ten minutes. His face was ashen, his eyes appeared translucent and dead to the world. His bony fingers were clasping a steaming cup of tea, but still his skin was like ice.

He sat in a chair in Linda's office, his shoulders hunched, face lowered, staring at the floor, looking physically diminished in stature and poise.

Linda sat behind her desk, her face visibly saddened by Jenkins's appearance. She gazed at him sympathetically with her hands clasped as if in a silent prayer.

Michael was sitting back in the same chair as before but had angled it slightly towards Jenkins. He had his notepad resting on his crossed legs, his pen poised, waiting for the right moment to begin asking his questions.

'I understand that Father Wainwright and you were very close friends, Mr Jenkins. I can't imagine just how hard this must be for you.' Jenkins looked up through his eyelashes and glared at Michael.

'You should be out there locking up whoever did this, not sitting here interrogating me.'

'This isn't an interrogation, Mr Jenkins. It's believed you were the last person, besides the murderer, who saw Father Wainwright alive yesterday. Can you tell me what time this was and the circumstances that surrounded the meeting?'

'It wasn't a meeting,' Jenkins snapped. 'I was out in town and I happened to bump into him.'

Michael glanced at Linda while making notes. 'You were not at work yesterday?'

'Free period.' Jenkins caught Linda's disapproving glance. Michael guessed free periods should be spent planning lessons, not shopping.

'What time was this?'

Jenkins rubbed his forehead with his hand and his eyes narrowed. He looked Michael straight in the eye. 'I had a free period at ten. I saw Malcolm about half-past. We spoke about the up-and-coming service on Sunday and that was it. I got back here at about eleven-fifteen.'

He turned to Linda.

'Yes, I was *slightly* late back to take my next class. That's my only crime.'

Michael paused, and glanced up at Linda. She looked irritated but it appeared to pass quickly. She leaned over and placed a comforting hand on Jenkins's shoulder. He gave a hard smile, and looked back at his now empty cup, still clasped firmly in his hands.

Michael was weighing up his explanation.

Wainwright had been murdered at approximately 11:30am on Wednesday morning. His body had been discovered around an hour later by his housekeeper, who had dialled 999 immediately before being taken to hospital herself with shock. They had a witness who saw Jenkins with Wainwright at the times Jenkins had stated.

He had a pretty tight alibi.

'How did he die, Sergeant? Did he suffer?' Jenkins's voice was abrupt.

Michael leaned back in his chair. 'His suffering was brief. It was over quite quickly, I believe.'

Jenkins sat open-mouthed, his eyes welling up once more. 'You *believe* it was quick, but you don't know for sure, do you?'

'Nothing is certain until we receive the pathologist's report. I'm sorry I can't be more precise.'

Michael looked down at his notepad. There was an awkward silence that seemed to last an eternity before Jenkins wiped his eyes with the back of his hands, and rose from his seat.

'Are we finished now? I have classes to teach.' He placed his cup on Linda's desk.

'I'm sending you home, Mark. I wouldn't expect you to stay after hearing this. In fact, take tomorrow off as well. We'll see you Monday, assuming you feel up to it of course.'

She smiled at him and he nodded, placed his hand on hers and mouthed the words, 'Thank you.'

Then he turned to face Michael.

'If it's all right with you, Sergeant, I'd like to be with my family. Malcolm was a dear friend and my family knew him well. My wife and daughter will be very upset.'

Michael nodded, closing his notepad. Linda helped Jenkins from her office and out to his car.

Michael watched them from the office window. He noted that the receptionist had brought Jenkins's things from his classroom: a dull brown overcoat and a tan briefcase. Michael wondered what secrets he kept in there. He watched Jenkins tremble as he climbed into his old Volvo.

When Linda returned, Michael was already on his feet. He extended his hand towards her. 'Thank you for your time, Miss Wallis. I hope I may have your cooperation again should we require any further assistance.'

Taking his hand firmly, Linda narrowed her eyes. 'I don't think that'll be necessary, do you, Sergeant?'

He held on to her hand when she tried to release it from his. 'All the same…'

Linda stared at her hand in his, and then her eyes rose to meet his stare. She smiled reluctantly. 'You may rely on me if needed.'

CHAPTER 11

Michael spent the rest of the day feeling disillusioned with everything that had happened in the last few days. He'd returned to the station after his talk with Jenkins, and kept his head down, avoiding Claire and Matthews as much as possible.

That became impossible by late afternoon, when Claire summoned him to her office along with Matthews to discuss the Hargreaves case and, when Michael officially handed everything he'd worked so hard on over to Matthews, he felt the resentment building up inside him.

The only consolation was that he caught the look on Claire's face when she was less guarded. He saw the sadness in her eyes when he caught her looking at him.

Maybe she wasn't doing this to him out of some petty personal vendetta after all. In any case, he didn't wait around to find out. By the time he left her office, he gathered his things from his desk, told Harper he could be contacted on his mobile, ignored the advice to clear it with Claire first, and headed out of the station.

The drive home seemed to pass in a blur.

When Michael parked in the street about four houses from his own, he released the seatbelt and rested his head against the steering wheel.

A loud bang against the windscreen made him jolt upright.

'Sorry!'

It took him several seconds to register what had happened. Then he saw Robby, the kid from next door, holding a football which had hit his car, with his mates beside him, laughing.

Michael got out from his car and allowed himself a small smile.

'Sorry,' Robby said again. 'I kicked it too hard.'

'No worries,' Michael said, and headed towards his house.

Once inside, he glanced out of the window. Robby and his friends were moving on, walking in the direction of the local park. They were good kids and in this town, that made a change.

Michael was fond of Robby. He saw a lot of himself in the kid, despite the fact their childhoods couldn't have been more different.

Robby's mother was a kind woman who worked every hour God sent to make sure her son had all the things he deserved in life. She kept a clean and tidy house, safe and warm. Michael knew this first hand because she'd invited him in a few times for a coffee. She was around his age and he knew she had a soft spot for him, but he wasn't attracted to her in a romantic way.

The wonderful childhood Robby had was a stark contrast to his own.

Michael's mind drifted back to one particular memory.

His mother.

She'd been wearing the same dirty clothes for a week. Her hair was tangled, her lips scabbed and sore, her soul torn.

She'd just kicked out another worthless boyfriend and the house looked ransacked, dirty, unloved.

A sad place to be, to exist.

He remembered that they were facing eviction. At the time he'd had no idea what that meant. He'd just wanted his mother to stop crying, something that rarely happened.

There were always tears in their strained existence.

There were no sweet bedtime stories, no teddy to clutch against his young skin to offer comfort from the monsters that were literal, not something imagined.

He remembered the song she used to sing to him.

A beautiful melody that would quickly dwindle into a sorrowful lament.

'*...My breast is as stone, my breath smells earthly strong; And if you kiss my cold clay lips, your days they won't be long...*'

Then his mother would kiss him, a cool caress on his lips. It wasn't the tender kiss that should come from a mother's love for her child, nor was it born from passion – a sinister unnatural incestuous longing.

Michael closed his eyes.

He heard his mother's voice in his head, and for a moment he was back there, in that old house, a mere child. He could feel the gentle vibrations of her breath against soft innocent skin, as she leaned over him.

'*...The stalk is withered and dry, sweetheart, and the flower will never return. And since I lost my own sweetheart, what can I do but mourn?*'

There was death in her voice. The nightly ritual for her became something entirely different to him, but it was never something he could accurately explain.

'*...When shall we meet again, sweetheart? When shall we meet again?...*'

Later he found out that this was an old English folk song. It was about a man who mourns his true love. When the spirit of his lost love complains she cannot rest, he begs a kiss. She tells him it would kill him and he should be content to be alive.

It took Michael about ten years from the last night she sang it to him to realise this nightly ritual was really about his mother's loss of his father, who had died suddenly aged thirty, while she still carried Michael in her womb. She'd never recovered from it and longed for a way out.

The melancholy that surrounded his mother had threatened to swallow them both whole, and all of it born from her own tormented mind.

Michael's eyes flicked open.

His mouth was dry and his eyelids were heavy.

He'd tried to erase this memory altogether, but it was as if it was to be forever etched on his soul.

He gazed from the window again. He watched Robby disappear from view.

The sound of his phone ringing brought him back to the here and now. It was Claire.

He didn't need her messing with his head any more today.

He killed the call.

CHAPTER 12

Claire stared at the screen of her BlackBerry. The call she'd placed moments before had diverted to voicemail too quickly, not leaving much time to ring, so she knew Michael had hung up on her.

She'd spent the day organising her team, and compiling everything they knew about Father Wainwright, and after the draining experience at Gladstone Court, she was exhausted.

She walked out of her office and surveyed the incident room, eyes landing on the photographs on the opposite wall of the room. Photographs of Wainwright were spread out across it, pinned together like some twisted jigsaw, the pieces yet to match smoothly. It was a gruesome collection showing one of the worst traits that lurked inside the rarest of individuals.

Claire had seen some violent crime scenes before, but she was entering uncharted territory with this one.

She checked her BlackBerry in case there was anything from Michael.

Nothing. No email, no text.

No explanation.

She knew it was handing the Hargreaves case over that'd got him pissed at her, something she expected would be the case. But still she wondered if the underlying issue ran much deeper, more personal than either he or she were comfortable to admit to.

'Guv,' DC Harper said, interrupting her thoughts.

'Gabe,' she said, trying to shake the sadness from her.

'CCTV picked Wainwright up in Toralei's restaurant the night before he was murdered. With his housekeeper.'

Claire exchanged a look with Harper. 'Do many priests go to dinner with their housekeepers, I wonder?' she said, voice dry.

'I'm still getting over the fact priests can afford housekeepers.'

Claire smiled. 'He's got no dependants, invested his money well…'

'I'm still having a hard job seeing it.'

Claire's BlackBerry pinged from inside her pocket. She reached for it, saw a new text message had come through.

Sorry. Bad time to talk. I'll email you later.

Claire frowned at the words.

'You all right?' Harper said.

'It's Diego.'

'I take it he's no longer MIA?' he said, smiling.

The BlackBerry pinged again. Claire flushed.

xxx M xx.

'Give us five minutes, will you, Gabe?' She walked away before Harper could answer.

CHAPTER 13

It was around 7:30pm when Claire returned home. She was tired and pissed. Michael couldn't be reached and she was having a hard job explaining his disappearing act to her superiors let alone to her team.

She was eager to leave the office and forget about him for a few hours if she could.

She pulled up the driveway to her detached house in the sleepy village of Hexton, just outside of Hitchin, approximately a half-hour drive from Haverbridge.

Claire knew how lucky she'd been in working her way to the top. Being fast-tracked to a DCI by the age of thirty-seven was definitely something to be proud of and made others envious. Her success was reflected in her appearance and personality. Her home was no different.

She lived in a four-bedroomed house that looked like something out of a *Homes & Gardens* magazine, with its bay windows and the old country feel about it.

She had of course added some modern elements over time and had had a large extension and double garage built just a few years ago, even though she didn't seem to spend much time there of late.

Coming home was just a means for her to freshen up and catch some sleep. There seemed little time in her life for much else.

She stifled a yawn as she turned the key in the door and let herself in. She stepped over the day's mail, which was sprawled across the mat, and kicked off her shoes and went to the kitchen.

She flicked the light switch and dumped her bag on the kitchen table, as the spotlights came to life above her head. She found the last of the supply of ready-meals in the freezer and put it in the microwave, then retrieved the mail.

She flicked through it: some pizza leaflets, a water bill, a letter from her mother Iris and a small white envelope with just her name, printed by a computer, on the front.

She frowned, inspecting either side of it with suspicion.

It had obviously been hand delivered.

She carefully opened it and pulled out a thin piece of paper, folded in half. Her eyes narrowed as she folded it back and read the contents, which had also been typed on a computer.

What revelation lies within the beauty of a rose? With its thorns sharp yet perfume so bewitching, you must breathe in the scent, be it foul in its reason for being.

Claire frowned as she took in the words. She repeated the whole verse in her head and out loud, trying to make sense of it.

She heard the microwave finish, and headed back to the kitchen. She left the letter on the table and dished up her food, the scent of the shepherd's pie making her mouth water. She realised then that she hadn't eaten anything since that morning, which would explain her terrible headache.

She shovelled most of the food into her mouth before returning to the table. She poked at the rest of it with her fork while reading the letter again. Ten minutes passed and she ran out of patience. She slammed her fork down on her plate and screwed the letter up and put it in the bin.

Putting it down to nothing but kids playing a prank, she went upstairs to change.

***

Claire tied her dressing-gown tight around her waist as she returned to the kitchen. She pulled out her BlackBerry, notepad and her personal file she'd already compiled on Wainwright.

She poured herself a glass of wine, then headed for the living room, collapsing on the cream-coloured sofa. She sat for several minutes, sipping from her glass, before checking her BlackBerry for any new emails and found there were three new messages.

There were several missed calls and voicemails relating to what had happened at Gladstone Court the previous day.

She certainly didn't need the stress of it right now. That visit she'd tried hard to conceal from Michael had zapped her energy. She longed for the day that she could wash her hands of the whole sorry mess.

Claire deleted the call list and the voicemails without listening to them properly.

She drained the last of her wine from the glass in one large mouthful and she looked across at the one photograph of herself with both her parents, which sat on a bookshelf in the corner. It was taken when she was first in uniform. On that day, even her father had managed to behave himself and her mother had managed to curb her bitter tongue.

They were still married then, although Claire never really understood why.

They hated each other.

But still, it had been all smiles that day.

Claire drew her attention back to her work. She checked through her emails.

The first was from Michael saying he'd spoken with Mark Jenkins, who would be providing a statement, but he'd discuss it with her tomorrow. He'd sent it shortly after he had disconnected her call earlier.

The second was from Matthews, thanking her again for letting him take over the Hargreaves case.

Claire grimaced as she read it. *Pull your tongue out of my arse, Matthews.*

It hadn't been a difficult choice to reassign the Hargreaves investigation to Matthews. Claire knew it was a case below what Michael should be working on, despite Matthews's seniority over him. Michael was wasted on this one.

She often thought he should've been recommended for Inspector, before Matthews, despite his ego.

She remembered the third email and deleted Matthews's message from her account before opening the final one. It was a reminder about the up-coming Charity Ball being held in a few weeks' time in Covent Garden at the Mayflower Hall.

Claire winced as she read it was a 'plus one' event.

The dress code was black tie and the ladies were expected to wear stunning evening dresses as well as meet and greet with the Mayor of London. This part didn't faze Claire – she'd met the Mayor before – but the thought of turning up without a special guest in tow did.

Her thoughts drifted back to Michael.

She knew she'd been out of line towards him lately but couldn't help herself. They had too much history between them for it ever to be normal again. She thought back to the moment she'd first met him and how she'd fallen completely in lust with him.

She'd resented being married from that moment on but it'd been a few years after that first meeting before they'd struck up an affair.

Now it was over and Claire knew she had to push him from her mind, no matter how reluctant she was.

She put the BlackBerry aside and began reading over her notes.

All she had to go on so far with regard to Wainwright's murder was Mark Jenkins. He'd been the last to see him alive. She read over her notes thoroughly; Jenkins was married with one biological child but had previously fostered three other children. One called Emily still lived with him, but the other two had since moved on leaving no forwarding addresses. There was no documented reason as to why they had left and Claire thought it strange. They seemed to have vanished.

Then of course there was his biological child.

What was Jenkins like behind closed doors?

She thought about this for a few minutes before making a call to the station. DC Gabriel Harper answered the phone at the other end.

'Harper, it's Winters. Just a shot in the dark here but can you run a name for me? Chloe Jenkins. See if anything comes up?'

'Didn't you go home already?' he asked.

Claire sighed. 'You know how much I enjoy taking my work home with me.' Harper laughed as he typed the information into his computer.

'Right…we have a Chloe Jenkins. Twenty years old, lives at 52 Boston Court, Haverbridge West. She was brought in last year for minor drug offences but released with a caution.' Harper paused. 'Is that who you're after?'

Claire wrote down the address. 'Anyone listed as next of kin?'

'No. No one listed.'

Claire had thought as much. She rang off and glanced at the clock opposite her; it was 9:00pm. Tomorrow morning she'd pay Chloe Jenkins a visit, but for now tiredness was overcoming her.

It was only while brushing her teeth that Claire remembered the letter from her mother that she'd not opened. She retrieved the letter from downstairs and opened it when she eventually climbed into bed.

When her parents had divorced Claire's mother had emigrated to Spain. The only time Claire saw her was when she came back to England, which was only when absolutely necessary. Even when Claire had gone through her own divorce she'd only come over once.

Hardly the doting mother.

Instead, Iris wrote to Claire at least once every two months, since she didn't believe in emails or text messages. Even the ability to pick up the phone was alien to her, and Claire wondered why she defended Iris so much whenever her father launched into a tirade of abuse about her.

Claire frowned as she skimmed over her mother's delicate handwriting. This letter was nothing more extraordinary than usual.

It read predictably; her mother asked about her work and hoped she wasn't doing too much all at once. She enquired about Simon, Claire's ex-husband, and if there was any possibility of them at least becoming friends again. *No chance there*, Claire sniffed. Then she asked the one question Claire dreaded: how was her love life?

Groaning out loud, Claire tossed the letter onto her bedside cabinet and switched off the light.

CHAPTER 14

It was 9:30am when Claire arrived at Boston Court the next morning. She'd overslept but it didn't bother her too much, considering all the late nights she was beginning to notch up.

She glanced up at the twenty-odd-storey tower block in front of her. It looked depressing, with its grey brickwork and dirty-looking windows. The parking area didn't look like somewhere Claire felt comfortable leaving her Mazda either, even if very briefly.

She saw a group of teenage boys dressed in hoods and baseball caps kicking a ball around and up against the wall of the block. They were right in front of the entrance. Claire sighed inwardly and headed towards them.

One of the teenagers looked up, staring at her as she approached. He nodded to his friend, who turned and spat on the floor in front of Claire, narrowly missing her boots. She paused and looked up at him, but the youth just stared back with a vacant expression on his face.

'Shouldn't you be in school?'

The youth squared up to her. 'Mind your fucking business.' His friends laughed.

Claire shoved past him. 'You kiss your mother with that mouth?' she said as she walked inside the block.

'Only yours, love,' came the cocky reply. Claire ignored him.

There was a main corridor leading to a stairwell but she decided to take one of the two lifts in front of her. She went into the nearest one and immediately a waft of urine hit her. She held her hand to her nose and looked at the panel listing the floors. It had some sort of clear beaded slime covering it. On closer inspection she deduced that it was spit, and fresh.

She swore when she saw the button for floor ten, flats 50 to 53, was covered in it. Pulling a tissue from her pocket, she wrapped it around her finger before pressing the button.

When she reached the tenth floor she noticed the smell of urine followed her to flat 52. She knocked on the door and noticed it was decorated with a red graffiti tag.

A few minutes passed before she knocked again, harder this time, but still there was no sound of movement.

Then the lift behind her opened, making her jump. A young girl, no more than sixteen, appeared pushing a pram, which was laden with shopping bags. She was struggling to get the pram out of the lift, and the doors began to close.

Claire rushed over to help and noticed that the girl was heavily pregnant. The girl looked at her and smiled.

'Thanks. Can't wait until I don't need this pram any more.'

Claire gestured towards her stomach. 'Looks like you'll need it for a while yet.'

The girl glanced down at her stomach, pulling her top down over her. She pulled a face. 'Yeah, worse luck.'

Claire faked a smile. She saw the girl go to open the door to flat 53 and her eyes flashed instantly. 'You don't happen to know the girl who lives here, do you?' she asked, pointing over her shoulder to flat 52. 'I've knocked but I'm not sure if someone's in or not.'

The girl glanced up. 'The Jenkins girl.' She nodded. 'Yeah, I know her.' Claire waited for any further information but it was not forthcoming.

'Well, is she in or does she work during the day?'

The girl looked Claire up and down. She was nervous. 'Why? What you want with her?' Claire held out her warrant card and the girl's eyes widened. She began fishing out her keys from her bag. 'You might've said you were filth.'

Claire looked her up and down but stayed silent.

'Usually I can guess you lot straight away.' She avoided Claire's eyes. 'Chloe works nights. She's probably sleeping.'

The girl shrugged and opened her front door, manoeuvring the pram inside. Claire helped her when the wheels caught against the door frame. The girl smiled and nodded a thank you. She began to close the door but Claire caught it with her hand and pushed it back.

'Sorry, it's important that I speak with her. Do you know where she works?' The girl paused and stared at Claire, unsure of her motives. 'I asked you a question.'

The girl sighed. 'I don't know if I should say really.' Claire shot her a hard look. The girl was trying her patience. The look prompted the girl to cooperate. 'She's one of them dancer girls.'

'Dancer girls?'

'She's a *stripper*.' The girl's demeanour came over all superior. 'She, you know, prances around in front of men who're married and should know better.'

The girl seemed to have an afterthought.

'It pays real good money apparently. I could do that, you know, I don't wanna live on benefits forever.' She glanced down at her stomach and frowned. ''Course, no one's gonna pay for me to shake this thing around, not when I'm this big.'

Claire knew there was an exotic dancing club in town but had no idea what it was called or where it was exactly.

'Do you know the name of the club she dances at?'

The girl thought for a moment. 'It's behind the leisure complex somewhere and I think it's called Paradis or something like that. *His* father used to go there a lot,' she said, gesturing to the toddler in the pram. 'One of the reasons we split up.'

Claire knew she could find out more back at the station so she thanked the girl and headed for the lift. Since their conversation, someone had called the lift a few floors up.

A sly smile spread across the girl's face. 'I remember the way he used to look at Chloe.'

Claire glanced towards her as she pressed the button to call the lift back down. 'I'm sorry?'

The girl's eyes met hers, something in them this time that was different from before. 'My ex,' she said. 'He used to give Chloe this look when he saw her. He still lived here with me, but that didn't stop him flirting. He was wasting his time though.'

The lift arrived at their floor, and the doors pinged open. 'Sounds like you're well shot of him,' Claire said as she entered the lift.

'She'd never have looked twice at him,' she said, voice smug. 'She only shags girls.'

Claire just looked at her as the lift doors closed. She pressed the button for the ground floor, and shook her head. Chloe's sexual preference didn't bother her, but her choice of job did. She'd only been in a strip club once, and that was to arrest a suspect.

It hadn't been a pretty sight.

As Claire exited the building she saw the youths had moved on, and she walked back to her car. As she approached the Mazda she noticed one of her brake lights had been smashed.

You little fuckers.

She looked around but knew the youths could be anywhere, so she climbed in her car and drove back to the station.

CHAPTER 15

Claire's office was quite large but cluttered with filing cabinets and chairs, making it appear smaller. She'd left the blind up the night before, so the early morning sun had flooded the office with intense light, leaving the room stifling.

Claire placed her coffee on the desk, opened the window wide, and then lowered the blinds. She picked at her nails, waiting for her computer to bring up the internet.

She accessed Google and typed 'Paradis' in the search box. She hit enter and it brought up lots of links. She glanced down the page and saw the link to the main website.

She looked through the glass partitions.

The incident room was busy. She doubted anyone would need her for the next ten minutes or so. She felt embarrassed at what she was about to look at.

She clicked the mouse and a half-naked lady popped up on the screen, accompanied by dance music, as the menus for the website dropped down in a fancy animation, followed by a swirling title appearing on the screen in the shape of green ivy.

It formed the words 'Welcome to Paradis' and pulsated on the screen. The woman had changed position and was now holding a red apple, about to bite into it seductively.

Claire cocked an eyebrow. *'Really?'*

Just then Michael pushed his head around the door. Claire glanced at him then back at the screen, looking flustered.

'Is now a bad time to compare notes?' he asked. Claire tried to turn the volume down on the monitor. Michael frowned then walked towards her. 'What's that shit?'

She tried to turn the monitor off before he saw the screen but he grabbed her hand as she went to hit the standby button. He saw the half-naked lady with the apple.

He looked at Claire.

'Whatever you're thinking, Diego, you're wrong.'

Michael held up his palms in defence. 'Hey, it's your lifestyle choice, not mine.'

'Piss off, it's work-related. Mark Jenkins's daughter works there.'

Michael sat in the chair opposite her and swung back on it. 'Jenkins has children? He doesn't strike me as the type.'

Claire clicked on the link to the 'How to find us' page on the website and brought up a map. 'Have you ever been to Paradis?'

'No. Not my thing… You didn't answer my question.'

She avoided his eyes, feeling the weight of his stare. She hated this tension between them. Every time they were together it was there, even when she tried to forget they had never been anything but work colleagues. She wanted to bury her head in the sand, and hope everything would sort itself out.

Claire sighed and rubbed her forehead.

'Chloe Jenkins is the only biological child. He used to foster children and they left the family, for unknown reasons. Their whereabouts is unknown. I think it's strange, and it might be nothing, but I think it's a good idea to see Chloe and ask her about her upbringing. I need some more background on Jenkins before I rule him out as a suspect.'

Claire highlighted the page of directions and hit the Print button. Her printer whirred into life next to her and produced the page. She picked it up and shoved it towards Michael. He glanced at it.

'Want to check it out with me later?'

Michael looked again and shook his head. 'No thanks. I'm not working late tonight anyway.'

He passed the page back to her. He noticed her staring at him.

'It's Friday night…you remember Friday nights, don't you? Going out drinking too much, dancing like a moron and trying to pull someone, then regretting it the next day with a massive hangover?'

Claire rolled her eyes. She remembered how much she loved his playful side and she smiled inwardly at the thought. She took a sip of her coffee, closed the web page and brought up her emails. Nothing new had come in since last night.

'What did you find out from Jenkins yesterday?' she asked, still looking at the monitor. 'Team briefing before lunch, but I'd like a heads-up.'

Michael opened his notepad. 'Not a lot. Head teacher wasn't very obliging either. I got the impression she was glad to see the back of me.'

Claire raised her eyebrows. 'I thought you'd be used to that by now.' Michael glanced at her. She was provoking him. He ignored her throwaway comment.

'Anyway, he seems a very stern teacher. I certainly didn't like him, really cold eyes,' he said, shivering at the thought. He glanced over a few more pages. 'He seems well-liked by the head of the school though and, more importantly, he has an alibi. He was teaching when Wainwright was killed around 11:30am.'

He snapped his notepad shut.

Claire sat back in her chair and picked up her stapler, flicking the spring back and forth. 'I still want to see his daughter,' she said at length. 'I'll get Gabe to try and pick up Jenkins on the CCTV from Town Centre management ASAP.'

Michael nodded in agreement, and got up to leave. As he reached the door, he turned to face her, grinning.

'I'll think of you watching the ladies thrusting their crotches at you this evening. Never know, you may enjoy it, batting for the other team,' he said, before ducking out of the door as the stapler came hurtling towards his head.

CHAPTER 16

Chloe Jenkins ran her tongue along her upper lip, tasting the thick red lipstick painted expertly along her fleshy Cupid's bow.

The overhead lights flashed in various sequences as she wrapped her slender leg around the metal pole and swung her body a quick 360, ending by casting her legs out and sliding to the floor in an expert 'splits' finish.

She awaited the inevitable jeering that accompanied her signature move, and tonight they seemed louder than usual. She stared at the black tribal design tattooed on the inner wrist of her right arm. She focused in on it, helping her drown out the surroundings like she did every time she performed.

A loud jeer broke into her thoughts.

Smile. Entertain. Repeat.

She turned, smiled at the row of men who edged closer to the stage runway, watched by the careful eye of the club's security.

She grabbed the pole with one hand, using it to pull herself up, her legs sliding back together slowly until she was upright, teetering on her six-inch high heels.

The music changed tempo and the bass line rose, accompanied by the strobe light. Chloe began to strut down the runway in time to the music, the gold locket she never removed swinging with each movement.

She tried to count how many bank notes were stashed inside her red G-string. She lost count at a hundred pounds, when she caught the eye of a woman watching her, standing with her manager across the room at the bar.

They were staring at her and exchanging conversation every now and again.

Chloe tried to concentrate, finished off her routine and picked up her discarded bra before leaving the stage, as other girls took her place.

She rushed down the corridor backstage, pulling her bra back on. When she reached her dressing room, a small box-room with battered furniture, she pulled out the notes from her underwear to count her earnings.

She heard her manager Joe Carter enter the room without knocking. Chloe certainly didn't have anything he hadn't seen before. He walked towards her, when she didn't look up.

He stood close, staring at her reflection in the mirror opposite them.

His dark-brown eyes narrowed.

He stared at the tattoo on her wrist. He'd asked her about it once, in general conversation, comparing his own ink to hers. She had withdrawn into herself in an instant, shutting him out, so he never asked her again.

His eyes moved over her, taking in every inch of her long blonde hair hanging down her small skinny body and then back to her blue heavily made-up eyes.

Eventually Chloe raised her eyes to their reflection.

He stood so close to her that she could smell the stale scent of cigarettes, and feel the coarseness of his black jumper against her arm.

Unable to stand the closeness, she stashed the cash into her handbag and turned to face him.

'Am I in trouble?'

'What've I told you girls about not bringing shit to the club, Chloe?'

She looked confused, her eyes narrowing as she looked into his. 'I've no idea what you're talking about.'

'Then why is there fucking pig filth sitting in my office asking to speak to you?' he spat, leaning in closer to her face.

Chloe sank backwards, her face twisted. 'No fucking idea.' She saw the doubt in his eyes. 'Joe, it's the truth.'

'She ain't here for nothing, is she?' He leaned in closer and she could almost taste the alcohol on his breath. 'Get it sorted or you're sacked.'

***

'Mind if I smoke?' Chloe said, pulling out a cigarette from the carton with her lips. Now fully dressed in casual clothes, and sitting in Carter's office, she faced the harsh cold eyes of DCI Claire Winters.

Claire tipped her head towards the No Smoking sign on the door behind her.

Chloe rolled her eyes and reluctantly replaced her cigarette. She sat with her legs crossed, her foot tapping in the air, her mind going over the last few weeks trying to find a reason why she was here, her job at risk.

After a few minutes of silence and Claire's frozen stare she found her voice. 'You gonna tell me why you're here? I hope you realise you've pissed off Joe. He doesn't want you lot in here, unless you're paying.'

Claire smiled. She knew there were a few men on the beat who visited the club and paid for the odd private dance or two. She couldn't understand what was so attractive about these women. Most looked malnourished, hungry for their next drug fix, and Chloe looked no different with her dyed blonde hair and tired expression. The girl had the usual signs Claire was used to seeing: the vacant expression, hollow eyes and the yellowing teeth from years of smoking.

Claire noted the track marks twisting their way up Chloe's skeletal arms, one scar partially hidden, the pinky-coloured line disappearing though a black tattoo. The rest showed signs of obvious attempts to camouflage them with make-up. She thought about what could've happened to this girl, the only biological child of Mark Jenkins.

Chloe saw Claire's eyes hover over the scars on her arms, and folded them quickly.

'I'm Detective Chief Inspector Claire Winters, Haverbridge CID. I'm investigating the murder of Father Malcolm Wainwright yesterday afternoon.'

Chloe barely flinched. 'I heard about him. What's that got to do with me?'

'We have a witness who states that your father, Mark Jenkins, was the last person to see Wainwright alive.'

Chloe leaned her head back against her chair. 'So? I have nothing to do with my father and haven't since I was seventeen. I left home because I hate him.'

Claire looked up in surprise.

'Does that shock you?' Chloe looked down at her fingers and started picking the chipped red varnish from her fingernails, not waiting for an answer.

Claire's voice was flat. 'Not much shocks me in my line of work.'

She studied Chloe's face, feeling a little sorry for her. Here was a girl who somewhere along the way became lost and felt she had to leave her family. Claire thought about what her parents would've wanted for her. A decent job, a nice boyfriend, and good prospects and hopes in life.

'Chloe, I understand you've obviously had a tough time and I know you felt you had to leave home. I'm interested in the reasons why.'

Fighting back tears, Chloe raised her eyes and studied Claire's face carefully.

Why should I trust you? Chloe had nothing to do with her family any more and with good reason.

But what harm could there be in talking to this woman?

'I left home because I couldn't take the religious shit any more,' she said under her breath, barely audible, but Claire understood. It was what she'd expected to hear.

'Go on.'

'What do you want to hear? My life story from my earliest memory or the day I decided to leave?'

'Let's talk about the day you decided to leave. At seventeen, you must've been scared. Leaving home is hard for anyone financially and emotional for you. How have you supported yourself?'

'I moved in with my boyfriend at the time. He worked and offered to support me until I got a job waiting tables. The pay was crap, and I was always told I had a good body and a pretty face, so a friend recommended here. Soon I had enough money to rent the flat I'm in now.'

'Tell me about why you left.'

'I told you. I wouldn't swallow Dad's religious bullshit any more.'

'Help me understand. Are you saying you clashed about your beliefs or does this go deeper than that?'

Claire was becoming impatient; she wasn't used to playing the sympathy card and it wasn't getting her any further. She knew Mark Jenkins was involved in this case somehow. Whether it was directly or indirectly, she knew something about him and his family didn't ring true.

'He didn't abuse me, if that's what you're implying,' Chloe snapped.

'So what could someone possibly do to have made you leave home? Just because he had different views to you? There are thousands of teenagers out there who don't agree with their parents – hell, I was one of them. That's life, but I think it goes beyond that.'

'Why do you care?'

Claire paused, kept her face neutral. 'Humour me.'

Chloe sighed.

Music and cheering could be heard from the stage area up the hall. She wished she was back out there fleecing the men for all they were worth. Anything sounded better than being here, facing this woman with her cold eyes and hard stare.

'Ever since I can remember,' she said, 'Dad was preaching his faith daily. Not just when we needed to hear it but over trivial things. I can remember him grounding me when I ate an extra slice of bread. He made me watch all these films about third-world poverty.'

She sneered at the memory.

'It ranged from things like that, to keeping me a prisoner when I wanted to go out, especially if it was a boy I wanted to see. He'd shout at me, calling me a whore for Satan, shit like that.'

She paused.

'With Dad, it's all about control. If he can't get inside here,' she said, tapping a finger against her temple, 'he'll attack you here.' She lowered her hand to her heart. 'I never let him get close enough to do any real damage and in some ways, that just made him worse. It was and always has been *his* way or no way.'

An uncomfortable feeling washed over her body. 'Then of course there was the Manor house which we spent a lot of time in. It brought out the worst in him *and* me.'

'Manor house?'

Chloe pulled a face of disgust as she remembered. 'Yeah, Shrovesbury Manor, owned by Father Manuela… disgusting man. A lot of children at the local parishes attend there for what my father called "extra direction in the fulfilment of divine enlightenment".'

She looked at Claire. 'I refused to go when I was older.' She let out a mock laugh. 'Oh, Daddy *loved* that… A woman, *thinking* for herself and disobeying him?' She shook her head. 'That was never a good thing. It was like brainwashing and something about all of it didn't feel right.'

Claire shifted in her seat. 'In what way didn't it feel right?'

'It just…didn't. The atmosphere was horrible. I still have flashbacks. I remember other children used to tell stories, rumours really. Some of us were scared of Father Manuela. There's also this Chapel that he had built in the grounds, and the other kids used to scare us younger ones with stories of children going missing there. I never believed that…at least I kept telling myself I didn't… Father Wainwright was there a lot of the time as well,' she added, watching Claire's reaction.

Claire stared hard at Chloe.

She didn't know how much of this was truth and how much was just the ramblings of a bitter young girl trying to score points against her father. After all, who was going to believe an exotic dancer against men of the cloth? And besides, Mark Jenkins had a very good reputation in the community, as did Father Wainwright.

Something didn't sit right about any of this or the circumstances of Wainwright's death. Claire had known this from the start.

She threw Chloe a curve ball. 'What about the foster children?'

Chloe shot her a surprised look. She was caught off guard by the question, and Claire saw the dread that appeared in her eyes.

'How'd you know about them?' Chloe's voice croaked from the back of her throat.

'It flagged up on various systems.'

'Then you don't need me to tell you about them.'

'Most of the information's missing. A lot of data was lost when social services merged various software.'

Chloe's eyes narrowed a fraction. 'Can't you ask my father?'

Claire stared at her in silence. This was a tried and tested method for her. She knew the pressure would entice Chloe to talk. She would feel obliged to. After an intense minute, Chloe sighed, giving in.

'Mum and Dad took in foster children to try and make up for me being such a failure in their eyes.'

'They said that?'

'They didn't have to. I saw it on their faces every day.' A tear began to slowly roll down her cheek. She sniffed and wiped the back of her hand over her eyes, smearing her make-up.

'Did they experience the same treatment from your father?'

Chloe wiped her nose and tried to pull herself together.

'They fostered three children. I have nothing to do with them and I don't know where they are. I was never close to them. After all, they were there to replace me, someone else for Dad to mould into the *perfect* child.'

She paused to think, searching for a memory she'd tried hard to lock away. 'I was almost six when they got the first kid, Stephen. He was with us for less than a year. Dad thought he could "save" him or whatever,' she said, shaking her head, embarrassed by her own words.

'He left soon after he hit sixteen anyway, couldn't take the religion either. I was only young but I think he was like Dad's experiment or something. He'd been passed from foster home to foster home since he was very young. He had issues. Dad got another kid just before Stephen left, called Emily. She might still be with them.'

Claire was making additional notes. She knew about Mark Jenkins's foster children, but only the basics of their ages and where they'd come from.

Anything else she could pick from Chloe's scarred mind was a bonus. She didn't know if any of this would be relevant but she was in need of a lead…and a potential motive for the murder of Father Wainwright. She looked up at Chloe, who was now staring at her feet.

'You said there were *three* foster children?'

'The third was Amelia. She came to us almost as soon as Stephen did. Weird kid.'

'Why weird?'

Chloe pulled at the locket hanging on the chain around her neck, and bit her lower lip, smearing what remained of her lipstick on her teeth. 'She's like a lot of kids taken into care. Fucked up,' she said at length.

Claire wrote the names of the Jenkins household on her notepad in large capital letters and drew lines between them with the word *Connection?*

She had enough information on them for now at least. She could tell Chloe was more than uncomfortable talking about them. She made the decision to move on.

'What was your father's relationship like with Father Wainwright? Were they close friends?'

'Yeah, I'd say so. He came to the house at least once a week – Mum made him Sunday dinner after the ten o'clock service was over. Greedy bastard always had seconds,' she said, the memory disgusting her. 'Like I said, he was at the Manor often as well.'

'Did you like him?'

Chloe's eyes narrowed.

'In your *opinion* what type of man was he? He was in a position of trust and had regular involvement with your family. Did you resent him?'

Chloe had every reason to hate Father Wainwright.

He hid a lot of secrets.

She thought about the day he was murdered. If this detective checked, she'd see she didn't have an alibi. That might stir up old tensions, uncover barely healed wounds.

Chloe had a split second to decide which card to play.

She smiled and her eyes met Claire's. 'I resent what he represented, but that's my father's fault, not his, I guess.'

Claire looked at her sceptically but wrote down her words before folding her pad closed.

***

Claire shook Joe Carter's extended hand. She had all she needed from Chloe for now and was now eager to leave Paradis as soon as possible. Judging by Carter's body language, it was a feeling shared.

He followed her out of the club, trying to act normally around his clients. He saw Claire to her car outside and tried not to look agitated.

'I hope Chloe's not in any kind of trouble, Chief Inspector?'

Claire was expecting this question and looked at him, smiling. 'Not at all. I'm just making some routine enquiries, that's all.'

She reached in her jacket pocket and pulled out her card and handed it to him. 'I gave Chloe my card but I'd like to leave one with you, just in case she misplaces hers.'

Carter studied the card briefly and forced a nod.

He waited until she'd driven out of sight before folding the card in half, ripping it to pieces, and letting them fall, curling and fluttering along the pavement in the gentle evening breeze.

CHAPTER 17

Music raged from flat number 15. The constant thudding baseline from the stereo seemed to rattle the doorframe to the very core.

The huge Rottweiler was pacing the living-room floor, staring at its owner, who was fast asleep on the sofa, the remote control for the television sliding from his hand before thudding onto the exposed floorboards.

The dog padded over to his owner's hand, sniffed before licking it and whimpered gently. A long trail of drool was hanging from its huge jaw, its pink tongue hanging at one side, panting.

Ashe Miller's body suddenly jerked, waking him from his slumber as he fell in his nightmare, just catching himself before he fell off the sofa.

The dog barked at him, as he balled his hand into a fist and rubbed his eyes hard. He glanced up at the television, still set on mute as he'd left it.

He shifted his stocky body from the sofa with a grunt and pushed the dog away when it tried to jump up at him on its hind legs. 'Get down, Clyde.'

Ashe staggered to the bathroom, Clyde in hot pursuit, bounding alongside him, his tail wagging.

Ashe stared at his reflection in the mirror hanging over the small wash-basin and stuck out his tongue. It had a nasty-looking white coating on it, and he pulled a face of disgust.

He leaned in closer to the mirror, pulling at his cheeks, examining his eyes.

His pupils were like saucers. His shock of jet-black hair stood up on end, making him more scarecrow-like than ever. His brown eyes looked like hollow black pits, with dark circles underneath.

He sniffed at his reflection and ignored the sudden knocking at his door. He could just about hear it over the stereo and, as it continued, Clyde began to bark again.

Ashe poked his head around into the living room and stared at the door. He glanced down at his clothes: a faded olive green T-shirt and black boxer shorts.

The knocking continued and Ashe glanced through the spyhole. He banged his forehead hard against the door in frustration and cursed under his breath.

It was another resident and all Ashe knew was that they lived above him.

He threw open the door and stared at the man in front of him, dressed in his pyjamas and dressing-gown. Ashe's arms were outstretched, gripping either side of the doorframe.

'Do you have any idea what time it is?' said the man, his voice raised over the din of the stereo. 'It's nearly midnight and I've to get up for work in five hours.'

Ashe shrugged his shoulders. 'How is that my problem?'

The man frowned, taking a step forward. He was taller than Ashe but at least ten years older.

Ashe may have been quite short for a man, but what he lacked in height, he made up for in girth. His T-shirt pulled against his stocky frame, a mixture of muscle and fat caused by too much alcohol.

Still, the man squared up to Ashe and uttered some profanity before hearing a snarl.

Looking down he saw Clyde at Ashe's side, his teeth bared, ready to strike at the first command. The man looked back at Ashe who grinned, grabbed the collar around Clyde's neck and yanked him back.

'He wants to play,' said Ashe. 'Shall we see who wins?' Clyde barked, his jaws and teeth smashing back together, drool splattering over the floor.

The man backed off, pulling his dressing-gown tight around his body. 'If you could turn the stereo down, I'd appreciate it.'

Ashe made a gesture of a salute. Clyde pulled forward as the man rushed back up the stairs to his floor. Ashe yanked the dog's collar hard, bent down and tried to soothe him with hushed words. When Clyde had calmed down, he licked Ashe's face, and followed him back inside the flat.

Ashe stopped his CD from playing and replaced it with another one. He hit the play button, turned the volume up higher and grinned before returning to the bathroom.

He found his stash of skunk hidden in a small bag inside an aftershave cap, still attached to a half-empty bottle.

He went back into the living room, slouched on the sofa and reached for the bottle of whisky on the coffee table.

He knocked back a few swigs of the amber-coloured liquid from the bottle and flicked stations on the silent television. He nodded his head to the pounding rhythm from the stereo, and rolled his joint.

***

It was an hour later when Ashe awoke again, still sitting on the sofa. Clyde had gone to his bed in the kitchen and Ashe realised the CD had ended.

So what was that banging noise that'd woken him?

He sat up, listened, and realised someone was knocking on his door again.

He slumped back into the sofa, hand rubbing his forehead. His head was pounding and he struggled to see.

The knocking continued.

Getting up, he stumbled towards the door and peeked through the spyhole. All he could see was red.

He blinked his eyes tighter, then opened them wide as he moved away from the door, deciding whether to open it or not.

Someone knocked harder on the door again and, with anger rising in his gut, Ashe retrieved his baseball bat from the bedroom. He came charging back and yanked the door open with force.

'You've got a death wish, mate!'

He blinked harder as his vision tunnelled.

The neighbour he'd been expecting was replaced with a young woman, around his age with flowing red hair and piercing green eyes.

'Oh, it's you,' he said. 'What are you after this time?' He stood aside and let her in. He looked her up and down before closing the door after her. 'I'm out of cash, so if you want paying like last time, I'll have to owe you,' he sniggered childishly. 'You can tie me up this time, if you want.'

The dog snarled at her as she moved to the middle of the living room.

'Quiet, Clyde. You know she's dope.'

She eyed the dog with defiance, staring into his eyes, which provoked him further. He barked, splattering more drool on the floor. He looked ready to attack her.

She felt the knife against her leg inside her jeans pocket. She squatted down to the dog's level. She smiled as she outstretched one arm, beckoning him towards her.

A concerned look flashed across Ashe's face. 'Maybe you shouldn't do that, he's pretty hyper right now.'

His words were sluggish, which meant the timing couldn't be more perfect for her. 'You saw me the other day, didn't you.' It was a statement rather than a question. 'You overheard what you shouldn't have.' she said, turning her head to glance at him over her shoulder. 'That's your problem, isn't it? Always listening behind doors, lurking in shadows…'

Ashe tried to remain poker-faced.

The dog snarled again. 'You should go,' Ashe said at length.

'But I've not stroked *Clydie-baby* yet,' she said, returning her attention to the dog. The knife seemed to burn through the fabric of her jeans, right through to her skin. 'Come on, *Clydie-baby*… I've brought you a treat.'

Stokebrook Secure Hospital NHS Trust, Buckinghamshire 2011

Amelia stared down at the identification tag fastened loosely around her wrist. She looked around the room that had been her prison for the past three years and longed for the pain and the charade to end.

Stokebrook Secure Hospital is a high security psychiatric hospital in the Buckinghamshire countryside. It houses two hundred patients who have been detained under the Mental Health Act 1983 for mental illness, severe mental impairment or psychopathic personality disorders.

Amelia Williams fell into the latter category and was housed in the Dangerous and Severe Personality Disorder Unit (DSPD). This is the second hospital of its nature in England alongside Rampton Secure Hospital in Nottinghamshire.

Three years ago, Amelia had attempted to murder a man who she claimed had tried to rape her. She'd been found unfit to plead in a trial and had been placed at Stokebrook for her own safety and that of the general public.

It'd been little consolation to Amelia that she'd escaped trial and a prison sentence. She'd pulled off the perfect act, making doctors and psychiatrists believe she had a personality disorder and was therefore not aware or responsible for her actions.

In reality Amelia had always known exactly what she was doing. She just didn't care that she enjoyed her thirst for violence.

But being in Stokebrook hadn't been plain sailing like she'd envisaged. Locked up with others like her in nature (or worse) and having to maintain her act was starting to take its toll.

Amelia was tired.

And restless.

Every time she closed her eyes she could still see the images of the past. A bloody staircase. A broken body at the bottom, close to death.

She'd heard the screams many times in her head, night after night, relentless. Sometimes she thought back and wondered whether she'd done the right thing in keeping quiet about what had happened. Then she'd think about her long-term plans, once she was out of here. She'd been right then and was right now. Hers and God's revenge would be sweet.

She'd used her time wisely.

And now she wanted out.

She looked at the woman opposite her. Volunteer Melanie Steward, who had been talking away while Amelia had pretended to listen, was now smiling at her.

Stokebrook had a patient befriending scheme that had worked to Amelia's advantage. Volunteers under the scheme were allowed to visit patients who otherwise had no contact with the outside world. Trained and given a thorough Criminal Record Bureau check, they were then closely matched with a patient.

Rules were strict and volunteers were warned about the potential to be taken in by the manipulative nature of some patients.

Melanie Steward had already fallen at that first hurdle two years ago, although she didn't know it yet.

'Am I boring you?' Mel said.

Amelia looked away. 'Did you bring it?'

Mel's hands twitched nervously. 'Is that all you wanted? I thought you liked my company?'

Amelia tried to sound convincing. 'I do but I hoped you'd help me.'

'And I said I would, whatever you want, no matter if it's against the rules.' Mel's hand swept across the bed

and clasped Amelia's. 'I never thought that meeting you would make me feel this way... I'm breaking all the rules, Amelia. You helped me realise what I've always wanted.'

Amelia looked away. Mel blushed, believing Amelia's gesture was out of modesty at knowing the love Mel held towards her.

The reality was much darker.

Amelia was repulsed by her.

After the first few visits from Mel, Amelia knew the woman was a homosexual. A fact that had at first seemed to be a setback had presented itself as another opportunity.

No stranger to being intimate with women, Amelia had played Mel like a pro.

A few well-planned questions and the chance to move physically closer to Mel had told Amelia all she needed. Melanie Steward was trapped in a loveless marriage with a man she couldn't bear to be touched by and the look in Mel's eyes had told Amelia that she was more than a little attracted to her.

'Amelia, I...' Mel trailed off and got up from her chair. Amelia's eyes widened as Mel began to raise her long skirt.

Not again, Amelia thought. She pushed herself further into the bed when she saw Mel's hands disappear inside her knickers.

Amelia closed her eyes tight. She heard the sound of tape ripping across bare skin.

'Here,' Mel's voice quivered. 'I brought it for you.'

Amelia inwardly breathed a sigh of relief as she eyed the intricate cut-glass statue of the Virgin Mary that'd previously been taped against Mel's inner thigh. Anything made from prohibited materials or sharp objects was strictly forbidden but Mel had broken yet another rule to please her.

Mel handed the statuette over and Amelia turned it over in her hands. The figure was just four inches long but was exactly what she'd asked for. 'It's perfect.'

'Really?' Mel beamed. 'I'm so pleased. It fitted the exact description you gave me.'

'Nobody suspects anything?'

'No, I was careful, just how you showed me.'

Amelia leaned forward and kissed Mel softly on the lips. 'You won't regret this… You'll come back later?'

Before Mel could reply, her breath caught in her throat as Amelia grabbed the pendant around her neck. 'What's this?' Mel saw the change in Amelia's eyes. She looked at the small fabric rose at the end of a fake gold chain.

'Don't you like it?'

Amelia's mind took her back to the Rose Garden at Shrovesbury Manor.

Rebecca…

She held back tears as the face from her past appeared before her, like it always did. Firstly, as a beautiful mirage of messy brown hair with wide dark eyes. Her face bore a few freckles which made her look younger than her sixteen years.

Then came the vision Amelia always dreaded, as the pretty face was replaced by a twisted mess of blood and smashed bone. Rebecca's once full light-pink lips now reduced to a menacing grimace of dried blood and events of unspoken evil.

Amelia ripped the chain from Mel's neck, making her gasp, her hand reaching for her neck. Amelia threw the chain into her face. 'Get rid of it.'

Mel was stunned. She avoided Amelia's eyes and looked around the room. She caught sight of the small shelf filled with a few books from the hospital library. Her eyes landed on a particular title. She knew many pages inside had been drawn over in red pen, many passages underlined or crossed out.

She'd helped Amelia do it herself.

Now she felt the twinge of regret deep in her gut as she read the gold writing down the spine of the book.

It read Holy Bible.

***

It was almost 8:30pm when Amelia heard the lock turn in the door.

Mel was early.

More importantly, she'd pulled off their plan thus far without any major problems.

Mel's face was ashen, her eyes dark and puffy as though she'd been crying. She had a small bag clasped tightly to her chest. She closed the door but didn't speak.

Amelia got up from the bed. She reached out to tuck a strand of hair behind Mel's ear and felt her flinch under her touch. Amelia's eyes narrowed, forcing Mel to look at her. 'Is everything in place?'

Mel's voice sounded hoarse when she spoke. 'I managed to bribe security to let me in this late and he agreed not to check the bag.'

Amelia smiled.

George, the night security guard, had been easy enough to bribe. Amelia had managed to pay him a midnight visit herself in exchange for him allowing Mel access into the building discreetly by the side trade entrance.

All men are weak, she thought. It'd come easy for her to manipulate but she saw it'd been much harder for Mel.

Amelia kissed her cheek. 'This'll be over soon.'

It was like Mel hadn't heard her, and was locked away inside her own mind. 'All our life's savings... Twenty-five years we've been married. Frank will be devastated when he realises what I've done.'

'You're in a loveless marriage, Mel. It's time you found happiness.' She kissed her on the lips passionately, tasting the sweetness of her mouth. When she withdrew, Mel was crying. 'I'm your future now. You don't have to fear what happens next.'

Mel pushed her away. 'I don't know if I can live a life on the run.' She tried to wipe away her tears as quickly as they fell. 'I love you, Amelia, but I don't know if I'm strong enough to do this. I thought I was but I was wrong. How can this be right?'

Amelia shushed her as she drew her into her body, comforting her as a mother does a child. Mel let herself fall into the embrace and they lay back on the bed.

'It's right because God says it is,' Amelia said. 'He'll forgive an act of true love, of true justice.' She closed Mel's eyes with her fingertips.

Mel sniffed back tears. 'God doesn't agree with us, what we are. What we do to each other.' She reached out for Amelia's body.

Amelia smiled as her lips brushed against Mel's ear. 'I wasn't talking about us.'

Mel felt the change in Amelia's body. When her eyes opened, Amelia had already retrieved the fragment of broken glass she'd concealed inside the mattress earlier.

Mel's eyes narrowed in confusion then fear as Amelia brought it up to her left eye.

It was what remained of the Virgin Mary statue.

'What're you doing?'

Amelia pushed her weight against Mel's chest and sat astride her, knees pinning Mel's arms down hard against the bed.

'I'm sorry I've had to smash this, Mel, after you took all the trouble to sneak it in, but how else was I going to do this?'

Mel felt bile rise in her throat as the realisation hit her. The last two years had been nothing but a lie.

'God had a plan for me from the moment I was born. I've used my time to plan His dream and now it's time for me to put all His words into practice.'

Mel's eyes locked onto the Bible on the shelf but was too stunned to speak.

'You must understand none of this is personal.' Amelia leaned closer to look into Mel's eyes. *'He wants revenge and only I can do this.'*

Mel felt her voice catching in her throat as she spoke. *'Who wants revenge? Revenge for what?'*

'God...talks to me. But He's stopped. There's no more guidance He can give me unless I get out of here. Don't deny the will of God, Mel. You were sent to help me. This was God's plan for you. He sent you to me. Sacrifice yourself for me and there will be a place for you in Heaven despite the sins you've committed by lying with women and committing adultery.'

Amelia clamped her hand down over Mel's mouth as she went to scream, drowning out the sound before she could call for help.

She brought the glass back to Mel's eye, so close that her eyelashes flicked the glass tip each time she blinked.

'I'll give you something to really scream about if you don't shut the fuck up, you stupid bitch,' Amelia hissed, her mask slipping.

At that moment Mel saw just what really lurked underneath the beautiful face that she'd grown to love and her eyes circled the room, desperate for a way out.

She saw the panic button near the door and tried to throw Amelia from her but Amelia's knees dug harder into her arms.

'I want you to know that every touch, every kiss and every word was a lie. Every time I touched your body, every time I made you forget the sadness in your life meant nothing to me but a means to an end. Every time I made you cry out for me...all lies. Nothing was real.

'Know this... I scrubbed myself until I bled after each and every time you touched my skin. I faked every cry of pleasure but now it's my turn. I want to make you scream... for your life.'

Each and every moment Mel had shared with Amelia came into the forefront of her memory and it made her feel sick. The reality of Amelia's words had taken hold of her body, but now the heartache was giving way to the adrenaline that now ran through her body.

The survival instinct began to kick in and Mel pushed all her emotional pain deep inside her body.

She blinked hard, tried to think clearly.

She was heavier than Amelia. She could use this to her advantage. With one surge forward she bucked her body forward, throwing Amelia from the bed.

The sound of Amelia's head hitting the floor was sickening.

Mel scrambled from the bed.

She stood, her heart pounding, staring at Amelia's limp body blocking the door. Her only hope of escape.

The glass was still in Amelia's hand and she edged closer, bent down and snatched it away before jumping back.

She stared at Amelia's body again until she was satisfied she was unconscious and edged towards the door. As she reached for the handle a leg rose up and kicked her hard in the ribs, knocking the wind from her.

She fell to the floor, doubled up in pain. Through her tears she saw Amelia pulling herself up from the floor and cradling her head.

Then Amelia stared down at her.

Mel swung the glass wildly, trying to fend her off, but Amelia was soon down on her like a lioness against its prey. She wrenched the glass from Mel's hand and brought it down hard into her throat.

Mel's eyes were wide as she spluttered, shots of blood gurgling from the wound.

Amelia stood above her, her eyes cold, looking down at Mel's now outstretched arm.

She picked up the leather bag Mel had brought with her. Inside there were bundles of notes, £10,000 in cash, a brown wig, a purse and Mel's security card that opened the hospital doors in the secure areas.

Amelia frowned. She cast her eyes back to Mel. 'You didn't pack my change of clothes?'

Mel's eyes were beginning to look glassy, but still they twitched.

A silent 'fuck you'.

Amelia reached down, grabbed a fistful of hair and yanked her head up. 'You forgot them, didn't you?' Mel blinked hard and Amelia let her head drop back to the floor and kicked her hard in the gut. 'You stupid cunt.'

Mel barely made a sound.

Realising she'd have to improvise, Amelia grabbed the sheet from the bed and wrapped it around Mel's head, covering her face and neck. She then started to remove Mel's clothes, careful not to get any more blood on them than there was already.

Soon Mel stopped moving and blood soaked through the white sheet.

Amelia stripped from her nightwear and put on Mel's clothes: a thin purple jumper and black skinny jeans that hung off Amelia's body. Not ideal but it was necessary.

She looked down at Mel's body.

She knew there was a toilet across from her room which had a safety mirror in it. She dragged Mel's body to the other side of the bed, so it was unseen from the window in the door.

She searched her trouser pockets and pulled out a five-pound note, a hair band, and a set of house keys. She removed Mel's shoes and pulled them on. They were a size too big and they rubbed the backs of her heels as she walked to the door.

She switched off the light and slowly opened the door, checked the corridor was clear and ran into the toilet opposite her.

Inside the small toilet was a wash-basin and the safety mirror.

Amelia stared at her reflection. Her hair was tousled in a wilder mess than usual. She found the hair band and pulled her hair into a rough ponytail. She picked up the wig.

Mel had shoulder-length brown curly hair. She'd had a wig custom-made with a view to helping Amelia escape by posing as herself. At a quick glance, no one would've questioned her. But in Mel's haste to please, she hadn't quite thought about how she would've got out herself. There had never been a time when she'd doubted Amelia's words.

A mistake that'd proved fatal.

Amelia pulled the wig over her ponytail, adjusted it, then stared back at her reflection.

Not bad.

Her eyes fell to the front of the jumper.

She used some water to dab off the spots of blood around the collar and shoulder. There was little she could do, and she gave up as the blood smudged to a dark-coloured stain. Against the purple fabric it wasn't too noticeable and at this time of night, there would be few staff and security around to stop her. Government cuts had led to staff shortages, which worked nicely in her plan.

She took a deep breath and stepped out into the corridor, Mel's bag slung over her shoulder, security pass swinging on the lanyard around her neck.

She walked quickly.

She kept her head down low as she passed each security camera mounted up high on the walls. It'd just be George manning them tonight and Mel had seen to him to buy his silence.

The bright white corridors seemed to wind on forever, but soon she came to the first set of security doors.

She held Mel's pass over the sensor pad and breathed a sigh of relief as it beeped and the door clicked open. She navigated two more doors until she came to the side trade entrance Mel had used to enter the building.

There was no one there.

George had left his post.

Once outside, Amelia found herself in the visitors' car park, partially lit in the darkness.

She still had Mel's keys with her but taking her car was out of the question. She headed towards the security booth that would be the last barrier she had to pass before reaching the road ahead into Stokebrook village high street.

As she approached the booth, she saw it was occupied as expected.

She dipped her hand into her pocket and felt the tip of the shard of glass she'd retrieved from Mel. She pressed the edge against her fingertip.

The man in the booth watched with some curiosity as she approached the pedestrian walkway.

It was George.

***

Amelia had been free for half an hour, climbing over fences and running over farmland, George's blood mixed with Mel's on her jumper.

Stokebrook village was surrounded by farmland and a wood, and Amelia had passed at least two other sleepy hamlets in the last half hour. Despite the isolation, she'd been careful to keep to the fields that ran behind the hearts of the villages.

She paused for breath behind a wooden outbuilding on some farmland.

The night was silent with only the light of the moon to illuminate her surroundings. She was tired from running and needed somewhere to sleep. She peeked inside the unlocked outbuilding.

There was nothing but hay inside, and although it smelt musty she curled up in the middle of it, pulling it all around her so she was hidden.

Using Mel's bag as a pillow, she rested her head and closed her eyes.

***

It was almost 7:00am when she awoke the next day to the sound of her stomach growling.

She was starving.

She rolled over and pulled out strands of hay that had caught in her hair. She sat up and pain surged through her skull. She grabbed the back of her head, rubbing it.

She inspected her fingers and saw dried flaky blood. She realised she'd cut her head when Mel had pushed her to the floor.

Ignoring the pain, she peeked outside and saw that morning dew had soaked the grass and a low mist still hung in the hills ahead of her. She was cold from the lack of food and proper clothes. She walked a few minutes down a small country lane to try and get her bearings.

She came across a small cottage with some clothes hanging on a washing line. She crept as quietly as she could and felt the fabric. Everything was damp from being left out overnight, but Amelia didn't care.

She grabbed a child's pink baseball cap, tracksuit bottoms, a top and zip-up fleece from the line. She ran behind some dense bushes and pulled off Mel's now grass-and-mud stained clothes and changed into the stolen ones.

The elasticised tracksuit bottoms fitted her fairly well, but the top drowned her. She pulled the fleece on, which fitted more snugly, before pulling the cap down low, obscuring her face with the peak. It was too tight, but not noticeably so.

She stood quietly for a while and could hear traffic somewhere in the distance, and wondered whether to risk hitting the main roads or not.

The hunger in her stomach made the decision for her.

After walking for half a mile she saw the main road through the trees, the cars zipping past in a blur. She saw a road sign for a service station and followed through the fields that ran alongside the main road until she saw the Welcome Break services ahead.

She walked through the car park towards the main entrance. No one seemed to notice her dressed as she was, and she blended in with the crowds of people resting in the many eateries.

She could smell the strong scent of fast food, burgers, fried breakfasts and muffins. Her stomach growled as she made herself walk past and towards the small WHSmith ahead.

She couldn't afford to be noticed by anyone. It would be less of a risk to blend in a fast-moving queue. She grabbed some water, crisps and a few chocolate bars and paid.

Soon she was ripping the wrappers from the chocolate and stuffing them into her mouth without really chewing, before washing it back with the water.

She was sitting in the picnic area away from most of the cars, gripping Mel's bag tighter, thinking of the money inside that would help her on her journey for revenge.

She looked around and saw the pay phone.

She had less than a pound in coins, but didn't want to risk going back into the services complex. She put all the coins in the slot and dialled the number she'd committed to memory, and waited.

'Hello?'

Amelia almost cried at the sound of that voice. Her eyes shut tight.

'It's me...I need your help.'

CHAPTER 18

Samantha Jenkins placed steaming hot bowls of roast potatoes and vegetables in the centre of the dining-room table. She'd already sliced up the roast beef joint and carved slices for each plate. She'd set out four plates and wine glasses.

Emily Jenkins was already seated at the table after helping her mother in the kitchen all morning, and was now eyeing the food.

Samantha was just bringing in the gravy when Father Manuela appeared with Mark Jenkins at his side. Today was Sunday and Manuela was joining them for a traditional Sunday lunch.

Manuela glanced at the food on the table and smiled, but it didn't reach his heavily-hooded eyes. They were a dull gun-metal grey, which always reminded Samantha of clouds in the sky as a storm was brewing. Manuela huffed as he sat his tall thin frame in the nearest chair. His salt and pepper-coloured hair was slicked back, a sheen of sweat on his brow.

'Well, this looks and smells wonderful, Sam,' Manuela said.

She smiled as she pulled out a seat for her husband. They all ate in silence after grace was said, helping themselves to food from the bowls. Emily helped her mother clear up afterwards while Manuela and Mark locked themselves away in the study.

'When's the funeral?' Jenkins's voice sounded weak.

'It all depends on when his body is released to the family. Father Wainwright is still with the pathologists... At the moment, he's their best piece of evidence – the police's words, not mine, I hasten to add.'

Manuela took a seat in the old tatty red leather chair at Jenkins's desk.

Jenkins poured a double whisky in a cut-crystal glass and offered it to Manuela, but he declined.

'Any word from David yet?' Jenkins said as he knocked back his drink in one mouthful.

'Nothing. I've left him countless messages but...' He trailed off and shook his head. 'Father Hawthorne – David – has distanced himself, as you know.'

Manuela rubbed his forehead hard and a heavy silence hung in the air.

Jenkins sniffed trying to hold back tears but they started to fall, heavy and hot down his cheeks.

Manuela handed him a tissue from the desk in front of them. 'Come, now,' he said. He smiled, but once again, it never reached his eyes.

Jenkins dabbed at his brow, and nose. When he looked at Manuela, his eyes were red-rimmed. 'It's not just Malcolm,' he said, fighting back more tears. 'I saw Chloe the same morning as Malcolm was kill—'

'*Chloe?*' Manuela said, cutting him off. His face grew red and what light there was in his eyes faded. 'You spoke to her?'

'I wanted to. She walked right past me when I was with Malcolm. Stared right at me, walked past like she's above everyone else, above *me*.' His mouth pulled into a grimace. '*Bitch*.' He looked nervous and he lowered his voice. 'Malcolm said he'd seen her around. Just days before...' He gave a strangled cry and brought the tissue to his eyes again.

Manuela reached out his hand, grasped Jenkins's shoulder. 'She always was poison, you know that.'

Jenkins nodded.

'You can't think she had anything to do with this?'

Jenkins shrugged. 'The way she was when she left us, the things she said. Those disgusting accusations she made against Malcolm and you?' He shuddered. 'Anything's possible, isn't it?'

Manuela's face was stony. Chloe was always a thorn in his side. She always *resisted*...

Jenkins swallowed nervously when he saw Manuela's cold reaction to his words. His face barely registered anything. He certainly didn't rush to defend Malcolm or himself.

'This isn't the time to speak ill of the dead,' he said, as if reading Jenkins's mind.

'Oh, no, of course not,' Jenkins said. 'I...'

He paused, then looked over his shoulder to make sure the study door was still closed.

'I haven't said anything to Samantha, but a detective came to see me at work.'

Manuela looked up, his face confused. 'Whatever for?'

'They say I was the last one to see Malcolm before he was... It was just a routine enquiry but it's still shaken me.' Jenkins lowered his head and sniffed back tears. 'He was a good man. Who could do something like this? I can't understand it, none of it.'

Manuela tried to think rationally, but kept seeing an image from his past that he'd tried so hard to bury. He thought he might be next in line for a visit from the police and it scared him. He rose from his chair.

'Mark, I have things to do at the Manor. Please try not to think about Chloe or dwell on all of this. There are some very evil people in this world. There's no use trying to make sense of it all. God will judge them. It's not for us to intervene.'

Jenkins forced a smile and showed Manuela to the door. He was just putting on his coat when Emily appeared. She smiled sweetly, her natural blonde hair twisted in a loose ponytail. 'Did you need a lift, Father?'

Manuela smiled at her but declined. He gave them his regards to Samantha and left.

***

Her local park was busy, the relentless heatwave showing no signs of ending, drawing people out in their droves.

Claire had to remain focused as she dodged around wayward toddlers, irritated mothers, and dog walkers, their pets straining at their leads, as she jogged around the outer path.

Circling the kids' splash park, Claire pulled off her sunglasses, wiped the sweat that trickled from her forehead into her eyes, and came to a stop beside a bench. She stretched her legs out, and tried to catch her breath.

She usually found that going for a run helped clear her head, but not today. And she was craving a cigarette. Claire silently promised herself when this investigation was over, she'd quit.

***

When Claire got home, and had showered, she headed into the kitchen, tying back her wet hair, smoothing it off her face. After making herself a drink, she picked up her BlackBerry from the kitchen counter and unlocked the screen.

She had one missed call, a voicemail and a text from Michael in response to her message to him the night before.

Hesitant, she listened to the voicemail. It was about the continued problems at Gladstone Court and Claire deleted the message halfway through listening to it.

Then she opened Michael's text message.

I'll catch up with you tomorrow. M

Claire tightened her grip on the phone. *Was that it?* She slammed the phone back on the counter top, and stared up at the kitchen cupboards on the wall.

Taped across the length of them were copies of the scene of crime photographs from Wainwright's murder.

All in their vibrant bloody red hues, flesh and bone, twisted into some kind of macabre sculpture.

Reaching out, Claire ripped them from the cupboards and fought back the tears. When she'd finished only scraps of sellotape and fragments of paper remained.

She leaned on the countertop, breathless, and let the tears fall.

What was happening to her? Usually so controlled and at times stoic, everything now seemed to be closing in on her. She felt caged, the door unlocked, so easy to escape, yet she hadn't the mental strength to do so.

She wiped the back of her hand across her eyes, and stared at the text message again.

Releasing a guttural scream, she hurled her mug across the room. It smashed against the far wall, cold coffee dripping down onto the fragments of china on the floor.

With her back now to the counter, Claire's body gave way from under her, and she slid down, hitting the floor hard, jarring her back. Pain shot up her spine but it barely registered.

Inside she was numb.

CHAPTER 19

The early morning brought light rain, but it did not ease the humidity. There had been a violent thunder storm during the night, through to the early hours, and Claire had spent the whole time watching it sat in the kitchen doorway, not caring as the rain had lashed down, drenching her to the bone.

She'd watched the lightning tear through the sky, the jagged light mesmerising. By the time the rain had eased, Claire had been shivering despite the muggy air, arms wrapped around her legs that were drawn up towards her body.

It had taken every ounce of strength she had remaining to get ready for work.

Today will be better, she told herself. *I am in control.*

She'd arrived at the station early. Nothing of note had been picked up by the night shift, and as they filtered out, bleary-eyed, Claire made a start with the report the pathologist, Danika Schreiber, had had expedited at Claire's request.

She now sat staring at it, one hand supporting her head, arm propped up on the desk.

She frowned at the pages. She'd read and digested it several times in the last hour, and this was the last thing she needed after working all weekend with very little sleep.

She called Michael to her office.

She stared at him as he sat in front of her desk, his hair messy and his face unshaven. He had dark circles under his normally clear eyes and his shirt didn't look like it'd seen an iron in a long time.

'Nice weekend?' she asked. 'Or should I say, eventful?' She eyed him up and down. He shot her a sleepy look but ignored her question. 'Judging by the look of your shirt, I'd say eventful.'

He stared down at his notepad, vacant expression on his face. Claire grew annoyed.

Leaning forward she clicked her fingers in front of his face. 'Are you even fit to be in work, Diego? I've called a team briefing in twenty minutes and you're looking fucked.'

'Sorry,' he managed. 'I guess I overdid it.'

She stared hard at him and felt the slight twinge of jealousy.

She remembered that look of his. It hadn't been that long ago that she'd been on the receiving end of his wild nights out. It was obvious to her that this weekend he'd been showing someone else a good time, and she hated the thought of it.

He's got over me too quickly.

'What's her name then?' she said after a prolonged silence.

'What makes you think I was with a woman?'

'OK then. What's *his* name?'

Michael laughed and looked at her. Her expression was blank and he tried to read her thoughts. It was becoming more obvious to him recently that Claire Winters, the county's most feared ice queen, was maybe starting to regret ending their affair.

'I just had too much to drink and ended up in someone else's bed. You'll be happy to know that my stomach is paying the price. And yes, *Mum*, I used protection.'

Claire hid her irritation, flicked her hair over her shoulder and turned to her computer. The email about the Charity Ball, with its 'plus one' invite, still sat in her inbox, silently mocking her.

'Diego, don't confuse me with someone who gives a shit…' She reached for the pathologist's report and passed it to him. 'I've been reading this for an hour. Now it's your turn, but I'll say this much, whoever did this, is one sick individual.'

***

Seventy-five-year-old Lily Ward opened the tin of cat food and emptied it into Jessop's bowl. The little black cat rubbed its head lovingly against Lily's tired legs, before tucking into the meal of tuna chunks and gravy.

Lily smiled, bent down and stroked the cat's head.

Jessop was her best friend, since she had lost her husband a few years back. Her daughter had bought her Jessop when he was a kitten to help keep her company. Now they never left each other's side.

The cat purred after finishing his meal and bounded after Lily as she sat in her usual chair in the living room. She picked up her knitting and switched on the television. She placed her glasses low on her nose and soon the sound of clicking needles began. Lily turned the television up loud, as her deaf ears strained to pick up the BBC One lunchtime news. Jessop snuggled down beside her feet and drifted off to sleep.

The sound of arguing outside Lily's flat woke Jessop soon after he'd dozed off and he darted off towards the front door, but Lily remained seated, engrossed in her knitting.

She'd grown used to hearing everyone else's business at all hours of the day.

This was what life was like in one of the little flats in town, above a shop, with neighbours on two floors above.

Hardly ideal.

Her daughter had kept urging her to move to accommodation which specialised in looking after the elderly, but Lily had refused, being as independent as ever.

Soon the sound of arguing had died down and Lily smiled at her knitting, admiring it. She was making a new jumper for her little grandson and had chosen a baby-blue wool.

Then something made Lily pause.

She thought she'd felt a light tap against her forehead. Dismissing the thought, she carried on knitting before stopping again.

A medium-sized smudge of something dark had appeared on the wool.

She squinted as she brought the wool closer, when another drop landed on her hand. She looked at the sticky congealed blob and slowly looked above her head.

She cried out, her hand clasping against her mouth.

She reached for her telephone and dialled 999.

CHAPTER 20

The scene looked like all the town's residents had descended on it at once. Uniformed police struggled to keep people behind the police tape which had cordoned off part of the town centre. People began to film on their mobile phones and speculate as to why SOCOs clad in white overalls were entering the flats.

When Claire and Michael arrived, a team of journalists pushed through the crowds to get to them. Ignoring a series of questions, Claire flashed her warrant card at a uniformed officer and he allowed her and Michael through.

The lift to the flat was broken so Claire and Michael took the stairs.

They were met by senior uniformed officer Inspector James Warrington at the top of the stairs. He nodded as Claire approached him.

'Ma'am,' he said and showed her through to Lily Ward's flat.

Claire could hear sobbing coming from the kitchen and peered around the door. She saw the old lady being comforted by a younger one, while speaking to another officer. Claire turned to Warrington.

'That's Mrs Ward in there?'

'Yes, Ma'am.'

Claire nodded as she looked around the small living area. 'And she called in the incident, but hasn't been upstairs and seen anything?'

'No. She was doing her knitting when she noticed the drops come from the ceiling.' Warrington pointed above Michael's head.

They all looked above and Michael wrinkled his nose at the sight.

Blood had seeped though from the flat above and was now a darkened stain around the light fitting, shade and bulb.

'It appears to have been there for a day or two but Mrs Ward hadn't noticed it. It's OK for you to go up now. Officers are currently doing a door-to-door. Photography and video have been taken with the body still in situ. The pathologist is still upstairs…' Warrington trailed off, his face looking grey. 'It's not a pretty sight up there, Ma'am.'

He shifted uneasily. Claire looked at him and then turned to Michael.

'I'll speak with Mrs Ward,' she said. 'I'll follow you up.'

***

Climbing the stairs to the floor above, Michael passed several SOCOs, barely acknowledging any of them, until one caught his eye.

'Hello again… DS Diego, isn't it?' Principal SOCO Jason Meadows pulled his face mask over his head and smiled.

Michael managed a nod.

'Is the SIO here? I'll show her up.'

'No,' Michael said, 'that won't be necessary.' Meadows frowned at him. 'DCI Winters is with Mrs Ward.'

Meadows nodded and turned on his heels. 'Everything's ready for you to go in. I'll get you a suit,' he said, as he padded back up the stairs. He showed Michael along the corridor leading to the flats and they were met by forensic pathologist Dr Danika Schreiber's extended hand.

'Sergeant Diego, nice to see you again,' she said, her German accent much diminished since moving to England ten years ago. Michael smiled and exchanged pleasantries.

Her long dark hair was pulled back into the usual ponytail, she wore no make-up, and her body was clear of jewellery. She was already wearing her Tyvek suit and shoe covers. She pulled the hood up over her hair, and nodded her head towards the door of flat 15 as she put her gloves on.

'We're in there.'

Meadows handed Michael a suit and overshoes. He pulled them on, then Danika led them through to the flat.

Michael tried to ignore the fetid smell at his nostrils as he stepped over the threshold. 'Jesus…'

Several bluebottles were buzzing around the room, flying past his ears. It made his skin crawl and he longed to scratch every part of his body.

Meadows pulled his face mask up again. 'In this heat, if no one had noticed the blood in the flat below, someone would've soon noticed the smell.'

'No shit,' Michael said from behind his own mask.

The front door was open wide and he saw the huge blood spatters covering the back of the front door when it was closed after them.

He saw smeared bloody hand prints dried onto the door and surrounding walls. Meadows made eye contact with him and nodded towards the stains.

'The spatter marks across the door would indicate the victim was already bleeding before being hit and with some ferocity. There're even spatters on the ceiling.'

Michael looked up. The yellowing Artex was spattered with arcs of dark lines.

'I think the fingerprints will match the victim's here,' Meadows continued, gesturing towards the door again. 'The victim must've made for the door and these smear marks are where he was clutching for anything to stop himself from being pulled back into the kitchen.'

Michael followed the dried bloodstains across the bare floorboards with his eyes.

The stains led in thick trails into what Michael assumed to be the kitchen.

'Is that were the body was found?' he said, gesturing towards it.

'Yes. On inspection of Mrs Ward's flat downstairs, the layout of her flat is exactly the same as this one,' said Danika.

'But the blood in here isn't enough to leak through the floorboards onto her light fitting though, is it?' he asked, looking around the floor. Danika pulled a sad face as she showed him the other side of the coffee table.

'Christ!'

Michael took a step back when he saw what was left of the Rottweiler.

'The floorboards are old. It's the dog's blood that has leaked through to Mrs Ward's flat.'

'The dog must've been killed first, but the mutilation would've happened afterwards. After whoever did this was finished with our friend in the kitchen, I mean,' Meadows said.

Michael took a deep breath. 'Let's get this over with.'

Meadows nodded. 'I'll leave you two to it,' he said and left the flat.

Danika let Michael enter the kitchen first.

What he saw could only be described as a mess of blood and flesh. He scanned the kitchen walls, which seemed alive with dried blood. Fat black spots buzzed past his ears – bluebottles, feeding on the decaying blood.

The floor was stained a deep brownish red, which led to a heap of flesh, blood and bone.

Ashe Miller's face was battered, almost beyond recognition, and his head lay to one side, his eyes open in a glassy cold stare.

Danika slowly approached Michael and pointed towards the body. 'Now you know why we called you and Claire in for this.'

Michael nodded. He recognised the obvious similarity instantly.

Ashe Miller's chest had been cut open, his muscle mass and flesh roughly peeled back, exposing parts of his ribcage.

'I've inspected the throat already. There's nothing obstructing the windpipe that I could see, but I'll do a thorough check during the PM.'

Danika tried to gauge Michael's reaction but his face was now expressionless and turned away from her. He stared down at the body, looking for a stab wound.

'What happened? Do you have a time of death?'

'It appears he was beaten about the face before being slashed repeatedly with a very sharp instrument. You can see some of the slash marks about his torso, legs and arms.' She paused and gulped in some much needed air, albeit putrid in smell.

'On examining the hands, I found various lacerations, indicating he tried to protect himself. It appears loss of blood would've killed him eventually, but his killer cut his throat in a left to right movement, suggesting the murderer is right-handed. Desecration of the chest was done after the victim died. I've estimated the time of death between one and three Saturday morning.'

Michael gave the body one last look and left the room. He stripped off the overalls and handed them to a SOCO to bag, as Danika followed after him. He stood in the corridor with his hands on his waist.

'Wainwright's throat wasn't cut,' he said, clarifying the fact for himself more than anything.

Danika moved in closer. 'Do you need me to see Claire?' she asked. 'Sorry, DCI Winters,' she corrected herself when Inspector Warrington appeared in the corridor. Danika and Claire had known each other for many years but Danika always made sure she kept the professionalism when officers were in earshot.

Michael shook his head. 'She'll be up to see the body when she's finished downstairs.'

***

Claire sat opposite Lily Ward and watched the scene unfold with ever-growing annoyance. She'd asked the old lady what had happened and whether she'd heard anything unusual in the last few days.

What were straightforward questions to Claire seemed altogether too difficult for Lily.

'I've told her time and again to move, but she won't listen,' said Gina Moore, with her arm around Lily. Claire stared hard at the woman she'd ignored for the last five minutes. Her eyes narrowed and her face hardened.

'I'm sorry but you are?' Claire asked.

Gina looked affronted, open-mouthed, as Lily continued to cry into her tissue. 'I'm her *daughter.*'

Claire offered no apology and returned her attention to Lily. 'Mrs Ward, again, in your own time please.'

There was another barrage of sniffles and Claire noticed Michael standing in the doorway.

He motioned his head to her.

She looked towards DC Harper sitting next to them. 'Could you finish with Mrs Ward, please, Gabe?' She left the room without waiting for a reply and followed Michael out into the corridor.

She listened, anxious, as Michael explained to her about Ashe Miller's body.

After digesting the information she went upstairs to view the body. Michael waited for her. There was no way he was going back to the carnage unless he had to. When Claire returned to him her face was pale.

Michael shrugged. 'Copycat on our hands, or the real deal?'

'None of the information on Wainwright's mutilation has been given to anyone outside the investigation, and I doubt his housekeeper would've voiced it to anyone. She couldn't even speak when officers found her.'

Claire saw Warrington appear on the stairs above them. Her face hardened. 'I want residents in the blocks down at the station to give statements.'

CHAPTER 21

A team briefing was called as soon as Claire was back in the incident room. She needed to bring her team up to speed on the developments of the Wainwright investigation and the possible connection to Ashe Miller, making sure everything was recorded in the Policy Book, in the event of a review process.

'I want the statements we have so far on HOLMES and any inconsistencies flagged up,' Claire said, as she attached a photograph of Ashe Miller to the board, next to Wainwright.

The Home Office Large Major Enquiry System (HOLMES), developed in the 1980s, contained all the information on the investigation, allowing for very sophisticated searches, and it could eliminate the possibility of any important links and information being missed due to human error, providing the information was inputted correctly.

Claire looked around the room. 'I want you, Harper and Cleaver,' she said, pointing at the two constables, 'to take statements from the residents in Ashe Miller's block.'

They nodded.

'I want mobile phone records for Miller, a list of known associates and their addresses. Where were they when Miller was killed? Miller was the stereotypical Haverbridge lowlife. He has a previous conviction for possession of drugs with intent to supply and a list of enemies a mile long. Even the Council have a file on him regarding anti-social behaviour complaints by other residents.' She looked around the room. 'You get where I'm going with this.'

'Sounds like he got what was coming to him,' Matthews said.

Claire shot him a look. 'That's not helpful.' She looked at DC Richard Lloyd. 'Lloyd, I want you to get me the CCTV footage from the communal areas. Sadly there's no cameras on Miller's floor. You can work with DC Harper and I want more officers going into the local shops. See if anyone saw anything unusual.'

Lloyd made notes and nodded. 'Yes, Guv.'

Claire's eyes returned to Matthews. 'I want you to speak to the town centre management team to get access to the CCTV footage for the rest of the town centre.'

He nodded.

Looking down at the witness statement from Lily Ward, Claire's eyes narrowed. She looked up and addressed the whole team.

'There's one shred of evidence we'll use as a starting point. Mrs Ward said, when asked if she saw anyone near Miller's flat the night he was murdered, that she'd gone upstairs to the third floor. Another elderly resident is in hospital and Mrs Ward had promised to check in on their pet bird. She took the stairs because the lift was broken and on her way down from the third floor, she caught a glimpse of a woman who appeared to be leaving Miller's flat.' She paused for breath. 'There happens to be one resident that somewhat fits her description.'

Claire looked around the room.

'The only description she could give was that the woman had, and I quote, long red hair the colour of blood.'

CHAPTER 22

Amelia picked at her fingers as she waited in the stuffy little interview room. She was on her own, but she knew she could leave at any time so she didn't feel nervous and had learnt to perfect the appearance of an innocent young girl long ago.

It seemed hours since she and the other residents had been asked to attend the station, and she realised she'd not eaten since Sunday night.

She was surprised it had taken so long for the body to be discovered. She thought about how she could've taken more time to dispose of the evidence, if she'd known it would take this long. She dismissed the thought though, knowing she had been so very careful.

She was quietly confident when Claire and Michael entered the room and sat in front of her. She stared at Claire, taking in her face, hair and clothes.

You're a hard-faced bitch. Amelia didn't like those cold piercing eyes. Her attention turned to Michael and, after giving him the once over, she dismissed him.

'I'm DCI Claire Winters and this is DS Michael Diego,' Claire said, reading from an A4 sheet of paper. 'You're twenty years old, live in flat number 18, Swanton Place, and you live alone. Is that correct?'

Amelia nodded. Claire looked at her delicate frame. 'Do you understand why you're here, and that you can leave at any time?'

'Yes.' Amelia's voice sounded small. She kept her eyes lowered, only occasionally meeting Claire's brutal stare.

'Where were you on Friday evening through to the early hours of Saturday morning?'

'In bed from about eight,' Amelia said. 'I had a headache so I went to bed early.'

'Can anyone confirm that?'

'I was alone. I didn't wake until about nine on Saturday morning.'

Claire paused as Michael made a few notes. He glanced up, feeling uneasy.

Amelia was staring at him. He felt uncomfortable, especially in front of Claire.

Claire had noticed Amelia's gaze and pushed her jealousy deeper within, cursing herself for still feeling anything for him. Michael was an attractive man, it was perfectly normal for anyone to stare at him, but nothing could contain her jealousy for very long.

'Did you know the deceased?' Michael asked, breaking the silence.

'No.'

'Did you ever have any dealings with him?'

Amelia lowered her face. Michael rephrased his question. 'What type of neighbour was he?'

Amelia scoffed at the question. 'Vile. Anti-social. He played his music too loud and kept a vicious dog. I kept my distance from him.' She glanced at Claire. 'He did a lot of drugs too.'

Exchanging glances with Michael, Claire leaned forward. 'How do you know? I thought you kept your distance?' Amelia's eyes innocently wandered from Claire to Michael.

'It wouldn't take an idiot to work it out,' she said. 'Whenever I did see him about, his eyes were always the size of saucers. He smelt of weed and I know he had shady visitors. My guess is he pissed off the wrong man and they got revenge.'

'What makes you say it was a he?' Michael said, glancing at Claire.

Amelia thought for a moment. 'From what I heard, Ashe got cut up bad. He was a tough guy. No woman could overpower that.' She smiled, smug. 'Surely you've already thought of that one and ruled it out?'

Michael sat back in his chair.

Claire didn't like Amelia. There was something about this girl that didn't seem right to her.

'We have a witness who said they saw a woman who looked like she was leaving Miller's flat around the time he was murdered…a woman with long red hair.'

Amelia's eyes shot up to Claire's. She grabbed a few strands of her hair, twisted them around her fingers and smiled. 'Then I guess that means I'm guilty.'

Claire frowned at her.

'That wasn't a confession, Chief Inspector,' Amelia said. 'Plenty of women have red hair. It doesn't make them guilty of anything.' She paused and leaned forward in her chair. 'I didn't go anywhere near Miller's flat. I was afraid to. I even hated walking past it in the daytime.'

Michael's eyes narrowed then flicked across to Claire.

The corners of Amelia's mouth twitched, hinting at a smile. 'I think I'd like to leave now.'

'You're free to leave at any time,' Michael clarified.

Amelia stood up, scraping the chair legs back across the linoleum floor.

'Just one more thing,' Claire said, her hand raised. A flicker of rage passed over Amelia's eyes but soon disappeared. She nodded.

'Do you have any next of kin?' Claire asked. Amelia looked at her, face blank, but offered no response.

'Amelia?' Michael prompted.

'I have no one.'

Claire's face hardened, not believing her. 'Where're your parents?'

'Dead.'

Claire stared at her a few moments longer before looking towards Michael. He cast her another sideways glance.

'Amelia, I need you to sign a statement before you go. If we need anything more from you, we'll be in touch,' Michael said in a well-rehearsed voice. Amelia looked at him from beneath lowered lashes and smiled.

It made Claire feel nauseous.

CHAPTER 23

'I'm not buying that innocent girl act,' Claire said, watching Amelia walk away from the station from her office window.

Michael cast a knowing glance. 'I can't imagine why.'

She ignored him and returned to sit behind her desk. She picked up a pen and played with it, twisting it between her fingers, thinking.

'My mind's been working overtime here. What links Wainwright's murder, a priest held in high regard, to some lowlife no one dared go near?' She paused. 'What's the significance of mutilating the torso?'

Michael sat in the chair opposite her. 'What's the significance of anything?' He exhaled slowly. 'Maybe it's just some psycho picking people at random. Maybe it's a religious nut targeting people of the same religion.'

Claire threw the pen down. 'Somehow, I doubt Miller was a church-goer. Call me cynical here, but there's no way he's meeting St Peter at the pearly gates any time soon.' She sat back in her chair and folded her arms. 'The guy was scum.'

A knock at the door startled them both. Claire waved someone to enter and Michael saw the familiar grin of David Matthews. He glanced at Michael, but didn't acknowledge him.

'I've taken a call from Dr Schreiber. Wainwright's body has been released back to the family, now we've got all we can from him. I know it's sooner than usual, than circumstances would normally allow… His funeral's being planned as we speak.' His smile was broad across his face. It irritated Michael.

You want a pat on the back or something?

Claire nodded and Matthews hovered briefly, before leaving. Michael shot Claire a look and shook his head.

'He's a prick.'

Ignoring him, Claire pulled the pathologist's report into Wainwright's death across her desk. 'You've read this too. They found a note buried inside him.'

'We're waiting for forensics to analyse it, although I doubt they'll find any trace fibres or DNA that didn't belong to Wainwright. We'll have to see what it means. Could be the killer messing with us though.'

Claire opened the report and flicked through to the page in question and passed it to him. 'Here,' she said, pointing to the text that was found on the note. 'Read this for me out loud.'

Looking at the text Michael began to read aloud.

'Section 5.2. Upon further examination there appeared to be a folded piece of paper which had been printed using a computer. This was found between the folds of muscle and tissue of the abdominal area of the deceased. Text reads as follows: "What revelation lies within the beauty of a rose? With its thorns sharp yet perfume so bewitching, you must breathe in the scent, be it foul in its reason for being."'

Michael looked up at Claire and frowned.

'You've gone pale.'

She drew a deep breath. 'I received the same note a few days ago. It was hand-delivered to my home.'

Scanning the report again, Michael looked shocked. 'Are you sure?'

Claire went to the window, wrapping her arms tight around her body. 'Of course I'm bloody sure. You don't forget something like that.'

'Of course. Sorry, Claire, it's just – I don't understand. Why have you kept this quiet? Where's the note now?' He watched her closely as she remained at the window, her back to him.

'I thought nothing of it. I put it in the bin.' She turned to him. 'I thought nothing of it until I read the report this morning. I mean, why should I?'

'But why not say anything at all…to me?'

'We got caught up in the Miller murder and besides, I wanted to go home, find the note and make sure I had it right.' She turned away from him again. Sensing she was upset, Michael joined her at the window.

'I can come back and look with you.' She stared at him hard and he raised his hands to her in defence. 'Not that you scare easily. I just thought you could do with the company as well.'

'I don't need your help,' she said, 'or your company.' She shoved him aside and started shutting down her computer.

'I know, but the offer's there all the same.'

Claire looked at him and told herself not to give in.

CHAPTER 24

Father Manuela looked pale when he saw the caller ID flash across his mobile phone.

David Hawthorne.

He debated in his head whether or not to answer it. After it rang a few more times, he pressed the answer button. 'I didn't think you'd call.'

The strain in Father Hawthorne's voice at the other end was obvious. 'When's the funeral?'

'Within the week. The family assured me the funeral director is dealing with the paperwork as a matter of urgency.' Manuela paused. 'It's not been easy for them. It hasn't been easy for any of us.'

Hawthorne listened but felt nothing for Wainwright. He owed them nothing and Manuela knew this.

'I'd be grateful if you could let me know the date and time. I'll be there to show my face. After that, I want no more contact from you. That part of my life is over. Is that understood?'

Manuela sighed and hung up the phone. He didn't need to utter another word to Hawthorne. Enough damage was already done. He only hoped Hawthorne held his nerve for both their sakes.

He buried his face in his hands. This had been much harder than he could ever have envisaged.

After a few moments, he peered out of the window in his study and gazed down at the Rose Garden.

The rose bushes cut a sombre shape in the shadows under the moon, and he felt shivers creep along his spine. He shuddered involuntarily and moved from the window.

He looked at the large cross opposite him on the wall and knelt on the floor.

He clutched his rosary and began to mutter a prayer. Tears welled in his eyes as he gazed at the relic.

'God *will* forgive me.'

CHAPTER 25

It'd been a quiet journey in the car, as Claire drove them back to her house. Michael had been observing her the whole time. She'd remained stiff in her seat, eyes staring dead ahead at the road.

She offered no small talk, but it didn't bother Michael.

He could tell she was uncomfortable with taking him home with her, but he could also tell there was a glimmer of relief in her eyes.

They pulled up the drive and she let them in the front door. There was another letter from Claire's mother on the doormat. He passed it to her, and she stuffed it inside her trouser pocket.

He wandered into the kitchen. 'Still as I remember it,' he said. He saw Claire stiffen. He avoided her eyes. 'Sorry.'

There was an awkward silence.

Claire picked up the kettle. 'Tea?' Michael nodded. He waited until she'd made them both a cup and drank half of it before asking the burning question.

'Is it in that bin?' he asked, looking behind her at the stainless-steel barrel. She nodded. He set his drink down and lifted the lid.

'You don't mind if I take a look?'

'You might need these,' she said, throwing him a pair of rubber washing-up gloves from the sink.

He took off his suit jacket, rolled up his shirt sleeves and started to delve in amongst her rubbish. He pulled aside many ready-meal cartons, tutting to himself.

'What's that supposed to mean?'

Michael laughed, holding an empty bolognese carton. 'Very healthy.' Claire flipped him the middle finger.

Searching deeper he then came across the squashed letter. He took it to the table and carefully rolled it out and read the message. He leaned against the sink.

'No mistaking that,' he said, pulling off the dirty gloves and tossing them aside. 'It's definitely the same message.'

Claire took a seat at the table and buried her head in her hands. Unsure what to do, Michael remained where he was and stared at the floor.

'We have to have forensics look at this…and maybe you should consider getting someone watching over you and the house.'

Claire bolted upright. 'Have you lost your mind?'

'Just a precaution.'

'I'm not living my life under surveillance. I can take care of myself.'

She grabbed the letter and stormed into the living room. Michael followed her at a distance. He watched her pull a clear resealable bag from a drawer and put the note inside.

'That'll do for now, although it's already pretty much ruined. You won't find any trace evidence on it we could use. I'll hand it over tomorrow. For now I just want to rest.'

She flopped down on the sofa.

'Have the last few days been better for you?'

Claire's eyes flicked towards him. 'What do you mean?'

Michael perched on the arm of the sofa. 'Well, you've not had to run off on something that's *top secret*,' he said, miming inverted commas at the last two words. 'And I've not seen you all jumpy, ignoring personal phone calls.'

Claire looked away, her eyes wandering towards the photograph of herself with her parents. She had an innocence about her then, despite everything.

'I hope you've got everything sorted now,' he said.

'You know what I'm going to say, don't you?'

'That it's none of my business?'

'It isn't.'

'Well, it is when we're working on a tough investigation.'

'What happens in my personal life doesn't affect you any more, now does it? You gave all that up.'

Michael sighed, and shifted awkwardly on the sofa. 'I just want to know if you're OK.' He glanced at her. 'That all right with you?'

Claire felt her stomach knot, but couldn't tell if it was because of anxiety or that pang of excitement he used to induce in her.

There was silence for a few minutes before anyone spoke again.

'I don't feel comfortable leaving you here alone,' he said, wary of her reaction. She glared at him, but then her face softened.

'I'll be fine. Go home, Diego.'

Michael thought for a moment, then sat next to her. 'Slight problem there.' She frowned at him. 'My car's still at the station. It's a bit far to walk back to get it, you being slightly out in the sticks.'

She sighed. 'Sorry, I was so wrapped up in everything, I didn't even think about how you'd get home.'

He looked around the room, avoiding her face.

'I didn't.'

They stared at each other before her professional judgement came into play.

'I'll call you a cab.' She reached for her phone. Michael was testing her resolve and she knew it. 'There're worse things than a psychotic killer out there, Diego,' she said, waiting for the taxi line to pick up.

He smirked and looked at her. 'Really?'

She smiled. 'Yeah.' She paused. 'Your libido.'

***

It was nearly 4:00am when Amelia awoke to the sound of her mobile ringing. She sat up in bed and realised she was in the comfortable hotel room she'd decided to check into.

She couldn't bear the thought of going back to her own flat right now. There was too much police activity in the block.

The mobile was still ringing.

She saw the '*G*' flashing on the screen and answered it quickly. She listened to the static on the line with bated breath.

'*What did you think you were doing?*' came the familiar voice she had longed to hear.

'I'm sorry. He overheard things from the other day, when we spoke over the phone. He was hiding in the stairwell and the money was drying up. The last time I fucked him, he refused to pay. I need more than you're giving me to keep this up, you know that.'

The Guardian was seething deep within.

'*You could've blown the whole plan, you stupid bitch!*'

Amelia jumped. Sweat began to bead on her forehead. 'I'm sorry, I was very careful. Be proud of me, I did it like you taught me, covered my tracks. They'll find nothing to lead back to me or you, or any evidence I've been in his flat, I swear.'

The caller was silent, calming themselves.

'If anything can be traced back to you, I'll cut all ties. I'll leave you to face the consequences if you deviate from the plan again, do you understand me?'

Amelia stifled a whimper. She knew what the Guardian was capable of. She'd been witness to it living under the same roof as them.

Amelia squeezed the phone in her hand tighter. She sensed there was more to come.

'Something's wrong, isn't it?'

She heard the soft intake of breath.

'I saw Mark with Wainwright that morning.'

Amelia froze. 'You said you'd been careful.'

'I was!'

'Keep a distance; follow towards the church, *that's* what you said.'

'Amelia—'

'You're giving me shit about Ashe, when Mark could've seen you!' The Guardian was silent. *'Did he see you?'*

'It's not relevant.'

'Like fuck it isn't.'

The line went dead.

Amelia stared at the screen, her thumb poised above the call button, ready to redial. She switched the phone off instead, and pulled the duvet tight around her and was deprived of sleep for what remained of the night.

CHAPTER 26

The day was colder than it had been but still warm and enjoyable for those lucky enough not to be trapped inside an office. The day of Father Malcolm Wainwright's funeral would be a glorious one.

Claire and Michael had missed the service itself but had slipped among the procession just before the coffin was being lowered into the earth. They quietly observed the mourners, who ranged from close family and friends to members of the public, with some kind of morbid curiosity.

Claire's eyes examined those around her. She nudged Michael when she caught sight of Manuela's strained face, staring hard at another man several feet from him.

Michael followed his gaze and signalled to Claire.

They both saw a man of medium height, slender and gaunt, staring at the freshly dug grave. He was dressed in simple dark trousers, with a white shirt covered by a dull brown cardigan.

After a few minutes of silent prayer, the mourners started to disband and talk in hushed tones amongst themselves. Michael saw Mark Jenkins giving him a cold stare and eased himself from his line of vision. Claire followed him, and they stood beside some gravestones, away from everyone else.

Claire watched Manuela walk over to the man in the brown cardigan.

From their body language, she could tell neither was comfortable being in each other's company.

'Interesting that,' she said, nodding her head in their direction. Michael ignored her, too busy watching Jenkins with his wife and Emily.

'That must be the foster kid still with the Jenkins family,' he said. Claire glanced over and nudged his arm in frustration.

'Yes, but we should be more interested in what's going on over there.'

Michael stared at the two men.

The one with the brown cardigan was gesturing a lot with his hands and looked sad, but there was anger in his eyes too. The other man seemed to be trying to calm him down, while looking around to see who was watching.

'I think that's Father Manuela,' Claire said. 'No idea who the other one is.'

Michael grunted in agreement but he had caught sight of something else through the trees, far off in the cemetery. 'I'll be back in a minute.'

He hurried towards a path that disappeared between much older gravestones. He walked along the ragged path that led him deeper into the cemetery and stopped to look around him.

He knew he'd seen someone darting behind the nearby trees, watching them, or at least, he thought he had.

He stood still for several long minutes, and heard nothing but nature around him.

Birds twittered in the lush green foliage of the trees and he could smell the strong perfume of flowers in bloom. Shards of sunlight cut through the branches overhead, the spots of light standing out in stark contrast to the green of the grass around him.

He looked up when a bird fluttered its wings, flying from a tree and disappearing into the bright blue sky.

He was about to turn and head back to Claire, when he heard a voice behind him.

'Hello, Sergeant. Were you looking for me?'

Michael slowly turned around and saw a familiar face with wild red hair flowing in the breeze.

'What're you doing here?'

Amelia smiled, walking closer to him. She was nearly at arm's length from him when he saw her face change.

She backed away, and then hurried back to the far entrance to the cemetery. Michael turned around and saw Claire walking towards him.

'Was that the Williams girl?'

'Yeah.'

'What did she want? What did she say?'

'I don't know… *You* scared her off before she could say anything.'

'You don't think it's weird she's here on the day of Wainwright's funeral?'

He shrugged. 'Not really. There're plenty of the curious here today…' He glanced over Claire's shoulder and saw a cameraman from the BBC. 'Plenty of hacks too.'

Claire looked behind her and frowned.

'Well, while you were playing hide-and-seek, I've been doing some police work.' She gestured with her head for him to follow her. 'That man with Manuela is called David Hawthorne. *Father* David Hawthorne, or at least he used to be. He was an old friend of Wainwright's until he suddenly took off, turning his back on the priesthood. He used to help Manuela run Shrovesbury, then one day he just left.'

'Who told you this?'

'One of the church-going coffin-dodgers. It's funny how the so-called pious ones are the first to dish up gossip to a perfect stranger.' She grinned. 'There's some irony in that.'

***

Back in her car, Claire turned to him. 'We've been invited back to Jenkins's home for the wake. I said we'd be delighted.'

Michael turned towards her. 'What the hell did you do that for? How shit is that going to be?'

'Just an hour, I promise.'

'I can just imagine the reception we're going to get once they all find out who we are.'

'Look,' she said as she switched on the engine, 'I want a chance to talk to that old woman again. She said Hawthorne left after a tragic event. I want to find out what that was.'

She was about to pull out and follow the rest of the cars heading towards the Jenkins' home when she felt Michael's fingers close around her wrist. It caused her to stall the engine and it whined to a halt.

'What are you doing?'

'I don't see what this has to do with anything.'

'Call it a hunch.'

Michael released her wrist and shook his head. 'Whatever's going on in your private life is affecting your judgement.' He looked at her hard in the face.

Claire half laughed. 'Don't tell me you're actually worried about me?'

'I'm worried about this investigation, and yes, actually, I *do* worry about you. Why wouldn't I?'

She stared hard into his eyes, trying to find any hint that he was stringing her along. To her surprise, she couldn't. She felt a knot form in her stomach, and her throat felt like it was going to seize up.

'Don't tell me you're lost for words,' he said, a smile playing on his lips.

Feeling uncomfortable, determined not to let him see she still had some feelings for him, feelings she didn't quite understand herself, she gripped the steering wheel and looked ahead, eyes focused on anything but his face.

'I said we'd follow the rest of them,' she said at length, gesturing to the other cars that had manoeuvred around them, heading in the direction of the Jenkins' home.

Michael placed his hand over hers, locked on the steering wheel, knuckles white. He felt her flinch, just a little. 'You do know that despite everything, I do still care about you, don't you?'

She swallowed hard. 'Don't turn this into something it isn't.'

'Turn what?' She stole a look down at his hand over hers, looked away just as quickly. 'You used to like me touching you.'

Claire started the car again, flicking his hand off hers in the process, moved forward a little, then stopped abruptly.

He studied the side of her face, admiring the curve of her lips. He saw her swallow hard, the veins in her throat pulled tight under the skin.

'I can't deal with this,' she finally said. She shot him a look. 'I've got—'

'Too much going on?' he said, cutting her off. 'Yeah, you keep saying that and to be honest, you need to tell me what it is, otherwise…'

Her eyes narrowed. 'Otherwise what?'

Michael sighed, propping his elbow on the side of the door, and let the side of his head rest in his palm. He looked straight ahead.

'Otherwise *what*, Diego?'

Michael risked a glance in her direction. 'I'll be forced to tell DSI Donahue that you're letting your personal life get in the way of things.'

Claire shifted around in her seat, turning to face him face on. 'You're taking the piss, aren't you?' He avoided her stare. '*This*,' she said, gesturing between them both, 'whatever it is we have going on between us, is hard enough to ignore, without you adding any pressure on me, and empty threats.'

He twisted in his seat to face her. 'So you admit there *is* something we need to get out in the open, about us, and whatever else is going on with you right now?'

'For fuck's sake, we're *not* going to turn this into some psychological study. It's none of your business what I do outside of work.' He went to speak, but she cut him off. 'It stopped being any of your business a long time ago.'

Michael felt a twinge inside him. It didn't take him long to realise it was the pain of being struck by her words. Did he really mean nothing to her?

He was too proud to show her that she'd touched a nerve. He looked ahead. The silence seemed to drag on for several seconds before he said, 'Don't assume that I'm dishing out idle threats.' He paused. 'I'm a man of my word, you know that.'

A small queue of cars was now building behind them and someone honked a horn in frustration. They were blocking the way out. Claire ignored it and looked Michael hard in the face.

'You're talking about Donahue?' She leaned in closer. 'Tell him what you like.' She let the sentence hang in the air for a moment. 'I'll be sure to tell him that you've disobeyed my command, potentially hindering this investigation.'

'This is pathetic. You're being petty now.' He laughed then, riling her further.

'We *are* going to the wake.' She paused. 'You're refusing to go?'

Michael flinched as he heard a barrage of more car horns. 'I'm not refusing anything.'

Her eyes narrowed. 'You're attitude is pretty shitty, Diego. I'm SIO on this investigation—'

'And don't you like to keep fucking reminding me.' He looked at her face as it slowly grew redder. 'You know what?'

'Oh, this ought to be good,' she said, staring ahead, and gripping the steering wheel tighter again.

'You weren't worth anything.'

Her eyes flicked to the side, to stare at him. More car horns were sounded behind them. 'We're holding up the queue, Sergeant. If you've got something to say, spit it out.'

Michael's face was serious. 'You weren't worth risking my job over. If I'd known *this* is what I'd be putting up with when I ended it, I'd never have touched you.'

'You know what, Diego? Get over yourself. You want to make Inspector one day and it's this attitude that's going to stop you.'

'And you, if you can.'

'If I have to.'

He paused, then opened the passenger door and got out. As more car horns sounded behind them, he leaned back into the car. 'Go fuck yourself, Claire.'

He slammed the door hard behind him.

Claire watched him disappear from view. She was seething as she pulled out onto the main road, narrowly missing a car coming from the opposite direction.

CHAPTER 27

David Hawthorne waited until Manuela had closed the door before reaching out and grabbing him roughly by the collar. He forced him back against the wall.

Manuela's eyes bulged as Hawthorne tightened his grip. He brought his face up so close to Manuela's that he could smell the faint stale aroma of whisky creeping from David's mouth.

'I can't believe you're prepared to do nothing!' Saliva sprayed Manuela's face. 'Even after Malcolm's death, you act like what we did never happened.'

They were in Mark Jenkins's bedroom, while the celebration of Father Malcolm Wainwright's life had commenced downstairs and the house was heaving with guests.

Manuela struggled to release David's iron grip. 'My dear friend, please understand we must remain dignified through this terrible time.'

David's face screwed up tight in anger and he released his choke hold on Manuela's neck. 'Someone knows,' he said, pointing a shaky finger in Manuela's face. 'Someone knows what we did and *we're* next.'

'How could anyone know? After four years, David, nothing has happened.'

'Look what has *happened* to Malcolm!'

'His murder could easily be a random case. Tragic, but random. They found the body of a young man in the same state. He's unconnected to the church. See reason, David!'

'I saw Chloe in recent weeks.'

Manuela froze at his words. Mark Jenkins had told him the same thing. After all these years, Manuela had only seen her once, despite living in the same city. Even then, it'd been *he* that had seen her. She'd been preoccupied with food shopping.

Then the obvious struck him.

'You've been back here, to Haverbridge?'

David gave a slight nod. 'I visited my sister. I had hoped to go unnoticed.'

'You never tried to contact me?'

David's voice rose. 'Why would I?'

Manuela's face screwed up as he spoke. 'You're taking this too far, David.'

'Chloe saw me. What if she knew more than she ever said? I have to wonder—'

'Don't be ridiculous!' Manuela dismissed him with a wave of his hand. 'Think about what you're saying!'

'I won't wait around to be hacked to pieces. We must do what we should've done four years ago. *I* should've done it years ago.' He reached for the door, but Manuela pushed him back.

'Are you mad?' he said, just above a desperate whisper. He inched the door open a crack to check no one was outside. 'We made a pact, David. The secret goes to the grave.'

'We may be in ours soon enough and I know where our souls will be. Damned for eternity.'

Manuela closed the door again.

David sank down on the bed and held his face in his hands. A few moments passed in silence. 'I can't live with the guilt any longer, Jeremy. I can't wrestle with my conscience. Even if it means imprisonment for the rest of my wretched life, I don't care any more.'

Manuela felt the cold sting of betrayal deep inside him, as he dissected David's words carefully inside his head. With little emotion, he watched as his old friend wept before him. He pushed his own guilt deep down, convincing himself that what they did had been necessary.

'Are you suggesting we move her?'

David looked through his tears and nodded. 'Maybe we should think about *her*. She had no Christian burial. In the eyes of God she's in limbo. Her soul will never be at peace if we do nothing.'

Manuela pursed his lips in anger, but tried to control his rage.

'I'm sure nature has done its job in these four years. Why cause more hurt to us and the church? Think of Malcolm's legacy. He'll have none if we speak out now.' He sat beside David on the edge of the bed. 'What's hidden must remain so.'

David went to utter a protest but saw the cold look in Manuela's eyes. He'd seen what this man was capable of and even now it scared him to the core.

'Besides, if you speak out now, I'll deny any involvement.'

David turned his face to Manuela, fear in his eyes.

'And who do you think they'll believe?' Manuela said, placing his hand against his chest. 'The man who has held this community together these thirty years, devoted to the one true faith, or the man who turned his back on God, deserting his post and obligations?'

He let his words sink in.

'Think carefully, David.' He walked to the door and opened it slightly. 'What you choose now will make or break you. Either way, I beg you, choose wisely and dare not cross me.'

Manuela left the room and David heard him join the mourners downstairs.

He sat on the bed for some time, unmissed by those below. He contemplated his next move and began to pray for the salvation of his soul.

1998

Chloe waited by her mother's side as the girl with hair the colour of flame walked up the path towards the house, hand clasped in her father's.

Chloe squeezed her mother's hand when the little girl in front of her stopped dead in her tracks, pulling on Mark Jenkins's arm, staring Chloe hard in the face.

Samantha Jenkins gave her daughter a gentle push towards the girl. When Chloe resisted, coming behind her mother's legs and wrapping her arms around them, Samantha turned and knelt down to her daughter's eye level.

'What did I say to you earlier?' She spoke softly, but there was an edge to the words that Chloe, even at her tender age, understood all too well. 'Be nice, Chloe.'

Mark had encouraged the girl beside him to walk the rest of the short distance to the front door.

Watchful green eyes looked at Chloe from head to toe.

'Here she is,' Mark said, smiling at his wife.

'Pleased to meet you,' Samantha said, and with more force than before, manoeuvred Chloe from her until she stood directly in front of the girl.

The girl's eyes widened, taking in every inch of her. She hugged a teddy bear under one arm. Squeezed it tighter.

Chloe held her breath.

Here we go again. Another like the first, *she thought.*

She swallowed hard as the girl let go of Jenkins's hand, fingers reaching out towards Chloe's face.

Chloe flinched as soft fingertips brushed her cheek. She went to take a step back, but felt her mother's legs behind her digging into her back.

Samantha placed her hands firmly down on Chloe's small shoulders.

'*Chloe's been very much looking forward to meeting you,*' she said, a forced smile plastered across her heavily made-up face.

Chloe looked back into the bright green eyes, saw them narrow a fraction before they changed. They seemed to soften.

A smile played on the girl's lips. She took Chloe's hand in hers.

'*My name's Amelia.*' She gave Chloe's hand a gentle squeeze. '*I know we're going to be best friends.*'

CHAPTER 28

It'd been two days since Michael had walked out on her at Wainwright's funeral and Claire was like a ticking time bomb waiting to explode. Everyone had been giving her a wide berth and hadn't bothered her unless absolutely necessary.

She'd found out very little by attending Wainwright's wake and had decided to visit Father Manuela instead.

Shrovesbury Manor sat in the leafy outskirts of Haverbridge. The redbrick Victorian building, designed in the typical Gothic style of its time, cut an impressive shape on the landscape. With its oriel windows, creeping ivy clinging to brick, and chimneys rising into the cloudless sky, Shrovesbury was without a doubt a beautiful building.

This fact was lost on Claire as she pulled up outside the large iron gates and read the sign ahead.

Welcome to Shrovesbury Manor
A place of religious enlightenment
Established in 1864

She pulled a face but drove on through the gates, along a private road flanked with beech trees on either side, until the view opened up to reveal the Manor in all its glory.

The heat from the sun felt intense as she climbed from the car. The Manor cast dark foreboding shadows down upon her as she approached the main doors giving her some respite.

Father Manuela emerged from the entrance like a serpent preparing to strike its prey. 'Good morning,' he said as she approached him. He offered his hand and Claire took it, forcing a smile.

His hand felt limp and clammy.

'Father Manuela. So glad you agreed to see me.'

'Please, call me Jeremy.'

Manuela showed her into the drawing room and waited until she settled on a large dark-brown leather sofa, before wheeling over a tea trolley from the corner.

Claire noticed the musty odour from the sofa immediately, or maybe it was just the room in general.

The wallpaper was a dark-maroon colour with a faint pattern embossed across it, slightly worn over the years. The darkness of it all made Claire feel caged and oppressed.

She took in her surroundings in a split second; she noticed how the tall slim bookcases were filled with dusty tatty books, many religious in nature, but with a few well-known classics thrown in for good measure.

Everything seemed to be dusty, old and eccentric, much like their owner.

'It's a shame we didn't get a chance to talk at the wake. It was a glorious service you missed at the church as well,' he said, pouring her a cup of tea.

He handed her a dainty little cup, and smiled. His eyes were heavily hooded by his droopy eyelids, and his expression seemed troubled. Claire waited until he'd settled in his chair and was giving her his full attention.

'I'm sorry if my colleague and I appeared to have intruded at the burial. Believe me, it was not our intention.' She tried to gauge his reaction.

Manuela just looked at her, nodding and showing the faintest of smiles. His teeth were yellow and jutted out in odd angles at the bottom. His lips were dry and had started to crack and Claire looked away when he wetted them with his tongue.

There remained a brief silence between them.

Claire sipped her tea, flinching at the lukewarm milky liquid. She only just stopped herself from spitting it back into the cup.

'The Manor looks quite something,' she said. 'I knew it existed but I've never known what it was used for. I noticed the sign said it dates from 1864.'

Manuela looked at her over his teacup, his smile genuine this time, happy she was showing an interest in his home.

'The Manor has been in my family for most of those years. I took over after my father, as his father did before him, and so on.' He reached forward and placed his half-empty cup on a small table to the side of him. 'It wasn't always used for religious purposes though. Originally my family's home, they then allowed it to be requisitioned for a training school and officers' mess during the war in 1939.'

Claire smiled, gesturing for him to continue. *Keep him talking and opening up.* 'Please go on.'

Manuela looked at her sceptically at first, then nodded. Passion for his family's work and history flowed through his body and he relished the chance to boast about the greatness of Shrovesbury.

'Well, by 1960 the Manor was used as a girls' residential school, mainly for problem students, I might add,' he said, frowning.

'What happened between the war and then?'

'It became my family's home again after the war. The idea for the school came about around 1947 but it then took a further ten years to push it through and it didn't open until 1960. After another ten years my father changed it into a place of religious enlightenment.'

Manuela leaned forward as if to keep the next part a secret between them both.

'He didn't like the fact that the girls who studied here were all delinquents and possessed less than Godly thoughts. They lacked a purpose in life.'

His eyes seemed to look through her as he continued. 'Christ gave his life so that they could fulfil theirs. My father had a Chapel built within the grounds to aid in the salvation of their souls. I took over from him in 1979 and have tried to carry on his vision and beliefs ever since. We have had and indeed still have a great success rate here.'

Manuela sat back in his chair and folded his arms, feeling an overwhelming sense of pride.

Claire processed all the information Manuela had given her. She thought Manuela appeared to be a nice man, pious and a pillar of the community, but then she remembered the scene she'd caught a glimpse of between him and the former Father David Hawthorne.

Manuela seemed less than likeable then. His face appeared to be a mask for something he kept repressed, something just hovering at the surface ready to take hold at any point.

'Father, I—'

'Jeremy, please,' he cut in.

She ignored him. 'I'm guessing you know I'm here for another reason; as fascinating as the Manor's history is, I have another agenda.' She saw the change in his face. His eyes frightened her as he tried to appear unaltered by her words.

'Chief Inspector, I'm not sure I understand your meaning. Father Wainwright was here on a regular basis offering salvation and wisdom along with the rest of us and he will be sorely missed. I don't know what more I can tell you.'

Claire raised her eyes, a little taken back. Manuela pushed himself from his seat and walked towards the window, his arms now clasped behind his back, facing away from her.

His fingers fidgeted uncontrollably.

'He was a good man. I won't have anything said to the contrary.'

'What makes you think I'm here to refute what you're saying about Wainwright? Everyone we've questioned so far speaks as highly of him as you do.'

Except Chloe Jenkins.

She could tell Chloe's disdain for the man was strong. She could almost smell it that night.

Manuela kept his back to her, staring out of the window.

'Why else are you here, if not for furthering your investigation?' His voice sounded agitated. 'That's the real reason you were at his funeral as well, I assume. Although who knows what you hoped to see there among his well-wishers.'

His head turned towards her but she remained silent. He smiled to himself and returned his gaze towards the window looking out on the gardens.

Claire took her time before she spoke. It was part of her game plan and she wanted to gauge Manuela's reaction without missing a single detail.

'Actually, Father…it was Father Hawthorne I was interested in talking about.'

Manuela's body stiffened but then he turned towards her and smiled. 'I'm only too happy to oblige, although I can't see why he should be of interest to you.'

Claire waited for him to sit but he didn't move.

'I think I'll get us some more tea,' he said and left the room.

Claire remained on the sofa.

She'd touched a raw nerve.

***

It was ten minutes later before Manuela entered the room again. Claire watched as he topped up her cup with a large quantity of milk, and her face turned sour. She looked away and waited for him to sit down.

'So,' she said, sitting back and crossing her legs. 'Father David Hawthorne. That was who I saw you …' She tried to search for the right word, making Manuela feel uneasy. '… *converse* with at the funeral?'

'I spoke with many people.'

'Let me be more specific. You spoke with a man similar in age, dressed somewhat dowdily, even for a funeral, and who appeared very agitated.' She watched Manuela carefully. His mouth was set firm, expressing no obvious emotion.

'Again, I spoke with many people.' He sipped his tea.

'You were arguing with him.'

'Arguing?'

'Yes, Father. Why was that?'

Manuela's eyes narrowed at her, as he tried to work out her agenda. 'I wouldn't call it arguing. Merely *conversing*, as you put it.'

'About what?'

'I fail to see what this has to do with anything, and I'd appreciate you not wasting my time. I'm a very busy man.'

Claire stared at him until he shifted uncomfortably in his seat.

'Father Hawthorne used to work here as well as being stationed in another local church, but he left very suddenly, both Shrovesbury and the priesthood,' she said, watching his eyes with care.

Manuela nodded. 'You're correct. But again, what has this to do with Malcolm's death? His *murder*.'

Claire noticed his stress on the last word.

'I thought it odd that after the death of a beloved friend, you should be arguing at his funeral. Father Hawthorne appeared very upset over something other than Malcolm's death. He also left the priesthood a little over three years ago, and I gather there's some controversy surrounding this?'

Manuela turned to stare at the door, his complexion draining of colour.

'You think our cross words have something to do with Malcolm's death? You couldn't be further from the truth, Chief Inspector. However, you're right in saying David's departure from us was upsetting and, as you put it, controversial. It's certainly not the norm for anyone to suddenly leave the priesthood.'

'Why did he leave? What could've happened for him to just walk away from everything he knew?'

Manuela rose from his chair, walked to the largest bookcase, and scanned the titles on the spines with his index finger. He navigated a few rows before finding what he was looking for, pulling it from the shelf with considerable care.

Claire noticed it was a large burgundy-coloured faux leather book, its pages bulging. Manuela laid it upon a small table and thumbed through it carefully.

Now Claire could see folded pieces of old newspaper stuck crudely onto the yellowing pages. It was some sort of scrapbook.

After turning towards the middle of the book, he brought it over to her and placed it in her lap, before returning to his seat. Claire studied the pages, at first not really understanding.

She saw a picture cut from a newspaper of a teenage girl, around fifteen or sixteen years old, with large pretty features. Her eyes were a very dark shade of brown, almost black in appearance, with shoulder-length brown curly hair.

Claire could tell the girl would've been of average build from the size of her face and shoulders, but she was drawing conclusions from a head shot only.

Above the girl's picture was a heading of 'Local Girl Missing' in bold lettering. On the other page there were a few newspaper articles pasted into the book; all had large creases where they'd been read many times before they'd been secured in the scrapbook.

Claire noticed the largest one had been folded in half again to accommodate it within one page. She pulled open the fold.

'Gently please,' said Manuela, watching her closely. Claire ignored him as she began to read.

LOCAL GIRL MISSING

Fears are mounting for the safe return of missing local schoolgirl Rebecca Turner, who disappeared on Sunday. Rebecca (16) was last seen leaving her home for Shrovesbury Manor to study at her usual Bible class. Concerns were not raised until Rebecca failed to return home that evening.

Rebecca's mother, Abigail Turner, first contacted police after repeated attempts to contact Rebecca on her mobile.

'I tried for hours but her mobile kept diverting to voicemail,' Abigail (47) told us. 'I tried her friends but they hadn't seen her. I contacted Father Manuela at the Manor, but he said my Rebecca hadn't shown up for her Bible study class. It just isn't like her. I fear the worst.'

Father Jeremy Manuela, resident and proprietor of Shrovesbury Manor, was unavailable for comment when *Heart of Haverbridge* went to press, but an official statement was released, reporting that those who work and attend Shrovesbury are in a state of shock for their 'dear Rebecca', and hope that the press and public appreciate that this is a difficult time for her family. They ask that they are given the privacy they need until Rebecca is brought safely home.

Eye-witness accounts, reporting to have seen Rebecca not far from Shrovesbury Park, have proved unreliable.

Haverbridge Police are continuing the search and ask anyone with any information to contact the incident room on non-emergency number 101, quoting reference H/12/3891. All calls will be treated in the strictest confidence.

Claire finished reading and looked at Manuela, who was staring at the door again. She skimmed through the other smaller articles on Rebecca and shook her head.

'I don't understand. There's no mention of Father Hawthorne in these articles.'

Manuela sighed and looked at her, his face solemn.

'Rebecca and David were very close. I'd even go as far as to say they were friends. He took her disappearance rather badly, blamed himself, although he had no way of knowing what could've happened to her. None of us did. All we know is that she didn't turn up that day.'

'Was that normal for her not to turn up?'

'Other students, yes, but not Rebecca. She was a very bright and well-loved student. She took her Bible studies very seriously.'

Claire studied the face of the missing girl hard, trying to see if she could even remember the case. After much thought, she realised she didn't. She tried to remember what case she was working at the end of 2009.

All Claire could recall was a major search for men involved in an armed robbery. Her time had been taken up working that case. A missing girl story would've meant nothing to her then and didn't mean much to her now. She felt a slight twinge of guilt at her attitude.

'Is Rebecca the reason Father Hawthorne left the priesthood?'

'Yes. As I said, he took it badly.'

'Was this alone enough for him to give up his life, his identity? Forgive me if I don't seem to grasp this, but why leave?'

Manuela stared at her. His eyes seemed to be trying to read her mind, a look that even she found nerve-racking.

'He felt he could've done more for her.'

'But her disappearance wasn't treated as suspicious. At least, it's not mentioned here in these articles as being a possibility.'

'Rebecca could be…easily led sometimes. It's probable she ran away of her own accord. There were occasions when she'd go missing for a few hours. This was kept from the press. Her mother thought it might make the police not take the disappearance seriously and stop looking for her. If you check your records, Chief Inspector, I think you'll find that was the case.

'Anyway, David felt he should've done more to save her from her own misguided nature.' He reached for his teacup, the liquid now cold, but he finished it regardless.

Claire read the main article again.

'The official statement given to the press at the time reads as if she were dead.'

Manuela shot her a nasty look. It took every ounce of strength to suppress the urge to smack her across the face. 'She may as well be, all the pain she's caused her family by disappearing. Sometimes it's worse not knowing.'

'No matter how bad the reality is?'

Manuela immediately stood up and glared down at her.

'Forgive me, Chief Inspector, but I'm not comfortable talking about this. It's too upsetting.'

He left the room and his footsteps could be heard thundering across the hallway towards the back of the Manor.

Claire gave it a few seconds before following him. She headed across the hall and past a huge staircase. She craned her neck to try to see past the landing above but realised she'd have to climb the stairs in order to see anything properly.

She found the kitchen with an extension built to the side of it, with large French windows leading out into part of the vast garden.

She let herself out onto an immaculately kept lawn, the grass a deep shade of green, with pretty flowers and bushes lining the borders and a very old sundial in the middle of the green.

Claire walked further from the Manor and saw Manuela's head just disappear beyond her to the right.

She hurried along the lawn and followed him through to a small area hidden at the side of the Manor, complete with an elegant-looking bench, a small bird bath and beautiful rose bushes, flanked on one side by a lone tree. The tree offered some shade against the raging sun.

Claire fanned herself as a line of sweat trickled down her hairline. She raised her hand above her eyes and moved to stand beside Manuela under the shade of the tree.

He gazed at the array of light-pink roses and smiled. 'Aren't they beautiful?' Claire looked at them half-heartedly.

'I had these planted a few years back. I come here at least once a day, just to take in their beauty. It's become my obsession, keeping this bit of garden just for me. It's here that I clear my mind.'

Manuela turned to her and smiled, taking a seat on the bench and offering her a seat next to him.

'I'm sorry if I seemed rude back there,' he said as she sat beside him, wiping the seat before sitting. 'I just find it hard to talk about.' He leaned closer and smiled, baring his yellow teeth again.

Claire paused. 'What can you tell me about Mark Jenkins and his family?' She felt his body turn towards her and she looked at his face. He seemed genuinely surprised at her question.

'What would you like to know? He's one of our Patrons. He helps fund a lot of events to keep this place going. He's well-liked and respected as is his wife.' He looked back towards the house. 'Though I can't help but wonder why you ask.'

Claire had anticipated this. 'He was the last person to see Father Wainwright alive.'

'But he has an alibi. He's a good person and so are his family.'

'And what about his foster children?'

Manuela's face dropped.

'Did they attend here?' she asked, not looking at him, keeping her gaze ahead. She felt him shift on the bench next to her.

'Yes, although the church wasn't for them. Emily, who is still with them, she still attends sometimes, but she's older now so has less time on her hands.'

'I've not met Emily, only Chloe.' She saw Manuela stiffen. 'She told me her fellow students would talk about bad things happening here.' He looked at her, his face stern. 'Although I suppose they're just children's stories.'

Manuela blinked. 'I suppose she told you about the secret passage as well?'

He saw Claire's eyes narrow.

'The house has a secret passage left from the old dungeon of the previous Manor built in the 1500s. It used to be part of St Albans Abbey lands. This one was built after the old one was knocked down. The passage offered an escape route for anyone loyal to Rome, when Henry VIII made himself head of the church, ordering the dissolution of the monasteries.'

He looked at her and held her gaze. 'Everything a child needs for a very convincing ghost story, wouldn't you agree?'

He stood and offered her his hand.

'I hope I've been of some help, Chief Inspector. It's been nice to meet you, although I do hope for the last time.' Claire hesitated before taking his hand. 'I hope you understand?'

'Don't worry, Father. I think I've satisfied my curiosity for now.' She went to leave but something stopped her. She turned to him. 'There was just one other thing.'

She watched him stiffen, but he smiled at her regardless.

'What was Rebecca's state of mind during the weeks leading up to her disappearance?'

CHAPTER 29

2009

'I've thought about how I can get him back,' Amelia said, her voice just above a whisper. She watched Rebecca move in closer, eyes showing her eagerness. 'I've been thinking about it a while actually, not just because of the scars he's left me with... I've promised myself it'll be the last time.'

'Tell me?' Rebecca said, looking around, checking the door was shut.

'The Chapel. It's like his baby. I've been thinking about how I could destroy it, like he's destroyed me and my faith.'

Rebecca gasped, raising her hand to cover her mouth, but her eyes were alight with excitement.

'That was my idea.'

Both girls looked across the room, staring at their friend as she lay back on the floor, eyes forever watching their every movement.

'You said to damage the Chapel,' Amelia said. 'It was my idea to burn it.'

'Still my idea.' She frowned. 'You're just trying to impress her,' she spat.

Rebecca shifted, uncomfortable. She'd seen her temper before and wasn't keen to ignite it. She tried to smile, soften her voice. 'Don't be like that, Chloe.'

Chloe's eyes shot towards her then.

Amelia saw it and stirred, as if she anticipated a fight. She'd fight not flee, as usual. 'Envy is such a destroying emotion...'

'Fuck's that supposed to mean?' Chloe said, sitting bolt upright.

'Hey,' Rebecca said, moving between them. 'It doesn't matter whose idea it was.'

'It matters to me,' Amelia said. She ran her hand over Rebecca's thigh. She stopped just as her fingertips edged under the hem of her denim shorts. Rebecca looked uneasy as Amelia looked at Chloe, gave her a grin.

'Stop it.'

'You love it,' Amelia said, laughter in her voice.

'You're a complete cunt sometimes,' Chloe said, and pushed herself up from the floor.

Rebecca slowly removed Amelia's hand from her thigh. She knew she had to ease the tension.

'The Chapel,' she said.

Both of the other girls looked towards her.

'You wouldn't dare, would you, Amelia? Burn it? He'd *know it was you.'*

Amelia smiled, pleased to have Rebecca's attention back on her.

'Not necessarily. It doesn't have to be me who does it, Becks. I can give myself the perfect alibi, by being at home. She *said she'd help.' Her eyes flicked towards Chloe. 'Didn't you, bitch-tits?'*

'I said I'd help get the shit together, not start the bloody thing. You know I don't like the flames.'

Amelia dismissed her with a wave of her hand. 'Bitch, please...'

Chloe flipped her the middle finger.

Amelia laughed, enjoying watching Chloe rise to the bait. 'We've been growing closer,' Amelia said, eyes still on Chloe. 'As much as she wants to resist it.'

Chloe looked away, slightly ashamed. 'Fuck off.'

'That's not what you said the other night.'

Rebecca flushed red.

Amelia started to giggle. 'Can you imagine his face, though, B?' she said, pulling Rebecca's hands into her own. Her eyes were alight with excitement.

Rebecca smiled as she thought about seeing Manuela's face, horrified as he watched the fire raze his beloved Chapel to the ground. As she thought to herself she hit a flaw in the plan and she frowned.

'But if it isn't you or Chloe who does it, then how can you pull it off?'

'And here it comes,' Chloe said, disdain in her voice.

Amelia ignored her, smiled at Rebecca instead. 'I've spoken to Stevie.'

'You haven't!'

Amelia raised her finger to her lips, urging her to keep quiet. 'Keep your voice down!' She listened for any noise coming from the landing. She was certain the Fathers were all downstairs still, but she couldn't be too careful.

'I've seen him, Becca,' she said, satisfied they were safe to talk. 'I climbed out my room the other night and met him in secret. I told him what happened and he wanted to help. He said we should go to the police at first but I talked him round.'

Rebecca thought hard. 'Maybe we should just tell the police. They can help you.'

Amelia's face turned red with rage and she reached out, slapping Rebecca hard across the face. 'Don't be so fucking stupid.'

Chloe smiled then.

Rebecca reached for her cheek and rubbed it, her eyes brimming with tears. Amelia looked deeply into her eyes and felt a twinge of guilt. 'I'm sorry, Becks, but sometimes you say stupid things. It's OK for you, they leave you alone.'

'I don't even get a second thought. Least you get attention,' Chloe said.

Amelia scowled at her.

'It's me they hate. Me they want to ruin. I can't do anything right, and even if I do they find a way to make what I've done seem bad.'

Rebecca wiped a tear from her cheek and nodded, reaching for Amelia's hand, clasping it tightly.

'I know… I just don't think involving Stevie is right for you.' She glanced at Chloe. 'Or you.'

Amelia frowned at her words.

'He's bad news,' Rebecca continued, 'and you're forbidden to have any contact with him.'

'They only forbid me out of spite. Only Stevie truly understands me, Becks, you know that.'

Chloe's body stiffened. Amelia's words stung more than she could ever anticipate, but she'd be damned if she let any more of her guard down tonight.

'He says the plan will work,' Amelia said. 'Get Father Manuela where it hurts, hurt him from my vantage being on the inside. I'll still need you to help with a few details though. I know you won't let me down, B.'

Amelia moved her hand from Rebecca's and glared at the cross hanging from the wall in front of them. 'I'll make him pay for what he's done.'

Rebecca gazed at Amelia and noticed her hair seemed more of a mess than usual, the red seeming to glow with the light coming from the small lamp beside them.

'*I have to ask this. Apart from telling him about this plan, what else happened with him?*' she asked, embarrassed by her own words.

Chloe turned to face them now. Tried to hide the hurt in her eyes.

Amelia smiled, her face flushing.

'*You don't want the gory details, B, really.*'

'*Yes I do. I want to know what it's like.*' Rebecca listened to her own words and felt dirty. '*Not that you should be doing it anyway. He's too old for you for a start.*'

'*I'm sixteen, Becks, I can do what I want. It's legal.*'

'*He's still too old for you.*'

Amelia laughed. She rolled over on her side and switched on the television. She thought about what Rebecca had said but dismissed it. She had her plan set up with Stevie and if Chloe kept her word, they would make the Fathers suffer over time. As long as she had them, she would be safe.

Three lost tormented souls.

Together, they could achieve anything.

CHAPTER 30

Father Manuela watched Claire leave, unaware that he was holding his breath. He exhaled once her car had retreated down the driveway, and he raised his hand to his chest.

His insides felt like they were on fire and he collapsed in a seat beside the window.

He looked down at his hands and watched them tremble. He tried to pick up his cut-glass decanter of whisky and pour himself a glass. He spilt some of it onto the desk in front of him and raised the decanter to his lips instead, and drank deeply.

He glanced at the scrapbook he'd shown Claire and frowned. He reached for the cordless telephone beside him and dialled, his fingers clumsy, stumbling over the keys. He heard a voice at the other end which was not familiar. Realising he'd dialled the wrong number, he hung up without saying a word.

He redialled.

He sighed when he heard David Hawthorne answer at the other end.

David listened to Manuela with care and shook his head. 'I think you should think about what I said at the funeral.'

'No!' Manuela said. 'I'm letting you know, in case you get a visit. If you do, just be cautious with your answers. Besides that, you will do as I say, David.'

'It's as if God wants her to be found.'

There was a silence at the other end.

Manuela glared at the picture of Rebecca in the scrapbook; her face had slightly yellowed over time, the newspaper wearing.

'God will forgive us, David. Trust in that. God will know his own.'

CHAPTER 31

Claire sat at the desk in her office and surveyed her notes from the meeting with Manuela. She'd made some further enquiries regarding Ashe Miller's murder and checked in with David Matthews about the Hargreaves case before studying her notes, but by this time she was tired and hungry. It was then that she realised she hadn't eaten since very early that morning.

She stood and grabbed her bag, when Michael walked into her office, tapping on the door to get her attention. Her eyes narrowed when she saw him and she looked down at her bag, pretending to rummage.

'I came to apologise,' he said, closing the door behind him, after she failed to invite him in. 'I was out of line the other day and I'm sorry. It wasn't my intention to upset you.' Claire ignored him, and leaned down to her computer to lock it. Michael edged a little closer and stared at her. 'Claire? Did you hear me?'

'I heard you.'

He tried to make eye contact but she stared at the desk in front of her. 'Are we good?'

Then she looked at him. He waited for her next sentence with bated breath.

'If you think that by apologising now, after avoiding me for the last two days and after what was said is OK, then the answer is no, we're not *good*.'

He frowned. 'I think you're going a little OTT there, Claire, don't you?'

'I think I'm being more than a little *kind* to you, considering I could have you suspended for your behaviour.'

Michael sighed and shook his head.

'And by the way,' she added, 'I still might if you insist on challenging me and bringing up the past. I'm not going to put up with your attitude, Diego, am I making myself clear?'

'Then why don't you?'

She glared at him. 'Excuse me?'

'Why don't you suspend me? It's not the first time you've threatened it.' He watched her face, realising he knew the answer. 'Oh, I think I see.' His lips pulled into a grin.

'You don't *see* anything, Diego. Don't flatter yourself.'

Michael stood with his hands on his hips, staring at her. He was fighting a losing battle. He nodded at her reluctantly. 'OK. You're right.'

She grunted to confirm she was done speaking to him and picked up her bag, swinging it over her shoulder.

'I'm off to a very late lunch.'

Michael seized his chance.

'Actually,' he said, standing in front of her, 'I had meant to offer you lunch. On me, I mean.' She looked at him with caution, trying to check if he was being sincere or not. 'As a peace offering I guess you could say.' She noticed his eyes had almost danced back to life again, teasing and testing her.

'You can't buy your way into my good books with food, Diego,' she said, with half a smile.

'Well, we'll see…'

***

Prezzo's was still very busy, even for late afternoon, when they were shown to a table. Claire ordered a white wine as soon as she sat down. Michael cocked an eyebrow at her.

'Unlike you to drink on the job.' She passed him a sideways look and shrugged. Michael ordered a soft drink instead, and waited until the waiter had gone before picking up his menu. 'I'm starving,' he said.

Claire already knew what she wanted, so ignored the menu and when her glass of wine arrived, she downed most of it in one go. Michael waited until the waiter had taken their order before looking at her, his eyes serious.

'Is it PMT?'

Claire shot him a look.

'It is, isn't it?' A grin pulled at his lips.

'Piss off.'

He laughed. 'OK, it must be serious then.' He thought for a few seconds. 'My second best guess is that the Miller investigation hasn't turned up anything of use yet, Hargreaves is still on our streets and then there's Wainwright.'

'Yes, thank you for stating the obvious.' She struck her fingernails on the table. 'Besides, it's not just that. I saw Father Manuela today.'

'And?'

'I don't know. I just feel there's something not right about him... Or any of them for that matter.' She played with her wine glass, moving it around the table.

'To be fair, you only went to see him for the sake of routine. You didn't have, and still don't have, any evidence about anything.'

'Other than Manuela having a heated argument with Hawthorne at Wainwright's funeral, yes, Diego, I know that,' she said, cutting him off. She sat back in her chair, frustrated. 'As I've said before, call it a hunch.'

They sat in silence until their food arrived. Michael started on his pasta as soon as it was put in front of him, wolfing it down as if he hadn't eaten in days. Claire watched him fleetingly before picking up her fork.

She took a few mouthfuls then set down her fork, and shoved the plate away from her.

Michael eyed her until she felt the weight of his stare. When she looked in his direction, she said, 'I wasn't as hungry as I thought.' She sipped some of her wine.

'Well, that's bollocks.' He wiped his mouth on a napkin and leaned forward, his arms resting on the table. 'Come on then…a problem shared, and all that psychobabble shit. I know I was out of line the other day, pressuring you to tell me, but it might make you feel better.'

Claire avoided his eyes. As if on cue, her BlackBerry vibrated across the table. When Michael leaned towards it to see the caller ID, she snatched it up from the table.

He sighed. 'You've been getting these calls for weeks now.'

She shot him a defiant look. 'What calls?'

'These "private number" calls, the ones you never answer, the ones that turn you into an even more moody cow than usual.'

'Don't start this again. I've told you, it's—'

'None of my business, yeah, I heard you loud and clear before.'

'So take the *hint*.'

'What kind of a friend would I be if I did that?'

He smiled at her when she looked at him.

'You class yourself as my friend now?'

'What would you call me?'

She found herself suppressing a grin. 'Don't tempt me…' Her face turned serious then. 'I'm fine, don't worry about me.' She paused a moment, then her eyes flicked back to his. 'Did you mean what you said the other day?'

'Which bit? I said quite a few choice words,' he said, voice teasing.

She shoved his arm. 'About things affecting my judgement?'

Michael leaned back in his chair and folded his arms, remaining tight-lipped. He stared at her until she relented.

'You're not going to stop until I give in, are you?'

He gave a slight shake of his head.

She sighed, then said, 'It's nothing, not really.' She blew out her breath slowly. He sat forward again and she mirrored his position. Her lips parted but no words escaped them. Her hands began to shake a little, and she laced her fingers together, hoping he wouldn't notice.

'You know, there was a time,' he began, making her look at him square in the face, 'when I would've dismissed the idea that anything could faze you.' Before she could stop him, he reached out and clasped her hand across the table. 'You're clearly going through something right now that's got nothing to do with the investigation.'

She looked away. She pulled at her hand, but he refused to release it. 'Let go of me.'

He shook his head. 'Sorry, I can't do that.' He smiled and squeezed her hand gently.

Feeling the spark of energy and desire she once yearned for stirring within her now, Claire's eyes hardened. 'What about you, then? The other day?'

Michael frowned.

'When you walked out on me at Wainwright's funeral? Where did that come from?'

This time he relaxed the grip on her hand a little. He silently weighed up the pros and cons of revealing parts of himself, emotions he'd rather have kept hidden, with finding out what was going on behind the mask Claire liked to hide behind.

'I go, you go,' he said.

Claire shrugged, and a deep crease appeared on her forehead. 'What's that supposed to mean?'

'I tell you things, and then *you* tell me things, what's going on in here,' he said, tapping her head lightly with his finger. 'It's like a win-win situation.'

Claire waited for him to start laughing, confirming that this was a joke, but when he held her gaze, she scoffed and managed to pull her hand from his this time.

'This is childish.'

Light seemed to dance in his eyes. 'Childish maybe...I prefer the term *playful*. I always thought you liked that side of me.' He leaned forward again. 'Some say it's positively charming.'

The faintest of smiles pulled at Claire's lips. She tried hard to bury it.

'I'll go first,' he said. 'I walked out on you the other day because I find it hard to be around you. Sometimes I look for an excuse to be anywhere but in your company.'

Claire paused, swallowed hard. 'At least you're honest,' was all she managed.

He laughed. 'You misunderstand me.'

'Oh, I think you've been more than clear.'

'Not clear enough, obviously.' He paused, and took a sip of his drink. 'I can't handle being around you sometimes, because I'm unsure of what my feelings are for you. I keep trying to distance myself because I think it's for the best.'

'What's best for you, you mean?'

'What's best for us *both*.'

'And that's why you walked out on me? You tried to get me to open up about things, my personal life,' she said,

184   *T.M.E. Walsh*

frowning in disbelief. 'That hardly seemed like you wanted to run away from me.'

He nodded. 'Yeah, I know. I told you, I feel...*conflicted*. I think you know what that feels like more than anyone.'

The brick wall Claire had been trying to build up began to come down, slowly, one brick at a time.

'You remember after we found Wainwright's body, when I rushed off when we were back at the station?'

He nodded.

Claire lowered her eyes, stared at the table. 'I went to see someone and it didn't...' She trailed off, rested her head in both her hands, elbows propped up on the table, supporting her. '...It didn't go so well.'

Michael edged closer. 'Who did you see? What's this all about?'

Claire looked at him, holding his stare. She relived that afternoon.

'It's my father,' she said.

Gladstone Court – The afternoon after Wainwright's murder

Claire stood in front of the door to the flat and steeled herself inside.

She pushed her spare key into the lock...

Almost immediately the door swung open, making Claire stumble forward.

'What time do you call this, girl? I've left countless messages. I nearly called the station!'

Cursing under her breath, Claire wrenched the key from the lock and pushed her sunglasses up on her head.

She stared at the gnarled fingers that clasped a walking stick in a tight fist. Her eyes took in the figure in front of her, tall and thin, but slightly stooped, with stiff joints. Then she stared back into pale blue eyes, not too dissimilar to her own.

'Afternoon, Dad,' she said, her voice flat, as she stepped inside.

Claire gave a cursory glance around her surroundings. There were unopened letters addressed to a Peter Winters on the table in the small dark hallway. Judging by the franked mark across the envelopes, they were from Haverbridge Hospital, and New Temple Housing, the warden-controlled complex based in Scotland. Soon to be Peter's new home.

Claire stared at the envelopes, and ran her hand across them, before picking them up. 'Did you want me to check these for you?'

He snatched them from her hand. 'I can open my own letters. I've been fending for myself all bloody morning anyway.'

'Hilary not been yet?' she said, turning to Peter as he slammed the door behind him.

'*Have you even bothered to listen to the messages I sent you?*' he said, as he ushered her towards the small living room.

'*I pay all this money and they don't even turn up on time,*' he muttered, easing himself into his favourite tatty armchair. His face winced, pain shooting through his joints.

Peter had suffered with rheumatoid arthritis for some years now, the disease gradually getting worse over the years, but accelerating in the last few months. Claire's parents had been divorced nine years now, after a very turbulent marriage. During this time Claire had been the only one to keep in touch with her father, since he'd pushed away everyone else in the family with his bad temper and stubbornness.

Peter eyed his daughter with some disdain, as if his condition were somehow all her fault. '*You're late.*'

'*I can't just drop everything and run whenever you call me, Dad, you know that. I've just come from a pretty nasty crime scene.*'

Peter dismissed her words with a wave of his hand. '*I've not been able to have a bath yet.*'

'*That's what Hilary's here for. To help you.*'

'*But she's not here, is she? You can run me a bath,*' he said, using his stick to manoeuvre out of the chair again, with some difficulty. Claire went to steady him, but he batted her arm away with his free hand. '*I can do it!*'

Claire took a deep breath, held it in a moment, and then let it out slowly. She cast her eye around the room. '*Have you eaten yet?*'

'*Not hungry.*'

'*You have to eat.*'

'*Says who?*' he snapped, pale eyes now staring at her, silently daring her to argue the point. '*I'm barely sixty,*

I'm not completely senile yet. I know when to eat if I choose to.'

Claire folded her arms across her chest, and chewed on the inside of her lip.

'You can help me bath,' he said.

'I can give Hilary a ring, see where she is.'

'No,' he said, raising his walking stick at her, stabbing the air in her direction. 'You'll do for now.' He looked her up and down. 'You should have more time for your old man, instead of always gallivanting around, like it'll make a difference.'

Claire's eyes narrowed. 'I'm a police officer, it's not a regular nine-to-five—'

'Don't I know it!' he bristled, and began to slowly make his way towards the door, heading off towards the bathroom. 'Sixty years of age, and reduced to begging my daughter to help me wash…bloody degrading.'

Claire watched him until he was out of sight. 'Degrading for me too,' she said to herself.

***

Twenty minutes later Claire helped ease her father into the bath. 'I'll speak to the council about having another rail fitted in here,' she said, as he waved her away from him, 'just until you move.'

'Fuck the council, bunch of sadists,' he said when she turned her back as he began to wash himself. 'They don't care what happens to me, so long as the end result is freeing up the housing stock.'

'Ever the pessimist, aren't you, Dad.'

'You don't know what it's like—'

'To be you?' she said, bending to pick up discarded dirty clothes from the floor. 'I can see what it's like.' She began loading the clothes into the basket beside her.

'*You know what your problem is,*' he began, the malice clear in his voice, '*you're just like your mother...*'

Claire's body stiffened. She counted to ten inwardly. '*I'll put a wash on for you before I leave.*'

'*Fucking bitch. If anyone deserves to be crippled with pain and knotted joints, it's her.*'

Claire spun around. '*I've told you before, don't talk about Mum like that.*'

Peter gave a mock laugh. '*There you go, defending the great bitch.*'

'*Dad... I've warned you. You need to stop.*'

'*Or what? You'll leave me to fend for myself? You do that enough already,*' he said, pointing at her, before letting his hand fall back down into the water with a splash. '*Ignorant, wilful thing, you are. You never got that from me, girl. That's your mother's disease. It's in you through and through.*'

Claire threw the rest of the dirty clothes to the floor in anger, and slammed both hands on the edge of the bath, making Peter jump. She leaned in close to his face, eyes wide.

'*Mum has her faults, but it was you who ruined your own life.*'

Peter's mouth opened indignantly. '*Now you listen—*'

'*No, you listen,*' she interrupted. '*I've spent the last few years helping you where I can, when I could've easily walked away, after how you treated Mum, after how you treated me.*'

Peter jabbed his thumb hard repeatedly against his chest. '*I gave you a roof over your head, girl, and what do I have to show for it? Disrespect. Reduced to having my own daughter help me bath and shooting your mouth off with it.*'

Claire's eyes narrowed. She leaned in closer. '*Fend for yourself. You move in a few weeks, so you'd better start*

getting used to having no one but strangers to scream at.'
She looked him over with contempt. 'I'm done.'

She pushed herself away from the bath.

Peter paused, shocked at first, then his face hardened once again as she headed out of the bathroom.

'You make me sick, like your mother, you never knew when to keep your mouth shut!' he shouted after her.

Claire went into the living room, fighting back the tears that pricked at her eyes. Peter was still hurling insults. She could hear the sound of him thrashing in the bath, water spilling onto the floor as he tried helplessly to get out of the bath.

'You fucking bitch!' he screamed, just as Claire headed back into the hallway. She stopped dead in her tracks.

Hilary, her father's carer, was standing by the front door, key in hand retrieved from the security box mounted outside on the wall.

Her mouth was open a little, clearly unsure of what she'd just walked into.

'I'm...sorry I'm late,' she said, closing the front door behind her. 'I did try to call. We're severely understaffed today.'

Claire swallowed hard, her mouth dry, and she lowered her sunglasses back onto her face to hide her eyes.

'He's in the bath. He's not eaten, says he doesn't want to.' She paused, then tried to move past Hilary. 'Let him starve for all I care.'

Hilary grabbed her upper arm. 'What on earth's happened? You look like you need to sit down.'

Claire tried to toughen up. She would not, could not, cry in front of her. 'I'm fine.'

Hilary tightened her grip a little. 'Come and sit down in the living room, I'll sort your dad out, then we can talk.'

'I don't have time for this. I already dropped everything and came here when I shouldn't have done.'

Claire shook her arm free.

'You need to take time for you.' Hilary stared at her with sympathy. 'It doesn't help to bottle things up.'

Claire pushed her hand on the front door until it slammed shut, and leaned in closer to Hilary, who was a good three inches shorter than her.

'Has she finally arrived?' they heard Peter shout from the bathroom.

'Won't be a moment, Mr Winters,' Hilary called out, her eyes never leaving Claire's. They heard him mutter some profanity in response. Hilary smiled with a kindness Claire wasn't used to. 'We don't have to talk here, we can go for a coffee. You look like you need someone who will listen to you.'

'What I need,' Claire said, 'is the next few weeks to go quickly, so I can move on with my life.'

'You're angry, and that's understandable, but don't you think—'

'Don't try to tell me what to think. He's moving soon. Any paperwork will be copied to me. It can't come soon enough. I've done all I can.'

'Think what it's like for him.'

Claire's jaw set firm, her patience with this woman waning. 'I have been thinking about what it's been like most of my adult life.' She jabbed a finger in the direction of the bathroom. 'Believe me, he is not the injured party here.'

Claire paused, trying to make sure that the next words out of her mouth were carried by a voice that didn't crack.

'I have my own life to live…I've been living in his for far too long.'

'You make it sound like after the move, you'll never see him again.' Hilary's eyes looked sad then.

'I've done all I can for him.'

Hilary placed her hand gently on Claire's forearm. 'But he doesn't have anybody else.'

Claire snatched her arm away. 'That's because he's spent most of his life pushing everyone away. I'm thirty-seven years old, I shouldn't be still picking up the pieces after all this time...after my parents' failed marriage.'

Claire turned and opened the front door again. She paused on the threshold as Peter shouted at Hilary again, something crude.

Claire turned to look at Hilary's face. Her skin was sallow and lines ran in deep furrows across her forehead, making her appear older than her forty-eight years. Claire looked at her dyed blonde hair.

'The sight of a woman with blonde hair angers him,' Claire said, sadness in her voice. Hilary frowned, deepening the creases in her skin. 'It reminds him of his own mother, of Mum...and me.'

After Claire had told Michael about her father, his illness, the move to Scotland, and some painful scattered memories of what it was like to live with two highly volatile parents, she felt like a weight had been lifted from her shoulders.

She winced inwardly at the thought of almost finding it therapeutic.

'Brings a whole new meaning to the phrase, *daddy issues*, doesn't it?' he said. When Claire didn't raise a smile to match his, he let his face fall. 'Sorry. I'm not trying to trivialise anything.'

'Don't repeat any of this to anyone.'

'Obviously. I wouldn't do that. My past isn't so sunny either.' She looked at him, curious. He smiled, reading her mind. '*That* can wait for another day,' he said. 'Too heavy for a lunchtime conversation.'

***

When they'd cleared their plates and ordered another drink each, Michael leaned in closer.

'I've been thinking lately, about the Charity Ball coming up.' He watched her straighten in her seat. 'Completely off topic and you can say no, and I'll understand. I guess it could end up pretty uncomfortable, but I was wondering if you wanted to go...with me?'

He watched her carefully as her face changed. He would even have sworn to anyone that he'd caught her smiling.

'I haven't given it much thought,' she lied. 'I don't think it'd be a great idea.'

'Why not?'

Claire looked at him. 'I can't believe you even have to ask.'

He shook his head and reached for her hands, holding them tight. 'It's not what you think. Perhaps you shouldn't read too much into it.' He looked at her from beneath his eyelashes, his head lowered. 'Don't flatter yourself, as you may put it.'

Claire looked at him and couldn't help but smile inside. Outside, however, she remained calm and unfazed, removing her hands from his.

CHAPTER 32

Mark Jenkins sat away from everyone else in church that evening. Although this was a midweek gathering, the pews were over half-full, almost double the usual. Jenkins sat gazing at the spot where he imagined Wainwright had died and bit his lips, holding back tears.

He nodded occasionally when someone greeted him in passing but offered no encouragement to polite conversation. This in itself drew some disapproving looks from those who never missed a gathering, be it routine or social in nature.

Jenkins didn't care.

He mimed his way through a few hymns and shut off his mind when the sermon dragged on. In all his years of dedicating his life to God, he'd never felt as he did now; despondent and his faith waning.

How could anyone murder a man of the true faith? How could God allow this to happen?

He waited until he was the last remaining person sitting amongst the pews after the service before he went over to light a candle for those in need of prayer.

He watched as the flame on a large candle lit the small wooden splint he was holding. He lit a smaller candle placed the furthest away from him and sighed.

In his thoughts, he prayed for Father Wainwright, but through the mirage of images circling inside his head, he saw past Wainwright's face and saw a haze of red cloud his thoughts.

He drew in a sharp breath and closed his eyes tight.

The vision of red become brighter, moving closer to him, and after a few seconds he saw it was shades of red hair, on top of a face so delicate, it hurt to behold.

His eyelids tightened when he realised it was the image of a girl, walking closer to him, her eyes burning into his, inside his skull, inside his very being. Her eyes shone an emerald green and soon he saw the shape of her mouth, and she seemed to speak to him, whispering in a sweet voice, like a siren.

I won't tell, if you won't.

Jenkins's eyes popped open with fright.

He found himself gasping for breath, and realised he was drenched in sweat, his underarms wet, with stains seeping through his shirt.

He whisked his body around several times to make sure it was nothing more than a vision, causing his head to spin.

He was alone.

He gazed back at the candle he had lit, and realised more than ever that he would always be alone in more than one sense of the word now that Wainwright was gone.

***

1998

The day had been a mixture of the elements. The morning a bright sunny one, if a little cold with the northern wind, changing to warm but damp by the afternoon.

Despite the muddy ground where the rain had fallen, Amelia sat curled up, her knees stained with wet grass, small cuttings sticking to her skin. She'd been in the Jenkins' back garden for around an hour, quite content to be by herself.

Mark Jenkins had returned from doing the weekly food shopping, and called out to Chloe, Stephen and Amelia from the bottom of the stairs. He always insisted the children put the shopping away, just as he always insisted they did almost everything else he demanded whether it was fair or not.

Chloe skulked down the staircase, her head lowered. She was met by her father at the foot of the stairs.

'Where's your brother?' His face looked stern. His hands were on his hips. 'The freezer food will be melting.'

'Dunno. Don't care, and Stephen's not my brother. Stop calling him that.'

Jenkins frowned, his forehead set in deep furrows. 'Where's Amelia?'

Chloe hesitated. 'Digging.'

'What?'

'In the garden. Digging.'

She went to the kitchen and started to unpack the first bag of shopping she laid her hands on. Jenkins followed her and grabbed her hand as she pulled a can of beans from a bag.

'What do you mean, digging? What for?'

'I dunno, she just said digging when I asked her.'

Jenkins looked down at his daughter with disapproval before letting himself out into the garden. His eyes scanned the back garden and saw nothing at first, until he saw a flash of red hair.

Amelia was sitting right in the middle of a row of bushes at the far end of the garden. Her back was to him, her legs tucked under her, and Jenkins could see mud caked on her bare legs and on the hem of the new dress Samantha had bought for her to wear to church the other week.

Marching towards her, his fists balled at his sides in anger, he called out to her, but she seemed to be engrossed in whatever it was she was doing. As he got closer to her, he could see there were smears of dried blood streaked up her legs.

Rather than call out to her again, he edged closer and it was then he noticed fur scattered on the grass.

Some clumps were stained with blood.

He swallowed hard and gingerly peered over her shoulder. As he did so, Amelia whisked her head around, and as he looked down at her face, he gasped.

'What in the name of God...' He tailed off as his hand instinctively reached up and covered his mouth. 'What have you done?'

Amelia smiled innocently, her eyes bright, wisps of her flame-coloured hair hanging around her face, some strands sticking to her forehead in the damp air. Her cheeks appeared rosy at first, until he looked closer.

Smears of dried blood and mud tainted her beautiful face, etched in lines and spatters over her cheeks and forehead.

The collar of her dress was damp from her sweat, and he saw the dried blood on her bare arms, leading down to her hands, which were buried in a plume of fur around the belly of a dead cat.

'I'm sending the soul to heaven, Daddy. See how I cut the chest? That sets the soul free. In case Mr Cat needs help leaving his body,' she said, pleased with herself.

As Jenkins recoiled, bile rising inside his throat, he caught sight of the sharp rock, it too caked in blood, lying beside the cat's open chest.

This was a new evil.

Sick and depraved...and Amelia seemed to enjoy it.

***

Upstairs in the house, Stephen lay on his bed, the headphones slipping from his ears as he dozed. Despite the music playing in his ears, he heard her cries over the din and his eyes flew open.

He pulled the headphones from his ears and bolted from the bed.

He listened. He heard her voice wail again. He ran to the window and looked down into the garden.

He saw Jenkins with his hand around Amelia's wrist, dragging her towards the garden shed. He saw her clothes and legs stained and her bloody hands clasping at thin air, as she tried to dig in her heels, arching backwards away from Jenkins.

He bolted down the stairs and nearly knocked Chloe over as she came from the kitchen.

'Just let it happen,' she shouted after him.

***

Jenkins forced Amelia inside the large wooden shed with such force, she slammed her shoulder into a row of shelves, sending empty planting pots and a watering can crashing to the floor.

She began to cry as she rubbed her shoulder.

'What about shedding some tears for the poor animal you just butchered?' he shouted at her, as he began to pull the belt from his trousers.

'It was dead already,' she said, tears pouring down her face.

'You cut open its body!'

He raised the belt above his head.

Amelia cowered in the corner on the floor, her knees together up under her chin. As Jenkins went to swing, a hand reached out and grabbed his wrist, bending it back with force.

He cried out in pain and his eyes were met with Stephen's as he wrenched the belt from his hand.

'How about you pick on someone your own size for a change?'

Jenkins glared at him and forced his hand from Stephen's grasp. He wound the belt tightly around his hand and snapped it taught.

'It'd be my pleasure, boy.'

***

It'd been a few weeks since Stephen had finally had enough and he'd packed his bags.

'You'll forget about me,' Amelia sniffed, her body curled up in a ball on his bed, hugging her teddy. The teddy Stephen had won for her at the local fair a few weeks before the cat incident.

He reached out and ruffled her hair. 'That's not likely, is it? I look after you. Look out for you. I'll still do all those things, just not from here. Besides,' he said, watching as Chloe came into the bedroom, 'you've got each other. Isn't that right, Chloe?'

Chloe nodded.

Amelia reached out and touched the fading bruise on Stephen's face. He winced.

'It's my fault,' she said.

'You're just a little girl, darling. It's not your fault.'

'Daddy says it is. He says I'm evil.'

Stephen sighed. 'He isn't your daddy, and never will be. He's the evil one.'

Amelia jumped down from the bed and looked out of the window. After a while she looked back at him, as he added a few last items to his rucksack.

'God is supposed to punish the wicked, isn't he, Stevie?'

He nodded. 'Yes, but not everyone it seems. Sometimes, God needs a helping hand.' He swung the rucksack over his shoulder and bent down to her eye level.

'Take me with you.'

Chloe's mouth fell open. 'You can't.'

Stephen looked at her, shook his head. 'It's your job now, whilst I'm not here any more. Look after her.'

'What can I do?'

Stephen glanced at Amelia, then returned his gaze to Chloe. 'Be strong for each other. Love each other.'

A cry escaped Amelia's lips. 'Please, don't leave me here. Take me with you.'

He smiled at her but shook his head. 'I can't. Not yet anyway.'

'But I'll never see you,' she said, flinging her arms around his neck, squeezing tightly.

'Yes you will, don't be silly.' He pushed her back, his hands on her shoulders. 'I'll be watching over you. You've got Chloe. You know she'll do anything for you, and I'll come and see you, often. I just have things I need to do. Things I need to set up.'

Amelia pulled a face. 'What things?' Then her face grew excited. 'Can I help?'

'I wish you could but you're too young. One day, though, you will. Both of you,' he said, eyes now watching Chloe intently. 'What I need to do will take time.'

'I...I don't know if I can do this,' Chloe said.

'How much time?' Amelia cut in, ignoring the pained look on both Chloe and Stephen's faces.

'A while,' he said, eyes never leaving Chloe's. An understanding passed silently between them. Despite her years, Chloe understood. An old soul trapped in the body of a child, he'd always thought.

'How long? Days?' Amelia said, pushing her body into his. She cocked her head to one side.

'Years, darling, but it'll be worth it in the end, you'll see.'

Amelia smiled. She reached for Chloe, beckoning her closer. Reluctantly, Chloe joined them. She held Amelia tight, but hesitated when Stephen's arm slid around her waist.

'It's all right,' he said, drawing her to him. He kissed her head, then smiled down at Amelia.

She looked back at them both, light dancing in her eyes.

'My old foster mother said we all had Guardians. Like angels, every one of us has one.' She hugged them both tight. 'My Guardians,' she whispered. 'Both of you.'

CHAPTER 33

Claire sat staring at her reflection in her dressing-table mirror. She sighed as she pulled at the dark circles underneath her eyes with her fingers. It'd been a long few days, but she felt better when she relived the moment Michael asked her to the Charity Ball.

She'd tried to show him she was indifferent to his suggestion but deep down she felt like a teenager awaiting her first date all over again. She smiled to herself as she began removing her make-up.

When it came to removing her work clothes, she reached for her silk nightdress, rather than the usual scruffy oversized T-shirt she'd grown accustomed to. She eyed herself in the mirror and patted her stomach, promising herself no more ready-made meals.

It wasn't until she was ready to turn the light out and settle down that she remembered she had to pick Iris up from the airport tomorrow, putting her instantly in a bad mood.

She'd planned to look for a dress in Milton Keynes and the thought of having her mother there while she chose it was not a comforting one, especially when she found out Claire had a date which wasn't her ex-husband.

***

Luton Airport was a nightmare to drive around at the best of times, but this Friday morning was the worst Claire had seen it.

'Slow down!'

The shrill voice in Claire's ear sent a shiver down her spine. She ignored her mother's request and put her foot down a little more just to piss her off.

Claire hated Luton and hated driving within any distance of it, and as she slowed down at a set of traffic lights, she heard her mother in her ear again.

'Where're we going again?' she asked for the third time.

'Milton Keynes.'

'And what're you looking for a dress for? *You* don't wear dresses. I remember you as a little girl crying at your aunt Grace's wedding because I made you wear a dress. You ruined the whole service.'

Claire cringed and knew it'd be a long day. She wondered if she could get away with losing her mother in the vast shopping complex.

'It's for the Charity Ball tomorrow,' she said.

Iris pursed her lips and shook her head. 'Nothing like leaving it to the last minute.'

'I didn't know I was going until the other day.'

There was a long pause before Iris turned to her, open-mouthed and a little excited. 'Will Simon be there?'

Claire groaned inwardly. The ever-wonderful ex-husband, in her mother's eyes, was bound to have been mentioned but Claire had hoped to avoid talking about him.

'I don't know. Maybe.' She cast a sideways glance at her mother, who'd suddenly perked up considerably.

'Well, we'll have to make sure you get the *right* dress then, just so he knows what he's missing.'

Cringing again, Claire put her foot down.

***

The shopping centre was busy, but Claire found a good parking space regardless and began dragging Iris around almost every woman's clothing store. After trying on countless dresses, Claire was at the point of desperation when Iris picked out the perfect dress in Monsoon. Claire eyed up the strapless figure-hugging dress in a deep shade of red.

'Isn't that a little sexy for your taste?'

Iris looked at her daughter then back at the dress. 'Normally yes, but Simon will be there. Remember that.'

Claire frowned and took the dress towards the fitting rooms, Iris following in tow. 'I said he *might* be there, and besides, I'm hoping he won't be and even if he is, it makes no difference to me.'

After a few minutes Claire emerged in the dress and even if she said so herself, she looked good. Iris made her turn round several times before giving her approval.

'Well, this will turn heads.' She pulled at the price tag. 'What's the damage then?' She eyed the tag and shrugged. 'Well, it's worth it, I suppose. Simon would approve.'

'Mother!' Claire said, as she disappeared behind the curtain. 'I have a date, and sorry to disappoint you but it's not Simon.'

***

Iris waited until the dress had been paid for and took Claire to a posh coffee shop. She studied her daughter's face. Claire was thinking to herself when she felt her mother's stare.

She flushed red.

'Who is he then?' Iris asked, clear disdain in her voice.

'Just a DS, Mum. It's purely business. Neither of us had a date but had to attend, so we thought we'd go together. It's no big deal.'

Iris stifled a laugh and sat back in the booth. 'So that's why you just bought the no-big-deal dress then?' Iris shook her head. 'I know I'm an old cow but I'm not blind.'

Claire buried her face in her coffee mug, for a rare moment in her life admitting defeat.

Iris sipped at her coffee and then set her cup down, and rubbed the faded white mark around the ring finger on her left hand. The wedding band had sat there for too many years, she knew, and even after she'd removed it, nine years on, her finger still bore the mark.

'I had a call from one of Peter's carers yesterday,' she said. Her light grey eyes watched Claire's reaction. 'Hilary, I think she said her name was.'

When Claire's eyes rose to meet her mother's, Iris tucked a strand of her dyed soft-blonde hair behind her ear. 'You going to tell me what's going on?'

'How'd she get your number?' Claire said, frowning.

'I asked her the same thing,' she sniffed. 'I mean – and I said this to her – he's not my responsibility any more.'

'And what did she say?'

'That the move is just days away. She said that he's got no one else, that none of the family will return her calls, and that you,' she said, eyeing Claire with a degree of sympathy, 'have been making the arrangements for everything through emails. She said you won't *actually* speak to her, or *him*.'

Claire scrunched up her used napkin in her hand. 'He's not made any attempt to contact me. In the messages she's sent me, she always says he's asked for me, that he doesn't want to leave here, leave *me*, with how things were when we last spoke, but…'

'You know it's a lie.'

Claire nodded. 'You know Dad better than anyone. He'd die before admitting he was wrong, before ever saying sorry.'

Iris shifted her small frame in her seat, crossing one leg over the other. 'Hilary said that you argued. She said it had been about me.'

Claire shook her head. 'Not just you, but… I don't want to talk about him.'

'You don't need to defend me to that *bastard*,' she said. Her eyes appeared hard when Claire finally looked at her. '*You* need to look after number one, my girl. No one else is going to.'

***

Saturday morning flew by and soon it was late afternoon and Claire was getting ready. She had her hair curled and flowing down her back, with a few delicate-looking diamanté hair grips in various places.

She'd spent a long time perfecting her make-up before slipping on her dress. She took all the compliments from Iris before a long black limousine pulled up in the driveway. Michael grinned at her as she stepped inside and sat on the white leather seat beside him.

'Over the top, isn't it,' he said, gesturing to the limo. He reached for the bottle of champagne beside him. 'Want some?' he said, offering her a glass, filling it before she could respond. He took a sip from his own glass, eyeing her over the rim. 'You look nice. New dress?'

'No,' she lied, sipping from her glass and trying to ignore his stare.

They sat barely making conversation on the journey there. They picked up a few colleagues along the way, and

Claire was relieved when Michael turned his attention to them rather than her.

When the limo pulled up outside the Mayflower Hall, they were hustled through the main entrance.

Inside was opulent in décor. The colour theme was deep shades of red and gold. Velvet draped across the ceilings, and everything seemed to sparkle and gleam.

Claire instantly felt out of place. She hadn't been here for the last few years, and had forgotten just how grand and over the top everything was.

She stopped and stared at a sweeping staircase in front of her and swallowed hard. She felt someone slip their arm inside hers.

'Shall we?' said Michael, smiling at her.

He led her through the crowd and towards a waiter carrying a tray of canapés. He helped himself and she watched as he stuffed them into his mouth, pulling a face. He picked up two flutes of champagne and handed one to her.

He paused when he saw her face. 'What?'

'You always did eat like a pig,' she said, taking the glass and turning her back on him. He shrugged, helping himself to more food.

Claire looked around at the other ladies in their finery and glanced at her reflection in a large mirror across the room. She looked better than most of the women present and she raised her head high with her shoulders back as she walked across the ballroom floor to meet the Mayor.

Michael, oblivious to Claire's departure, carried on filling a plate with finger food before he became aware of someone standing next to him. He glanced up and was faced with the smug grin of David Matthews.

Michael swore inwardly, but managed a smile. Matthews stood with his hands in the pockets of his fine ivory-coloured suit trousers, a big grin cut across his face.

'Did you know you're the one they say will tame the wild beast, Mickey?' He nudged Michael's arm.

Michael frowned. 'I don't understand.' He stuffed more food into his mouth. 'And don't call me Mickey.'

Matthews gestured towards Claire, who was busy talking to the Mayor, laughing at his jokes and taking his compliments on her dress. Michael saw Claire's ex-husband, DCI Simon Forester, walking towards her.

He must have paid her a compliment, judging by her body language.

'Come on, mate, you know what I mean,' Matthews continued, leaning in so close that Michael could smell the alcohol on his breath. 'Reigniting the old flame with the ice maiden.'

Michael tried to walk away but Matthews put his hand on his shoulder and laughed. 'Come on, it's just a bit of banter between friends.'

Michael watched as Matthews took a champagne flute from the table and swallowed half of the expensive fizz in one go. He could easily punch him in the mouth right here and now, and not care.

'Just so you know, and I know I can say this because we're quite alike you and I—'

'I doubt that,' Michael said.

'I just wanted to say well done… Well done for getting the best fucked-up case we've seen in a *long* time, and I just wanted to say no one, and I mean no one, thinks you got in on it because you're in and out of the Guv all day and night.'

Matthews leaned in closer and winked suggestively.

Nothing prepared him for what happened next.

His alcohol level had dulled his senses considerably but he was still more than aware of Michael's fist hurtling towards his face at high velocity.

Even though he felt no pain at first, he heard the sickening crunch of his nose and felt his blood gushing down his face. The last thing he saw was red streaks over his clothes and Michael being dragged away by security, his legs and fists straining to get at him.

CHAPTER 34

It'd started to rain that evening, despite the heat and sunshine of the day, and the streets in the old market town of Hitchin seemed to form a miniature river on the uneven cobbles on the Market Square.

Adrian Brown cursed under his breath as his expensive suit soaked up the water, as he dipped and weaved in between people also seeking shelter.

Despite the rain, the pubs and clubs were still heaving with people enjoying their Saturday night before the drudge of Monday morning crept upon them again all too soon.

Adrian didn't know the area too well, so he stopped under the light of a nearby lamp post and glanced at his mobile phone. The message he'd received earlier had told him to be in the Red Hart pub at 9:00pm sharp and if rumours were to be believed, he should abide by that.

It was just before nine and Adrian recalled the phone conversation he'd had with the man earlier.

Adrian had asked how he would know the man.

The reply had been unnerving; the man would know him and he should sit at a table in the corner furthest from the bar which would be kept free for them to conclude their business. He should wait to be approached and not ask any questions before then.

As Adrian headed towards the pub, a youth bumped hard into his shoulder. A surge of pain ravaged its way through Adrian's nervous system and he gripped the wound on his shoulder.

Deep inside, he cursed Amelia Williams and strode on ahead.

***

The pub was heaving with patrons of all ages and Adrian immediately regretted wearing his suit. This was a rockers' pub and everyone was dressed in a variety of clothes representing their taste in music, from punks to indie boys.

Dating back to the 1500s, the Red Hart was not only the oldest public house in Hitchin but also the last place where the town had held a public hanging. Adrian couldn't help but raise a smile when he'd read that on the internet earlier that day.

How apt.

As he pushed through the entrance he was faced with a huge man, both in girth and height, dressed in leather, head shaven. He loomed over him, arms folded.

Adrian swallowed hard and sweat began to bead at his brow. The man gestured for him to follow, and he led him to two chairs and two pints on a dirty-looking table.

Adrian stared at the large man, then the table.

The man pressed a huge meaty hand on Adrian's shoulder, forcing him down into one of the chairs, casting him a hard glare before returning to the bar.

Adrian stared around the pub.

Everyone was having a good time, talking, drinking and behaving rowdily. Everyone seemed to ignore the table and free chair opposite him, despite the pub heaving with bodies and lack of seating.

After a few minutes eyeing the pint in front of him, he picked it up and downed half of it in one mouthful to steady his nerves.

A further five minutes or so passed before a shadow fell over the table.

Adrian looked up, swallowing hard.

In front of him stood a tall fat man of about forty with receding brown hair. His eyes were close together, sunk deep within his skull, with a thin mouth and large nose. His huge gut hung over his black jeans and tried to burst free of his Black Sabbath T-shirt.

He inspected Adrian like he was an insect he wanted to squash, before sitting down in the spare chair. He remained silent, just staring.

'Mr Hargreaves?' Adrian's voice was somewhat less confident than his usual bravado.

'You can call me Gavin.'

Adrian offered his hand but Hargreaves just stared at it, face blank, until Adrian retracted it, looking embarrassed.

He was out of his depth associating with thugs like Hargreaves, but Amelia had given him no choice.

He'd acquired Hargreaves's mobile number after a chance meeting with an old friend who thrived in the gang culture in London. Adrian had confided in his friend, who'd recommended Hargreaves as someone who could make problems disappear but at a price.

'You're not what I expected, given the nature of your problem, Mr Brown,' Hargreaves said, his voice low and gruff with a hint of a Scottish accent still audible, twenty years after leaving Falkirk. 'I hope you have a photo of the subject?'

He reached for his beer and drank deeply from the glass.

Adrian reached inside his jacket pocket, produced a photo, placed it face down on the table and pushed it across the rough wood.

Hargreaves's eyes remained on Adrian as he casually picked up the photo and raised it to his face, before finally looking at it. He grinned. 'Pretty.'

Adrian nodded and pulled out a folded piece of paper from his jacket and passed it to Hargreaves. 'Don't be fooled by her appearance. She's stronger and tougher than she looks,' Adrian said, rubbing his wounded arm. Hargreaves looked up and laughed at him.

'You tell me she took you by surprise. I tell you,' he said, pointing a finger in Adrian's face, 'I wouldn't have let her get so close in the first place.'

Adrian felt somewhat annoyed at being made to look less of a man by the thug sitting in front of him. 'I don't think you understand. She's unstable, unpredictable.'

Hargreaves looked at the paper Adrian had passed to him. It had Amelia's address printed on it. Hargreaves frowned.

'This is the same flats where the Miller murder took place. It'll be crawling with filth… It'll not surprise you that I'm known to them.'

Adrian shrugged.

'I don't care where you do it, just as long as it's done, and quickly.'

He reached for what was left of his beer and finished it, glancing around him, hoping not to see anyone he knew.

Hargreaves's ability to intimidate was not through getting angry and losing his temper. He only had to use his words and eyes to strike fear into any man. He leaned forward, beckoning Adrian closer.

'Have you ever physically hurt anyone, Mr Brown? Heard their screams and felt bones break in your hands? I judge by your expensive suit and well-groomed face that this is not a life known to you. *My* life, for instance.'

Adrian shook his head. *Not bloody likely.*

Hargreaves raised his finger in Adrian's face, pointing at him before continuing.

'You tell me you've been laundering money and fixing the company's books for some time. Then you meet this girl and promise her cheap rent. Have I got it right so far, Mr Brown?'

Adrian nodded, feeling drained. He wasn't cut out for this.

'I'm curious. What do you get from her in return?'

Adrian blushed and thought before he answered. 'Like you said, she's a pretty girl.'

Hargreaves smiled. 'So she's rejected you and you want revenge.'

'She wanted to break the deal and continue getting reduced rent, then she stabbed me in the arm,' Adrian said, raising his voice.

'Hell hath no fury…as the saying goes,' Hargreaves said, his stomach heaving up and down as he laughed.

Adrian frowned and leaned across the table.

'I'm paying you. It shouldn't matter to you why I want the bitch out of the way.'

'Money is something I have plenty of.' He leaned closer. 'Tell me why I should help a piece of shit like you?' Adrian dared not answer. 'You come in here acting all superior in your flashy suit and turn your nose up at people like me, yet deep down we're alike.'

'I'm *nothing* like you.'

Hargreaves ignored him. 'You didn't care about this girl, you used her and now you want my help to do what you're not man enough to do.'

'I can make it worth your while.'

'How so?'

'You said yourself she's a pretty girl…you could do whatever you wanted to her before you frighten her off. That and the money is a fair deal, I think,' Adrian said.

'I could do that anyway. She's not yours to give.'

He eyed Adrian closely and could see he was in way over his head. 'Tell you what I'll do,' he said. 'You lure her to meet you somewhere, away from her flat. Me and my boys will pick her up, rough her up a little and scare her off, and make her give up the flat immediately. All it will cost you is 4k.'

Adrian practically jumped from the table.

'What! That's double what we originally agreed!' Adrian saw the man who showed him to his seat earlier suddenly up close beside him. He looked at Hargreaves, who remained seated and unfazed.

'Sit down, Mr Brown. Don't make a bigger cunt of yourself than you have already.'

The big man forced Adrian back into his seat again. 'You're being unreasonable,' Adrian said, fighting his nerves.

'Your *request* is unreasonable. From what I can see, you deserved what she did. I like the sound of this woman and I won't enjoy hurting her. You must understand I *have* to like my job, Mr Brown, and four thousand pounds cash would be sufficient to take pride in my work. I guarantee she wouldn't bother you again.'

He leaned back in his chair and placed his huge hands on his stomach. 'And judging from what I've seen, you can more than afford it...take the offer or leave it.'

Adrian thought for a long time, considering Hargreaves's deal.

Reluctantly he offered his hand to Hargreaves across the table.

'You've got a deal. Make her suffer.'

CHAPTER 35

Michael knew he was getting off lightly, as he sat in a back office with a security guard, while Claire patched things up outside with the Mayflower Hall's night manager.

He flexed his fingers and bent his hand in several different directions, a dull ache growing in ferocity across his knuckles. Despite the pain and redness where he'd cut the skin, he felt satisfied when he thought back to the look on Matthews's face.

He smiled at the security guard, who stood opposite him, arms folded.

'Don't suppose I can smoke in here, can I? I feel like celebrating.' The guard ignored him.

After a few minutes Claire and the manager entered the room.

'Mr Matthews has decided not to press charges. It could have been a lot worse for you I think, Mr Diego,' the manager said in a thick Romanian accent. His tone was so stern that Michael felt like he was back in a school classroom.

'That's *Sergeant* Diego,' he said.

'Then act like it,' Claire snapped. She then addressed the manager. 'Thank you for being lenient. My colleague is under some pressure at the moment and isn't always thinking straight. Although that doesn't excuse his actions, I do hope you'll accept my apologies once again.'

The man smiled warmly at her. 'Of course.' He waved his hand to the security guard to leave the room. 'Take as long as you need but I want him out. He's not to go back to the Ball.'

Claire turned and stared at Michael. He sat looking at the floor.

'You could've broken his nose, Diego.'

'I should've hit him harder then.'

'I should have you suspended,' she said, her voice sounding as tightly wound as a piano string. 'I don't know what's got into you, but you can cut the crap right now… I'm beginning to regret signing you up for this case. You're making a fool out of me.'

Michael remained silent, letting her vent her anger.

He thought about telling her why he hit Matthews. He doubted she'd feel so loyal then and would probably congratulate him. He decided against it though, and stood up to leave, but she blocked him.

'I'll call you a cab, until then you're staying here,' she said, pushing her hands against his shoulders. As she did so, he grabbed her around the waist and pulled her down on top of him in the chair, forcing his mouth against hers in a rough kiss.

Claire pulled away and slapped him hard across the cheek. She struggled in his arms, but he held her too tight.

She glared at him.

As his eyes met hers, all the old feelings she once had for him began to surface, and she felt herself giving in to an old habit, which had died hard not so long ago.

February 2012

'*Simon suspects something,*' *she said, lowering her eyes and staring at the stark white messy sheets on the hotel bed. All she could hear was the sound of her own heartbeat as she awaited his response.*

She raised her eyes to stare at his torso as he lay close to her, his chest rising and falling as if he were in the midst of a peaceful slumber.

Claire studied his face and realised that he had indeed fallen asleep. She cursed. Why did men always fall asleep after sex? She'd thought Michael would be different but after several weeks of hiding her secret, she'd realised that her colleague wasn't much different to any other man she'd slept with.

Better, but not different.

She sat up and gave him a sharp dig in the ribs. He bolted upright with a yelp and stared at her, confused, rubbing his side with his hand.

'*What was that for?!*'

'*I would've thought it was obvious.*' *She studied his eyes and remained poker-faced. After a few seconds of looking at his blank face, she sighed.* '*You fell asleep.*' *He looked at her and rolled over on his side, his face screwed up in disbelief.*

'*Crazy bitch.*'

He felt her get up from the bed and she appeared beside him, completely naked. He opened one eye and stared at her stomach, his eyes lowering further. '*Are you presenting?*' *he asked with a grin.*

'*We need to talk.*'

'*About what?*'

'*About Simon.*'

'Why's it always about Simon?' he sighed, rolling onto his back again. She sat perched on the side of the bed, staring at him.

'Because he's my husband.'

He stared back into her eyes and felt himself sink inside. 'Look, Claire, we've been over this. When we're together, we're here to forget about everything else and just concentrate on each other.' He looked bitter. 'I don't want to keep hearing about him.'

'It's a little hard not to think about him. He's my husband.'

'Isn't it a bit late to suddenly have a conscience?'

'I feel guilty.'

'That's 'cos you are.'

He saw her recoil. He reached for her hand, but found it hard to offer her much sympathy. 'You should've thought about this before you started sleeping with me.'

Claire was hurt but knew he was right.

She started thinking back on all the lies she'd told to get where she was, here in this luxury suite, to which they were regular visitors.

Surprisingly to Claire, she didn't care that it was obvious to the hotel staff what they were up to. All that had mattered was being with Michael, but now she was not so sure.

Their relationship had always been love-hate, even more so when Claire thought back to the day they'd shared their first passionate kiss. They were in their element when together in passion but once it was over, they reverted back to sniping at each other.

The next days and weeks would follow the same cycle. For some reason they lived for it. Neither one wanted it to end, but Claire could feel his lust dwindling, while hers *grew until she began to fear it could take on a new identity and grow into something she feared.*

Something she'd originally married Simon for.

Love was a game best played with two willing parties, and Michael, she feared, might be losing his game face.

It was several weeks later when Michael called her to end the affair. She was cold, calm and collected over the phone, agreeing with him, and it appeared a mutual decision, but inside she was screaming.

She cursed herself for letting herself get so emotionally involved with him, for starting to feel more than lust. Then her thoughts turned to Simon and how their fairy-tale romance was long gone and dead in the water.

For Claire, there was only one option.

CHAPTER 36

Claire awoke to the sound of her BlackBerry vibrating on the cabinet beside her. She forced herself to reach for it and hung up without bothering to check who'd been calling.

She opened her eyes, squinting at her digital clock, glowing a bright green in the half-light of her bedroom. It was after 10:00am, late rising for her, even for a Sunday.

She stretched her arms out and hit something warm lying next to her.

Turning her head to one side, she saw his familiar shape lying close. She could smell his aftershave along with a twist of sweat.

Oh fuck it.

She eased herself from the bed, reaching for her dressing-gown when she realised she was completely naked.

Michael didn't stir.

She grabbed her BlackBerry and headed for the kitchen. She sat at the kitchen table waiting for the kettle to boil, and checked her call history.

It'd been Matthews calling her. She was glad she'd missed his call. He hadn't left her a voicemail though, which bothered her. Maybe he wanted to press charges against Michael after all?

Pushing the thought from her mind, she logged in to her inbox.

Among the usual official emails, she saw an email from Matthews. It was titled 'HARGREAVES'. Clicking on the heading, she scrolled through the text.

It appeared Gavin Hargreaves had met with a male unknown to the police and not connected to any of the unsolved cases involving Hargreaves.

'So?' she sniffed aloud to herself at the words on the screen. 'Could've been anyone and about anything.' Just before she went to exit the message, she noticed the lines of text she'd previously missed.

Reports showed the man had become agitated by Hargreaves but they appeared to have struck some kind of deal; both men shook hands at the end of the meeting.

Before she could hit the Reply button, she was startled by someone's hands suddenly upon her shoulders. She jumped but was held down in her seat.

'Easy,' he said. 'It's only me.' Michael's face then appeared in line with hers. He smiled at her, trying to gauge her reaction. She remained cautious, her face blank. 'Was it that bad then?' He removed his hands from her shoulders and took a seat opposite her.

She avoided his eyes.

'No...' she managed. Michael looked quite pleased with himself. '...and yes.' He froze as he reached for an apple sitting in the fruit bowl in front of him.

His eyes found hers.

'I didn't hear you complaining.' She smiled, and it stung. In that moment he felt vulnerable and he hated every second of it. 'I don't think it's funny, Claire,' he said as he bit roughly into the apple.

'You and your ego, Diego,' she said, shaking her head. 'I meant it was bad because it shouldn't have happened.' She leaned in closer to him across the table. 'It won't happen again.'

The kettle boiled. Claire got up and made them both a mug of coffee, put his down beside him and took her seat opposite him again.

She watched him as he gnawed at the apple, a defiant look on his face. His eyes were dull this morning and his stubble thicker than usual. He looked animal-like with his messy brown hair.

Deep inside Claire began to feel guilty. She'd wanted last night as much as he did and here she was telling him it wouldn't happen again, even though she wanted nothing more than to pick up where they'd left off.

She found herself in a rare moment of weakness, reaching for his hand.

Michael was startled by her sudden moment of tenderness and refused her hand, instead studying her eyes intently, unsure how to react. After a few moments he let her fingers intertwine in his. She squeezed his hand and smiled.

'We have to remain professional, Michael.'

He smiled to himself. She rarely called him by anything but his surname.

You must really mean it, he thought.

'I gave up being professional long ago,' he said. 'I know I don't want any of what's happening between us right now to stop.'

There, he'd said it, and as soon as the words were out of his mouth, he regretted them, despite knowing there was truth them. He didn't want to appear the vulnerable one.

He couldn't read the expression on her face. Did she look pleased? He couldn't be sure.

Claire's BlackBerry began ringing again, making them both jolt, their hands separating. Claire glanced at the caller ID.

DI David Matthews.

She gave Michael a long lingering look, before she answered the call and walked away from the kitchen, letting herself out into the garden.

'So you think there's something significant with this man who met with Hargreaves?' Claire said, reiterating what Matthews was telling her.

'Yeah, I do. Call it intuition.'

Claire walked around the winding stone path leading further into her large garden. She glanced at the beautiful hanging baskets her gardener had planted recently and walked over to the nearest one, mounted on the brick wall to the annexe. She sniffed at the delicate flowers cascading over the side of the basket.

Then she remembered last night.

'Hang on a minute. You were at the Ball last night getting your arse kicked, how'd you know about this meeting?'

'He *wasn't* kicking my arse. He just caught me off guard. I could've taken him. He's lucky I didn't press charges and—'

'*And* the meeting, Matthews?' She cut in to his sentence like a knife through butter.

Matthews hated her when she did that. She was renowned for her rudeness and way of getting to the point. He'd been warned from his very first day in CID to let it ride over his head. Let it go over his head he did, for the most part, but nevertheless, he could never get used to it.

'I had my team working on it.'

Claire stiffened and pursed her lips. 'Oh, it's *your* team now, Matthews?'

'Sorry, Guv. I just meant—'

'It's irrelevant.' Claire cut him off again, mid-sentence. 'I don't want you taking up too much time over this mystery stranger. Could be something, but more likely nothing.

Concentrate on the assault charge. I want Hargreaves in court and off the streets.' She hung up before he could respond.

She went to go back inside when she noticed her rose bushes. She thought back to the letter found on Wainwright's body.

She saw Michael emerge from the patio door and head towards her.

'What did that twat want?'

'Nothing important.'

'Couldn't it have waited until tomorrow?'

'It was about the Hargreaves investigation,' she said, 'which doesn't concern you any more, does it?'

There was no mistaking the change in her body language and tone. Any chance he had right now of a repeat of last night was gone.

Damn Matthews.

Claire looked to the roses again. 'Just think about Wainwright's murder.' She began walking back to the house. 'And Miller as well,' she called back over her shoulder. 'It can't be a separate unrelated murder.'

Michael watched her go back inside the house and glanced at his watch, scowling. Why did he have to complicate everything?

CHAPTER 37

Adrian Brown hated Monday mornings. He glanced at his office phone and saw the new message indicator flashing red: six new messages.

He told Mary to bring him his usual coffee and to have the audio dictation tape he'd left on her desk done by midday before he went to conduct another viewing.

He waited until she'd left, closing his office door before he began to listen to his messages on loudspeaker.

He barely listened to the messages from either landlords or tenants, enquiries about ground rent, broken boilers and nuisance neighbours, dismissing each one as they went.

Until he came to the sixth message.

He recognised the underlying Scottish tones as the voice crackled from the machine.

Adrian almost fell from his chair.

How did Hargreaves get his office number? This wasn't part of the deal.

He lifted the phone receiver, taking it off loudspeaker, and began to sweat as he listened to the message. As soon as it ended, he hit the Delete button, and slumped back in his chair, his hand covering his mouth.

Tonight is the night, he thought. *It's so soon.*

He loosened the tie around his neck and undid the top button on his shirt. He called out for Mary and asked her to dig out the file for Amelia's flat. Within ten minutes she'd brought it to him. She studied his face, and noticed how flushed he was.

'Would you like a cold drink? You don't look well.'

He ignored her, staring at the file instead. She waited a few more seconds before leaving his office.

Adrian couldn't stop his hands from shaking as he looked over the file.

Soon Amelia would be warned off and he'd be free of her.

He'd been sloppy, he knew that, but he'd been dazzled by her beauty and charm. The wound on his arm stung as he turned a page in the file and he remembered how unpredictable she was, how violent she could turn on a whim.

He tapped his fingers on the well-thumbed file before closing it. He tried taking a few deep breaths before picking up the phone receiver and making the call. It only steadied his nerve by a mere fraction but still he went ahead regardless.

It was a necessary evil.

Afterwards he emailed Mary to ask her to cancel all his appointments for the day. He had no wish to talk to her again.

Mary blinked hard at the email when it popped up in her inbox. She read the text and frowned:

Mary
Cancel my appointments for today. Make an excuse. I'm not to be disturbed by anyone, and this includes you and any phone calls. I still need the letter typed by noon and sent out in tonight's post. Pls PP it for me.
Adrian.

Mary scoffed, drawing a few glances from her colleagues, but reminded herself she needed the job, which paid reasonably well, so she returned to typing Adrian's letters.

***

Amelia was shocked when she saw the caller ID flash Adrian Brown's name across the screen and debated whether to answer it or not. After several rings she pressed the answer button.

Twenty minutes later when she'd hung up, she dialled the contact in her phone labelled as '*G*'. The call was answered and after Amelia had explained everything Adrian had said to her, the Guardian was stunned.

'*He asked you to dinner?*'

'Yes, can you believe that?'

'*What's he up to? I don't like it.*'

'He just said he wanted to apologise. Men like him don't apologise in my experience. Only one way to say for sure though.'

'*You told him yes?*'

'I did… Was I wrong?'

There was a long pause and static plagued the line.

'*Yes. I don't like this… Give me the details. You're not going alone.*'

CHAPTER 38

It was almost 7:30pm when Amelia arrived at the Italian restaurant. She spotted Adrian, already seated at the far side of the room. He waved her over and Amelia removed her coat as she walked towards him.

Another one of her tactics.

He eyed her from head to foot several times.

He took in her red hair, which she'd tamed into a loose ponytail, her fitted blue shirt, right down to her black pencil skirt, and followed her legs to her very high stiletto heels.

He felt a twinge of guilt inside when she greeted him with a soft smile but then remembered the stab wound on his shoulder, which would leave an unsightly scar.

'I didn't think you'd show,' he said as she sat down in front of him. He waited until a waiter had taken her drink order before leaning in closer across the table. 'I'm very glad you did.'

The waiter brought over a large glass of wine for Amelia and Adrian scowled at the man when he caught him eyeing her suggestively.

She rolled her eyes. 'It shouldn't bother you. Other men look. Deal with it.'

'I didn't ask you here so other men could distract us.'

'Then why did you ask me here?' She folded her arms.

'I told you, I wanted to apologise for what's happened. I shouldn't have taken advantage of you when I knew you needed money.' Amelia looked at him sceptically, her eyes unusually dull in colour. 'I hope you'll accept my apology.'

Amelia glanced out of the glass front of the restaurant and into Haverbridge town plaza. She searched the ordinary faces of the people outside before she saw her Guardian sitting on a bench nearby, looking in on them.

She knew what to do.

'I accept,' she said, her eyes wandering back to his. 'And I hope you know I'm sorry for what I did to your arm. It's my head... My past is...' She struggled to find the words. Adrian reached for her hand, clasped it between his fingers and smiled.

'We all have skeletons, Amelia. Everyone.'

'I know. Maybe we could go somewhere and talk after dinner?'

Adrian smiled. She'd walked into his trap easily with minimum effort from him. It was better this way.

***

After they'd left the restaurant, Adrian put his arm around her shoulders as they walked across the plaza. Amelia looked around and saw her Guardian following at a discreet distance behind. The Guardian always did turn heads, and Amelia saw a few give a second look as they walked by.

No one ever suspects beauty can do evil things...

Adrian stopped as they approached a long side road next to some fast food outlets. He turned towards her. 'How about you come back to mine and we'll talk? See if we can't sort this mess out.' He smiled, stroking her cheek with his hand.

Amelia looked towards the dark side road. She could only just make out some parked cars and rows of wheelie bins which backed off behind the takeaway shops. They were overflowing with rubbish.

'You parked down there?'

'It was closer to the restaurant. You know what Haverbridge is like for parking.'

She immediately knew something was off. '*You* parked your flashy car down there?'

Adrian paused but smiled to reassure her. 'I know people who work around here. They keep an eye out for me.' He gestured with his arm, directing her down the narrow road.

Amelia checked over her shoulder. She'd lost sight of her Guardian but she knew they were there, in the shadows, watching. Waiting.

She walked with Adrian into the darkness.

A few neon signs ahead were the only light in the oily blackness.

They were about halfway down the stretch of road before Amelia felt alone. She reached out for Adrian but grabbed nothing but air. She spun round but all she could see were vague shadows.

'Adrian?'

Then she heard a faint sound. Something was moving in a van parked right next to her.

She paused, her breath catching in her throat.

Then strong arms grabbed her from behind and lifted her off the ground. She tried to scream but something was sprayed into her mouth. It burned her throat, making her retch.

Someone grabbed her legs, lifting them high. She was being carried by two large men, as far as she could tell in the darkness. She tried to kick her legs free.

The back doors of the van were opened and some rushed words were said in strong accents.

Her heart raced as she was forced into the back of the van and pulled to the floor. The metal was cold against her skin and she felt a crushing weight pushing down on her torso.

Someone was sitting on her back.

Soon hands were on her ankles and feet, so she kicked out hard, her heels cutting into someone's face. Someone yelled and Amelia felt a hard blow across her face.

The force nearly knocked her out cold and she had no way of avoiding the blindfold which was then tied around her face.

She began screaming but someone covered her mouth. She snapped her teeth hard and fast until she found flesh. She pressed down hard until she could taste the copper of blood.

A man screamed as she bit against his fingernails and he began hitting her hard across the face but she refused to let go.

Then she froze.

Something cold was pressed hard against her temple.

'Let go or I'll blow your brains out all over the van.'

Amelia released the other man's fingers from her mouth. She felt his blood trickle down the corner of her mouth.

'Who the fuck are you?' she screamed before someone struck her hard across the face with the butt of a gun.

All she knew then was darkness.

***

The Guardian cursed as the the van drove off. They wished they had followed her down the side road.

They had lost sight of Adrian and were waiting to see what would happen. The Guardian had hoped Amelia would meet them on the other side of the road but then they had been helpless when the men had grabbed Amelia.

The Guardian leaned back against the wall and tried to think what to do next. Then the sound of approaching footsteps was all that could be heard in the darkness…

The Guardian

I ran on ahead and ducked into a shop doorway. The sound of footsteps were getting closer and I could feel my bowels tighten with a mix of intoxicating excitement and apprehension.

I held my breath.

The footsteps were almost upon me.

Adrian walked right past me and back towards the restaurant, his hands in his pockets. He was whistling, like nothing had happened.

I released my breath, and my lungs ached. My head swam. It felt soft, my ears straining to hear properly. I felt like I was sinking, my head dipping below water.

At least I'd remained unseen.

But what to do now? Amelia can hold her own. Always did, especially when growing up. She'd survived worse than most.

But was she strong enough for *this*?

My stomach knotted. Do I follow Adrian or trace the van and rescue Amelia?

To be honest, I think I knew the answer as soon as it happened.

Think of the bigger picture.

I stepped out from the doorway and followed the whistling.

CHAPTER 39

Claire sighed as she heard Dr Danika Schreiber's voice on the other end of the phone.

'Nothing on Ashe Miller? Not even one clothing fibre?'

'No. What's confusing is the way he died. Cause of death was the cut to the throat but he has a deep laceration to his abdomen. This alone would've been enough to kill him. This attack was particularly violent – unnecessarily so. Whoever did it must've hit him hard and fast. He died from loss of blood and his chest was cut open down to the ribcage as with Wainwright after death.

'Except Wainwright died from *asphyxiation*, and of course had that letter tucked inside the skin folds. You either have the same killer who was disturbed and therefore had no time to finish, or a copycat. I understand the letter was not made known to the press?'

'No, it wasn't,' Claire said.

'So it could've been someone who read about Wainwright's murder and tried to copy it through Miller… just not successfully.'

'It's a reasonable assumption but I can't help feeling we're missing the bigger picture here,' Claire said as she rubbed her forehead.

'You sound tired. Maybe you're taking on too much.'

Danika liked Claire. They'd worked on many investigations together over the years and Danika was one of the few people Claire respected.

'That bloody letter,' Claire said. 'Forensics turned up nothing on that either.' She swung around in her office chair in frustration. 'Do I assume we've got some loony out there, cutting up priests and junkies, while playing fucking John Keats on me?'

Danika laughed. 'God, I hate Keats.'

Claire reached inside her desk drawer and pulled out her version of the letter. She read it several times to herself.

'You still there, Claire?'

'Yeah… Listen to this, see if you understand it. "What revelation lies within the beauty of a rose? With its thorns sharp yet perfume so bewitching, you must breathe in the scent, be it foul in its reason for being." What the hell does "reason for being" mean?'

Danika paused for a moment and wrote it down on her own notepad. She stared at the passage and racked her brains. 'It's the rose, isn't it?'

'What's the rose?'

'The reason for its *being*. The reason it's alive, why it's there,' Danika said, feeling smug.

Claire stared at the words at her end. 'The reason why someone planted it you mean… "be it foul in its reason for being."'

Danika looked at the words again then almost jumped from her chair.

'I've got it!' Claire screwed her face up at her words. 'Don't you see it? When it says what lies beneath the rose and be it foul the reason for why it's there, it's saying it's covering something. Like underneath a rose. Something foul but you must smell the rose regardless.'

'Smell the rose? I don't see wh—'

'Investigate the smell. Investigate what's foul underneath or *buried* beneath a rose.'

The penny dropped for Claire. 'That's why it's there. It hides something.'

Danika laughed and boasted at the other end, while Claire racked her brains for a rose.

The word 'rose' doesn't have to be literal. It could be a metaphor for something.

She glanced at the scene of crime photographs of Wainwright's body and remembered her visit to Shrovesbury Manor.

She remembered Father Manuela's precious Rose Garden.

CHAPTER 40

The Guardian

I followed Adrian at a safe distance, just closely enough to see where he was heading.

I kept to the shadows, following him to the multi-storey car park on the edge of the town centre and climbed the stairs two at a time when Adrian took the lift to the third floor.

By the time I reached the doors at the top, Adrian had just stepped out of the lift.

I slipped through the doors and darted in between the concrete pillars with minimal sound as Adrian headed towards his car.

I jumped as a shrill *beep* sounded in the empty cavernous space when Adrian pressed the fob in his pocket, the headlights of a silver Aston Martin flashing in the corner. The lighting in here was dim and cast large shadows around Adrian.

It allowed me to slip close, unnoticed.

Adrian pushed the key into the car's lock and opened the door.

I saw his face reflected in the glass of the car window. He saw me then. His mouth dropped open a fraction.

I swung the metal bat I'd brought with me, which I'd previously concealed in my rucksack.

The last thing Adrian saw was a flash of steel reflected in the car's windows, before my bat connected with his head.

Darkness overcame him. Blood trickled down his face.

And I smiled, genuinely, for the first time in years.

***

The room spun and bright white lights danced in the dark behind his eyes, as Adrian awoke, dazed, and with a killer pain raging through his skull. It felt like a bomb had gone off, turning his brain to pulp.

He tried to raise his hands to cradle his head, but found they wouldn't move. He tried to move his body but his torso was firmly held down, by what felt like rope.

He tried to open his eyes, but gasped in agony as he tried to peel his eyelids apart.

Sharp pains pierced his skin. He felt bruised. He couldn't open his eyes no matter how hard he tried. He shook his head from side to side and tried opening his eyelids again but with more force.

Pain shot through his face. This time he tried to scream, but his mouth wouldn't open.

Now panic-stricken, he rocked violently in his chair, straining his eyelids, until a small amount of light hit his retinas. He tried again, and felt something pull then slowly begin to rip at his skin.

He screamed again.

His mouth pulled back together, and he could taste blood. He flicked his tongue along the inside of his mouth and wrenched his lips apart again.

Thick thread criss-crossed along his lips.

He rocked against the chair, leaned too far to one side and felt himself falling. He hit the wood floor hard and heard his shoulder crack.

Ignoring the pain shooting through his shoulder, he strained his eyelids. He willed them to open, until he felt whatever was there snap away and blood blurred his vision.

His arm felt like it was on fire – his shoulder had been dislocated. His breath came in short sharp bursts. His chest tightened.

Blinking fast, he tried to make out his surroundings. He recognised the television and floor lamp standing in the corner. Then an expensive-looking sofa came into focus.

He was in his own living room.

He concentrated on the large mirror in front of him, which hung on the wall from floor to ceiling.

He saw his reflection and tried to scream.

Thick black thread was stitched into his mouth, holding it closed, crossing through his thin pink lips. Blood had dried in all the cracks and had trickled down his chin.

Tears started to roll down his cheeks when he saw his eyelids. Moments before, they had also been sewn together.

Then he saw the large gash at the side of his head, now crusted with congealed blood and bruised skin.

He pulled at his bonds but could barely move against the tall wooden chair. The rope cut into his wrists. He tried to kick out with his legs but they too were tied securely to the chair.

Mustering as much strength as he could, he screamed until his face turned red and the thread began to give way. Flesh began to pucker and tear, but he kept going until all the thread had snapped free.

With his mouth released, he cried for help until his voice was hoarse, but it was useless.

No one could hear him.

He'd moved into a new-build penthouse suite a month ago and there wasn't anyone living on the floor below him or next door. He could scream for hours and no one would come.

The pain in his shoulder was becoming too much and he broke down, his body shuddering with uncontrollable sobs.

Then something creaked.

***

The Guardian

He'd heard me open the door to his bedroom. Arching his head around towards the living room door, he struggled against the rope. His line of vision was slightly off. A few inches to his right and he would've seen me by now.

Then he spoke.

'Who's there?'

I walked forward from the shadows. I marvelled at my handiwork. The stitching had been a nice touch.

'I said who's there?!'

'*Shhh,*' I said. '…No one can hear you. You'll need your breath. I suggest you don't waste it.'

I came into the dim light. And then he saw me, well, a different version of me, anyway.

He turned his head, and took me in from head to toe. I saw his confusion over my appearance. Head to toe in plastic overalls. Hood over my hair, gloves on my hands. I was naked underneath.

His eyes widened, not believing what he was seeing.

'Who're you?' Adrian said. 'Please, help me. My eyes… my mouth… God help me.'

I smiled at those words. In all my years growing up, it was always about God. All it ever came down to.

'It's interesting that you should now ask God for help,' I said.

Adrian watched me as I sat down on the sofa. He twisted his head up to look at my face. 'Please…'

I inched forward, lowering my face closer to his.

'You live your life as if you were fearless. Fearless of pain, of violence. Fearless of redemption,' I said.

'Please, take anything you want. My arm's dislocated. I need a doctor.' Adrian began to sob.

I shook my head. 'Even now you think your wealth will be enough to save you. That's the extent of your arrogance.'

'Why are you doing this? My eyes…my mouth?'

'Did you like it?'

His face screwed up with the pain.

'So that you may appreciate what it's like to feel vulnerable. To be alone at the mercy of others… Like Amelia Williams, for instance.'

Adrian's heart must have been pounding. The adrenaline would be surging through his veins. It would be relentless.

I pushed myself up from the sofa and it took all my strength to get a strong enough hold on him in the overturned chair. I hauled him upright.

Adrian whimpered when I glared at him, my eyes boring deep into his own. The way he trembled told me that he truly believed I was looking into his soul. In a way, I was and I was disgusted with what I saw.

'Amelia Williams!' I screamed into Adrian's face. 'Don't try to deny anything.'

Sweat poured from his face.

'Where're they taking her?'

'I don't know… I…'

I've learnt a few things in my job. I've learnt to hold my own, to fight back, and defend myself against woman or man.

I drew my arm back and brought my fist straight into Adrian's jaw, the force even taking me by surprise.

Adrian's eyes rolled back inside his skull. He tasted fresh blood in his mouth. I let Adrian regain his composure. 'Let's try again, shall we? Where are they taking her?'

Adrian's head was reeling. I could tell by the way his eyes took their time to refocus on mine. He mumbled and blood leaked at the corners of his mouth.

'Where're they taking her?' I said, and grabbed hold of both sides of his face and slapped both cheeks. 'Come on, you piece of shit. Where is she?'

Adrian whimpered, and pulled against the rope.

He glared at me then.

And then I saw it.

Rage began to surge inside him, overcoming his pain and weakness.

I smiled, and cocked my head to one side, looking back at him.

'You value your life more than anything else on earth. Tell me where she is, and the pain will end.'

Adrian's defiance urged me on. It gave me a high. I wondered how he'd react when I upped the stakes a little. I pulled back, went behind the sofa, and grabbed the can of petrol.

Adrian's eyes widened.

That look sent electric charges burning through my limbs.

'Don't tell me what I want to know, and I will kill you. Be certain of that.'

Adrian blinked away dried flecks of blood. 'Who are you?'

And this is the part when they try to make you do a U-turn. Make you see them as a person, not an object. In theory it should make me less inclined to harm him.

In theory…

'Who I am makes no difference to you,' I said, placing the petrol can on the floor in front of him. 'It's what I'm capable of that should scare you... Where's she been taken?'

'You need help. We can get you medical help. I have money, I can pay. I can help you...and Amelia.'

'I don't need your money or your help.'

Adrian tried to move his arm again. I saw his face crumple with a fresh wave of pain.

I grabbed at his shoulder, squeezing it hard.

Adrian let out an agonising scream and thrashed around in the chair. 'Fuck you, you sick fuck!'

I couldn't help but smile. 'Amelia, Mr Brown.'

'Let me go!'

'Tell me now and the pain will end.' In some way it would, but maybe not how he envisaged.

Spittle flecked Adrian's mouth, his chin and then his lips pursed. He spat blood and mucus into my face.

It was warm. Revolting.

Adrian froze, watching me carefully as I casually wiped the mess from my face and then picked up the can of petrol.

I unscrewed the cap, breathing in the scent that hit my senses. I shook my head. That's when he lost control entirely.

In that moment his eyes filled with a slow realisation of what was going to happen.

'OK, I'll tell you! Just stop this!' he screamed at me.

I threw the cap down on the floor. 'I'm listening.'

'She's with a man called Hargreaves. *Gavin* Hargreaves.'

Whatever I was expecting, it wasn't that. Not that name.

I tipped a small amount of petrol on top of his head.

'No, please! I had to do something, just to scare her off. I can give you the address, just promise you'll let me go. I won't tell anyone about this!'

I stared down at him, cowering in my very presence. I love this power. Either sex, male or female. They all bend or cower to me in the end. I walked towards the far wall, and began to douse it in the petrol. Then I moved on to the furniture.

Adrian began babbling.

I cupped my ear, half indifferent, half curious. 'You'll have to say that again? I can't quite hear you.'

'She's at Blackley Farmhouse, Haverbridge West. Now please, let me go, you promised!'

Yeah, I guess I did.

I turned and picked up another can of petrol from behind the sofa. Then I let my gaze fall on Adrian. He just stared, eyes pleading.

'You said the pain would end.'

I carried on tipping the petrol over his head. 'It will.'

The liquid seeped into Adrian's open wounds and he screamed, struggling fiercely against the rope, especially when he saw me pull something small and silver from my overall pocket.

It was a lighter.

Adrian looked like he was barely able to breathe.

As much as he tried, he couldn't even scream. He sat there open-mouthed, trying to speak. A last ditch attempt to save his life.

Death is a release not a punishment. I forget who said that, but it's a wise motto.

I flicked the lighter's wheel, watched the long yellow flame burn before my eyes.

Then I cast it into the air.

Within less than a second of the lighter hitting the floor at the far side of the room, flames ignited the petrol and soon engulfed everything in its path, swallowing Adrian in a burning mass of yellow and orange.

CHAPTER 41

Claire finally managed to get hold of Father Manuela and he couldn't hide the annoyance in his voice when he answered her call.

'I'm sorry to call so late, Father, but it's very important that I speak with you. I've come across some new information and I wonder if I can come and see you at the Manor.'

'Surely you can't mean tonight, Chief Inspector?'

'If it isn't too inconvenient.'

'Well, it is. It's late and I have things to do.'

'Of course, Father. Perhaps tomorrow?'

Manuela checked his diary and sighed. 'Tomorrow at 9:00am. Honestly though, I have no idea how I could be of any further assistance. This is becoming quite tedious, I don't mind telling you that.'

After she'd hung up the phone she glanced over the letter found on Wainwright's body and the one which had been delivered to her own home.

'What are you hiding, old man?' she said to herself. 'There's more here I've yet to see.'

She turned to her computer and brought up the internet, accessed Google, typed in Shrovesbury Manor and waited.

The search engine brought up many links, including the main website. Surprised Manuela was able to run his own web page, she clicked on the link and entered the site.

There were many sections about the history of the Manor, the Mission Statement, a photo gallery and a section on existing and former members and staff, both members of the clergy and the public.

Claire clicked on the heading and it took her to a page with separate links for years both past and present.

Remembering what Manuela had said about the dates Rebecca Turner had gone missing, she clicked the link labelled *2008–2009*.

She scrolled through a long list of names until she found Rebecca's. Claire clicked on her name. Another page opened detailing everything from her religious achievements, through to the news stories of her disappearance. There was also a section for photographs.

Claire clicked on the page and a few small thumbnails were brought up which would appear at the full resolution if selected. She glanced through a few, most showing Rebecca receiving communion in the Chapel, singing in the choir, and a few shots of her at the sixteenth birthday party that'd been thrown for her.

Flicking through the photographs half-heartedly, she saw an image that caught her off guard. Staring hard at the image, she squinted against the glare from the computer screen.

She saw a few girls sitting next to Rebecca, smiling for the camera, posing with cards and gifts wrapped in birthday paper. One girl had caught her eye among the few ordinary faces.

This girl had bright green eyes, a small frame, and a pretty face with a wild shock of flaming red hair. Claire read the names along the bottom of the photograph.

Amelia William-Jenkins.

Reaching for the notepad she'd taken to Paradis, she flicked to the page listing the names of the children Chloe

Jenkins had said her mother and father had fostered. She saw the name Amelia.

She stared at the picture on the screen again. She was sure this was the same girl she and Michael had interviewed over the Miller murder.

She clicked back to the current and past members' page and searched for Amelia's name. After a few seconds she found it and brought up a small selection of photographs and some accompanying text.

Claire's eyes widened as she read the words in front of her.

Amelia William-Jenkins joined Shrovesbury Manor in 1999, aged six. The former foster child of one of our Patrons, Mark Jenkins, whose name she took, left Shrovesbury in 2009. Amelia learnt many lessons to equip her for a very fulfilling life during her time at the Manor, and maintained many loving friendships along the way. She will be a familiar face sadly missed by all those at Shrovesbury.

Claire scrolled through a few pictures of Amelia with her friends and Mark Jenkins. There were pictures of Amelia with Wainwright, sitting on his knee as a little girl, and with Manuela and Hawthorne.

Highlighting the pictures, she clicked the Print button and sat there holding her head in her hands.

She stared at her notes from her interview with Chloe Jenkins. She read over the key points and found herself staring at her own words written in capital letters: *CONNECTION?*

2009

Stephen stretched out, arms above his head, his fingers splayed, his leg easing out of the cramp that had travelled down one side of his body. His back arched like a cat stretching lazily on a summer's day, content, until something inside him cracked.

He felt the long thin arm lying across his stomach flinch.

Amelia raised her head which had been resting on her arms, a dishevelled mass of hair framing her face. 'I hate it when you do that,' she said, and lightly pinched the skin on his upper arm.

He laughed, and encircled her into his body with his right arm, her warm bare skin comforting against his.

Amelia kicked her legs haphazardly, the grass tickling her toes. A shiver danced up her spine as the wind gently blew through the branches of the trees overhead.

They were in a part of the local wood into which few rarely ventured, stretched out, semi-naked on a dusty old picnic blanket that Amelia had found at the Manor. The weather had been kind to them, the sun beating down, kissing pale skin, and for a small amount of time, at least, they had felt contented.

Then Amelia shifted her weight, propping herself up beside him on one elbow. Her hair hung down, covering her breasts, her lower back curved in at a sharp angle, her jeans sitting low on her narrow hips.

Stephen studied her face; each small line that creased her forehead when she frowned, and the light in her eyes as it slowly darkened with her mood.

'Have you given your name any more thought?' he said.

Her eyes slowly rose to meet his. She traced a long finger nail across his lower belly. She nodded.

'And?'

Amelia removed her hand abruptly, and shook out her hair in a vain attempt to detangle the strands. 'I'm not changing it.'

He let out a loud sigh.

'You can't make me.'

He propped himself up, resting his weight on his forearms. 'I'm not going to make you do anything...'

'But?' Amelia said, eyes widening.

'...but, I think you should.' He gripped her arm, as she went to move away from him. 'Your name is the first thing they'll check for.'

'My name's common. So's the surname. They can't hunt down every single one of us.'

Stephen tightened his grip on her arm a little. Her eyes lowered to watch his fingers squeeze her flesh. Then her eyes snapped back to his as she leaned in closer, her lips inches from his. 'I'm not changing it.'

He went to speak but she cut him off. 'All my life people have been taking what they want from me,' she said, whipping her arm from his grasp. 'My life, my fucking dignity, the power to control my own destiny. Everything.'

She sat up, eyes burning into his. 'I'll be damned if they'll take my name too.'

Stephen shrugged. 'What's in a name?'

'Everything...'

'We'll find you another, something beautiful, something worthy—'

'I am Amelia Williams,' she said, 'and nobody is going to take that away from me. Not you, not them.' She pushed herself up from the ground, retrieved her top and shook it out, stray blades of grass floating onto the blanket.

'We're in this together,' Stephen said, stopping her in her tracks. 'Don't force me to remind you of that fact.'

He let the sentence hang in the air a moment longer than necessary.

He flung her discarded bra at her. 'How about Laura?'

She stared at him, eyes never leaving his. 'What?'

'It's a pretty name, don't you think?'

'It makes no difference to me. That's not my name, Stevie.'

He smiled to himself as he gently eased himself back down on the blanket again. 'I could get used to that name…Laura…'

Amelia's eyes narrowed. She aimed a spiteful kick to his ribs.

He batted her foot away just in time. 'Don't be such a vicious cunt, Laura*…'*

She lunged at him, hands grabbing at his face. He laughed as she sat astride him, her mouth snarling, spitting out insults. She pulled her flick knife from her jeans pocket, unsheathed the blade and brought it down towards his face.

His hand caught her wrist and squeezed, fingertips digging into her flesh, making her gasp in pain. 'Don't play this game,' he said, voice low, calm, with an edge to it that frightened her. 'You won't win.'

'I'm not changing my name,' she spat.

Stephen bent her wrist to one side, making her hand release the blade, a small cry escaping her lips. He bucked his hips, throwing her off balance. He swung her like a rag doll, until she was now pinned beneath him.

'Do what you want to me,' she said, voice defiant. 'Whatever you do, it won't make a difference.'

A cruel smile pulled at his lips, as his eyes wandered over her face, over the cable-like taut muscles straining in her throat beneath delicate skin. A bead of sweat had formed in the deep well of the jugular notch. 'Don't tempt me…' he whispered.

She lifted her mouth up towards his.

'I am Amelia Williams…' she said, her breath misting against his skin, '…and my name will *be remembered.'*

***

Chloe watched them and waited until Stephen left, leaving Amelia alone in the wood.

Amelia was topless still, enjoying the rays of sun on her small pale breasts. She folded up the blanket when Chloe emerged from behind the dense trees, making herself known. Amelia didn't see her at first, and jumped when she felt Chloe's hand on her arm.

'Shit, how long have you been there?'

Chloe swallowed hard. 'Long enough.'

Amelia shot her a knowing smile. 'You can't be jealous?' When Chloe avoided her eyes and remained silent, she dropped the blanket to the ground. 'Can we not do this?' she said.

'He's wrong for you.'

'Oh, 'cos you're so special?'

'Better than him.'

'You're just a confused teenager,' Amelia said.

'Maybe you are too.'

'No, I know exactly what I want. You've no idea wh—'

Chloe leaned in and pressed her lips against Amelia's. An ill-judged and timed kiss, her teeth catching Amelia's with the force of it.

Amelia shoved her back, both hands pressing against Chloe's chest, making her stumble back.

They stared at each other, Chloe breathless and unsure what to do.

'I'm sorry,' she said. 'I shouldn't have done that.'

Amelia stood there quiet, watching. Her long hair hung down over both shoulders, just covering her breasts.

She saw Chloe's eyes lower.

Amelia felt a rush through her body, white hot heat building up inside her.

She tossed her hair back, so it cascaded down her back and slowly unbuttoned her jeans.

CHAPTER 42

Amelia had no concept of time when she finally awoke to find her body hog-tied and lying on her side on something soft. It felt like a bed but she was still blindfolded and could only concentrate on the pain in her jaw and the ache of her limbs.

The burning in her throat had subsided but she could still taste bitterness on her tongue. She wondered what had been sprayed into her mouth, but this was the least of her problems.

She tried to spit out the gag which was tied around her head and stuffed into her mouth, when she heard a low sound which sounded like someone laughing.

She froze.

She tried to twist her head from side to side to loosen her gag, when she heard a voice in the room with her. Then she smelt the strong scent of cigarette smoke.

'Please don't struggle. It won't do you any good.' The voice was deep with a slight accent.

Amelia stopped moving and listened.

After a few seconds passed, she tried to remove the gag again, rubbing her face against what she guessed was a mattress. It soon began to pull away from her mouth and she was able to breathe more easily. As she took in a mouthful of air, she heard someone clapping.

'Well done. You're a clever girl, Amelia, I can see that now. Not just pretty but brains too.'

She tried to process the voice. She couldn't place it. 'Who are you?' She was scared and struggled to keep her voice steady. She had to remain strong, at least for appearance's sake.

'It doesn't matter who I am. It's why you're here that should.'

Hargreaves watched her body tense when she felt him sit beside her, the weight of him dipping the bed considerably lower.

He plucked the cigarette from his mouth and blew smoke slowly into her face. She coughed and turned her head, as he laughed childishly.

Hargreaves stared at her for a few more minutes, taking in every small detail, from her head to her toes.

He stared at her naked feet inside her stiletto heels and reached out his hand.

The blood inside Amelia's veins froze when she felt his fat fingers caress the skin on her feet and slide up over her legs. His hand edged closer to the hem of her skirt, and he thought back to his discussion with Adrian.

Having some fun with her couldn't hurt.

His fingers dipped under her skirt an inch or two.

A knock on the door startled them both, giving Amelia time to think as Hargreaves removed his hand and barked a command in another language. She heard another man answer him but couldn't hear what was said.

She felt Hargreaves get off the bed and speak in a hushed voice outside the room.

Using what might be her only chance, she managed to work one hand loose. She forced herself backwards to lie partially on her back, her legs still joined by the rope to her other wrist.

She heard the door close and a key turn, locking them in.

Footsteps edged closer so she heaved herself forward, trying to free her legs, ripping them against her bonds. She misjudged her place on the bed and felt herself fall before two meaty arms grabbed her.

Hargreaves laughed as he sat on the bed, pulling her over his lap, and she felt his knees digging into her back. She kept her free hand out of sight as she felt his face come close to hers, his breath putrid, laced with strong sprits and ash.

'Almost lost you there,' he said, bouncing her body, like she was nothing more than a rag doll in his arms. 'Wouldn't that have been a pity?'

'Let me go.' Her voice was steady, despite the rage beginning to boil inside her from the pit of her stomach. It may as well have been the pits of Hell.

Hargreaves let out a huge booming laugh, his fat stomach bouncing hard. Then he was coughing, hacking into one clenched fist. 'You really have no idea why you're here, do you?'

'And *where* is here?'

'That doesn't concern you.' Hargreaves grinned. 'You're here with me because my client wants to send you a message. I'm here to make sure you read it loud and clear.'

Amelia frowned and shook her head. 'I don't understand. What client?'

'You know… Tall, dark, a lot less good looking than he thinks he is, more money than sense… Money launderer, among other things.'

'*Adrian.*'

Suddenly his disappearance made sense, along with his surprise dinner date. She'd walked right into his trap. She felt stupid.

Hargreaves's face changed from jovial to serious, relieved he no longer had to string her along. 'And so the penny drops.' His voice was unnerving. 'He paid me a considerable amount to put the frighteners on you and I can't be seen to disappoint.'

He lifted Amelia in one swoop from his lap, back onto the bed, and pulled a pocket knife from his jeans. He watched her heave herself onto her knees, and lean back on her legs that were tucked under her. She began pulling at the rope again.

Hargreaves released the blade he was holding.

Amelia didn't have to see it to recognise the sound.

'Interesting what you can find in a young lady's bedroom, don't you think?' he said, running his thumb along the outer edge of the blade. He saw Amelia's mouth open. 'Yes,' he said, 'I had a good look inside your flat. Courtesy of Mr Brown... He was most insistent I use this on you.'

She felt him sit beside her again. Then her own blade was lightly dragged along her exposed collarbone. She remained perfectly still, but this time she didn't fear him.

'I can pay you,' she whispered.

The blade stopped moving over her skin.

'Interesting,' he said.

Then the blade was moving again and was soon running up her inner arm, careful not to break the skin.

'Money's not something I need.'

She felt his other hand grasp around her ankles, his whole palm seeming to envelop her ankle bones.

'Now, you'll listen to me and know I'm serious... You'll go back to the flat and pack your bags. There's some money under the mattress for you to use getting out of Haverbridge. There's a letter on the table in the living room, saying you're giving up the tenancy with immediate effect. You'll sign it, take it to the estate agents and drop it through their letterbox.

'After you've done this, you'll go straight to the train station and go as far as the money will take you. I believe Adrian has left you enough to take you to the other end of the country. You'll never have any contact with him again.'

Hargreaves pulled her face to his, his eyes dark, glaring at her. 'You *will* follow these plans laid out for you.'

'And if I don't?'

Hargreaves pulled the knife against her throat. 'Your life won't be worth living.' He pushed the blade until it nicked her tender skin. 'You don't know what I'm capable of. I assure you your death would not be over quickly.'

Amelia flinched at the blade and felt blood beading at the cut. She breathed hard, ignoring the pain. *You don't know what* I'm *capable of...*

'I still think you and I could come to our own arrangement.' She found the courage within her as she listened to her own words spilling from her mouth. 'What I can offer you is worth more than what Adrian could ever pay you.'

She brought her face forward. She felt him recoil, unsure of her, but her lips kept searching until she could smell his breath, hot and moist on her face. Her lips arched upwards until she found his. She kissed him briefly, withdrew her mouth and smiled.

All men are weak...

Hargreaves took the bait.

He grabbed the back of her head, pulling her to him, his mouth clamping down on hers. His stubble scraped the soft skin around her mouth, as she fought back the urge to choke when his whisky-soaked tongue pushed inside her mouth. His arms grasped her shoulders and she realised he was no longer holding the knife.

Pulling hard against the rope, she managed to free her other hand.

Hargreaves mistook her struggling for passion and his hands were quickly at her chest, pulling at her shirt buttons.

In one swift movement, she reached out and grabbed his head firmly. She felt his tongue against her teeth and she bit down hard, gripping it in place.

Hargreaves's eyes shot open and he tried to scream but saliva and blood pooled inside his mouth, dripping down his airways.

He began to gag.

He grabbed at her, trying to force her from him, but her hands held firm against his head. He tried to pull away from her but felt like his tongue would sever at the root.

Amelia moved her thumbs around his face until she found his eye sockets.

She heard someone outside the room, frantically trying to open the door from the outside. She knew it wouldn't be long before they'd come through it and that'd be it.

Game over.

She mustered all the rage and strength inside her body.

She pulled Hargreaves's head closer to hers, and almost swallowed the length of his tongue. She bit down again, yanking her head sideways with force.

His body convulsed against her, and she jerked her head until she felt the muscle between her teeth start to tear.

His muffled screams rang inside her ears when, with one final pull, she wrenched her head to the left and felt something give.

A wet spray spattered her face, like drops of summer rain.

She pulled the blindfold from over her eyes and saw his mouth had become a bloody screaming 'O' in front of her.

Time seemed to slow and sound drowned out in Amelia's head. Her vision became tunnelled as her rage reached boiling point. She stared at the blood spurting from the stump where his tongue had been and smiled.

Her eyes met his and he knew she was enjoying his suffering. She stole a few seconds, watching him writhe in agony, satisfying her own pleasure, before she reached forward with her hands, her own screams filling the room.

The last thing Hargreaves saw were her eyes boring into his. Then her thumbs pushed into his eye sockets in one fluid motion as she hurled her body at full speed, sending them both falling from the bed.

She heard his head smack hard against the floor, and it was as if the life was sucked from him in an instant.

She had landed on top of him. Her thumbs pressed harder, deeper into his skull. She stared at his fat bloated face, lifeless in front of her. She felt his body twitch a little under her weight, but still she kept her position.

After a few minutes, her vision returned to normal, the ringing in her ears stopped and she felt all her senses return to her. She noticed the men outside the room had stopped kicking at the door, and there was nothing but an eerie silence.

She pulled her thumbs from Hargreaves's eye sockets, stared at his blood, then wiped the excess over her skirt.

She tried to push herself off from his body but fell to the side, realising too late that her legs were still bound.

She hit the floor hard, taking the brunt of the force on her shoulder. She stifled a scream as white-hot needles danced up the nerves in her arm.

She reached for the knife on the bed, despite the pain, and cut through the rope, then went to the door.

Slowly she tried the handle.

The door wouldn't budge. She remembered she'd heard the door being locked from the inside and her eyes came back to Hargreaves.

She went through his trouser pockets and smiled as her fingers encircled the key. She went to the door, slipped the key in the lock and slowly turned it. She waited with bated breath as she heard the door mechanism click and give.

Her hair was now soaked with sweat and Hargreaves's blood, and hung in limp tendrils around her face. Her body was also drenched. She shivered as she opened the door and a sliver of air from outside touched her skin.

Still holding the knife, now raised at her side, she opened the door wide and stepped outside.

CHAPTER 43

Amelia saw beautiful eyes staring back at her. Her Guardian clasped her tight as she fell into their arms and began to sob.

'I thought you'd abandoned me,' she said, kissing their mouth. The Guardian recoiled, tasting blood on her lips. Looking deep into her eyes, the Guardian smiled, and twisted a strand of her hair between cold fingers and kissed her forehead lightly.

'I'll never leave you... Look what I've done for you already.'

Amelia looked around the room, a large living area. She saw the bloody stains across the floor leading to the bodies of three men lying slumped against the far wall, with one gunshot wound in each man's chest.

She looked at the Guardian as they raised their gun, equipped with silencer, and grinned. She kissed them again until they were forced to push her away. The Guardian moved her aside and entered the other room.

Amelia waited with bated breath, her teeth chewing on her bottom lip.

'Fuck!'

She ran to the room and hung against the door frame. The Guardian was bent over Hargreaves, face now turning to stare at her.

'Have you any idea what you've done?'

'I'm sorry!' She slumped to the floor. 'He would've raped and killed me.'

'How can we go through with our plans when you keep deviating from them? You keep fucking up! What the hell's the matter with you?' The Guardian pointed at her. 'Do you want to be locked away again and never be with me? We swore on Rebecca's life to bring them to justice.'

'It's not just for her and I won't be parted from you again, I'll die first.' She pulled the knife so it crossed her throat and looked at him, her eyes glazed with tears.

The Guardian slowly moved to sit in front of her. 'Give me the knife.'

She complied, moving the knife away from her throat and it was pulled from her hands. They sat staring at each other. Minutes passed before the Guardian rose and stared at Hargreaves's body.

'Let's move. It won't be long before they find Adrian.'

CHAPTER 44

Claire walked up to the Manor door, making sure she'd put all the photographs she'd printed inside the file. After satisfying herself they were all there, she tucked the file under her arm just as a lady, about mid-fifties in age, opened the door before she had a chance to knock.

She eyed Claire from head to toe with a hint of a scowl. Claire's face hardened when the woman didn't speak. She waved her ID in front of the woman's grey eyes.

'I have an appointment with Father Manuela.'

The woman sneered at the warrant card before stepping aside. 'I know who you are. I'm his housekeeper, Mrs Lawrence. You're early.'

Claire looked at her with some intensity. Lawrence was a dowdy woman, with grey bushy hair and a very lined face. She looked a lot older than Claire guessed she actually was. She forced a tight smile across her lips and stepped into the hallway.

'In here, please.'

Claire noticed the room where she'd sat with Manuela before was empty. 'Where is he?'

'In the garden,' she said. 'Now, if you please?' She pointed to the room again.

'I think the garden's just fine for our meeting,' Claire said, pushing past her, and heading towards the gardens. Lawrence followed after her.

Once outside, Claire caught sight of Manuela and headed towards him. He looked up as they approached, puzzled, as Lawrence started yelling.

'She wouldn't listen, Father!'

Manuela stared at Claire, who was looking hard into his eyes. He knew she meant business.

'It's all right, Helen. It's far too hot to be stuck inside anyway.' He offered Claire a seat next to him on the bench. 'Please bring us some tea.'

Lawrence paused a second or two, sniffed at Claire and headed back inside. Claire's eyes followed her until she was out of sight.

'Worked for you long, has she?' She took a seat on the bench beside him. Manuela stared at the floor before answering.

'Yes, but only on a part-time basis.' Then he turned to face her. 'What's this all about, Chief Inspector? I answered all your questions the other week… Your methods are starting to grate.'

She pulled out the sheets of printed photographs from her file and handed them to him. She studied his face as he took the pages, a confused expression on his face. She watched him carefully as he looked at each picture. She thought she saw his eyes widen, but he handed the pages back and shook his head.

'I don't understand.'

Lawrence soon appeared carrying a tray. Claire waited until she'd handed them both their cups and had left before continuing.

'You don't recognise her then?'

'She was a former member here,' he said, before taking a sip of his tea.

'Is that all you can tell me about her?'

Manuela sat his cup back down on the saucer with a bang. 'Why are you asking me? Why aren't you out there finding out who murdered Malcolm?'

'Humour me.' She passed the pages back to him. 'Tell me her name, for instance.' Manuela took the pages again but didn't look at them.

He didn't have to.

'You got these from the website. It would've told you her name.' He eyed her with suspicion, and when he saw her face remain stony, he rolled his eyes and looked at the pictures again.

He saw the familiar bright red hair and green eyes staring back at him, smiling for the photograph taken alongside Rebecca at her birthday party. He cast his mind back to the many times he'd been forced to punish her for her insolence.

'Amelia William-Jenkins.'

'So she *is* Mark Jenkins's foster child?'

'Up until about four years ago.' He looked confused and gave her back the pages. 'You're going to have to help me here, why are you interested?'

'Why did she leave?' she said, ignoring his question. 'Where did she go?' Manuela sipped his tea again, his face turning dark, angry. She stared at his face. 'Father?'

'You'll have to ask Mark that question. He doesn't talk about her to me, or to anyone for that matter.'

'What can you tell me about her from back then?' She paused and looked at the pictures herself. 'What type of girl was she?'

Manuela finally made eye contact with her and a new kind of seriousness clouded his pale insipid eyes.

'I don't know where you think you're going with this, Chief Inspector, but I'm going to have to ask you to leave.'

He stood up.

Claire looked at the roses surrounding her. She couldn't back down now.

'Father, you will answer my questions. Either here or I'm quite prepared to do this at the station.'

Manuela was thrown by her outburst. 'You can't force me, I'm not under arrest.'

'Of course not, but I wonder whether you realise the seriousness of this and why I'm asking you.'

'You're asking me about a girl who I haven't seen in four years. What has she to do with me?'

Claire swallowed hard and set her cup down on the floor in front of her. 'Amelia Williams, who has now dropped the Jenkins' name, lives in the same flats as Ashe Miller, who was found brutally murdered. In fact she only lives a few doors down from the deceased.'

Manuela looked at her and scowled. 'And?'

'*And* Ashe Miller was found murdered in a similar way to Wainwright, who had very strong ties to the Manor, and I now know that Amelia came here and was once a foster child of Mark Jenkins.'

Claire watched the colour drain from his face.

He stared at the floor, his mouth open. Slowly he took his seat and looked at her. 'You think she has something to do with this? With Malcolm's death?' His voice sounded strained and weak, as if it hurt him to speak.

'I hoped you could offer me an insight into her life. A character profile, you could say.'

Manuela's face had frozen as if he had somehow finally made sense of it all. More worryingly to Claire, he didn't seem at all shocked.

'Perhaps we should go inside.'

***

Claire waited until Manuela had handed her his file on Amelia. Like the scrapbook he'd shown her when they last met, it too was scruffy and aged. She turned the pages with care and studied Amelia's background.

'So she was given up for adoption from birth, according to this?' she said, looking up at Manuela. He nodded, standing by the window watching her closely.

'Yes. She'd been adopted but by the time she was five, her new parents had enough of her and she was taken into the care system again.'

'Why did they do that?' She studied a photograph of Amelia, which had probably been taken when she was around six years old.

Manuela shook his head. 'The circumstances, as I came to understand, were that she'd become unruly.'

'Kids *are* unruly, Father.'

Manuela shook his head and took a seat opposite her. 'You didn't let me finish.' He leaned in closer to her. 'Amelia was unruly and at first, yes, they thought it was nothing more than a child acting up, for attention or what have you, but they were wrong. Amelia showed…signs of disturbing behaviour, both towards herself and to others.'

Claire pushed aside Amelia's file and gave him her full attention, moving her hands to encourage him to proceed.

'The couple who adopted her had thought they were unable to have children of their own, so they chose to go down the adoption route. Then, not long after they adopted Amelia, they were blessed with a child of their own making. Everything was going well and for a short period after the baby was born, they had a happy life, but something in Amelia changed and she grew jealous of the baby.'

'Isn't that natural in young children when a new baby comes into the picture? They no longer have all their parents' attention.'

'You're right, but Amelia conveyed her jealousy in more sinister ways and it became...*necessary* for them to pass her back to social care.'

'They feared for the life of their new baby.'

Manuela nodded.

Claire mulled over the information in her head. 'How is it that you know all this? You have your own file you've made up especially for her?'

Manuela shrugged his shoulders. 'Mark told me. He wanted us to try to help Amelia.' He sat back in his chair. 'Mark took pity on her, welcomed her into his family, and myself, Father Wainwright and Father Hawthorne tried our best to instil in her a good religious upbringing.'

'How did she adapt to that?'

'Very well at first but she was easily led astray. She seemed to always find trouble. We also thought that even though she appeared a well-rounded child from the outset, she possessed something inside her which led us to believe she was unsound, psychologically.'

Claire shook her head. 'Father, forgive me, but I have a problem.' Manuela raised his eyebrows at her. 'You speak of how she was unsound, psychologically, but you haven't given me any examples. If this is true, why wasn't she receiving the proper care?'

'She was prone to violent outbursts. One minute she'd be calm, the next...' He trailed off and looked at her. 'You should be talking to Mark. I'm not a psychiatrist, Chief Inspector, and she wasn't here every day. Mark has all the records that he somehow got from those in charge of the process.'

Claire drew in a deep breath and, despite Manuela's reluctance to talk specifically about Amelia's actions, she probed further.

'Did she have many friends?'

Manuela shook his head, but then stopped as he remembered something.

'She was close to a young man who attended here but it wasn't for very long. He was a less than desirable character and brought out the worst in her.' Manuela's face appeared sour, as if the very mention left a nasty taste in his mouth.

'What was his name?'

Manuela frowned at her question and thought before answering. 'Stephen, I believe. No, it was Stevie for short.'

She froze and stopped writing mid-sentence.

'Another foster child of Jenkins?'

Manuela raised his eyebrows. 'How did you know that?'

She ignored him. 'Were they close?'

'Somewhat,' he replied, not really sure why she was asking. 'How did you know about this, Chief Inspector?'

Claire debated whether or not to mention Jenkins's estranged child, but remembered that Chloe had been less than favourable regarding Manuela, and wondered if the feeling was mutual.

'Chloe Jenkins.'

She watched Manuela's face turn from confusion to indifference.

'I'd take whatever she says with a pinch of salt. A real bad egg that one,' he said, crossing his legs and rubbing his temple with his fingers. 'She was another one who…' he trailed off. He mulled over the words in his head before he spoke again. 'Well, let's just say, she didn't play well with others. When the three of them were together, it was hard. They bounced off each other.'

He sighed then, shook his head. 'I hate to speak with such venom about Mark and Samantha's biological child, but I speak as I find. Chloe was – is – not without her own problems. She was constantly fighting her own demons.'

'Why was that?'

Manuela bristled. 'It was certainly nothing to do with her parents. She was just born nasty and *that* way inclined, shall we say.'

Claire held eye contact. 'You mean she prefers girls, Father?'

Manuela shifted, uncomfortable. 'All in her head. Something she *chose* to dabble in. Filthy, if you ask me.'

'And not tolerated by you?'

'Not *tolerated* by God's holy church. It isn't natural.'

Claire held her tongue then. She did feel a flutter of doubt start to set in through her body. And Chloe was the cause of it.

Chloe Jenkins. Another name with too much association with all the players in this family and the investigation.

'Was there anyone else who Amelia was friends with?' Claire said, trying to push Chloe's image out of her head, for the moment at least.

She watched Manuela thinking and he eventually shook his head. Claire looked at the picture she'd printed of Amelia beside Rebecca Turner at her birthday party.

'What about Rebecca?'

She waited for his response and it wasn't until she looked into Manuela's eyes that she thought she detected a flicker of anger behind them.

'They were…friends.'

His answer was too guarded for Claire's liking. She remained silent, and thought of how to bring up the note found on Wainwright's body.

'It's quite hot in here, isn't it?'

Manuela looked at her face and noticed she was smiling at him, while fanning her face with her folder. 'I think it'd be cooler in the garden.'

***

Manuela was glad to show off the Manor's grounds and to be out of the stuffiness of the building.

He walked Claire around the neatly trimmed lawns and flowerbeds, naming each plant for her in turn. They drew closer to the Rose Garden and Claire seized her chance.

'Father, I'm going to go back to what I said about the body of Ashe Miller.' Manuela just looked at her and nodded. 'As I said, his death bears similarities to Father Wainwright's, with some exceptions, which I'm sure you've read about in the press.'

'I have.'

'Well, not everything was released to the media. We found a letter on Malcolm's body.'

Manuela stopped dead in his tracks and looked at her. Sweat beaded along his brow. All his thoughts went back to Hawthorne's words after Wainwright's funeral.

Somebody knows what we did...

'A letter?'

Claire nodded. 'Here,' she said, pulling a copy from her jacket pocket, and handing it to him. She'd committed the words to memory and repeated them to him as he read the text. He looked at her, and she noticed he'd turned white.

'Any idea what it means?' His voice sounded strained.

She shook her head and they carried on walking, heading towards the Rose Garden.

'It could just be the killer playing with us. Could mean nothing,' she said, turning to him again so his eyes were staring into hers. 'Then again, it could mean everything.' She nodded towards the Rose Garden. 'When did you have the bushes planted, Father?'

Manuela looked away from her.

'I'm not entirely sure.'

She followed him as he walked ahead of her. He stared at the rose bushes. 'Roughly?' she asked. Manuela thought for a few moments.

'About four or five years ago, I suppose.'

Claire edged closer to the rose bushes and kicked her shoes around the soil. She dug a small shallow hole with the tip of her foot.

'Please don't do that.'

She cocked an eyebrow at him.

'You're making it untidy.'

Claire mumbled an apology and stared at the roses. Her mind went over all the information she'd heard over the last hour, and was certain these rose bushes somehow held the key to the whole investigation.

CHAPTER 45

Glenn Wright had spent his entire fifteen years in the fire service saving lives, and slept well every night in the knowledge that he made a difference. He'd never lost a soul yet on his watch and had made a solemn vow never to do so as long as he was in charge.

It had come as quite a surprise when he'd been told by his colleagues that there had been a fatality in the penthouse suite they had been called to in the early hours of the morning.

'It's not a pretty sight, boss,' said the usually cheerful Matt Walker. Glenn looked at his colleague's soot-covered face and sad eyes, which stood out bright against the thick black smudges.

Glenn lowered his head and shook it. 'I guess you just can't save everybody.'

Matt placed a reassuring hand on his shoulder, as word got round that what they'd first assumed was probably the result of a faulty wiring system in the new blocks was now obviously a murder.

Inside the flat, everything was coal black and still smouldering. The flames had destroyed almost everything and the only recognisable shapes left were the charred skeletons of the expensive furniture Adrian had decorated his flat with.

Glenn entered the building holding his breath, bracing himself for what was to come. He took a deep breath before following Matt inside the flat.

Whatever he was expecting, nothing prepared him for what he faced now.

Adrian's flesh was a pulpy mess of black and deep crimson, fused to the chair he'd been tied to.

There wasn't much left of his face, the only recognisable feature being his jaw, which appeared to be caught in a silent scream.

Glenn took one look at what remained of the man and vomited. He stumbled sideways and Matt grabbed him before he collapsed on the floor.

'Shit!'

He started backing out of the room, holding Glenn, taking his weight on his own shoulders. 'Somebody help me here!' Two more firefighters shouldered Glenn's weight and they staggered out of the flat.

When they'd helped him outside and into the waiting ambulance, he was already unbuttoning his jacket.

As a paramedic wiped the vomit from his face, Glenn gripped Matt's shoulder hard and leaned in closer. His breath caught Matt off guard, the smell causing him to recoil. Glenn didn't seem to notice.

'Did you see his hands?' he said, his throat feeling raw. 'His hands, his arms, pulled back behind the chair.' Matt handed Glenn a plastic cup of water, which he pushed away. 'God damn it, did you see it?!'

Matt looked at him and lowered his head, nodding. He handed him the water again and this time Glenn took it and drank it in one go. 'What sick bastard did that?' he said, his breath coming in short sharp gasps.

Matt looked at him.

'We don't know what happened yet. Not for sure.'

Glenn leaned closer again. 'Someone must've tied him to that chair, Walker. No one would just sit there and burn to death.'

'He might've been dead before the fire started. We can't start making assumptions,' Matt said, looking the paramedic square in the eyes. She looked away, trying to ignore the conversation.

'We need the police down here now,' Glenn said, before bending forward and spitting onto the pavement.

'They're on the way as we speak.'

He put his hand on Glenn's shoulder for comfort. Glenn nodded his appreciation before reaching forward and vomiting again, onto the pavement.

CHAPTER 46

After leaving the Manor, Claire returned to the station and tried Chloe's mobile number she had on file. She got a voicemail service, and left a message. When she hung up, she found the number for Paradis.

After being passed between two different people in the office, she finally got put through to Joe Carter.

If he was irritated about her call, he hid it well.

'I've not seen Chloe yet, Chief Inspector. She's not due in for a few hours yet, but I'll be sure to pass on your message when I see her.'

Claire doubted that.

'It's really important that I speak with her,' she said, despite knowing it would mean nothing to Joe.

'I'm sure it is, but I don't control the girls' actions outside the club.'

Claire paused then.

'Is there anything else I can help you with?' Joe said.

He heard the line go dead.

'She's hung up,' he said, replacing the receiver in its cradle. He looked up, across his desk. 'I think it's about time you told me what the hell's going on, don't you?'

Sitting back in her chair, Chloe Jenkins lowered her eyes from his, and bit the inside of her cheek to stop herself from breaking down right there in front of him.

CHAPTER 47

'I hear you found yourself a crispy critter yesterday.' Michael leaned across Matthews's desk, and grinned. Matthews raised his face to look into his eyes, then returned to his computer screen and nodded.

He knew he was lucky to be the SIO on this investigation. If Claire hadn't been so involved with the Wainwright and Miller murder, she would've snapped this one up in an instant. It would be just another achievement on her CV, and Matthews had every intention of rising to Claire's level and higher, even if it meant losing friends on the way.

He judged from the jibe that Michael didn't think he was up to it. Matthews would prove him wrong.

'So, any ideas yet? I heard he was completely unidentifiable.'

Matthews remained focused on his computer, typing a few words into an email, not making eye contact with Michael.

'We need to get a positive ID from his dental records, but it's likely a man called Adrian Brown. That's the name on the mortgage agreement for the penthouse. If it *is* him, he's got priors.'

Michael nodded and picked up a file on Matthews's desk and opened it, flicking through the pages. He saw the crime scene photographs of Adrian's body and pulled a face. 'Nasty…'

Matthews snatched the file from him.

'That doesn't concern you, Diego.'

Michael frowned at him. 'Protective, aren't you? Just 'cos you're SIO…' He leaned in closer. 'It doesn't bother me. While I'm on the case that's gone national, you're knee-deep in charred flesh, scraping some twat off the bottom of your shoe.' He pushed himself away from the desk.

'That was somebody's son, you know.'

Michael stopped and turned his head to look over his shoulder. Matthews was now standing up, his hands at his waist. 'How would you feel if that was your loved one, tied down and burnt alive?'

Michael moved closer. 'This ought to be good.'

'I don't care for your attitude, Diego. Remember your rank… One word to Claire…' He trailed off. 'You're hanging on by a thread.'

Michael was now in front of his desk. He stared at Matthews, making him uncomfortable, before he broke out laughing.

'You're a funny man, David.' Matthews's face remained guarded, his jaw set firm. 'He's somebody's son and all that? Brown was an estate agent.' He paused and looked Matthews hard in the eyes. 'I reckon there's a few people out there now who are kinda glad there's one less of them in the world.'

'You're a sick son of a bitch,' Matthews said, as he sat back down in his chair.

Michael grinned and put his hand up to his face to rub his nose. 'How's your face, by the way?' Matthews looked down, ashamed by the bruising around his nose and eye. 'Still smarting?' Michael added.

Matthews went to respond but stopped when he saw Claire appear in the doorway.

She looked Michael hard in the face. 'Team briefing. Boardroom. Now.'

***

As they climbed the stairs to the top floor, Claire watched Michael carefully. 'You know, you should take my advice and stop yanking Matthews's chain every five minutes,' she said, as he turned to face her, blocking people from coming up or down the stairs.

'You're kidding me, right?'

She moved him to one side with her arm, and people filed past them. 'No, I'm not. I'm getting complaints about you.'

Michael avoided her eyes. 'For God's sake…'

'And it's not just from Matthews. I have someone to answer to as well, Sergeant. Best you not forget that.'

He looked at her, and noticed that this time she seemed to be offering genuine advice. Her eyes were silently pleading with him. After a few uncomfortable seconds, he nodded as he pushed past her and into the boardroom.

Everyone was helping themselves to the fresh orange juice and coffee that was sitting on the sideboard next to the large glass conference table. They were still waiting for some people to arrive, so Michael grabbed a handful of biscuits from a plate in the middle of the table.

After several minutes Claire was ready to start.

CHAPTER 48

Dr Danika Schreiber was glad of her surgical mask as she leaned in closer to the burnt corpse laid out on the slab in front of her.

She paused and checked her findings several times before she committed them to the tape. This was an expedited PM at Claire's request. She was rushed off her feet, but determined to remain calm, and allow herself no room for error.

'Looking at his skull, it's clear he sustained serious blunt trauma to his head before he was burnt alive,' she said to her assistant.

Paul Farringdon bent over the body for a closer look and grimaced.

Paul was only a trainee but he had grown close to Danika in the short months since his placement, and during this time he'd witnessed a lot.

He'd learnt how long it took maggots to eat through a decomposing body and how to gauge how long someone had been dead. He'd seen a woman's body jerk as it expelled gases, and nearly died from fright after first witnessing it.

He'd seen the bodies of cancer victims young and old, and observed the horrific effects that drug abuse can bestow upon its victims, along with the bodies of the homeless, who had died from the cold and starvation.

Then there were the babies that had been stillborn and he'd told himself that, for whatever reason, Mother Nature could be cruel and didn't discriminate against age and innocence.

Despite the horrific truth that lay in seeing death up close, these had been deaths by either natural causes or self-inflicted torment.

Adrian Brown was Paul's first murder victim, and although he knew it wouldn't be his last, he couldn't help but feel sick at the sight of what man could inflict upon his fellow man. The human condition, he'd surmised, could be brutal, cold, and unrelenting.

'Do you think he was unconscious in the fire?' he said.

Danika pulled a face and didn't look positive. 'I hope he was, but I think it's doubtful. Whoever did this had a lot of rage inside them. I think they wanted him to suffer as much as possible. They wanted him to feel every ounce of pain before the body shut down, unable to take any more.'

Paul swallowed hard, knowing how much it'd hurt when he'd burnt himself with his own lighter by accident when lighting a cigarette. 'I don't understand. Who was he, to deserve this?'

Danika shook her head. 'We're not here to ask why. We're here to help piece together the puzzle of how it happened.'

Realising she sounded a little cold, she turned and looked at him.

She pulled her mask over her chin. 'We can't become emotionally involved, as hard as it is sometimes, no matter what we see. We have to accept life can be this cruel. Some will not have the good fortune to die from old age in their beds at night, even if that's the least they deserved.'

Paul nodded. 'I'm sorry. I knew what I was signing up for but still… I guess you can never completely prepare yourself for this.'

Danika smiled and went back to examining the body.

After an hour she was ready to make her phone call. She didn't want to leave it until Matthews had read her report. She picked up the receiver sitting beside her desk and punched in the numbers. She waited a few rings before Matthews answered at the other end.

CHAPTER 49

Claire had finished writing the information about both Wainwright and Miller on the whiteboard in two separate columns. She'd written in bullet points what they knew about each man and the nature of their deaths, before turning and facing her team.

'I'm going to open this briefing up for discussion now. I want to hear your theories: Why the mutilation of the chest? Is it symbolic? What does this tell us about the killer? Do we think both men died at the hand of the same person?'

Michael was the first to speak.

'I think it's still too early to say if it's the same killer, but my guess is the mutilation of the chest area is symbolic.'

'I think the killer's just blood drunk. There's no meaning behind it. The killer did it just because they could,' said DC Brooke Fielding, a tall, skinny woman in her mid-thirties.

Michael looked at her with some disdain and turned in his chair to face her. 'I'd like to know what makes you think there's no meaning behind it.'

'Well, there's no significant link between either victim. They're miles apart in terms of their lives, social group and character. They didn't know each other, so we should assume there's no calculated reason to the mutilations. It's just a barbaric act.' She looked at the other faces around the table and felt quite pleased with her spiel.

Michael started to grin.

'Just because there's no obvious link between them doesn't mean there isn't one. If my previous work with killers with an agenda has taught me nothing else, I know that when somebody takes the time to carve open a chest and pull back muscle mass to the ribcage, you're looking at someone trying to make a point.

'They risk being caught by taking the time to do the act in the first place. We're dealing with someone who has a lot of strength, both mental and physical. A person who perhaps knows no boundaries and who is trying to tell us something. There's no randomness about them or their crime. The biggest proof we have of that is the letter left under the folds of Wainwright's skin. Perhaps our biggest clue.'

Fielding looked at him and then at the faces of those around her. She then felt stupid. They all seemed to be agreeing with Michael, and as reluctant as she felt to admit it, she guessed he had a valid point.

Claire decided to break the tension. 'Michael's right, but any ideas what this could be symbolising? Wainwright was a priest, so are we looking at this from a purely religious angle?'

'I think that's a strong possibility but Miller's the elephant in the room. He was a junkie with no known interest in faith but, having said that, our killer could be seen to be trying to instil faith in him,' said Michael.

Claire gestured for him to explain. 'How so?'

'Maybe allowing Miller to cross over or be accepted into God's arms. If you look at many religions, even the ones that go back as far as the Egyptians, Mayans or the Aztecs, they all believed in offerings to appease their God, or gods. If you believe the Bible story, Abraham almost sacrificed his own son to show his love for God. Maybe our killer is *offering* his victims.'

'Offering what? Their blood?' Fielding said.

Michael looked at her and shook his head. 'No, not blood. It goes deeper than that… I'm talking about the soul.'

Claire wrote Michael's idea on the board. 'So our killer thinks they deserve to die for whatever reason. Does he think God speaks to him?'

'Maybe. It's just a theory,' Michael said, shrugging his shoulders back at her. 'Maybe they did something wrong that the killer feels they should be punished for. Kill them all and let God sort them out, is something I've heard before.'

DC Gabriel Harper sat forward, gaining Michael's attention. 'Ashe Miller was a junkie, so he needed to pay his debt to a society he helped to fill with drugs and lives he helped destroy.'

Michael nodded. 'That's what I'm saying.'

Claire stared at them both as she processed the idea. 'That's all well and good…' she said, taking a seat. She pulled out a photograph which showed a wide-angle shot taken of Wainwright's mutilated body. 'But what did Wainwright do?'

CHAPTER 50

1999

'Amelia I know you're up there!' his voice called up the winding stairs. Stephen heard a little girl giggle, followed by footsteps racing along the landing above him.

He grinned and gave chase up the stairs, pausing on the landing to listen. All he could hear was the sound of his own breathing, slightly laboured from his little sprint up the Manor stairs. He strained his ears as he heard the front door creak open.

Father Manuela and Father Wainwright.

Stephen could hear their voices and he rushed across the vast landing.

'Amelia?' he hissed as close to a whisper as he could manage.

He heard the sound of tiny feet patter behind the door to Father Manuela's study.

Stephen listened for a few moments, making sure Manuela and Wainwright were not coming up the stairs. He heard Manuela's voice further off now, walking to the other end of the Manor.

Then the back door slammed shut.

Breathing a sigh of relief, he crept inside the study and over to the window which overlooked the Chapel in the vast garden.

Manuela and Wainwright were walking across the grass talking together and pointing at various parts of the Chapel exterior.

Realising he was holding his breath, Stephen exhaled and turned to look around the large room. His eyes found the old mahogany desk, cluttered with paperwork and files around a small fifteen-inch computer monitor.

There were various pens and empty coffee mugs scattered across the top, along with a small vial of Holy Water.

He picked it up and inspected the intricate cut glasswork pattern on the vial. It was half full, with a pretty plaited velvet cord wrapped around the top. He pulled the cord gently through his fingers and found a tiny statue joined to the end of it.

It was of the Virgin Mary.

He sneered and placed it back on the desk.

The dark wallpaper made the room seem smaller than it was, and he realised he'd never been in this room before. It was off-limits.

The room was a backwards 'L' shape and he walked past the desk into the far end of the room. Here there were religious pictures on the wall, and a large oak crucifix with a fake-gold Jesus hanging on the far wall. There was also an old tatty dark-brown leather sofa.

He observed the couch with interest as he caught sight of her hair visible from behind the nearest arm. He ran towards it, finding Amelia kneeling behind the sofa.

'Got you!'

He reached out and grabbed her small shoulder. Amelia shrieked and let out fits of laughter as he tickled her under her arms. He giggled as she rolled around on her back trying to escape him.

'Stop it!' she squealed.

He stopped and she sat up, grinning at him.

'*Come on, you,*' *he said,* '*we shouldn't be in here. Mark's in the Chapel still and Manuela has gone in there with Wainwright. We'll be for it if they catch us in here.*'

Amelia jumped up and clasped his hand. She looked up at him with admiration.

'*Why do you call Daddy Mark and not Daddy?*' *she said.*

'*Because he isn't my daddy, or yours.*'

'*But he's like a daddy, though. He does what daddies do.*'

Stephen sighed and knelt down to her eye level. He brushed her hair back behind her ears, away from her pale face. He noticed the little gold cross-shaped earring studs in each of her ears and frowned.

'*Baby-girl...nice daddies don't make you swallow all this religion bollocks every day.*'

'*You said a bad word!*' *she said, her hand covering her mouth. She grinned as he held out his hand for her to smack. She tapped the back of it.*

'*I don't understand what you mean though.*' *Her face pulled into a frown.*

*He sighed, standing up again, looking down at her. '*You're six. Of course you don't understand.*' He pulled her towards the door. '*If anyone asks, we were never up here, and certainly not in the study. Punishment will be more than Hail Marys. Downstairs, now.*'*

Amelia ran from the room and down the stairs, and he followed behind her.

Skipping across the parquet flooring, Amelia's black shoes sounded a noisy rhythm ahead of him. It made him smile.

As Amelia turned into the drawing room she stopped suddenly in the doorway, frozen. Stephen's brow furrowed until he too stood in the doorway.

Mark Jenkins was there with his hands behind his back, staring down hard at Amelia. His eyes rose to Stephen's before he turned to Manuela, who was sitting in an armchair, his hands locked together, his chin resting on them.

'You see, Father. He leads her astray,' Jenkins said, returning his glare towards Stephen. 'I rue the day, boy. Make no mistake about it,' he spat.

Stephen stepped forward, pulling Amelia from view behind him. The animosity between him and Jenkins was more than obvious. The tension hung heavy in the air.

'I've always known it. I've felt it right here,' Stephen said, taking his clenched fist and hitting it once against his chest.

Jenkins sneered and slapped him hard across the face, sending Stephen's head reeling.

Amelia screamed as Jenkins grabbed her arm roughly, pulling her towards Manuela.

Stephen ignored the pain in his face and rushed after her but Jenkins shoved him from the living room and slammed the door behind them, leaving Amelia alone with Manuela.

'Get out of my way!' Stephen screamed in Jenkins's face.

He tried to push past him, but Jenkins anticipated his every move. With force, he shoved him back onto the stairs. Jenkins was stronger than the boy, whose frame was no more than that of a lanky sixteen-year-old.

Ignoring the pain in his back, Stephen hammered his fists against Jenkins's chest, until Father Wainwright appeared from outside.

They both stopped to stare at him.

Stephen pointed at the door. 'Do something! Amelia's in there with him again!'

Wainwright looked at them both, pausing for a moment, his eyes sad. Then he turned, walked past them both and hurried up the staircase without saying a word.

In the living room, Manuela sat with Amelia standing in front of him.

Her head was lowered, sending her hair falling around her face.

Manuela stared at her, his weak heavily-hooded grey eyes watering a little. He sniffed and placed his reading glasses on his face, setting them low on his nose.

His light-brown hair, which had wisps of silver in it, had recently been cut and was now cropped closely to his head, making his nose and ears appear more prominent.

'Your father tells me you were supposed to be praying with him in the Chapel when you suddenly ran off. He says you knocked over a statue of our blessed Virgin Mother in your haste and broke it, ignoring him when he called after you.' He paused, sucking in a deep breath. 'What have you to say in defence of your crime, child?'

Amelia's eyes rose. She sniffed back tears.

'I didn't break it. It fell over but it didn't break.' Her voice sounded small, as if the light had left it.

'Are you calling your father a liar?'

Amelia lowered her eyes back to the floor.

She knew her father had broken it himself. This wasn't the first time she'd been punished for something she hadn't done. She was unsure what to say. She'd been taught never to lie, but considering what her punishment had been previously for telling the truth, she felt hopeless.

What do I do?

She remembered the bruises on her back, which were only now starting to fade, and she thought of how Stephen had tried to spare her a lashing by taking the blame himself.

Manuela glared at her, and lowered his head down to her eye level, his face pulling into a sneer. 'As I thought… I don't like liars, child, and we all know where liars go, don't we?'

'They go to Hell, Father.'

'Indeed they do.'

He began to unbuckle his belt and Amelia felt tears welling in her eyes. He removed the belt and began winding it around his hands, pulling it firmly.

The big brass buckle hung in front of her face.

Her eyes glazed in a mist of misery and loathing as she prepared herself for what was to come.

***

That night had brought thunder and lightning.

It was the fitting end to the horrors of the day. Amelia was sore. Bruised and broken, she lay on her bed crying into her pillow, Stephen by her side, holding her hand.

She was shaking. She'd barely stopped since it happened. The assault that was to be the first of many at Manuela's hands.

Manuela had done more than use his belt on her. He'd violated her in such a way that had shattered her already fragile world.

Stephen had cleaned her up afterwards. He'd wiped away the blood from between her legs.

He felt useless.

He knew no one would believe them if they reported it. He'd spent so much of his life being thrust into precarious situations, to be at the mercy of strangers, he had no respect for anyone who should've been there to protect him...protect her.

All he could do to help her right now was to hope the assaults would be few and far between.

Chloe had watched them, from her bed, in the room she shared with Amelia, too young to fully understand what had happened. She had been frightened by the blood.

That hadn't stopped her creeping from her own bed, snuggling in Amelia's and holding her hand.

Stephen had watched them both, a smile on his lips. He knew, as he stroked Amelia's hair, that their time would come. All three of them. It would be a sweetness worth waiting for.

CHAPTER 51

The boy called Jude was hiding behind the large grey van parked behind the building, in the courtyard. He knew his friends never thought to look here, three hundred or so yards from the playground in the park. He loved to play hide-and-seek, and his record time was about twenty minutes before being found.

All the children knew about the Blackley Farmhouse, which in fact wasn't really the farm the name would otherwise suggest.

There were fields attached behind it with a few acres of unused land that went in tow with the abandoned property but despite its potential, it had still sat derelict and empty for the past few years. There was a new sign at the front, Jude had noticed, with information about the property going to auction in a few weeks with an estimated guide price of a mere £90,000.

Jude hoped it wouldn't be sold, for it had been the focal point for his friends' stories that they told the smaller children around Halloween. They told tales about ghosts which haunted any child brave enough to go near its gates at night.

Jude, however, didn't scare easily and, ever brave, had decided to choose here as his hiding place.

The van outside hadn't raised any alarm bells in his head that there might be anybody inside the building. The game in hand was all he thought about.

That was until he saw the smear of something dark along the door at the back of the van, which looked like dried blood. He ran his little fingers over the stain and then scratched his fingernails through it.

He inspected the dirt under a fingernail, and raised it to his nose.

It smelt like copper.

He stared at the van door for a few seconds and looked over his shoulder.

He couldn't see anything or hear a sound other than that of his own breathing.

He tried the door handle, slow and steady. It creaked ajar. He noticed the smell from inside and grabbed the handle fully in his hand, pulling the door open wide.

He recoiled, covering his nose, and dared a look inside the van.

He saw three men slumped inside, surrounded by flies, their bodies piled on top of each other like soft toys, stuffing spilling on the outside.

Jude stared wide-eyed and turned to run but tripped over his own feet.

As the earth came rushing up to meet him, he put his arms in front of him, bracing for the impact. He lay back on the gravel, staring into the van, and screamed, but as much as he wanted to flee the horror, he remained frozen to the spot.

CHAPTER 52

Claire was nearly ready to wrap up the morning's briefing and scanned the faces sitting around the table.

'So, to summarise,' she said, reading her notes before looking up at DC Jane Cleaver opposite her. 'Jane, I want you to do some background checks. Find out what you can about past and present members at Shrovesbury Manor, including staff, especially Manuela. Anything that seems out of the ordinary, I want to know about it. Also find out who landscaped the Manor's gardens, and when.'

Jane nodded. Claire looked across to DC Harper at the far end of the table. 'Harper, I want you and DC Fielding to re-interview the last known people to have seen Wainwright alive during the last twenty-four hours before his murder. And Stefan,' she said, looking to a man sitting on the other side of Michael, 'I want to bring you in with Michael and me ASAP.'

Detective Inspector Stefan Fletcher looked a little surprised but also thrilled. Then he felt Michael's stare. Stefan shrugged at him.

Michael looked back at Claire and tried to hide the annoyance in his voice. 'Why are you bringing in Fletcher?' He turned to Stefan again. 'No offence meant, by the way.'

Claire looked at Michael and he knew the truth was hidden in her eyes. She didn't want him compromising the case after his behaviour at the Charity Ball. Maybe he shouldn't have wound up Matthews so much either.

Claire looked at the rest of the team. 'I'm temporarily taking DI Fletcher off another investigation. DSI Donahue authorised it this morning. DI Fletcher can offer a fresh outlook on the case. I believe you're all aware of the Mariner's case a year ago, where DI Fletcher broke the codes that were sent in by the killer, which led to the capture of Geoff Mariner and his ten-year-old hostage, Gemma Green.'

Claire looked at Michael.

'I believe his expertise could prove invaluable so I want him working closely with us.' Michael felt his face redden as the others looked at him and then at Stefan, who was trying to look neutral.

Claire broke eye contact with him and addressed the room. 'Any other questions?' No one raised any further issues.

Stefan waited until Michael was leaving the room before approaching him. 'That was embarrassing for me too. No hard feelings I hope?'

Stefan's blue eyes were shining under the fluorescent lights overhead. Michael looked at him and shook his head, but offered none of his usual chat.

Stefan watched him as he headed down the stairs. He raised his hand and pushed his floppy light-brown hair from his eyes and sighed.

'Don't worry yourself over him, Fletch,' Claire said, her body now close beside him. He turned to her as she leaned in. 'He's suffering from a bruised ego.'

'I'm not worried. Guess I'd be a bit pissed if the boot were on the other foot.'

Stefan started walking and Claire followed beside him, watching his tall lanky frame closely, but didn't offer any further conversation. When they reached the incident room, David Matthews was standing there waiting for them.

CHAPTER 53

Claire sat behind her desk and waited. Michael and Stefan sat to one side of the office, while Matthews stood holding a file.

'I've just had it confirmed that the body found in the penthouse suite on upper George Street is that of Adrian Brown, an estate agent at McCarthy Lacey & Co. Their head office is situated in Haverbridge town centre.'

'I thought this was about the Wainwright investigation? Who is Adrian Brown?' Stefan aimed his question at Claire. She ignored him and looked at Matthews, her face unreadable.

'I called McCarthy Lacey & Co. and apparently Brown had a large client bank and his area included Swanton Place.'

Matthews paused on purpose, watching to see if Claire had understood the significance of the name. By the look on her face, he guessed she had. Michael, already bored by Matthews's presence, crossed his legs and shrugged.

'And?'

Matthews turned to him and smiled. Then his eyes returned to Claire's, as if giving her permission to do the honours.

'Swanton Place is the flats where Ashe Miller was found,' she said, as if he should have recognised the name immediately.

There was an uncomfortable silence, until Matthews stepped in again.

'Miller's murder is similar to Wainwright's. The mutilation of the chest being identical suggests the likelihood of this being committed by the same person.' He opened the file on his lap and scanned the pages. He picked up a photograph of Adrian Brown and held it up.

'Brown was arrested in 2010 when his then employer, Homes & Property Ltd, suspected him of laundering money. The case was thrown out for insufficient evidence. He then moved to McCarthy's, where he's been a pretty successful employee, rising from tenancy officer to a manager almost overnight.'

Matthews risked a look at Michael, who was staring at the floor, his face blank.

'Go on, Matthews,' Claire said.

'Yes, Guv… You remember I informed you that on the night of the Charity Ball, my team were carrying out surveillance on Gavin Hargreaves?'

Claire nodded, risking a glance in Michael's direction.

'Hargreaves met with a man not currently known to the investigation and they seemed to be striking a deal, although our "John Doe" seemed reluctant to initially.'

Matthews handed another photograph to Claire, and she studied the picture taken from across a busy pub. She recognised Hargreaves immediately, his huge frame dwarfing the man sitting opposite him. After studying the picture, she handed it to Michael.

'Carry on.'

'We've positively identified the man as being Adrian Brown.'

Before Matthews could continue, Michael spoke up. 'What has this got to do with Wainwright?'

Matthews sucked in air and flushed. He looked at Claire for encouragement and she raised her hand at Michael to be silent.

'I looked in to Brown's other listed tenants occupying the flats in Swanton Place. I double-checked the list myself when I came up with one resident in particular, Amelia Williams.

'I believe you've already questioned her but, and I hope you don't think it hasty of me, I spoke to Brown's PA this morning. I asked her if there'd been anything unusual in the last few weeks with Brown and his behaviour. She mentioned that Williams had come into the office for a meeting with Brown and caused some kind of commotion. He then left the office saying he had a hospital appointment, which he hadn't mentioned previously. His PA thought it strange because normally, if he would be away from the office, he would tell her in advance.'

'Which hospital?'

'She didn't know.'

'Is Williams or this relevant?' Stefan cut in, looking at Claire.

She sat back in her chair. 'Her name keeps coming up. Is she the common denominator?'

She pulled out her file on Amelia and passed it to Stefan. 'She was a former foster child of Mark Jenkins, the RS teacher, who was the last person to see Wainwright alive. She also attended Shrovesbury Manor, where Wainwright volunteered when he wasn't looking after his own church.'

Stefan looked up from the file notes. 'And she lives in the same block of flats where Miller was found with his chest cut open.'

'Like Wainwright,' Michael added.

'Well, Matthews,' Claire said, 'we could have something here but my problem is Hargreaves. Where does he slot in to all this?'

'That's the killer question we need answers to and I'd pay him a visit but…he's gone missing.'

Claire bolted upright in her seat, making all three men jump.

'Missing!'

'Dropped off the radar.'

'How can he just drop off the radar, Matthews? He's not exactly incon-fucking-spicuous, is he?'

'I've got the team working on it. His van was last seen in Haverbridge industrial area. That's all we have so far, but I think all these facts link together somehow,' he said, his voice rising to match hers.

Claire took a deep breath and glared at all of them.

'OK, I want Hargreaves located. What's his significance with Adrian Brown? Matthews, that's your job. Find out who Brown's mobile network provider is. I want a list of incoming and outgoing calls made in the last two months.

'Stefan, go to all the local hospitals within a ten-mile radius. See if any of them have a record of Brown in the last few weeks.' She paused and looked at Michael. 'Diego, you're driving. I want to talk to his PA.'

CHAPTER 54

Mary Harris looked shaken, her face ashen, and her eyes red from crying. She pulled her tissue from under the cuff of her cardigan and blew her nose.

Claire eyed her desk and dismissed most of the clutter of stationery, files and food wrappers until she caught sight of a picture taken at an office party, crudely pinned to the partition wall of a row of desks beside her.

It showed Mary draping her arm around Adrian and smiling for the camera. Adrian's arm appeared to be circled around her waist, and even though there were other employees around them, posing for the same picture, Claire guessed there could be more to this than she first thought.

'Do you know who did this?' Mary sniffed, looking up at Claire. Michael handed her a fresh tissue from the box sitting next to her. She took it and mouthed a thank you.

'Did what?' asked Claire.

She'd seen the minimal press coverage and so far the fact they now had yet another brutal murder on their hands had not been leaked. Adrian's death was being portrayed as a terrible accident.

'We're not treating this as arson just yet.'

Mary ignored her and stared into space. Looking at Claire, Michael rolled his eyes and took the lead.

'Were you and Mr Brown close?'

'Adrian was a good guy,' Mary said, sniffing into her tissue. 'I know everyone's saying what a self-righteous prick he was but they don't know him like I do...sorry, *did.*'

'So he wasn't well liked?'

Mary shook her head. 'People just didn't understand him. Once you got to know him, he was a nice guy.'

Claire looked around the office. She studied the other members of staff and noticed none of them seemed at all cut up over the news of Adrian's death. They were just a bit quiet but she guessed that had more to do with her and Michael's presence than grief.

'Can you believe they didn't even let us have today off over this?' Mary said, more as an open question than to anyone in particular.

'I spoke to your area manager before we got here. He said you all had a minute's silence this morning,' said Michael. Mary shrugged her shoulders and looked at her computer. 'I'm sure everyone's just in shock but you can't stop all business because of one tragedy.'

Mary cried fresh tears into her sodden tissue and Claire rolled her eyes at him for his tactless remark. Mary was also drawing a lot of unwanted attention from other staff, so Claire leaned forward and put her hand on her shoulder.

'I think we should go somewhere more private, if that's OK with you, Miss Harris?'

Mary nodded and she showed them into a small, stuffy room, usually used for in-house meetings. Claire wasted no time in firing off her questions.

'You mentioned to my colleague Inspector Matthews over the phone this morning that Adrian had gone to hospital suddenly the other week.'

Mary nodded, wiping her eyes on a fresh tissue.

'He wouldn't tell me why, but I knew something bad had to have happened to him. It was out of character... He depended on me. If he'd been ill he would've asked me to call someone.'

'You said he'd had a visit from one of his tenants.'

'Yes. Amelia Williams. He wasn't scheduled to meet her but she called and demanded to see him later in the day. I booked her in and forgot to tell Adrian. He was angry with me, but I had so much to do that day I just forgot and—'

'Just stick to the basics, please,' Claire said, cutting her off mid-sentence. 'You say Williams *demanded* to see Adrian. Do you know why?'

Mary tried to recall everything in detail. 'She wouldn't say. She got really angry when I tried to schedule her for another day.'

'What did she say?' Michael asked.

'It's not so much what she said,' Mary replied, feeling a little stupid. 'It was more how she said it... I knew I shouldn't cross her.'

Claire and Michael exchanged glances.

'Mary, why don't you start from the moment Williams arrived? Take us through what happened,' said Claire, pulling out her notebook. Mary nodded, and took herself back to that afternoon.

After she'd explained the details, her face had turned white. She got up and poured herself a cup of water from the cooler in the corner of the meeting room, and sat down again. She took a few sips before setting the cup down.

'On Monday, Adrian was acting weird,' she continued without prompting. 'He came in and looked like he hadn't had much sleep. He sat in his office for a while without asking me to make him his coffee.' Mary looked up at Claire. 'Usually it's the first thing he'll ask me for. Anyway, when he did emerge he asked for the file for

Williams's flat, then locked himself away for a bit.' She paused to drink some more water.

Michael and Claire watched her carefully. Mary seemed to be in her own world, alone without them, until at length she spoke again. 'You know the last time Adrian spoke to me was in an email. I remember being angry about it.'

'What did it say?' Claire asked.

Mary looked up at her. 'Does it matter now?'

'It could offer us some insight as to Adrian's state of mind before he died. It's important. Whatever details you can give us, no matter how insignificant you may think it is, you must tell us.'

Mary nodded. 'Wait here a minute,' she said, before leaving the room.

In her absence, Michael turned to Claire. 'This is getting us nowhere fast.'

He wiped his face with his hand, waiting for her to agree with him. She offered no support; instead she watched Mary returning a minute or so later, a piece of paper in hand.

'Here,' she said.

Claire read the email and handed it to Michael. 'Is this typical of something he might've sent to you?'

Mary shook her head. 'No, not Adrian. Not to me at least. I mean sure, he could be blunt and to the point sometimes but never so… I struggle for the right word.'

'*Rude,* perhaps?' Claire offered.

'Exactly,' Mary said, smiling a little.

Claire looked at the email again. 'Can I keep this?'

'Of course.'

'Also, can I ask you to bring me the file you gave Adrian on Monday for Williams's flat?'

***

It was getting near closing time by the time Claire and Michael had sifted through the file Mary had brought them. Michael sat back in his chair and flexed his fingers, cracking them, making Claire cringe.

'I wish you wouldn't do that.'

He looked at her and then cracked the fingers on the other hand, grinning as she shot him a look. She was about to retaliate with words but stopped herself as Mary put her head behind the door.

'Sorry, but the office is closing in about ten minutes.'

Claire nodded and waited until the door was closed again. 'I'd put money on the fact there was something going on between them.'

Looking up from his notes, Michael raised his eyebrows. 'Maybe she just wanted there to be more.'

'I know these things,' she said, then fell silent when she realised what she'd said. Michael put down his pen and looked at her. He ran his hands through his hair.

'I've had enough.'

Claire glared at him. 'Of what?'

'Of clutching at straws,' he said, pointing at the file. 'What're we looking for exactly?'

Claire mulled over the question before answering. 'I'll know when I see it.'

'Oh that's really helpful.'

Claire ignored him and it wasn't until the last few pages of the file that she noticed something. 'This file is incomplete.' Michael looked up, vaguely interested, and glanced at the page.

'How can you tell?'

Claire turned the pages around for him to have a better view and marked out a few sections on the pages in front of him with her pencil. 'Here, here and here… The sums and figures are incomplete. They don't tally right either. Do the maths.'

Michael studied the page of numbers and breakdowns regarding the monthly rent. 'I was terrible at maths, I'll take your word for it.'

Claire ignored him and glanced at her watch. She got up from the table and left the room. She found Mary sitting by her computer.

'Mary, do you know Adrian's password for his PC?'

CHAPTER 55

As Matthews entered the farmhouse, he saw the blood spatters across the walls and floor. He prepared himself for the worst.

When he'd received the call that a local boy had found a van with three dead men inside, matching the description of known associates of Gavin Hargreaves, he'd immediately driven down to the crime scene himself.

He'd had a brief look inside the van and recognised one of the men, but had moved inside, and hoped the body he was about to see was not Hargreaves, as the SOCOs had been saying. He needed him alive and able to talk if he was to bring any justice to his past victims.

Once suited up, Matthews had entered the farmhouse and peered into the bedroom.

He now saw the familiar shape of Gavin Hargreaves lying on the floor with a pool of dried blood around his head. Matthews stared at the bloody scene and swore, smashing his hand against the door in frustration.

His outburst startled Dr Danika Schreiber, who'd been standing with her assistant. She pulled off her gloves as she approached him. 'I know this is the worst possible thing to have happened right now.'

Matthews looked at her and shook his head. 'We were that close to bringing him in,' he said, gesturing a small space with his fingers. 'Now the bastard's dead.'

Danika saw the anger in his face. 'Do you want a brief breakdown so far?'

He nodded, his eyes still focused on Hargreaves's body.

'My initial estimation is that he died from trauma to the head, probably caused as a result of falling from the bed. Judging by the pooling of the blood, spatter and position of the body, he died there instantly. He hasn't been moved.'

Matthews nodded, struggling to take in and process the information. Danika guessed he still hadn't heard about the wounds sustained before death so she pulled him to one side.

'I need your full attention, David,' she said, her eyes serious. 'Just looking at what's in front of me, I'm guessing Hargreaves and his men had someone tied up in here.'

Matthews's face dropped.

'Shit, I've just been reeling from seeing him like this. I hadn't even thought about why he's here.'

Danika put her hand on his shoulder. 'It's OK.' She moved him back through to the kitchen area. 'Hargreaves suffered before he died.'

'Suffered?'

'His tongue has been bitten off, and his eyes gouged out, probably by someone's fingers.'

'Jesus Christ…' His eyes widened at her words. 'By who? Whoever you say they had tied up in here?'

'I'm not sure, but by the way the bed sheet is tangled, I can tell there was a struggle. There's some dirt on the bed, from a shoe probably, judging by the shape. SOCOs have found some fibres which look like they came from rope, and judging by the heavies piled in the van, I'm guessing they transported someone in the back and into here for God knows what.'

Matthews glanced out to the courtyard and looked at the van, its back doors still open. 'Have you looked in there yet? Checked the bodies?'

She shook her head. 'I've not had a chance… Do you know how busy I've been with all these bodies mounting up? Seriously, what's going on?'

Matthews ignored her and looked back inside the room at Hargreaves's body. 'We're in serious shit,' he said to himself. Danika watched him carefully, and tried to think of something that might help.

Then she remembered the photograph.

'I might have something. Wait here.'

Matthews said nothing but watched her speak to a SOCO, who handed her an evidence bag. She brought it to Matthews.

'We found this in his wallet.'

Matthews stared at the small passport-sized photograph through the clear bag and pulled his mobile from his jacket pocket.

As he waited for someone to pick up at the other end of the line, he stared back at the pretty girl in the photograph, whose bright green eyes stared hard back into his.

CHAPTER 56

Claire ignored her BlackBerry as it rang in her pocket. She waited for Mary to type in the password for Adrian's PC. She watched the letters that she typed.

'Shakespeare1564... *That's* the password?'

Mary shrugged and smiled. 'Like I said, there was so much more to Adrian than people thought.' She returned her attention to the monitor in front of her.

'Adrian kept all the files on our in-house system but also kept backups in his personal files, or rather I did it for him. He was hopeless at saving stuff.' She accessed the main drive and selected a series of Excel files.

'All the account information is here?' said Claire. Mary nodded and got up from the chair, so Claire could sit. She instantly began sifting through information. Michael watched from over her shoulder. Claire looked at him after a few minutes.

'There're certain files missing for Amelia's rent account. Look, the dates don't match.'

Michael moved her hand from the mouse and used it to access the Recycle Bin, but it showed empty. He then right clicked the Tenant Account file and checked the Properties.

'This was last updated on Monday, at nine-forty.'

'What does that mean?' Mary asked from behind them.

'It means Adrian was hiding something in the accounts figures,' Michael said, turning to face her.

Claire went to speak but her BlackBerry rang again, and she fished it out from her pocket and answered it. Michael saw her face turn serious. 'Everything all right?'

'You're serious?' she said into the phone. She looked at Michael and held up her finger for him to be silent. 'Bring her in,' she continued. 'Arrest Amelia Williams immediately.' After a few seconds she hung up and swore.

'What's happened?'

'That was Matthews. It's Hargreaves. He's been found dead… Murdered, to be more precise.'

'What's going on?' Michael said, his voice not hiding his frustration. Claire looked at him, her face serious.

'A photograph of Williams was found in Hargreaves's wallet. She bloody knows something.'

'A photograph? That's weak at best.'

'She's the only specific suspect we have right now.'

'I think maybe we need to be looking closer at Chloe Jenkins.' Claire turned to him, surprised. 'She grew up with Amelia. That Manor was her stomping ground for a while. She knew Wainwright.'

'OK,' she said, folding her arms. 'So what does she have to do with Gavin Hargreaves?' When Michael's face looked blank, she arched her eyebrow. 'Exactly.'

'I'm just saying she's worth looking at again.'

Claire chewed at her bottom lip. 'Right now we get Amelia in. I'll speak to DC Harper about Chloe Jenkins. Leave it with me.'

Claire walked out of Adrian's office and Mary followed.

'What will happen now?' Mary said.

'I'll be sending some officers down to take away Adrian's computer. I'll need you to make a formal statement of what you've told us this afternoon.'

Mary just nodded, too stunned to really take in what was happening.

Michael rushed after Claire as she headed down the stairs to reception. She turned to him as the bemused receptionist let them out of the automatic doors from the building.

'You're sitting in on this,' she said over her shoulder. 'Let's see how deep the rabbit hole goes.'

CHAPTER 57

Stefan came rushing through the incident room as Claire was going into her office. 'Where've you been? I've been emailing you.'

'I haven't had a chance to read them. Have they brought Williams in yet?'

Stefan shook his head. 'Not yet.'

'I'm anxious to have her in custody.'

'Well, I've got something that might lighten your mood. I found out which hospital Adrian went to.'

'Where?'

'The QE2, Welwyn Garden City. He was given eight stitches for a wound to his arm caused by a sharp object. Doctor said Brown wouldn't say how he got the injury but she thought it was definitely consistent with a stab wound. She knew who I was talking about because she remembered how scared he seemed that afternoon and she said she'd make a statement.'

Just then, Michael appeared in the doorway.

'She's on her way.'

***

It had taken an hour before Amelia had been processed in the custody suite and a further hour before the solicitor had arrived and she was ready to be interviewed.

She'd come without a fuss when Matthews had arrested her. She was confident there was nothing but circumstantial evidence against her. She'd been too careful to have left anything crucial behind or lying around her flat should the police decide to search the premises.

The text message her Guardian had sent her the day before had given her the heads-up to expect something and soon.

She's getting closer.

That was all the message had said. Amelia had deleted it after she'd read it. It'd given her time to put a few things into place at least.

When Claire got to the interview room, Michael was waiting for her outside. He gave a wry smile. 'It's Carmichael, you'll be pleased to know.'

She sighed and rubbed her forehead. 'Why is it always Carmichael when I'm in a bad mood? He's not a solicitor, he's a bloody parasite.'

'He's fond of you too, Guv.'

Claire wasn't listening. 'That'll explain why he's taken so long to get here. He always uses the delaying tactic, not that he'll ever admit to it.'

'Just play him at his own game.'

Her face was stony when she looked at him. 'I'm in no mood for games. Let's just get this over with.'

Michael entered interview room one, which was hot and uncomfortable. Claire watched him place a plastic cup of water down on the table in front of Amelia, and then turned her attention to the man offering his hand towards her.

She stared into the cold grey eyes of Josef Carmichael.

'Chief Inspector,' he said, giving her a small nod. 'I'm sorry for the delay but I needed the necessary time to brief my client.'

Claire ignored his hand and glanced at the two-way mirror on the wall to her right.

Matthews and DC Jane Cleaver were watching through the mirror from the small dark room next door. Matthews watched Amelia's eyes bore into Claire's face; they were the only part of her that conveyed any emotion. She was sitting in her chair as if she were a waxwork mannequin but her eyes shone bright.

'She's just fucking creepy,' said Matthews.

Jane looked at him and sighed. Although she'd heard it all and despite her years of experience, she still detested the crassness of some of her colleagues, male and female alike.

'Any time you feel like putting a lid on the potty mouth, go right ahead.'

Matthews gave her a sideways look but didn't respond.

Inside the interview room Claire had started to state the relevant information for the benefit of the tape and made sure Amelia knew why she was there and that she was being interviewed under caution.

'Amelia,' Claire said, leaning forward in her chair, 'I believe you're acquainted with a man by the name of Adrian Brown?'

Amelia removed her eyes from Michael and looked at Claire. 'I thought this was going to be about some thug with my picture? That's what they told me,' she said, turning to Carmichael.

'I understood this to be about a Gavin Hargreaves, Chief Inspector,' Carmichael said. He clasped his hands together in front of him on the table and eyed her with suspicion.

Claire looked at him fleetingly, before casting her eyes back to Amelia, taking in her appearance.

Her arms were bare and her hair fell over her shoulders, leading down to a bright pink-coloured tube top. Her black jeans sat low on her hips.

Amelia began to click her flip-flop back and forth on
her right foot, her leg crossed over her left, swaying a little.
Nervous or cocky: Claire couldn't tell which trait Amelia
was conveying right now but the act irritated her.

Then Amelia suddenly stopped and looked at her. 'He's
not an acquaintance…Adrian Brown, I mean.'

'But you do know him?'

'Yes.'

'How?'

Amelia stared at her and then a smile broke out across her
face. 'Surely you know how? You're the detective, after all.'

'Answer the question,' Michael said.

Amelia looked at him and smiled. 'He's the managing
agent for the flat I rent. I've hardly spoken to him and have
only met him about twice, three times at most.'

There was a lingering pause, as Claire looked over her
notes. 'When was the last time you saw him?'

'It was a few Wednesdays back in the afternoon, in
his office…the twenty-first.' Claire looked up, surprised
Amelia was going to admit to being in his office with so
little effort on her part to coax it from her.

'And what was the nature of your visit?'

Amelia looked down at her hands resting in her lap and
smiled. She looked back at Claire.

'It was business.'

'Involving what?'

'Just rent issues.'

'How much do you pay monthly?'

Carmichael sighed and sat forward in his chair. 'Chief
Inspector, I must ask what is the significance of that
question?' Claire looked at him but fired off another
question instead.

'Are you aware that Adrian admitted himself to hospital
the same afternoon after your visit?' Amelia shook her

head, looking at the two-way mirror in front of her. After a few seconds, Claire turned to look at the mirror herself, then back at Amelia. 'Anything wrong?'

Amelia continued to stare at the glass but shook her head again.

On the other side Matthews and Jane exchanged glances, both a little unnerved by her fixating stare.

'I know the answer, but still…she can't see us can she?' Matthews said, his arms folded tight across his chest.

Jane didn't take her eyes off Amelia. 'No, she can't… but she knows we're back here,' she said, turning to look at him.

Back inside the interview room, Claire continued.

'We know that Adrian had to have stitches in his arm that afternoon. Why was that, do you think?'

'I don't know, maybe he fell. Who cares? Why are you asking me?' Amelia's voice raised a notch.

'We had a long chat with his PA earlier. She said he left shortly after your visit and she confirms he saw nobody until he left for hospital.'

'She's lying.'

'Why would she do that?'

'Why not?'

Claire looked her hard in the eye making Amelia break eye contact. 'Do you know a man called Gavin Hargreaves?'

Amelia looked up and sighed. '*No*,' she said, drawing out the word. 'Did you really bring me here just to fire off random names at me?'

'I wouldn't call them random.'

Amelia looked at Carmichael and gestured towards Claire. 'Seriously, can this stupid bitch really keep asking me this shit?'

Claire shifted in her chair, and Michael pressed his hand on her forearm before she reacted vocally. Carmichael turned to Amelia, hushed her, then addressed Claire.

'Chief Inspector, I must insist that you get to the point or release my client. Really, this is tedious.'

Behind the glass Matthews let out a surprised laugh.

'Carmichael either never learns or has one of the hugest set of balls I've ever seen.' Jane looked at him and pulled a face. 'Sorry, Jane,' he said, still grinning.

Back in the room Claire was trying her best not to show Amelia she'd got to her, and took a few deep breaths.

'Perhaps we should take a short break,' Michael said, rising from his chair but Claire grabbed his arm.

Carmichael turned his attention to Amelia, leaning into her to whisper in her ear, but his words were drowned out in her mind as she watched Claire.

Michael sat down again and Claire addressed Carmichael.

'You will advise your client to restrain herself. I will not tolerate bad language in this room, especially when it's aimed at myself or a fellow colleague.'

Her voice startled him and the room soon fell silent. Amelia's eyes bored deep into Claire's. Not to be outdone, Claire returned the favour and it was Amelia who looked away first.

'Let me help move this along, Amelia. I suggest that you have more than a purely "business" relationship with Adrian Brown, and I believe you know who Gavin Hargreaves is.'

'Your theory is based on what exactly?' Amelia's foot started swinging back and forth again.

'I've had a look at your rental agreement. I then looked at your monthly payments. Tell me,' she said, pausing, 'just what were you giving Adrian in exchange for a reduced rate?'

Michael's eyes almost popped from his head. 'What DCI Winters means—'

'She knows exactly what I mean,' Claire said, cutting him off. She leaned forward and shoved a file in front of Amelia. 'Why did he admit himself to hospital after your visit?' She opened the file and a photograph of Adrian's corpse stared back at her.

Amelia took one look at the photograph and her hands shot up over her face.

'Tell me why he's dead? Here's how the firemen found him: tied to a chair and burnt alive.'

'Stop this!' Amelia shook her head, refusing to look at the photograph again. Carmichael tried to protest but his words were drowned out by Claire's.

'Come on, Amelia. You're paying reduced rent. I have evidence mounting up that Adrian was fixing the books for you. He must've been getting something in return.' She paused, taking a breath.

'You say you don't know who Gavin Hargreaves is. I don't believe you. Adrian Brown was seen in some kind of meeting with Hargreaves last Saturday night,' she said, sliding another picture in front of Amelia, who risked a look at the grainy black and white photograph.

Despite the angle and quality of the photo she saw it was Adrian at a table with Hargreaves.

'Why is it that Adrian has turned up dead only two miles from where we found Hargreaves murdered, with a picture of you in his wallet?'

Amelia began muttering to herself. 'Adrian's dead?'

'That photograph of you will be tested. I bet Adrian's fingerprints are all over it. I'll want to know why. Why does a known violent criminal have your photograph?'

'I don't know. Please believe me…' Amelia shook her head and started crying.

Carmichael edged closer to her, offering some words of encouragement. Michael looked at Claire, and raised his eyebrows at her when she caught him looking. She spoke for the benefit of the tape.

'Interview adjourned for a short break at 19:43 hours.'

***

Matthews and Jane stared at Claire when she entered the room adjacent to where Amelia was still sitting.

'Why are you staring?'

'You basically implied she was selling her body for reduced rent,' said Matthews.

'She didn't deny it, did she?'

'Did she have a chance to?' He paused and leaned up against a chair. 'Look,' he said, pointing to Amelia through the glass. 'I've seen cold-blooded killers before…she doesn't fit the profile.'

Claire frowned at him. 'Fuck the profile! That's how we make mistakes if we stick to what we *think* we know about killers. There's always someone to break the mould, do something different and be something we've not seen before.'

'She's right,' Jane said to Matthews.

Claire pointed towards Amelia. 'She went from cocky little shit to a meek little girl in the space of ten seconds. *That* out there is an act.'

Matthews went to speak but thought better of it, instead heading out of the room. 'I'm going to get a coffee,' he said, slamming the door behind him.

***

Back in the interview room Michael sat watching Amelia. He handed her a tissue and she took it, wiped her eyes and gave him a little smile.

'I'm sorry.'

He felt sorry for her when her sad eyes looked at him from beneath her eyelashes. 'It's OK… You're not the first and certainly won't be the last she'll have in tears.' He looked at the two-way mirror.

Amelia picked up her cup of water and pretended to sip from it. Michael thought he heard her say something. When he looked at her she was looking deep into his eyes, her own appearing almost black.

'Did you say something?'

Carmichael shifted uncomfortably in his seat. 'Miss Williams, I must advise—'

'I said you're *fucking* her, aren't you?' Amelia broke out into a laugh. Carmichael went to apologise to Michael but he held his hand up, dismissing him. He stared hard at Amelia.

'Just drink your water.'

'I can tell, you know. It's in the way she looks at you,' she said, before drinking from the cup.

In the room next door, Jane gave a low chuckle as Matthews came back carrying two cups of coffee.

'What's funny?'

'She's a piece of work.'

'What's happened now?'

Jane turned towards him and took her cup. 'It's a good job the Guv ain't here to hear what she just said… Williams just asked Diego if he was shagging her.' She laughed nervously, watching Matthews's face.

Matthews paused before taking a sip from his cup. 'Well…she's perceptive, I'll give her that.'

CHAPTER 58

The interview commenced again and this time Claire decided to take the heat down a notch. She could feel every pair of eyes on her but, unperturbed, she carried on from where she'd left off.

'Amelia, I hope you understand that I'm just trying to piece together parts of what looks like a huge jigsaw here. Sometimes I need help finding the pieces of the puzzle. I think you should start being honest and tell me what you know.'

Amelia looked at her with contempt and turned her head to Carmichael. 'I don't know anything. I can't help them.'

Carmichael looked at Claire and shrugged. 'Charge my client with an offence or release her, Chief Inspector.'

'We can hold her for twenty-four hours. I'll decide when she can go.'

'I don't know anything,' Amelia said. 'We can keep doing this for as long as you like, but you've got nothing on me and do you know why?'

Claire's eyebrows rose.

Amelia sat forward. ''Cos I haven't *done* anything.'

'Why did Hargreaves have your photograph?'

'I don't know, but I may have an explanation for Adrian.'

She closed her eyes and sighed. When she opened them again, Claire was still staring at her. 'It's true, Adrian did offer me reduced rent if I...' She looked at Michael. 'Well,

I'm sure I don't need to draw you a picture. He expected me to sleep with him.'

Claire's eyes narrowed. 'And did you?'

'No,' Amelia said, her eyes returning to Claire's.

'And how did he react to that?'

'I got the impression he wasn't used to being turned down, but he still let me pay reduced rent and I didn't question it.' She shrugged. 'I mean, why should I? The flat's overpriced for a one-bed and I'm not made of money.'

Claire eyed her carefully before she spoke. 'How do you support yourself?

Amelia's eyes narrowed. 'Why is that relevant?'

Claire shrugged. 'Do you work?'

'I had money left to me.'

'By whom?'

Carmichael sat forward, his face agitated. 'We're going around in circles. Charge or release, Chief Inspector.'

Amelia raised her eyebrows at her, a smug look crossing her face.

Claire looked to Michael for support but he offered none. After a few seconds, she appeared to be admitting defeat.

She ended the interview and when Amelia walked into the hallway, Carmichael ahead of her, Claire said, voice low, almost a whisper, 'Chloe Jenkins.'

Amelia stopped dead in her tracks. Her head tilted towards Claire, but she didn't speak and her face gave nothing away.

Claire gave a small nod, as if silently confirming something unspoken to herself. Amelia followed after Carmichael.

Claire waited until Amelia and Carmichael left the custody area before she turned to Michael.

'I looked to you for backup. Where were you?'

He looked at her face and saw how tired she was. 'Claire, I don't think we've got the right angle on this.'

'How can you say that? After what we've seen on Brown's computer, and Hargreaves. The picture too.'

'It doesn't mean Williams had anything to do with their deaths.'

'What about the links? You're just not seeing it.'

Michael put his hands on her shoulders. 'I think we brought her in too early. We should've waited until we had something more concrete... Truth be told, I think you need some sleep.'

'Don't treat me like an idiot and stop patronising me.' She pushed his hands away just as Matthews came around the corner to look for them. He stared at them both and Claire pushed past him. 'Go home, Diego,' she said over her shoulder.

'Guv,' Matthews called after her. 'Gabe spoke to that Norman Tyler, one of the last people to see Wainwright in the last twenty-four hours before he was killed.'

He waited until she'd turned to face him and waved a file at her. 'Tyler saw Wainwright at Toralei's, having dinner with his housekeeper the night before he died, went over to say hello since he attends Wainwright's church.'

'We know this, Matthews,' Michael said.

'Yeah, but what Tyler didn't mention before, not until Gabe pushed him harder, was that he saw a woman who had been staring at Wainwright. He said she'd looked white as a sheet and angry. Gabe checked the security footage from the restaurant, recognised her straight away.'

Claire reached out her hand as she walked back towards him. She took the file from him. Inside were a few photographs – stills taken from CCTV footage.

The photographs showed a man sitting in the far corner of the room away from Wainwright and his housekeeper.

The man had his back to the camera from its angle in the corner of the room, mounted high to the ceiling. Claire couldn't make out anything recognisable of the man but she instantly knew the woman sitting opposite.

Chloe Jenkins.

Claire's face hardened. Michael looked over her shoulder.

'Shit…'

Claire's eyes rose to meet his. She turned and headed down the corridor without saying another word to either of them.

'Claire,' Michael shouted after her, but Matthews touched his elbow. Michael instantly snatched it away, giving Matthews a look of annoyance.

'Cool your jets, mate. Let her go.' Michael stared at the back of Claire's head as she headed out of the door at the end of the corridor. Before he could think straight, Matthews spoke again. 'Williams has just been released pending further enquiries.'

Michael nodded. Matthews's face grew uncertain, gesturing towards the door.

'She looks exhausted.'

'She'll be fine.'

'She's taken on both the Wainwright and Miller investigations, not to mention Brown and Hargreaves. I think she's going to crack.'

Michael shook his head. 'Don't underestimate her,' he said.

Matthews patted him on the shoulder. 'You and me have had our differences, I know, but…be careful you don't confuse the case with your own personal feelings,' he said, as he walked away.

CHAPTER 59

Despite the late hour Claire sat in her car trying to make sense of everything.

Her fingers massaged her temples, as a headache began to surface.

She slumped back in the seat and rolled down the window. Warm air rushed in and hit her flushed face. Even the night air brought little respite from the heatwave they were experiencing during the days.

She picked up her BlackBerry and went to the phone book. She scrolled through the list until she came to the one she was after.

Dad's house phone.

Her finger hovered over the call button. Then she thought better of it and threw the phone on the passenger seat. She sat there for a few minutes, her mind going over the last words she'd spoken to her father.

He brought it on himself, she told herself.

She watched Michael leave the station, cross the car park and light a cigarette. He leaned up against his car and arched his head back as he exhaled a stream of smoke into the air. He gazed up at the stars above.

She thought about going over to him, crying her eyes out in frustration and allowing him to comfort her. Claire made it a rule never to cry in front of anyone but for Michael she was willing to make an exception.

She watched him take off his suit jacket and throw it onto the back seat of his car. She felt guilty when her thoughts rushed back to the night of the Charity Ball. She noticed his shirt was sticking to his body with sweat and there was no doubt in her mind where it would lead if she did seek his comfort.

After another minute he squashed the cigarette under his foot, got inside the car, and the headlights lit up.

Claire ducked her head a little, even though she guessed she was parked too far away for him to notice her, and watched him pull away out of sight.

Forget about Michael Diego... Easier said than done.

She shook herself, pulling herself together, and her thoughts dragged her back to Chloe Jenkins. She glanced at her watch. Paradis would still be letting customers in.

She started the car and headed into town.

CHAPTER 60

Carmichael had done the decent thing and seen Amelia home. She had thanked him for his support, but it was clear his intentions were not strictly honourable.

Amelia was more than accustomed to using sex as a weapon, but she didn't feel inclined to use Carmichael in that way if she didn't have to.

'You could issue a complaint if you wanted to,' he said, eyeing her up and down. 'Perhaps I could come in and we could go over a few details.'

Amelia smiled but squirmed inside. She raised her arms and took his face in her hands, staring into his eyes.

'Thank you for what you've done for me.' She kissed his cheek. 'Perhaps another time,' she said as she withdrew. 'I'm tired.'

Carmichael's face was stern at first but then a smile broke out across his face, although it failed to touch his eyes. He nodded and headed back down the corridor.

Amelia's face lost its smile as soon as he was out of sight, and she went inside. She rested her head against the door, breathed out heavily and praised herself inwardly for her performance tonight.

She headed into the bedroom and pulled her hair up high on her head, securing it in place with a hair grip. She went to the window and opened it a little. Warm air rushed in but she relished the sensation as it touched the skin on the back of her neck. She closed her eyes, breathed in deeply and pictured her fallen friend.

Soon, Becca, it'll all be over...I promise.

***

She'd almost changed her clothes when she heard the turning of the key in the front door. She bounded over, just as the door opened, and flung herself against her Guardian.

She showered their face with kisses and tried to fight against their attempts to push her away. The Guardian grabbed her arms hard and forced her back.

'Have you burnt the sheets?' they said, as their fingers dug into the flesh on the inside of her upper arms.

She tried to read their face. 'Why would I burn the sheets?'

She watched the Guardian's face fall. 'I told you to burn them.'

The Guardian forced Amelia from the doorway and shut the front door. They dragged her by one arm into the bedroom and pushed her up against the wall, then started pulling the pillows from the bed and threw them at her. 'Put these in a black sack.'

'Why? I don't understand,' she said, pulling the bedding from their hands.

The Guardian stopped and looked at her. Amelia saw dark eyes, sinister-looking in the shadows cast around the room.

'You slept with Adrian on these sheets?'

'Yes.'

'Then we need to burn them. They've linked you to him already. We need to get rid of anything that could have his DNA on it.'

She watched as the bedding was piled in a corner. The Guardian went to the kitchen. Amelia folded her arms, annoyed that she hadn't thought of this already. She knew she'd been careless with Hargreaves as well.

That fucking photo.

The Guardian returned, holding a black bin liner, and began shoving the bedding inside it. All Amelia could do was stand there and watch.

After it was done, the Guardian looked at her and took a moment to catch their breath. Amelia stood wearing only her underwear and tube top, her arms pulled tightly across her torso, strands of her hair falling down around her face. The Guardian nodded towards her.

'I take it you've washed your clothes since he was here?'

She nodded, and sat down on the now-bare mattress. 'You still want to go through with this tonight? Even after I was arrested?'

'You have to.'

Her head shot up, her body jerking with frustration. 'Where's my alibi though? That bitch Winters, or whatever the fuck her name is, will pull me in again. I can't keep turning on the waterworks and refusing to answer questions.'

'We just have to push everything through ahead of schedule, that's all. First Hawthorne, then Manuela.' The Guardian paused, then reached for her hand. 'There won't be time for her to pull you in. Trust me.'

Amelia stared at her Guardian and her mind wondered if they would cut her loose if she were proven to be guilty. That detective was drawing closer, fixing the pieces together, making the links. Then she thought about how careful they had been in eradicating any trace of DNA to link them.

Amelia realised all the police had was just a theory, no evidence, not enough to convict anyway. More importantly, she knew her Guardian wouldn't let her down. She remembered what they had done to Adrian and Hargreaves's men.

She glanced at the bed. 'What am I supposed to do now? I can't sleep on this old thing with no cover.' Her face turned playful as she ran her hand over the worn mattress. 'I could always go back with you?'

The Guardian looked at her with longing at first, then shook their head. 'It's too risky.'

Amelia got up from the bed, wrapped her arms around their neck and kissed their soft lips. Arms circled around Amelia's waist, their embrace deepening with passion, until the Guardian forced her away again.

'They're getting closer. We must push ahead with Hawthorne.' The Guardian's breath was heavy against her lips.

'I don't want to do it without you there,' she said, as she sat back on the bed. The Guardian grabbed the bursting bin liner.

'You're going to have to. I'll be along later.' They handed her a set of rosary beads. 'Like Wainwright, as we've discussed.'

She took the beads, wrapped them around her fingers, and stared at the cross on the end. The Guardian then handed her the same knife and scalpel that they'd used on Wainwright.

'Don't forget to bring these back with you when you've finished.'

'I'm not an idiot.' She pulled the grip out of her hair and ruffled her tresses. She stared at the scalpel. 'So he's definitely still in the hotel? You know this for sure?'

A curt nod. 'I checked already.' As Amelia went to get off the bed, they reached out and grabbed her wrist.

'Whatever you do, don't deviate from the plan. We can't afford to be caught now.'

As Amelia looked into their eyes, she thought she saw fear for the first time since they had started their plan.

The priests had to pay.

Anyone else who was caught in the crossfire was an unfortunate casualty of their war. God would understand that sacrifices are sometimes made for the greater good.

She sneered and pulled her wrist from her lover's grasp.

'I don't care if I'm caught. At least I'll have done God's will.'

She got up from the bed and stormed into the living room. The Guardian was close behind her, and as she went to the kitchen, she felt all their power full force, dragging her by her waist and slamming her hard into the wall.

'I fucking care!' The Guardian grabbed her face so she couldn't avoid their eyes. 'We've worked too hard to get sloppy now. I don't have the option of going to jail, Amelia. I want to live and live well after this.'

'As long as I live long enough to avenge Rebecca, I don't care what happens to me. That's for God to decide,' she said, her mouth close to theirs. 'I'm His soldier.'

The Guardian stared at her and loosened the grip on her face. 'I don't believe in God. What is there left for me after this if we're not together?'

'But we can be together... All it takes is the courage.'

The Guardian turned away, freeing her from the wall. '*Suicide*,' they said, practically spitting the word as if it hurt to speak. 'You believe what you were taught. Suicides don't make it to Heaven, Amelia.'

'Then maybe I belong in Hell.'

She watched the Guardian sit down on the sofa, face in their hands. She edged closer and knelt beside them, her hands reaching out for theirs. The Guardian looked down at the small scars on her hands.

'Do you remember how I got these?' she said.

'How could I forget?'

The Guardian thought back to when they were kids. Remembered when Father Manuela had wrapped the barbed wire tightly around her hands, the sharp edges cutting her skin. Wainwright had looked on, making no attempt to intervene.

Then there was Hawthorne.

That man had known it was wrong and his protests only fell on deaf ears. He could've done so much more.

'He called it the suffering of Christ,' she said, as if reading the Guardian's thoughts.

'So that you may understand how grateful you should be to be living this life.' The Guardian finished Amelia's sentence for her, as their fingers traced the scar tissue, which had faded over time.

'I'm not afraid to do what's necessary.' She pulled her hands away. 'I've become accustomed to the feeling, that last moment when you hold someone else's life in your hands. They're at your mercy. Whether they live or die is up to you, you have all the power.'

The Guardian watched her face, looking as if she were in a daydream. A dark twisted fairy-tale, that was Amelia's mind, and they had always longed to be a character, playing out the role as long as they were needed.

'I must go. Tonight must be the night.' The Guardian got up from the sofa and collected the sack of bedding.

'Aren't you going to wish me good luck?' she said, smiling.

The Guardian looked at her, raising the bin liner. 'I'll dispose of this.'

Amelia nodded and opened the front door.

As the Guardian walked from her flat they glanced at the police tape covering the door that was once Ashe Miller's home.

The Guardian looked back at Amelia. Her eyes were dull, as if there were nothing else left behind them but evil.

The Guardian thought as they continued onwards that maybe that was all there had ever been.

CHAPTER 61

As Claire parked her car she noticed that Paradis, even on a weekday, was still teeming with customers, and as she walked to the entrance, she received a few wolf-whistles and cat-calls from the men hanging around the entrance.

A large bouncer stepped in front of her as she tried to enter, and she held up her warrant card.

Police ID seemed to Claire an understated weapon of choice; in the event of obstacles lying in the path, flash the warrant card, which almost had the power to make even walls move.

The bouncer eyed her with some disdain and asked her to wait by the entrance. After a few minutes he returned and ushered her inside, where she found Joe Carter waiting for her.

He pulled a smile and although it was dark inside, Claire could still make out his yellow teeth staring back at her.

'Don't take this the wrong way, Chief Inspector, but I'd hoped I wouldn't be seeing you again.'

'I've been getting that a lot lately,' she said, struggling to be heard. The din of the music pulsated so hard she felt the vibrations through to her very core.

'I take it you want to see Chloe?'

She nodded.

'She ain't in yet.'

'It's late though.'

'Yeah, tell me about it,' he said, motioning for her to follow him towards the back offices. 'She was due in half hour ago, the lazy cow.'

'So, where is she?' Claire asked, unease in her voice now.

'On her way apparently. She called about ten minutes ago,' he said as he opened the door to his office and stood to one side. He extended his arm and Claire walked in, turning to face him when he didn't follow her. 'Said she'd fallen asleep,' Joe added.

Claire could tell he was just as sceptical as she was.

'Feel free to sit in my chair,' he said with half a grin. Then he left.

Claire sat in the chair behind his desk, small beads of sweat forming along her brow.

She saw an elastic band on the desk and grabbed it, pulling her hair up into a ponytail, relishing the air circulating around her neck.

It was another fifteen minutes or so before Chloe entered the room.

She wore a pair of soft black gym shorts and a pink halter neck top. Her hair was down and dried sweat stuck strands of it to her neck. Her make-up seemed to be melting from her face, her eyes heavily smudged.

She gave Claire a smile. 'I ran,' she said. 'Bloody hot out there.' She dumped her bag down on the floor and sat in front of Claire. 'And tropical in here,' she said, picking up a magazine on the desk and fanning her face. 'Joe's too tight to fix the air conditioning.'

Claire gave a small smile but didn't waste time dragging it out; it was far too hot and uncomfortable, and she started to tell Chloe about what she had so far.

She explained about the new bodies of Miller, Brown and Hargreaves and their significance. When Chloe had looked confused, Claire had told her to bear with her and it would become clear.

She then explained about her meetings with Manuela and told her about Rebecca and Amelia. Then she told her about the letter that had been found and the Rose Garden. By the end, Chloe appeared shocked and if Claire hadn't mistaken it, a little scared.

'I know what you're going to ask me,' she said. 'You want to know about Amelia. If I think she had anything to do with this.'

'Well, you're right about that, but first,' she said, drawing the sentence out as she pushed the file Matthews had given her across the table, 'you can tell me what this is.'

Chloe frowned, her hand slowly hovering above the file. She opened it and saw the photograph stills.

All colour drained from her face.

'What's this?' she said.

'I was hoping you could tell me.'

'It's not what it looks like.'

Claire nodded, gave a mock-laugh. 'Right, OK.' She picked up a photograph, waved it in front of Chloe's face. 'So why don't you start telling me what this *isn't*?'

Chloe risked another look at the photographs.

'Well?'

'Joe took me to dinner.' Her eyes found Wainwright's face in the photograph. She swallowed hard. 'And there he was.' A tear rolled down her cheek. 'Bold as fucking brass, sitting there, not a care in the world.'

Claire tapped the file. 'This is about fourteen hours before Wainwright was killed.' Chloe wiped her eyes, smudging her make-up even more. 'So?'

'So?' Claire's eyebrows raised. 'I'm not too keen on coincidences. You must know why I'm here?'

Chloe bristled, sitting upright in her chair. 'Shouldn't you be doing this at the station? Making it official?'

Claire remained poker-faced.

'Because the fact you're here,' she said, leaning forward, an arm now on the desk, 'and not hauling my arse down there, tells me you've got fuck all.'

Claire pulled the photographs back across the desk, scooped them up and pushed them back into the file.

'Amelia Williams,' she said.

'That name again,' Chloe said, tired of hearing about it. She rubbed the tattoo on her wrist as she spoke.

'Tell me what you know, Chloe,' Claire said, the tiredness evident in her voice.

Chloe looked back at her. 'You're asking me if I think she had anything to do with any of this, what you've just told me.'

'Do you?'

Chloe lowered her eyes and sighed. She clutched and then pulled at the locket around her neck, sliding it around the chain, nerves getting the better of her.

Suddenly, she wasn't so cock-sure, and realised she was out of her depth.

'You know, I really didn't think she was serious.'

Claire sat rigid in her seat.

'Serious about what?'

'Before all this I didn't think it was relevant. She always did say things like that and never followed through. I just took her to be full of crap.' Chloe looked agitated.

'You must tell me what you know.' Claire made no attempt to mask her impatience.

Chloe looked at her and shook her head. 'I can't tell you here.' She looked hard into Claire's eyes. 'And if *he's* with her on this I want protection.'

Claire frowned and got up from behind the desk. She stood in front of Chloe and folded her arms. 'I don't understand. What protection?'

'You know what I'm asking…' She gestured with her hands as she searched for the right word. 'Like on TV.'

'You mean *witness* protection.'

Chloe nodded, wrapping her arms around her small body, shivering a little despite the heat.

'You're going to have to give me a good enough reason, Chloe. What do you know? Are you saying you know who committed these murders?'

Chloe gave a small nod. Claire squatted down next to her chair, so they were at eye level. 'All of them?' When Chloe didn't respond, Claire grabbed her shoulders, turning her towards her. 'Chloe!'

'Father Wainwright!'

Tears had already begun to well in her eyes, her mascara smudging underneath her eyes. 'And if I'm right, and I hope to God I'm not, but if I am,' she said, looking Claire directly in the face, 'Father Hawthorne isn't safe.'

CHAPTER 62

Amelia tucked her hair underneath her black baseball cap before creeping through the shadows to the garden at the rear of the guest house. She saw one bedroom light on and a light in the reception hallway for guests to find their way around should they return later than the landlady was willing to stay up.

Father David Hawthorne was staying here, this much she knew, but in which room was the burning question. She returned to the front of the guest house and tried the main door. It opened and she crept inside, listening out for anyone in the foyer.

Hearing just a faint sound of a television set, she headed further inside and saw the reception desk ahead of her. It'd been fitted recently and did not look in character with the rest of the surroundings.

The guest house used to be a large family home but had been converted some years ago. The décor was of yellowing beige and cream, and Amelia thought the two stars the AA had awarded it on the sign outside was being more than generous.

She climbed over the reception desk and found the reservation book. She scrolled through the names, running her finger down the page until she found Hawthorne's and his room number.

She was just in time. Hawthorne would be checking out later today and returning up north. She looked at her watch.

00:30am.

The wall behind the reception desk was a partition built using frosted glass blocks, which separated the guest area and the landlady's living room.

Amelia could see the shimmering light of a television set behind it. Her heart began beating faster as she strained her ears to listen for any movement.

Hearing nothing but the faint voices coming from the television, she swallowed hard and climbed up the stairs towards Hawthorne's room.

The stairs beneath her feet creaked in several places and she tried to distribute her weight. When she reached the top she saw there was now no light coming from any of the rooms on the landing and she was in total darkness.

She switched on her small torch and shone the light on each door, checking the room numbers. She walked carefully along the landing and followed a hallway which led further towards the back of the building.

A light flicked on in the room opposite her, and a dull yellow illuminated her feet from underneath the door.

She froze and held her breath when she heard the creaking of floorboards and the sound of the occupant going to their en-suite. After a minute or so, the light switched off and once again there was silence.

Exhaling slowly, she began to move again and shone her light on the door in front of her. The number ten stared back at her, which meant Hawthorne's room should be beside her. She looked and realised the final two rooms were right at the end of the corridor ahead of her.

She edged closer, careful not to make a sound above a whisper as she stood in front of room number eleven.

Reaching out, she slowly turned the door handle and pushed gently. The door didn't budge. Hawthorne had locked the door before turning in for the night.

The hotel still used the traditional lock and key rather than a swipe system to access the rooms, and Amelia crouched down, shining her torch through the keyhole.

The key wasn't in the lock on the other side.

She held the torch between her teeth and pulled out the lock-pick set secured to her waistband. She selected the correct picks and quietly thanked the man who'd once taught her how to pick just about any lock. The same man whose life she'd nearly taken once.

The reason she'd been sent to Stokebrook.

After a few minutes, she felt the pins move and the lock opened with a small click. She secured the picks, switched off the torch and slowly turned the door handle, slipped inside, and closed the door behind her.

She saw him in his bed, breathing heavily.

Amelia's eyes had become more focused in the dark, and the full moon outside added some much-needed light as it filtered through a pair of cheap thin curtains.

She edged closer to the bed, drawing out the knife from her inner jacket pocket. Hawthorne was wearing just his underwear and was lying on top of the sheet, the duvet cast aside.

She raised the knife and leaned over him, her hand hovering over his mouth. Just as she knelt next to him, the bed dipped and his eyes shot open.

Hawthorne had little time to react as she straddled his chest, pinning him down, clamping her hand against his mouth. He started to struggle and she brought the blade up close to his eyes, his body freezing with fear in an instant.

'One sound and I open up your throat. Understand?'

His eyes were fearful and he nodded slowly, searching her face.

He could see the outline of her hair, which had worked its way loose from under her cap. He saw the faint hue of red.

He had no time to take in anything more. Her fist caught him unawares, as it struck his face squarely in the middle. He felt a fine mist spraying his face and a sharp pain through his nose before darkness consumed him.

CHAPTER 63

Chloe sat in a small room just off from the incident room with her head in her hands, bent double, arms propped on her thighs.

Although she'd come willingly, she still felt uncomfortable, and with the heat, a headache was growing around her temples and the back of her head.

Claire sat opposite her with only a battered-looking table between them, observing her closely.

She looked at Chloe's fingers, raked back through her hair, and noticed how bitten down her nails were. She saw traces of chipped nail polish, red clumps clinging to her cuticles, and a nasty-looking bruise under one of her thumbs.

'That looks nasty,' she said when Chloe looked up.

She glanced at her thumb and shrugged. 'Comes with the job.'

'I could help you, Chloe.'

'You mean if I help you, you'll help me.'

'Something like that.'

Chloe looked to be contemplating the thought when Stefan walked in and placed a plastic cup of tea on the table in front of her. He took a seat beside Claire and folded his arms and looked at Chloe.

She looked back into his eyes, then at Claire, in confusion.

'This is Detective Inspector Stefan Fletcher. He's assisting in the investigation,' Claire said, seeing the reluctance in Chloe's face. It occurred to her that although Chloe had trust issues, this was clearly magnified by the presence of men.

'It's OK. He's safe to talk in front of,' she said, glancing at Stefan, as he shifted his weight, uncomfortable. Chloe scanned both their faces, then nodded at him.

'Tell us what you meant about knowing who killed Father Wainwright.'

Chloe wrapped her hands around the plastic cup of tea, still feeling cold in the stuffy room, and looked up from beneath her eyelashes.

'You should be out protecting Father Hawthorne.'

'You mean David Hawthorne,' Claire said. 'He's not a priest any more.'

Chloe ignored her. 'He could be dead now for all you know.'

'Yes, you've said that, but as yet I've heard nothing from you that can convince me. You need to tell me everything, Chloe. Tell me what you meant about Amelia.'

Chloe sat back in her chair. 'If I tell you, you'll protect me?' She paused and watched their faces. 'Otherwise I'm keeping quiet.'

Claire looked at her with some curiosity. 'Even if that meant another death?'

Chloe stared back at her, contemplating her answer first before she spoke. 'If it came to saving my life over his, so be it.' She looked at Stefan, her face serious. 'I know what they're capable of.'

Claire shot Stefan a look, to find he was looking back at her, confused, but also a little chilled by Chloe's remarks.

'Who are *they*?'

Chloe took a sip of her tea before telling them what she knew.

'Amelia, as I told you before, is fucked up. Living with us just helped fuel it with the religious bullshit, and her friendship with Stephen, Dad's first foster kid. I knew there was something weird about her from the start and although most of the time I blew her off for playing up to the fact she was different, sometimes I knew what fear felt like when I looked into her eyes.

'The thing you have to understand with Amelia is the art of not being sucked in by her.'

She lowered her eyes and shrugged. 'Sure, she's beautiful… She's small and delicate, almost like a china doll, so many people said when she was first introduced to our church.' Her eyes flicked back to Claire's. 'I knew different though. She's strong. *Powerful*. I knew never to cross her even then, in the early years.'

'And you think she murdered Wainwright?' Claire said.

'I *know* she did. They both did.'

'Both? I'm sorry, I don't follow,' said Stefan.

'You really don't get it, do you?' She took it in turns looking at them, back and forth, exasperation in her eyes. 'Amelia and Stephen… She called him Stevie. They grew very close, despite the short time before he left us. He looked out for her. I guess I should've too but I was jealous of her.

'I was never good enough for my parents, so they tried replacing me. I kept my mouth shut, even when I guessed she was seeing him later on as she grew older. Dad banned her from any contact with him. They blamed him for leading her astray. She used to say the priests were cruel to her and when she was sixteen she told me she planned to leave because of something they did. Something they had to pay for.'

'What kind of something?' Claire said, leaning forward.

'She wouldn't say. She just said it was bad.'

'Did this occur around the time Rebecca Turner went missing?'

'Yeah,' she said slowly. 'How'd you know about that?' Claire ignored her and pressed further.

'What else did Amelia tell you?'

'She told me her Guardian would help her.'

'Guardian?' asked Stefan.

Chloe nodded at him. 'That's what she started calling Stephen. She used that as a code name when others were around in case anyone overheard her. She told me God had come to her in a dream and told her to send *The Three* to Him, so that they may be punished for their sins. She truly believed God had chosen her.'

Claire exchanged bewildered looks with Stefan, and wasn't sure if he was buying Chloe's story.

'Who are The Three?'

'Wainwright, Hawthorne and Manuela. She said God wanted their souls.'

Chloe then buried her face in her hands and started crying. Stefan reached out his hand and placed it on her shoulder, but she carried on sobbing.

'I'm so sorry! I should've told you when Wainwright was murdered. I knew it had to be them once I found out about his mutilation, but I was scared.'

'Did she tell you in detail how they would murder them?' Stefan said.

'Not exactly. She told me she was planning to leave us and then bide her time before they carried it out.'

Claire swore and said, 'Do you know how much time you've wasted?' Chloe avoided looking into her eyes. 'Amelia's linked to six *other* separate murders.' She watched Chloe's face and the sight of shock and sadness was genuine.

'I didn't know!'

Claire was losing patience. 'Stop crying!'

Stefan held his hand up at Claire, and she folded her arms tightly as Stefan knelt down to Chloe's eye level.

'Did she explain anything about what they intended to do in detail? Why a rosary?'

Stefan's voice was soft and it made Chloe look at him properly for the first time. To her his face seemed soft, gentle, not what she was used to by a long shot.

She sniffed and wiped her eyes on the back of her hand, smudging her make-up. He handed her a tissue and she blew her nose.

'She said he'd choke on his faith, be lynched like Christ, and she'd prepare his body to release his soul.'

Stefan looked at Claire. 'Michael was right about the deaths being symbolic.'

'She planned on doing this to all three,' she said, rising from her chair. 'We need to find Hawthorne and fast. Get DC Harper, tell him to watch over Chloe, then I need you to get hold of Jane; I need a report on her findings at Shrovesbury and the landscapers for the gardens right now.'

Stefan nodded and began to help Chloe from her chair when Claire held out her arm quickly, stopping him. 'Wait.'

She made Chloe look at her.

'Why has she waited this long? She was sixteen when she told you all this.'

There was a long pause. Chloe remembered the promises Amelia had made her that were ultimately broken, the secrets she told her to keep, to take to the grave. After what Amelia had done, the feelings and misery she'd stirred and brought to Chloe's life, there was part of her that wanted to reveal everything. Their affair, the choices Amelia had made between her and Stephen.

Everything.

It was about time she lifted some measure of weight from her mind, regardless of the danger. She'd been quiet for far too long.

Chloe shrugged. 'I heard a rumour she ended up in hospital.'

'An accident?'

Chloe shook her head. 'A *secure* hospital,' she said, standing up again. 'But as I said it was just a rumour.'

CHAPTER 64

Hawthorne awoke to a pain in his nose and jaw. His eyes opened and bright light made him turn his head away, his eyes screwing shut again. When he dared to reopen them he did it gradually, peeping through his eyelashes.

He didn't see anything other than the room he'd spent the last several days in, and he tried to rub his face, but found his hands were tied behind his back.

He tried to talk but there was something wedged into his mouth and secured with tape on the outside over his lips. He realised he was still on the bed and tried to heave his body onto his side but before he could move very far, he felt strong hands grip him by the shoulders.

He winced in pain as his full weight crushed his hands underneath him, and his nostrils flared, trying frantically to draw air into his lungs.

It was then that he saw her clearly for the first time.

He instantly recognised the face and burning eyes as she stood at the foot of the bed, dressed in translucent overalls, naked underneath. He saw that the hood struggled to contain her wild hair.

His eyes shot around the room and to the bag she'd worn on her back, now cast aside by the door.

Then he saw the scalpel in her hand.

The blade gleamed under the overhead light, and he tried to scream, but felt the brute force behind her fist laid bare across his jaw.

Amelia's eyes watched him squirm in pain, no emotion in her face.

'Don't do that again.'

She crouched beside the bed.

His eyes frantically searched her face when she placed the scalpel beside him. She produced the rosary and dangled it in front of his face, watching his eyes follow the small cross attached to the line of beads.

'These were your favourites.'

Hawthorne recognised them instantly.

He remembered giving them out to all the children in his congregation at Christmas each year. He tried to speak, but his words were muffled against the gag. Amelia leaned forward towards his mouth.

'What's that? Can't quite hear you,' she said, cupping her ear.

He struggled again, trying to speak. She stared at him, then picked up the scalpel, holding it to his throat.

'I'm going to remove your gag. If you scream,' she said, brushing the blade against his throat, 'I'll bury this inside you. Understand?'

Hawthorne was frozen, his limbs seeming to grow heavier, the weight of his body cutting the circulation to his arms and hands. Somehow he managed to nod his head, his eyes watching her every move.

She used one hand to pull away his gag and braced herself as he drew in a large gulp of air and spluttered. After a few seconds of rapid breathing, he mustered up the strength to speak.

'Amelia… My child, why?'

Her mouth pulled into an unattractive line. 'As you can see, Father, I'm no longer a child.'

His head began to shake. 'I don't understand.'

'Oh, I think you do,' she said, pressing the scalpel harder against his skin, making him flinch. 'I'll give you a clue.' She leaned in so close to his face, he could feel the soft mist of her breath against his skin. 'She had curly brown hair, dark eyes, about 5ft 6 and was rather pretty.'

Her voice was teasing as she moved the blade across his throat and up towards his ear. She caught the look in his eyes: sadness, fear and a cold realisation of what was to come.

'Ahh,' she said, shifting her weight off his chest a little. 'The penny dropped.'

Tears began to well in his eyes and his voice croaked when he spoke. 'I…I didn't hurt her.'

'But you let them get away with it!' she screamed into his face.

'I tried to stop them! I tried to make it right.' His voice grew more desperate when he saw her shaking her head. 'Amelia, please. See reason, for the love of God!'

She rammed the gag back inside his mouth, choking him. He tasted bile against his tongue.

'I *lost* my faith in God that day! I couldn't understand why He let her die and not me. That's when He came to me, telling me she had to die for all *your* sins and that I had to send you all to Him so that there could be real justice. Now I believe again: in a different God than the one you preach about.'

Hawthorne tried to speak again and she ripped the gag away, her eyes wild with hatred.

'I can help you, Amelia! Please listen to me. This is *not* what God wants. I was kind to you, I tried to support you, but you refused my help. Let me help you now.'

The words meant nothing. She no longer wanted to hear him.

She drove the scalpel into his flesh, dragging the blade across his abdomen. As he screamed, she rammed the rosary inside his mouth. He tried to fight her, his teeth biting at the flesh on her hands, grazing her knuckles.

She flinched at the pain but pushed her fingers further down his throat, until she felt his body convulse, his gag reflexes kicking in.

She forced his bottom jaw up hard and ripped the end of the rosary apart. The cross on the end was now firmly lodged in his throat and, like Wainwright had done, he started to asphyxiate.

He rolled around on the bed, pulling at his bonds. He stared down at the gash, blood leaking from his belly. His eyes silently pleaded with her, and he tried to scream, the sound almost animal-like.

Amelia clamped her hand down against his mouth, drowning him out.

And she stayed there, staring into his eyes, watching every last drop of life ebb away, until it was gone and his body was still.

She removed her hand and stared at his bloody spit smeared on her palm. In disgust, she wiped it over the grey hairs on his chest.

Picking up the scalpel once again, she listened for any signs of movement from the rooms outside.

Satisfied no one had been disturbed, she made the next cut into his aged skin, and relished the sight, as the blade slipped easily through the tissue.

CHAPTER 65

It had only taken a brief call to locate Hawthorne. Claire had rung Father Manuela as soon as she'd left the station. She'd stressed the urgency to him without revealing what she'd learnt from Chloe, and after he'd told her Hawthorne was due to leave tomorrow morning, she only had a small window of time to find him.

She'd arranged for officers to head to the Newport B&B and driven ahead.

She plugged in her hands-free kit and connected to the B&B, and waited with bated breath as the phone began to ring. She drummed her fingers against the steering wheel in frustration.

'Come on, pick up.'

She knew she was taking a chance with this. She also knew she couldn't afford not to take Chloe seriously. With a bit of luck this all meant nothing and she'd find Hawthorne alive and well, annoyed that he'd been woken from a peaceful night's sleep, otherwise no harm done.

She was about to hang up when a voice of a lady sleepily answered the phone.

'This is DCI Claire Winters, Haverbridge CID. You have a guest staying with you by the name of David Hawthorne.'

There was a slight pause at the other end before she heard an answer.

'Is this some kind of joke? There's a law against nuisance callers, you know.'

'Listen to me! You have a guest staying there, David Hawthorne. You need to wake him and don't let him out of your sight until I get there.'

The lady the other end shook her head. 'What's going on?'

'Stop talking to me and go wake him up! He could be in danger.' Claire made the landlady jump and she dropped the receiver.

Claire heard it hit against the floor with a *clunk* followed by frantic movement. Then the line went dead.

Shit!

Claire turned off the main road and into a residential area. She looked at the sat-nav and saw she had approximately four miles until the destination.

She put her foot down.

***

Sally Parker had run the Newport B&B since 1996, after the death of her mother, proprietor before her. Never in her seventeen years since she came into ownership had she ever had the police at her door.

Sure, she'd experienced difficult guests over the years, but the most serious of these incidents had involved insects infesting an en-suite bathroom.

Claire's call hadn't even shaken Sally and she headed to reception, wrapping her pink moth-eaten dressing-gown around her more than ample body. She found her diary and scanned the bookings.

She had to shut her eyes hard and open them again wide, fighting back sleep. She rubbed her eyes and groaned.

She'd fallen asleep in her old chair while watching repeats on the television and was still not fully alert. She ran her finger over each name, squinting without her glasses, and sighed.

She didn't make a habit of remembering her guests' names unless absolutely necessary, and was about to give up, but decided to put her glasses on and read over the names again.

The second time she struck lucky.

Mr D Hawthorne, written in scruffy blue biro – *room eleven*.

'So you do exist.'

She sniffed, not sure what to do. She wasn't entirely convinced it wasn't a prank of some kind. She decided to head upstairs, making sure she grabbed the torch from under the reception counter.

She flicked the switch and the light came on but then winked out again. After hitting it a few times, then wriggling the batteries, she finally got the light to remain on and she started up the narrow stairs.

It was nights like these that Sally wished she wasn't so tight and had invested in air conditioning. The air felt thick and heavy as she walked quietly along the corridor by torchlight, and she could feel herself sweating through her dressing-gown.

When she reached room ten, she stopped and shone her light up the hall until she saw the number eleven staring back at her.

There was no light coming from underneath the door, and she hesitated before walking over to it and listening with her ear to the wood.

She heard nothing, not even the sound of heavy breathing that comes from someone in a deep slumber.

She turned the handle and to her surprise it gave a little.

It wasn't locked, which was unusual for guests, at nighttime especially. She opened the door a little and whispered Hawthorne's name in the darkness.

No response.

'This is ridiculous.'

She opened the door a little more, shone the torch inside the room and frowned.

The light illuminated patches of dark red on the carpet and the bed sheets. She followed the stains that led towards the en-suite.

A slow realisation began to flow through Sally's body, and she felt the sweat on her body cool, making her shiver.

She reached her hand around the door frame and switched on the light.

CHAPTER 66

Stefan sat facing a reluctant Jane, as she popped a couple of pills in her mouth and washed them down with warm water. She sighed, and when she realised he was watching her, she grimaced.

'Headache… Claire gave me a few days to compile this information. Why does she need it now, tonight? I'd just got into bed when you called.'

Stefan sat down next to her, the fluorescent lights overhead casting dark circles under his sleepy eyes. 'You know Claire,' he said, pulling the files she'd laid out in front of her closer for inspection.

'Where is she, then, if this can't wait until tomorrow?'

'Hopefully securing Hawthorne. He could be in danger.'

He opened a file. The first page showed a letter on headed paper, with a company's information laid out in a green design and logo. 'Connor's Landscaping,' he read aloud. '"Dear Constable Cleaver, we thank you for your letter"…' He continued reading to himself. When he'd finished he looked up at her.

'They landscaped the gardens at Shrovesbury in 2007?'

'That's what it says.'

'It breaks down all the work done in each segment of the grounds.'

'Yep.'

Stefan looked over the details laid out again and shook his head. 'This isn't right. Can't be right.' Jane watched him, then grew tired of waiting for him to explain himself.

'You've lost me, Fletch.'

Stefan looked up at her.

'There's no mention of the Rose Garden. It was added later.'

CHAPTER 67

Claire pulled her car into the driveway, narrowly missing two parked cars outside the B&B.

She saw that every light inside was on, shining from the windows. The front door was wide open and a young woman was sitting on the doorstep, a mobile phone attached to her ear.

She was hunched over, wearing a small camisole and bed-shorts, her other arm wrapped tightly around her middle. She was speaking into the phone, rushing her words, completely unaware of Claire's presence.

As Claire headed to the entrance, she saw a middle-aged man emerge from the building, almost tripping over the girl on the doorstep. He barely noticed as he stumbled outside, his feet bare against the gravel, his hand cupped over his mouth.

Claire's eyes widened. *I'm too late...*

'Oh my God,' the man said, as he stumbled further down the drive, almost bumping into her. He looked at her, his eyes full of fear. 'Don't go inside.' He placed his hands on her shoulders. 'We've called an ambulance and the police. There's nothing more we can do.'

Claire shrugged his hands from her and pushed past him. 'I *am* the police,' she said over her shoulder, and stepped through the front door.

She looked around and heard commotion coming from above. Her eyes travelled towards the stairs as she heard a woman screaming.

Then came the sound of other people running around the landing overhead.

Claire closed her eyes and took a deep breath.

She didn't have to see upstairs to know what had been discovered. She was about to ascend the stairs when she heard the sirens in the background, drawing closer.

Just then two more people came running down the stairs, a man in his late twenties and a woman a good few years older. They passed Claire, shock etched upon their faces. Claire reached for the man's arm.

'Hey!' Her fingers gripped around his shoulder. He looked back at her and shook his head.

'You should wait outside with us.'

'Where's the landlady?'

The man's face froze and he lowered his eyes. 'She's still upstairs... Room eleven... She won't stop screaming.' He shrugged off Claire's hand and ran through the front door.

Claire could hear the dull sound of someone moaning, like an animal in pain, and began climbing the stairs. When she reached the top, she saw nearly all the doors to the guest rooms were wide open, as if people had left in a hurry and not bothered to collect their things.

She followed along the landing and didn't need to check the door numbers; she followed the wailing ahead of her.

As she approached room eleven, she saw the lights were on, illuminating the trail of blood spattered over the carpet.

Then she saw Sally sitting in a heap on the floor outside the bathroom. Her shoulders were slumped forward and she was shaking, her face staring at the floor.

When she heard Claire approach, she looked up. Her eyes were caked in wet mascara, which rolled down her cheeks. She tried to speak, but her voice croaked and was inaudible.

Claire entered the room with caution, avoiding the blood, and didn't disturb anything as she drew closer. Sally threw her arms outwards towards her, making her jump.

'No!'

Claire stopped dead in her tracks. She paused, her eyes wandering towards the bathroom.

'You don't want to see this.'

Claire looked at her and hesitated, but only for a moment before turning her head and peering behind the door.

Claire had seen her fair share of gruesome crime scenes but this fact still didn't stop her from dreading dealing with each one.

This time was no exception.

As she came face to face with Hawthorne's mutilated body, she looked away.

As she could have foreseen, his chest had been cut open, exposing bone. His tongue hung sideways from the corner of his mouth, bloated and blue.

His eyes bulged.

Claire knew asphyxia was the cause of death before the mutilation and she knew when they inspected his mouth there would be a small cross lodged inside his throat.

Wainwright had been found on his back on the church floor, with no attempt made to move him into any kind of position.

Ashe Miller had been mutilated in the same way, albeit with subtle differences, but again he was found on his back, with no attempt having been made to rearrange his broken body.

Hawthorne was different.

Claire knew what she'd seen but still her eyes forced her back for a second look.

She stared at the body in the bath, hanging from the shower rail, the arms outstretched and secured by rope at each wrist.

The legs hung down but Hawthorne was too tall for them to hang inside the bath. Instead they hung outside, over the top, tied together at the ankles. A sliver of what was left of the rosary beads hung from his mouth.

Blood dripped to the floor.

There was no mistaking the symbolism of the rudimentary cross.

Claire sank inwardly.

The feeling was unbearable.

She looked back at Sally, who was crying but without tears, like she'd cried herself dry.

Heavy footfalls on the stairs jolted Claire back to reality. She turned and saw ambulance staff race across the landing towards her.

As they faced the mess in the bathroom, they paused, open-mouthed in shock and revulsion.

CHAPTER 68

It was early when Claire called the team briefing. She'd had little sleep, maybe a few hours at best, but had still managed to make it into the station. She stared at the wall ahead of her, charting dates and suspects, bodies and links.

The faces of death stared back at her, their bloody mouths fixed in cruel smiles, as if taunting her.

Ashe Miller's in particular caught her attention; nothing more than a deep red hole, the blood looked like a broad smile not too dissimilar from a clown's at a children's tea party.

She shook the thought away from her, and, when she glanced at Adrian Brown's black corpse, a detailed close-up of his face, she started to fear that maybe she was out of her depth.

Stefan was suddenly beside her, his eyes studying her face. 'Are you sure you're up to this?' She turned to look at him. 'You look like you haven't slept. I can take over if you want?'

Claire shook her head. 'I'm fine.'

She turned to face her team and waited – their cue to be silent. Just as she was about to begin, Michael entered the room and mouthed a quick 'sorry' in her direction, before taking a seat beside Stefan. She frowned at him and took another moment before she spoke.

Stefan leaned in to him, and whispered, 'Your head's for the chopping block if you're not careful.' Michael looked at him, his eyes narrowing. 'Just giving you the heads-up, mate.' Michael shifted uneasily in his seat.

Claire explained Hawthorne's death for all present. She pointed out the link to Wainwright and his death, along with Ashe Miller. She handed out a few copies of the photographs taken by the SOCOs at the scene.

'The landlady, Sally Parker, found the body after my phone call to her. When she found the body she was frozen to the spot… Quite literally in fact.'

She sat perched on the edge of a desk after she'd circulated the photographs, and waited until everyone had at least glanced at them before continuing.

'Out of the twelve rooms in the B&B, ten were occupied. There were fourteen guests listed and they're currently giving statements, and we've got uniform on a house-to-house, but reports have already come in that a woman, matching the description of Amelia Williams, was seen in the neighbourhood. Matthews is already in the process of going through the CCTV footage from the area.'

She looked at the crime scene photographs in front of her on the incident room's wall. She looked at the file photograph of Amelia and shook her head.

'Miss Parker was heard screaming by most of the guests, who rushed out onto the landing. It was then that Parker was found by the other guests in room eleven, screaming after discovering Hawthorne's body.

'Several attempts were made to remove her from the room, but she sat on the floor and refused. As it happens, she later told me, she'd been too frightened to move. She was paralysed to the spot with fear. She's going to need ongoing counselling for the foreseeable future.'

She shifted against the table, letting her words sink in. 'Early indications show that Hawthorne had been dead no longer than half an hour before being discovered. Maybe even less than that as the body was still quite warm. Hawthorne was almost certainly surprised while he was asleep; he had no defence wounds and there were no signs of a struggle.

'The killer entered the room through the door after picking the lock. The Principal SOCO at the scene said there was barely a scratch on the lock, indicating the killer used professional tools and had some experience in lock-picking.'

She paused and took a sip of water, swallowing hard. 'We know that Hawthorne's hands were tied, due to the ligature marks and bruising around his wrists.' She held up a close-up shot of the dead man's hands.

'Hawthorne most likely died from asphyxiation. Although we'll need clarification from the PM results, I suspect he was stabbed first, with a very sharp instrument in the abdomen, before being choked to death with a rosary which had been forced into his mouth.' Claire held up another photograph showing a small cross, caked in dried blood.

'This cross is identical to the one found in Wainwright's throat.'

She looked at the expectant faces watching her.

'As with Wainwright, Hawthorne's body was then mutilated, the flesh of the chest sliced back, exposing part of the bone of the ribcage, but with a subtle difference... Hawthorne was first dragged into the bathroom before being cut open, with what we expect was the same instrument used on Wainwright and Miller.

'Lastly, Hawthorne's body was moved again, after the mutilation; hung up in the bath, tied by his wrists to the shower rail, his ankles bound, then draped outside the bath.'

She held up the last shot in the air and heard a few gasps. 'I don't need to explain the symbolism, you can see for yourselves.'

There were a few more murmurs, out of shock more than anything else. Claire had been so close to preventing this grim outcome.

'The killer is evolving...using more force, becoming more savage, and the killer's message is growing stronger. Why else reposition the body? There'll be some kind of finale if we can't stop this and soon.'

Stefan shifted in his seat. 'Maybe if the Jenkins girl had been more forthcoming sooner, we could've avoided this.'

Claire looked at the floor. 'She didn't know.' Her eyes rose to meet his. 'We can't blame her. As soon as we locate Williams, I'll be happy.'

Michael pulled a face, his eyes looking back from Claire's to Stefan's. 'Jenkins girl?' he said, leaning forward.

Claire looked at him, her face stern. 'So glad you've been paying attention, Michael.'

He cast her a dark look.

'We pulled in Chloe Jenkins last night. We were too late... We could've prevented another murder.'

Michael took a moment to absorb the information. 'And Williams?'

'Amelia Williams is our prime suspect.'

CHAPTER 69

It was just coming up to noon when Mark Jenkins sat down to have his lunch. His wife Samantha was in the kitchen fussing over the cat and Emily, he assumed, was at college.

He hadn't felt well that morning so had called in sick. He sensed that the head hadn't believed him. Jenkins couldn't blame her really for being less than sympathetic. It would be her job to find another teacher willing to cover his classes throughout the day, and he knew there wouldn't be many takers.

He switched on the television and the lunchtime news filled the screen. He paid little attention to the newsreader as he bit into his tuna sandwich, and only when he heard the headlines for the day's top stories did he look up.

He stared open-mouthed as the reporter detailed yet another gruesome death of a man who used to be a priest.

A man who used to be his friend.

Jenkins cried out as a photograph of Hawthorne flashed up on the screen, followed by a media frenzy of reporters surrounding the Newport B&B.

He saw Claire pushing past reporters, refusing to comment further on the crime scene before she got into her car.

Then the reporter flashed up again and revealed that police had issued a photograph and the name of a woman they wanted to speak to urgently in connection with the murder.

Jenkins froze, his eyes growing wide as the picture flashed on the screen. He repeated the name over and over in his head, until he cried out loud, like a dog in pain.

Samantha rushed into the room.

'What on earth's the matter?' She stared at his pale face before looking at the television.

After a few moments the story changed to other news, and she looked back at Jenkins, shaking her head. 'That can't be right.' Her voice sounded small and soft. 'Not David...'

Jenkins stood slowly and tried to call Manuela, but received no answer. He sat back in his chair and stared at the wall. Not until Samantha was at his side, with her arms around him, did he speak.

'I need to speak to the police, Sam.' He felt her body stiffen against him, and he saw her eyes looking into his, confusion on her face. 'It's Amelia,' he said. 'She's alive, Sam.'

She pulled away from him and shook her head. 'That's impossible.' Her demeanour had changed, anger growing over her usually soft exterior.

Jenkins looked sad, his hand reaching for the telephone again, and nodded his head in her direction.

'She's back, Sam,' he said, as he dialled the number that had appeared on the screen moments before. 'She's back from the dead.'

CHAPTER 70

Matthews had been reluctant to take the call patched through from the call centre, until he heard it was about information regarding Amelia Williams.

He took the call straight away and passed the information straight to Claire, interrupting her briefing.

He saw her eyes burn into his as he entered the room, but her demeanour quickly changed as soon as she read his handwritten note. She looked at him and Matthews thought he detected just a hint of a smile.

Claire addressed her team.

'Mark Jenkins has come forward to offer information on Williams.'

'Have you located her yet?' Stefan said to Matthews.

'Officers are going to her flat now.'

'Good,' Claire said, and turned to her team. 'Jane, I want you to contact social services, Thames Valley Police and the Herts Probation Trust HQ in Stevenage. Chloe Jenkins said she heard Williams was held at Stokebrook Secure Hospital in Buckinghamshire last year, but didn't know why. If she *was* definitely a patient there and she's out, she must be reporting to and being assessed by someone... You don't end up in Stokebrook for nothing.'

'I've just spoken to Thames Valley Police,' Matthews cut in. 'I'm waiting for a call back. There was no one to bloody speak to me.'

Jane scribbled a few notes and nodded. 'I'll put in a call to Stokebrook.'

Claire looked to Harper. 'I want you to base yourself at Shrovesbury Manor. Manuela will most likely put up a fight – tell him it's for his own protection.' Harper nodded.

'Matthews, how far along are we with getting the link between Brown and Hargreaves?'

'We've been speaking to their known associates but they're reluctant to say much.'

'If there was a deal between Brown and Hargreaves, I want to know what it was.' She eyed Stefan and Michael. 'I need someone to re-interview Chloe.'

They looked at each other.

'I'll do it,' Michael said, standing up.

'Good. Try and get anything more you can out of her.'

'Is the Jenkins girl still here?'

Claire shook her head. 'No, she's back at her flat. A family liaison officer is with her. Just see what you can get out of her but do it gently. She's been through enough as it is.'

***

A few turnings from the Jenkins home, Stefan explained to Claire Jane's findings about Connor's Landscaping.

She slammed her hand against the steering wheel. 'I fucking knew it!'

Stefan jumped in his seat. She caught him looking at her, bewildered. 'I swear you have a problem and it's *medical*.'

She allowed herself a small grin. 'Don't you see, Fletch? Manuela lied to me. I think I see why.'

'You've lost me.'

'It's been staring us in the face from the beginning, ever since I got a copy of the letter left on Wainwright's body.'

'The Rose thing, you mean?'

'I think I know where Rebecca Turner is, Fletch. Those priests had something to do with her disappearance and someone is dishing out payback.'

'Williams is doing the payback, yeah?'

'Don't be fooled, Fletch. I know she looks like butter wouldn't melt. You heard what Chloe said.'

'I just can't envisage her pulling Hawthorne up in the bath and tying him to the shower rail on her own. Hawthorne had to be, what, six stone heavier than Williams. That's a *lot* of dead weight to be hauling.'

'You think I haven't seriously considered the involvement of this Stephen already? Of course he's involved, I just can't figure out yet to what extent. We need to find him.'

Stefan looked embarrassed; he knew Claire would have thought of every possibility.

As they pulled into the Jenkins' driveway, the front door opened. Mark Jenkins appeared in the doorway, arms folded tightly across his chest, a grim pout etched upon his face.

He tapped the watch at his wrist.

Stefan and Claire exchanged glances.

'Guess Diego wasn't exaggerating,' said Stefan through gritted teeth.

CHAPTER 71

As Michael parked his car in a visitor space, he looked up at the tower block and was filled with trepidation.

He heard loud music pulsating from open windows. He saw evidence of damage caused by kids, fly-tipping, and there were cigarette butts piled in the doorway to the block. He heard some shouting and swearing from a woman at someone Michael assumed was her kid, judging by the young cries which sounded afterwards.

He considered himself lucky he now lived in a nice two-bedroom house, in a reasonably nice area of Haverbridge. He had no worry that his days would be interrupted by what he called 'Urban Scum', and people who were 'thick as pig shit', that seemed to plague the housing estates he had once been raised on and had later in life policed on a regular basis.

For every kid damaging property and ripping out the potty mouth, he could guarantee a dog-rough mother, on her fourth pregnancy and fifth partner, and understood why the youth were no longer brought up, but dragged up instead.

As long as they weren't under their parents' feet, it didn't matter what they got up to, whose lives they made a misery, or what a strain they were on the housing system.

These people gave a bad name to honest hard-working families, who still held onto real family values for dear life, and Michael despised them, thinking back to his own childhood. Respect – there was none.

He walked towards the main door, and recognised the CID pool car poorly parked to one side on his left. The family liaison officer was still there.

As he went inside, he took the stairs rather than the lift, and soon regretted the strain the stairs placed on his thighs as the muscles burned.

When he reached the tenth floor, he stood to catch his breath. He caught a young pregnant girl looking at him as she pulled a pram out of her doorway from the flat next door to Chloe Jenkins's.

He waited until she'd disappeared inside the lift before finally knocking on the door. After a few seconds, the door swung open.

'Michael?' said FLO Clara Stewart. 'I didn't think they were sending anyone else over.'

Michael shook his head. 'DCI Winters wants me to take over from you, and ask Chloe a few more questions…and you do look like you need a rest.' He smiled. 'When did your husband last see you?'

Stewart laughed and ran a hand back through her hair. 'He's been calling quite a lot, don't you worry.' She glanced back into the flat. 'Chloe's asleep in the bedroom, been there for about an hour or so.'

Michael raised his eyebrows. 'Oh, well, I don't want to disturb her.'

'I've just been checking on her every half hour. That's all you need to do really if you're going to wait until she wakes up on her own.' Michael nodded and Stewart headed back inside the flat. 'I'll just get my stuff.'

Michael followed after her and took a seat in the small living room. The television was on but the volume was really low. Once Stewart had gathered her things she turned to him. 'Give me a call when you're done. I'm going back home for a few hours.'

'No problem. Tell Rob I said hello.'

'Will do,' she said, as she shut the front door carefully.

***

After skipping the pleasantries, and refusing anything to drink, Claire and Stefan got down to business in the Jenkins family living room.

The television was on but the sound had been muted. Claire noticed it was on Sky News and saw the reports of Hawthorne's murder running along the bottom of the screen.

Jenkins sat staring at the television, while Samantha never took her eyes from him.

'You said you had important information that could aid our investigation, Mr Jenkins,' Claire said. Jenkins looked up at her and nodded, but then looked back at the screen.

Stefan and Claire exchanged looks.

'Look,' said Claire. 'We don't have time for this. Two of your oldest friends have been murdered, brutally, not to mention six other bodies found in the recent weeks, which have strong links to this case. You said you had information on Amelia Williams, who we can't locate, and you refused to give any information over the phone to DI Matthews.'

Jenkins looked at her and scowled.

'You'll have to forgive my husband, Chief Inspector,' Samantha said from across the room. 'We had thought for over a year that she was dead.'

The room fell silent

'Dead?' Stefan said, sitting forward in his chair.

'Yes, we had it on good authority she was presumed dead.'

'Whose authority?' Claire said.

'Thames Valley Police. After her escape from Stokebrook last year, police found a body washed up on shore in Cromer. The body was badly decomposed after being in the water for so long, but the police were sure it was her. Everything from her height, build, hair. There were no dental records for Amelia – they'd been removed, but the clothes were hers.'

She paused, as if taking it all in again for the first time. 'We just assumed,' she added, fighting back tears.

Claire absorbed the information, her brow furrowed.

'I've spoken to your daughter, Chloe. She told me Amelia left of her own accord when she was sixteen, wanting nothing more to do with any of you. The social records back this up. How do you know all this? Amelia dropped off the grid. Chloe certainly didn't know any of this.'

By this time Mark had sat up in his chair; having listened to his wife, he was eager to speak.

'Just because she walked out on us doesn't mean we didn't care what became of her. She was a disturbed girl and it wasn't long before she got herself into trouble. She stabbed a man up in the Glasgow area, nearly killed him.'

He shook his head as he remembered. 'It was in all the papers. I forget all the particulars but she was declared unfit to stand trial and was placed in Stokebrook's personality disorder unit from where she escaped. She murdered two people in the process.'

Claire and Stefan exchanged looks, not believing what they were hearing.

'It wasn't long before we had a visit from you lot,' he continued, motioning with some disdain towards Claire, 'asking us if she'd been in contact and the usual. Several months later a body shows up, matching her description, her clothes. Everyone assumed it had to be her.'

'Had Amelia ever had links to that area?' Stefan cut in.

'What?'

'She was found washed up on Cromer beach. That's the Norfolk coast, why would she go there?'

Samantha spoke again before her husband could.

'We had a few family holidays there. She loved Cromer, so it made perfect sense that if she wanted to…take her own life, she would do it somewhere she knew.'

There followed a long silence. Claire watched Mark biting his lower lip, frowning hard. A vein pulsated in his temple. He was deep in thought.

'I think it's about time you told us about the day Amelia left your family, Mr Jenkins,' Claire said, ordering rather than asking.

She watched Jenkins's face turn to hers, his cold eyes boring into hers.

'I want to know everything.'

2009

It'd been a mere two days since she'd seen her friend's life ebb away into nothingness. Amelia had sat for what seemed like an eternity, trying to decide what to do.

Sure, she could go to the police, but what kind of justice would that entail? There was no better judgement than His, she'd thought, and she would send them to Him, of that she was certain.

Stephen would help her, he'd promised.

And Chloe…Chloe was less predictable. She hadn't taken it well when Amelia first told her she would leave soon with no notice.

'You'll be better off without me,' she'd told Chloe.

A part of her truly meant it, although she knew there would come a day when she needed Chloe's help.

Whether she would or not, only time would tell. She hadn't taken it well when Amelia had finally chosen Stephen over her.

Amelia was determined not to dwell on it.

She packed a small bag of her things and was now sitting in her little room, deliberating on when to leave.

She wondered how she should do it. She could leave in secrecy or go boldly, letting her final words to them cut through their religious flesh.

It took Amelia just seconds to decide.

She stood, pulling her bag onto her shoulder, grabbed the door handle and stepped onto the landing.

She listened carefully to the voices from the living room and guessed they were all in there together: Mark, Samantha, and Emily.

One big happy fucking family.

Chloe would be there too. The outsider in their apparently perfect world.

She took her time going down the stairs, counting each step as she went, like she used to as a child.

With her Guardian.

Her Angel Stevie.

When she reached the bottom, she went into the living room and waited for their attention.

Chloe was standing near the door looking out of the window, waiting for a taxi, when she caught sight of Amelia and her bag.

'And where're you going? You're not allowed out on your own.'

Amelia smiled at her words, delivered brilliantly. Chloe was a good actress when she wanted to be, but no words could disguise the pain she glimpsed in her former lover's eyes.

Since Rebecca had been reported 'missing', Jenkins was making sure the girls were kept safe.

Under lock and key.

Chloe, of course, was the exception to that rule. She carried on dating boys from school, kidding herself she preferred them.

Jenkins turned his attention away from the television and eyed Amelia suspiciously.

'You heard your sister, Amelia. You're not allowed out without an escort.' He caught sight of her bag. 'And what's that?' He stood up from his chair. 'Where do you think you're going?'

Chloe sneered and folded her arms. 'I bet she's going to meet up with him again.'

Amelia shot her a cold look that nearly broke Chloe's resolve, but before she could answer, Jenkins was shouting at Amelia.

'What does she mean "again"? Amelia, your mother and I—'

'She's not my mother!' Amelia eyed him with hatred. 'And you're not my father.'

Her eyes met his and there seemed to be an uneasy silence as he took in her words.

'If what you've shown me these years are what other mothers and fathers truly are, then I'm glad I have neither.' She glanced at Samantha, then back to Jenkins. 'You have no control over me. Not any more.'

Samantha's mouth dropped a little. 'Why are you doing this? Why are you saying these horrible things? After all we've done for you, Amelia.'

She cut herself off as she felt tears stinging her eyes and her voice catching in her throat. Jenkins's brow furrowed as he heard the hurt in his wife's voice.

'You see how you hurt your mother?' He was so close to Amelia that his face looked down into hers. 'I always knew you were poison,' he whispered.

Amelia let her bag fall off her shoulder and lowered her eyes to the floor before taking all her anger and years of unhappiness, pushing it way down in her gut and lashing out.

The force of her fist caught Jenkins off guard as the blow hit him square across the jaw so hard, he instantly tasted blood.

As he recoiled and fell back into his chair, gasps escaped everyone's lips. Cradling his mouth, Jenkins turned and looked at her. He watched a smug smile spread across her mouth.

She picked up her bag.

'You won't hear from me again,' she said to no one in particular and turned back into the hall.

Rage filled Jenkins as she gave him one last sneer and tossed her hair over her shoulder. He pushed himself from his chair and started after her.

'Mark, please!' Samantha screamed, rushing across the room. Before she got to the hallway she heard the anger in her husband's voice and Amelia cry out.

By the time she reached them Jenkins had his hands gripped tightly around Amelia's throat and had forced her down on her back against the stairs.

'Mark, no!'

Samantha tried to grip his arms and pull him back but he was too strong for her. He slapped her hard across the face and she fell back against the doorway, her head cracking back against the frame.

Amelia fought for breath and her nails scored the skin on the back of Jenkins's hands, when he returned them to her throat.

Her face was beginning to turn different colours and a desperate wheeze escaped her lips.

While Emily helped her mother, Chloe stared down in disbelief at the events unfolding before her very eyes. It felt as if she'd left her own body and was now looking down, separated from everyone.

She felt frozen to the spot.

Jenkins began screaming obscenities at Amelia as his hands closed their hold even tighter, but Amelia managed to force her knee up and caught him hard in the ribs.

As he fell to one side in agony, she saw her chance and sprinted for the front door. As she grasped the handle and turned it, she glanced back and her eyes met Chloe's.

She was so close to Amelia, their lips were close to touching.

Their eyes stared hard into one another's and their world seemed to stand still, a moment suspended in time.

Chloe swallowed hard as she realised Amelia would be free from her father forever. The sense of envy twisted from

within and cut through her bones and tissue. It cut deeper
than Amelia's betrayal with Stephen ever could.

'Just go,' she whispered. 'Run while you can and never
come back.'

***

Claire watched the tears roll down Jenkins's face as his wife handed him a tissue.

'That was the last we ever saw of her,' he whimpered. 'We guessed she'd gone to be with Stephen. They'd been seeing each other behind our backs, against my wishes. She must've thought he could offer her everything.'

Stefan shot a glance in Claire's direction. From her expression, he could tell she wasn't buying into the theatrics.

'Mr Jenkins, apart from what seems to have been a violent ending to your last moments with Amelia, I can't see how this would tie in to the murders of Wainwright and Hawthorne.'

Jenkins sighed and shook his head.

'She said she knew who killed Rebecca!'

Jenkins froze and looked towards his wife in disbelief.

After all this time, they had both agreed to erase that from their minds, and now here she was betraying his wishes.

Jenkins quickly looked at Claire.

'You must forgive my wife.' He turned towards Samantha again. 'She doesn't know what she's saying. It was a while ago. Words and memories become blurred.'

Claire shook her head.

'I think I'd like to ask your wife some more questions, Mr Jenkins… On our own.'

***

As Claire drove them away from the Jenkins family home, she shook her head. 'I can't believe they never took Amelia seriously.'

'To be fair, she was known for her stories, and she never disclosed how Rebecca was supposed to have been murdered or by who. Rebecca was – still is – a missing person and there never were any suspects.'

Claire mulled over the information.

'I know, but she's not stupid. I think she knows what happened to Rebecca and started dishing out her own justice. That spell in Stokebrook just set her back a while. I've got to see those records. And have Matthews run Stephen's name through the system again. Surname was Metcalfe, right?'

'That's what Jenkins said.'

She stared at the road ahead and put her foot down.

***

As Claire pulled into the station and parked in her usual bay, she caught Stefan staring at her.

'What?'

Stefan shrugged. 'It's nothing, not really.'

He could feel her eyes burning into the side of his face, and risked a look in her direction. She raised her eyebrows at him.

He sighed and turned his body around in the passenger seat, facing her head-on.

'Look, tell me if this is overstepping the mark, but I have to ask you something.' He watched her face. It was unflinching. He looked at his knees as he asked the question.

'Is there something going on with you and Diego?'

His eyes avoided her face, and inwardly he was squirming, anticipating her smacking him hard across the face. He would deserve it, asking such a personal question, but he had to know.

When no word escaped her lips, he finally looked at her. She was staring out ahead, instead of at him, and instantly he felt a little relieved.

'I think you've wandered a little off your pay grade there, Fletcher,' she said with an uneasy calm in her voice. 'You shouldn't ask me questions like that.'

She removed her seatbelt and got out of the car.

***

Once inside, Claire checked the drawers of her desk. She had a headache and usually kept Nurofen in her drawer in vast quantities, but today she found nothing but one empty pack. She swore to herself, before realising Stefan was waiting by the door.

'Jane needs to speak with us.'

'It can wait.'

'She says it's urgent.'

'It can wait until I find some bloody painkillers.'

She fished around in her bag. When she had no joy, she remembered Michael always kept some in his drawer. He wouldn't mind her quickly rummaging in his desk.

And if he did, she didn't care.

Stefan was still waiting with bated breath in the doorway. Claire felt a little sorry for him, as she noticed his soft eyes, unsure what to do.

'Look, I'll be with you in a minute. You go ahead.' She waited a few moments for Stefan to disappear before heading to Michael's desk.

She searched his top drawer and had no luck, but after rummaging through the second, she found the last two tablets in a blister pack on its own.

She sat down on his chair and popped the pills in her mouth, washing them down with warm water from a plastic cup still left on his desk.

She let out a long breath as she rubbed her temples with her fingers, her head hanging forward.

She was about to close the drawer when something caught her eye.

Stretching down, her hand clasped around a small white plastic case. On closer inspection she realised it was an empty contact lens case.

She ran her thumb across the name emblazoned upon the side, *4 EyeZ*.

She shrugged, snapped the case shut and threw it back into the drawer, and went to see Stefan and Jane.

CHAPTER 72

It was shortly before noon when Chloe woke from her sleep, rolled over and checked her watch.

She sighed and rested her head again, her hand covering her forehead, which was throbbing because she'd slept too long in the heat.

She pulled on a pair of soft shorts over her knickers and adjusted her camisole, before yanking a brush through her tousled hair. After checking her appearance in the mirror she opened her door and headed to the living room.

She poked her head around the door, expecting to see the officer who had looked after her all night and morning, only to jump when she saw Michael.

'Who the fuck are you?'

Michael held up his ID.

'Calm down, Chloe. Officer Stewart has a husband and family to look after besides you,' he said, returning his gaze to the television. 'Besides I need to ask you some more questions.'

Chloe bit her bottom lip, feeling more than a little embarrassed about her outburst. She stared at Michael for a few seconds longer, but his eyes remained fixed upon the screen in front of him.

'Can I get you a drink?'

Michael's eyes flickered briefly before nodding.

Chloe frowned. She wasn't used to men not responding to her, even if it was only regarding a beverage. 'Tea, coffee, juice, water, Coke?'

Finally Michael looked at her. 'Tea, white, no sugar.' He looked away. 'Please.'

Chloe half smiled as she went to the kitchen. As she filled the kettle, she heard him enter the room.

She turned around and gave a small smile, and he watched her closely while she retrieved the milk from the refrigerator.

The kettle boiled and Chloe could feel his eyes on her as she made tea for them both.

It made her nervous and as she turned around to hand him his mug, she saw a look in his eyes. She stared at his features as she watched him take a sip of tea, wincing at the heat.

CHAPTER 73

Claire headed towards Jane's desk and sat opposite her. Stefan was already sitting down beside her.

'I've spoken to DC Harper,' he said. 'Manuela refused him entry into the Manor so he's watching the place from the driveway.'

'That's good enough for now,' Claire said, as if she'd been expecting it. She laid her hands flat against the desk and leaned forward. 'What have you got for me, Jane?'

'Chloe was right. Williams *was* at Stokebrook.'

Claire looked across to Stefan.

'It gets better,' he said.

Jane pushed a file across towards Claire. 'Williams was sent to Stokebrook Secure Hospital in 2009 after being deemed unfit to stand trial for the attempted murder of Clark Andrews, a forty-eight-year-old father of three, living in Glasgow.'

Claire looked up at her, a little shocked. Jane nodded as she opened the file and pointed to several pages inside. 'She knifed him in the neck, narrowly missing the jugular vein…that was after she'd poured caustic soda over his genitals for an hour.'

Stefan physically shuddered.

Caustic soda, when mixed in hot water, was widely used as a cleaning agent to dissolve grease and oils. Used on human skin it can cause a chemical burn.

'That man can't even go to the toilet by himself any more,' Jane added.

'It says here she accused him of trying to rape her.'

'*If* it's true, I'd have bought her the caustic soda myself,' Jane said, as she pushed another sheet of paper towards Claire. '*If...*'

Claire carried on reading and wondered what Amelia was doing up north in the first place.

'"Volunteer Melanie Steward..."' Claire read aloud, '"... part of Stokebrook's befriending scheme...stabbed in the neck with broken glass."' Claire frowned as she looked to Jane, who nodded.

'I know. It doesn't make good bedtime reading, does it?'

Claire studied the next few pages. 'And security guard George Manning...also found murdered.' She paused and looked away from the file. 'What the hell happened? Stokebrook's like Rampton or Broadmoor...you can't just walk out.'

'She didn't,' Stefan said, pushing more paperwork towards her. 'Williams planned her escape in very fine detail from almost the moment she was admitted to Stokebrook. It's quite clever really when you think about it.'

Claire's eyes rose to meet his. 'Clever? She's an animal, that's what she is.'

Stefan shrugged. 'I agree with you, but you have to admit she's nothing like anything we've seen before.'

Claire eyed him carefully, her face unreadable. 'I need more.'

She turned to Jane.

'Jenkins said that Amelia was presumed dead around the time of her escape. He said that a body had washed up in Cromer, believed to be hers. Chase up Thames Valley Police. We need everything they have from their investigation.'

'I'm on it, Guv, but I'm going to need more hands.'

Claire nodded. 'When Diego's back he can help you.'

Jane paused, her face looking unsure.

Claire caught her eye and felt her stomach tighten. 'Is that a problem?'

Jane sighed and avoided Claire's eyes. 'There was something I wanted to talk to you about.' She glanced at Stefan. 'Well, both of you actually…in private.'

Claire looked around them. The incident room was half empty, with only a few DCs trawling through CCTV footage. No one appeared even remotely interested in the three of them.

'This team is tight, Jane,' Claire said. She failed to hide the unease in her voice.

'I know, Guv,' Jane said, 'but this is really sensitive.' Claire and Stefan exchanged nervous glances, as Jane got up from her chair. 'Please, Guv. This is for your ears only.'

Claire paused, looking at Stefan again. 'Whatever you need to say to me, Stefan hears it too.'

***

Claire pushed the door to her office closed and when she turned around Jane was staring at her, her face troubled, and Stefan's expression was intense.

'What's wrong, Jane?'

Jane shrugged. 'I don't know. It's all probably nothing…'

'Well something's got you spooked,' said Stefan.

'This is about Michael, isn't it?'

Jane looked between the two of them and started to fidget. 'I can't believe I even think it, let alone be able to say it out loud.'

'You can talk to us, you know that,' said Stefan, when Claire wasn't forthcoming.

Jane paused before she spoke. 'I don't know if you're going to take me seriously but…I heard something…back when Matthews and myself were watching you interview Williams about Brown and Hargreaves.'

Claire's face was serious then. 'Heard what?'

'Something Williams said to Michael when you terminated the interview for a break.' The words played over and over in Jane's mind.

You're fucking her, aren't you?

Claire's eyes widened as Jane revealed what she'd heard.

'What is this?' Claire said, looking to Stefan.

'She was talking about you, Guv,' Jane said, her voice starting to crack.

'What're you saying?'

Jane became flustered as she spoke. 'I don't know, I just thought it was wrong and then there're the other things, little things, like when you talk about Williams in team briefings. He changes.'

'Changes?' Stefan said.

'The way the light dies from his eyes. The way his body language alters… You're going to think I'm imagining it all, but there's also the way they looked at each other in that interview room.'

Claire listened to Jane's words and what Amelia had said to Michael.

You're fucking her, aren't you?

She analysed each syllable, and played the words in her head in two types of context.

After what seemed like an age in slow motion, her mouth opened, her lips dry.

Her body felt instantly cold and when she spoke, her voice was barely above a whisper.

'You think they…' Her voice caught in her throat.

'I don't think I'm wrong, Guv.'

Stefan ran his hand back through his hair. 'Christ, Jane. Think about what you're saying.'

Claire's eyes looked more icy than usual as she stared back at Jane. When she spoke again, her words were barely audible.

'You think they know each other.'

CHAPTER 74

Chloe had given up trying to make conversation with the man.

He'd given her nothing but muted answers here and there, showing no interest in her words, yet still she noticed how he never took his eyes off her.

They were in the living room again, and she was sitting perched on the arm of a chair, pretending to watch the television, even though the volume was very low.

Now and then she would look at him, hoping he'd stopped staring at her, but each time she was sorely disappointed. After the fifth or sixth time she'd had enough.

'When's the other copper coming back?'

Michael smiled thinly. 'I told you, she has better things to do.' He picked up his mug, still steaming with tea, and walked towards her. 'Why? Aren't we having fun?' he said, smiling.

Chloe felt the hackles going up on her back.

'She's nicer than you. At least she talked to me… Why do you keep staring at me?'

Michael edged closer and she stood up from the chair.

Their eyes were fixed on each other for several seconds before Chloe quickly looked away.

'I want you to leave now, please,' she said, her voice catching in her throat. 'I'll be fine.'

Michael ignored her and took a step closer.

'I don't think so.'

Chloe instantly felt her stomach in her chest, and she backed away from him. Her brain worked overtime as she tried to place his face. So familiar to her, yet she had no name to put to it to ease her mind.

'I don't understand,' she said, her voice a little shaky. She thought about how he could be a customer from the club, but still the idea didn't sit well inside her.

He smiled again, as he reached out to take her mug from her hands.

He noticed she was shaking.

He set the mug down with his own on a side table and reached out his hands, cupping her face.

Chloe was frozen to the spot, as he made her look deep into his eyes, his hands feeling firm against her cheeks.

Those strong hands…

'I don't feel as though I've properly introduced myself. Forgive me, Chloe, but it's been a long time. About fourteen years or thereabout, isn't it?'

His hands tightened their grip around her face as she tried to pull away from him, tears welling in her eyes.

'It can't be you… *Stevie?* It can't be you.'

Please don't let it be you…

The realisation hit her full force, so hard she felt like her bones would shatter underneath him.

She knew him, that attractive familiar face. His eyes were different somehow, his hair now dark, but she remembered him clearly now.

Michael smiled at her and there was a hint of laughter in his voice when he finally spoke.

'Hello, Chloe.'

'You're back,' she said, shaking her head from side to side in disbelief. Tears now fell down her cheeks, fear taking hold of her when she realised why he was there.

'Chloe, honey…' he said, his voice almost soothing, '…I never went away.'

Before she had any time to realise what was happening, he swung his head forward. There was a loud crack as his skull hit against hers.

The force knocked her out cold.

***

When Chloe woke again, only ten minutes had passed but what was to come would feel like hours.

The ache in her head and nose felt like an explosion had gone off inside her skull, and she could taste blood when she licked her lips.

She moaned with pain as she tried to roll over onto her side, but felt someone sit down on her torso, legs either side of her.

Michael's weight crushed her chest, and she started to cry.

'Now, now, Chloe, be a big girl,' he said and brought his face forward until she could practically taste his breath. 'You're a screamer, I know, but I can't have that.'

He reached behind him for the television remote and pressed the volume key.

The sound shot up and Chloe let out another scream, which was cut short by a sharp jab to her ribs.

She instantly felt sick. Coughing hard, she turned her head and spat bile from her mouth. It rolled down from the corners of her mouth, down her neck.

'You bastard…'

Her voice rasped with each breath and she thought she was about to pass out. She sucked in air and looked up at his face, shaking her head. 'Why?'

Michael laughed, and in what seemed like one fluid motion, he stood and dragged her up with him, his arms under hers, hauling her to her feet.

'I would've thought that was obvious,' he said, and without more than a second of hesitation he swung his fist and caught her hard in the mouth.

Her head snapped back hard. She tasted blood. Drops of it trickled from the corner of her mouth.

She stumbled back, grabbing her jaw instinctively, her eyes burning into his through a mass of her matted hair.

'You killed Father David,' she said, specks of blood spattering her pale skin as she spoke. 'You and Amelia, you're both crazy!'

She lunged at him, her fingers reaching for his face, itching to claw out his eyes.

He was too fast for her.

He caught both her hands and twisted them back.

She screamed at the pain, her voice almost drowned out completely by the television. Her body collapsed in his arms and he threw her on the sofa.

'Stay down!'

'Why couldn't you both have just stayed away?'

'I thought you'd be happy, Amelia back on the scene?'

'I moved on from her after what happened at Stokebrook.'

'Ah, yes, that. What did it feel like to help her after all those years? She took another lady lover in there, did you know that?'

'Stop this!'

'You never really did mean anything to her, you know that don't you? You were just her play thing, a distraction.'

Chloe tried to raise herself from the sofa, but Michael shoved her down again, batting her legs out of the way with his hands.

'There's so much you never knew, Chloe. Amelia played you good.'

Before she had time to think, he was on top of her, his hands at her throat, squeezing the life from her.

'I've waited so long to do this. You nearly took her away from me…'

She clawed at his hands and bucked her body trying to throw him off but he was far too strong.

Play dead!

Desperation was taking its toll on her, but before she had any more seconds to think, unconsciousness took its grip.

Soon there was nothing more than a curtain of darkness in her eyes as her body fell limp underneath him.

CHAPTER 75

'How could I have been so blind?' Claire sat at her desk, still in disbelief at what was unfolding around her. 'Why didn't you say something sooner if you had doubts?'

Jane shook her head. 'What was I supposed to do? Ask you if what Williams said was true? Ask if you're screwing Michael and compromising an investigation?'

Claire rose from her chair. 'Perhaps you should've done.'

Stefan moved across the room to gain Claire's attention. 'I think we need to take a step back and look at what we have here.'

Claire shot him a dark look but he remained composed.

'So Michael knows Williams. So what? He may have come across her during other assignments. Maybe they met and hooked up once. We just don't know. We need to ask him first, not jump to conclusions. After all the years he's worked with us, we owe him that much.'

Claire looked at him and shook her head.

'Come on, Claire, he's one of us.'

'Why didn't he say anything in the beginning, then, if it means nothing?'

'I can't answer that. Only Michael can and that's why we need to call him back in and ask him outright. There's got to be a reasonable explanation for it.'

His words were little comfort to her.

Suddenly all the looks that had been exchanged between Michael and Amelia were flashing back through her mind.

The day of Wainwright's funeral came back to the forefront of her memory. He'd been talking to her in the graveyard and Amelia had run off when Claire found them.

None of this seemed to make sense and she could feel her stomach pulling taut inside her as she explored every possibility inside her head.

How much did she really know about Michael outside of work? Outside of her bed?

She blushed when she realised she knew very little at all.

Here was a man she'd invited into her personal life, and only the other week she was contemplating reliving their affair all over again.

She realised all she knew was the basics. He never talked about his childhood, his parents or anything else in his personal life, and she realised that the man she spent most of her days with may as well be a stranger to her.

Claire watched as Stefan picked up the phone next to her.

'I'll try his mobile.'

Jane looked around and felt a little uncomfortable. She felt like she'd just walked in on a conversation she shouldn't be hearing.

'I'm going to call Thames Valley,' she said to no one in particular and left the office.

Claire watched Stefan's face. She let out a loud sigh and sat down in her chair when he shook his head, returning the receiver to its cradle.

'No luck. Not even diverting to voicemail.' He took a seat beside her. 'What do you want to do?'

Claire weighed up the idea before shaking her head.

'We've still not located Williams. From what information we got from Jenkins we know Amelia almost certainly faked her own death and I'm guessing this Stephen helped her.' She paused and shook her head again. 'I don't like the way this is going, Fletch. You go over to Chloe's, get Diego back here to see me.'

Stefan nodded and rose from his chair.

'What about Chloe?' he asked, looking back over his shoulder.

'Take a uniform with you in case Diego kicks off. The FLO should still be there to watch Chloe.'

He nodded and made for the door.

'Stefan, wait,' she called out.

Claire thought to herself for a moment and felt a little stupid as she heard her own words escaping her mouth, as if she had no control over them.

'This may sound stupid, but did you know Michael wore contacts or glasses?' Stefan shook his head.

'No. I couldn't see him having glasses. Can't say I've noticed or heard him talk about wearing them.'

'But what about contact lenses?'

Stefan looked confused and walked closer to her again. 'Claire, what's this about?'

'I don't know really. I just… I found an empty contact lens case in his drawer when I was looking for some tablets. It just struck me as odd.'

'What can I say? He's a dark horse. Maybe he's embarrassed by the fact he needs glasses. Loads of people wear contacts, Claire.'

'I don't think this looked like a prescription lenses case. Never heard of *4 EyeZ* before.'

Stefan let out a sound of recognition and Claire looked at him. 'That company specialises in lenses which are purely cosmetic. You know, if you fancied a change? I used to wear those cats-eye ones, just to freak my parents out.' Claire raised an eyebrow which did not go unnoticed by him. 'I went through a bit of a Goth phase, believe it or not,' he added.

'Even I can't imagine you wearing those, Fletch,' she replied. 'That still doesn't explain Diego.'

'I'm sure there's a reasonable explanation for all of this.'

Claire avoided his gaze and looked at her hands. 'I sure hope so.'

***

It had taken DC Harper about ten minutes to talk his way into Shrovesbury Manor, only to have Father Manuela all but force him out again with the help of his housekeeper less than ten seconds afterwards.

Cursing under his breath, he decided to sit in his car outside the main gates to the Manor. The turning into the grounds was overgrown, rounded off with two large willow trees, their branches obscuring the view to the main road.

Harper noticed how beautiful and tranquil the scene looked as he took in the view, contented.

After about half an hour he was growing hungry. He'd skipped breakfast this morning, rushed to work burning on nothing but a cup of tea that had gone cold, and now his stomach was raging.

He checked the glove compartment, which contained nothing but the usual and half a pack of mints, which were a little dusty.

Hardly appetising.

He let his head fall back against the headrest and stared at the roof of the car. Then he remembered the shopping bag in the boot, his emergency stock of energy foods if the occasion called for them.

Today it most certainly did.

He climbed out of the car and opened the boot, fumbled for the shopping bag, then rummaged inside.

His hands fell upon a bottle of cheap energy drink. He eagerly popped the cap, taking several swigs.

As he screwed the top back on he heard a noise and swung around, but before he could understand what was happening, he felt a hard blow to his temple and the last thing he remembered seeing was the ground rushing up to meet him.

Then darkness.

CHAPTER 76

Stefan parked his car in one of the allocated parking bays and shut off the engine. PC Brennan pulled a grimace as he looked around.

'Don't think you can park here.'

'We won't be here for long. Residents won't argue with us about it.'

Brennan pulled a face. 'I wouldn't be so sure on this estate, Guv.'

Stefan ignored him and got out of the car. Brennan followed suit and they headed into the tower block towards the lifts.

As the steel doors closed them in, Brennan noticed the graffiti on the walls.

'Have you read that one?' he said, pointing to a rude message and a telephone number for some girl known only as Stacey. Stefan read the message. 'Bet her mother's proud,' Brennan added.

'Enough of that. Remember why we're here.'

'Babysitting some stripper into showing off her gash, yeah, word already got round.'

Stefan shot him a hard look.

'Her name's Chloe. She's a vital witness, Brennan, and we're trying to protect her, not babysit, or disrespect her.'

Brennan knew he'd overstepped the mark. He nodded and remained quiet.

They arrived at Chloe's floor and Stefan knocked on her door and waited. No one answered.

He tried again, then several times more. When no noise came from the other side he began to worry. His stomach pulled tight as he remembered what Jane had told them earlier.

'You said DS Diego is supposed to be watching her now?'

Stefan didn't answer, as his fist hovered against the door, ready to knock again.

Then he had a better idea. He pulled his phone from his pocket and dialled Michael's number.

The call diverted straight to voicemail.

'Shit.'

'Maybe there's no signal in there?'

'He would've heard us knocking.' Stefan pushed his ear to the door and listened. He heard nothing. He stepped back and thought for a minute before looking at Brennan. 'We've got to force it.'

'Is that wise?' Brennan's eyes narrowed with disapproval.

'We've got no choice.' Stefan placed the palms of his hands flat against the door and ran them across the surface then along the hinges. 'Something's not right in there.'

'Maybe Diego took her out?'

'Bollocks. He knows better,' Stefan said as he took a few steps back from the door.

He stared at it a moment and gathered that the wood was more like chipboard than oak, flimsy and unreliable like most of the others in the older council blocks falling into disrepair.

He took a deep breath and hurled his foot at the door in one fast swoop.

The wood groaned but remained intact. He kicked at the door again, only this time towards the hinges, but still it stood fast.

Brennan rolled his eyes. 'Do much breaking and entering in CID?'

Stefan looked at him hard in the face, feeling a little berated. 'Shut up, Brennan, you're not helping.' He took a few steps back. 'Last time I broke a door down, I had an Enforcer…'

Taking a bit of a run-up, Stefan hurled himself at the door, leading with his shoulder, his whole body weight right behind him and with a loud crash, the door collapsed inward, swiftly followed by Stefan.

Pain shot through his shoulder as he landed hard on his side against the door itself but he pushed it back down inside him.

Chloe was the priority.

He looked up the small hallway. There was still no sign of Chloe.

Brennan stood open-mouthed at the space where the door had been seconds before, then leaned forward to help Stefan to his feet.

He went to speak but stopped when they heard the locks from the flat next door unbolt and the door swing open.

They were faced with a pregnant girl staring at her neighbour's door, then back at them in disbelief.

'Who the hell do you think you are, fucking Rambo?' she said. 'What have you done to my neighbour's door? You just woke my kid up.'

Stefan raised his warrant card to her face and saw her demeanour change instantly. 'What's Chloe done?' she said, her voice now a little shaky.

'Just stand back, please,' Stefan said. The girl hesitated and glanced through the doorway. 'Better still, PC Brennan, take this lady back inside her flat,' he added.

Brennan looked as reluctant as the girl did, but nevertheless he motioned her back inside.

Stefan lingered a moment, but when no one else came to investigate the noise, he stepped through over the broken door.

'Chloe?'

When he heard nothing, Stefan felt his stomach start to shift. He began to feel uneasy and he could feel his heart beating faster inside his chest the further he ventured inside.

He turned the corner leading to the bedroom and pushed the door open gently without stepping inside.

'Chloe?' he called out with some caution in his voice. He inspected the room, then headed towards the living area.

When his eyes caught sight of spatters of blood on the cream-coloured carpet, he froze.

CHAPTER 77

Claire hung up the phone, slamming it down into the cradle. 'Voicemail again,' she said to Jane.

'Same with Harper,' said Jane, as she hung up on her own mobile. 'I've left him two voicemails already.'

Claire stared at her computer screen and tapped a pen against the desk. 'I don't like this... Send uniform to the Manor.' She picked up the phone again and began dialling.

'Who are you calling now?'

'Manuela.'

Claire's BlackBerry started to ring and vibrate across her desk. Jane glanced at the caller ID.

'It's Stefan.'

Claire hung up on the landline and answered her BlackBerry before she'd even brought it to her ear. 'Stefan, have you—'

She stopped mid-sentence when she heard screams in the background from what sounded like a young woman.

Stefan was shouting at PC Brennan, something about getting the girl out of the flat. Claire repeated Stefan's name into the phone until she heard him clearly.

'Claire...it's Chloe, she's...' The line began to crackle and his voice sounded far away.

'I'm losing you, Fletcher,' Claire shouted. 'Where's Chloe?'

The static on the line disappeared and Stefan's voice was suddenly loud in her ear.

'There's a lot of blood…'

Claire's eyes grew wide. 'Stefan, what the hell is going on? You're not making any sense.'

Stefan looked down at Chloe's battered face and the red imprints around her neck. He cradled her head, lifted an eyelid carefully, and saw her pupil react to the light.

'Thank God… Stay with us, Chloe.'

Claire heard him drop his phone and shout to Brennan to call an ambulance before running back to the phone.

'Fletcher, where're Chloe and Michael?'

'I've found Chloe. She's been badly beaten and strangled almost half to death. Christ, I thought she was dead, but I can just make out a faint pulse now.'

Claire's mouth went dry and her hands tightened around the phone. 'Stefan, where is Michael?'

There was a short pause from the other end.

'He's gone, Claire.'

'What do you mean he's gone? Gone where?' She felt a knot tie in her stomach.

'I don't know…wait, I think Chloe's trying to say something.'

He dropped the phone again and looked down at Chloe's face.

Her eyes were still shut, and there was deep purple bruising spreading out from her nose and around her eye sockets. Just then, her lips began to move. Stefan moved in closer to her mouth.

From the other end, Claire could hear him gently coaxing Chloe awake, and reassuring her she was safe now.

She heard him ask where Michael was.

She waited with bated breath and realised Jane was still at the door listening, a worried expression on her face. Claire looked at her.

'Is she OK?'

'I don't know…' Claire trailed off, pressing the phone closer to her ear, so hard it pained her.

She heard Stefan pick up the phone again.

'Don't tell me…' she said before he could speak. 'I think I know.'

He blew out a deep breath. 'Chloe's saying Michael did this.'

Claire shut her eyes tight and felt her heart in her mouth, betrayal sweeping across her body. She felt she might buckle at his words.

'Michael…he's…'

He paused.

Claire couldn't believe her own words as they escaped her mouth. 'He's Stevie.'

CHAPTER 78

Amelia grasped one end of DC Harper's unconscious body and pulled him into a thick row of bushes alongside his car. After she was satisfied he was completely out of sight, she stretched her aching arms.

'You could've helped. The bastard's heavier than he looks.'

She eyed the long metal pole being wiped clean of Harper's freshly spilt blood by a pair of strong hands.

Michael's hands.

He looked at her and smiled, his lips set cruelly against his usually handsome face. 'You could benefit from more heavy lifting. Build your strength up, considering what happened with Hargreaves.'

Amelia stared at him. She wished she could be more angry with him, after what he'd done with that detective he worked alongside, built up trust in…shared a bed with.

'She'll find out about you and me.'

Michael swung the metal pole behind his neck and balanced it there with both hands, cocking his head towards her.

'It doesn't matter now.'

'She won't want you any more.'

'Like I said, it doesn't matter. She was never special to me. Soon all our plans will be complete and there won't be time for anyone else other than you and me.'

Amelia looked sceptical and he could see that inside she was eaten away by bitterness and jealousy.

She looked away from him and towards the Manor. 'It was only supposed to be you and me in the first place.'

Michael swung the pole back down to the ground with one arm, cutting into the grass beside him with a thud. He looked into her eyes and she raised her eyebrows at him when he didn't answer her.

He looked away and walked around the trees and hedgerows which led towards the Manor gardens, rather than straight up the driveway to the main door.

Amelia followed, trying to block his way, jutting her shoulder out so he walked into it, but he didn't stop.

He carried on walking to avoid her eyes.

Amelia watched him increase the void between them until she felt a boiling anger rise up inside her that she just couldn't ignore.

Her pace quickened, and soon she was matching his stride. She threw her arms forward and shoved him hard to one side, the force catching him off balance.

'Don't ignore me. I said it should only have been you and me. Why did you have to fuck her again?'

Michael turned to look at her. He saw her hair was a mess of red as usual, and her eyes looked sad and tired.

'Stop being so jealous. What I did was…necessary.'

'And Adrian was *necessary*?'

'Yes.'

'Bullshit!'

Michael dismissed her with his hand, pushing her from him.

Amelia came running up beside him, her face red with anger. 'Adrian deserved many things but not to be burnt alive.'

She punched him hard in the shoulder but he refused to look at her. 'You're a sick bastard, Stevie… How could you do such a thing? It wasn't part of the plan.'

'You cut up the priests and Ashe Miller and fucking enjoyed it,' he said, turning around on her, anger in his face. 'Shall we try and analyse what that says about you? Ashe Miller was *never* part of the plan either.'

'They were different, and Ashe knew too much. He was a threat.'

'I'm starting to believe maybe you enjoyed what Adrian was giving you,' he said, walking away from her again. 'You're lucky I'm not the jealous type or he'd have got a lot worse before he burned to death.'

'Don't walk away from me when I'm talking to you.'

Michael turned around, let the pole fall to the ground and rested his hands on her shoulders to calm her down.

She screamed in his face. 'Don't touch me!'

She tried to push his hands from her but he tightened his grip. 'You need to calm down.'

Amelia smacked him hard across the cheek. When he showed no obvious signs of pain, she struck him again, then once more until he let out a guttural roar and shoved her down on the grass, his weight pinning her chest.

'Don't test me, Amelia.'

'Get off me!'

'We're so close, don't blow this now. There's only ever been you, you have no reason to be jealous of Claire. I did what I *had* to do.'

'And Chloe?'

He saw the tears brim in her eyes.

'You knew there would be *sacrifices*.'

The last word sounded like venom forced from his lips, and Amelia digested his words, but inside she refused to believe them.

She raised her head off the grass towards him until her lips were inches from his. 'You say you're not the jealous type? Don't make me laugh. You hated how close I grew to Chloe. All she helped me with after Stokebrook, and you...' She fought back tears, anger grief and frustration coming to the surface. 'Why couldn't you have left her alone?'

'You chose me over her, or have you forgotten so soon? There wasn't room for both of us in your life to love you, give you what you needed. You know that.'

Amelia blinked away her tears. 'Don't you speak her name to me.'

He shook his head. 'This is pathetic.'

'I wouldn't hesitate to feed you to the wolves if it meant I could get away... You remember that... If it came to it, I'm strong enough.'

Michael stared down into her eyes. 'You don't mean that.'

'Don't I?' She cocked her head to one side. 'You prepared to take that risk?'

'You know what I'd do to you before you got that far,' he said, shaking his head. 'You're not the one that makes you strong, Amelia... *I* made you who you are. *I* helped you channel that rage of yours.' He stabbed a finger hard against her forehead. 'Your head was already fucked up...those seeds were already sown, I just watered them day by day.'

She batted his finger away from her head and raised her knee up into his chest, catching him hard in the ribs. He stifled a groan, reached for the pole beside her and got to his knees. He swung it above his head.

'Fucking do it!'

Michael's breath was coming in short sharp bursts as the weight of the pole pulled against his hands. His face was red, his mouth set firm as he swung the pole forward.

Amelia's arms rose instinctively as the pole narrowly missed her, landing hard on the grass beside her head.

Slowly, lowering her arms, she looked up at him.

His breathing was heavy and his face pained. 'Next time I won't miss.'

After a few seconds Amelia nodded her head and he helped her to her feet. He retrieved the pole from the ground. 'Let's do what we came here to do.'

She let him push past her.

She knew she'd overstepped the mark but despite the fact she'd almost driven him to kill her, the anger she felt inside wasn't directed at herself.

Far from it.

She knew that if she ever got the chance to meet Claire Winters on her terms, she would take her time showing her how far jealousy can drive a person.

She stared at the Manor through the trees, nothing but hatred in her eyes.

CHAPTER 79

Claire had wasted no time after she ended her call with Stefan. She had called Jenkins and asked if he had access to a fax or email account.

'What the devil for?' he said.

'Do you have access or not?' She was losing any fraction of patience she had with him.

He sighed. 'Yes, a fax machine, but I can't work it. I leave that sort of thing to Sam.'

'Are you any closer to finding a photograph of Stephen?'

'Sam's been looking since you left.'

'When she finds one can you get her to fax it through immediately, the latest image you have of him before he left.' She heard him swear and another sigh.

'I know I told you we'd look but I don't think we have any. I think I threw them away. We didn't want him to be a part of our lives.'

'This is really important. Think.'

He dropped the receiver and she could hear raised voices coming from him and Sam in the background. After a few minutes he grabbed the phone.

'What's your fax number?'

***

Twenty minutes passed and Claire was now perched on her desk staring at the fax machine, her hands clasped together.

She was so lost in her own thoughts that she didn't hear Matthews enter the room, with Stefan and Jane in tow.

Matthews cleared his throat. She ignored them until she realised Stefan was there.

'How's Chloe?'

The feeling of a genuine sense of compassion towards Chloe, though she barely knew her, was a strange emotion for Claire. Stefan looked less than positive.

'She lost consciousness again when the paramedics got there. She's fallen into a coma.'

Claire's eyes widened.

'When I left, she wasn't responding to anything. She has a fracture in her arm and a broken nose... He used her head like a punch bag.'

Claire couldn't bring herself to look at him. 'She's not alone, is she?'

'PC Brennan's with her at the hospital... We need to tell her parents.'

'No. Not yet.'

'Claire, they need to know.'

'Not yet!'

She brought her attention back to the fax machine and waited. Matthews and Stefan exchanged glances.

'We've found some evidence that Hargreaves was hired by Brown to rid himself of Williams,' Matthews said. 'Something concrete, I mean.' Claire gave him a sideways glance. 'We've now got phone records, text messages and emails. Williams was trying to blackmail Brown regarding the money he was laundering.'

Claire nodded and lowered her eyes.

Matthews stared at her, a little annoyed. 'I thought this is what you wanted.' Stefan stepped forward in her defence.

'Amelia is working with Stephen.'

'Metcalfe?' Matthews shook his head. 'I've run his name, there's no trace of him on the social since 1999. He's not on the PNC and the Missing Persons Bureau hasn't had any updates since 2000.'

Claire jumped as the fax machine started spooling paper beside her. 'This one's colour, isn't it?' she asked no one in particular. Jane muttered what sounded like a yes.

Claire practically tore at the paper as it gradually fed through the machine. Matthews ignored her but Stefan noticed her ashen face.

'Claire?' he said, moving towards her. She let the paper in her hand loose and it floated down onto the table beside her.

'There's a reason you won't find anything under the name Stephen Metcalfe...and the reason is staring you right in the face. Hiding in plain sight of all of us.'

The others looked down at the fax and saw a photograph of a boy aged around sixteen, with a mop of floppy blond hair framing the face. Claire studied his eyes. The jaw cut a familiar shape, along with the boy's wide grin.

'My God,' Stefan muttered under his breath. 'How did Jenkins not see him?'

'He's changed a lot. Apart from the fact he's now fourteen years older, he's dyed his hair.'

Matthews looked up at them both and pointed at the image. 'You're not telling me what I think you're telling me?'

They remained silent.

Matthews shook his head. 'He's got different colour eyes for a start.'

Claire looked at Stefan.

'Contact lenses,' he answered on her behalf.

Claire sat down again.

'Jane, I need you to contact Harper, tell him backup is on its way, and he's to enter the Manor immediately, regardless of what Manuela has to say about it. Tell them we're on our way. Let's hope Manuela is a bit more cooperative when he knows what's been planned for him.'

CHAPTER 80

The blues and twos drowned out anything else from the streets, as marked police cars cut their way through traffic towards Shrovesbury Manor.

Claire put her foot down in her own car, causing Stefan to grasp hold of the handle above his passenger window. He exchanged glances with Jane, who was in the back seat. Claire saw her hang up her mobile in the rear-view mirror.

'Any luck?'

Jane shook her head. 'No. It's going to voicemail, and that's not like Harper.'

'You think they got there first?' Stefan said.

Claire glanced at him but didn't answer. Jane's face screwed up, still trying to comprehend what was happening.

'Why did Amelia kill Ashe Miller? He had nothing to do with her past.' Claire looked over her shoulder and narrowly missed clipping another car.

'Maybe he found out about what she was doing. She needed money to help fund all this and she's used to using sex as a weapon. You put two people like that together and you've got yourself one hell of a ticking time bomb ready to explode. Miller was just collateral damage,' she said, looking back at the road. 'Like Melanie Steward, George Manning, Brown and Hargreaves. Wrong place, wrong time.'

'I'd say she did us a favour with Hargreaves,' said Stefan.

'What about Brown?'

Claire shook her head. 'I don't think she killed him. I think Diego took care of him before helping her with Hargreaves and his boys.'

'You mean Stephen,' Stefan corrected.

Claire paused, staring ahead at the road.

'Whatever he calls himself, the bastard's going away for a long time.'

7ᵗʰ December 2009

  The room smelled of blood, so thick she could almost taste it.

  Amelia leaned as far back into the wardrobe as she could and held her breath. Blood pounded in her ears and her body shivered uncontrollably. Her heart raced inside her chest so hard it felt like it would suddenly burst from her body.

  Outside, all was silent once again.

  For the moment at least.

  She knew they'd be back to clear up the mess and she dared not reveal her hiding place after witnessing so much evil.

  The minutes ticked by and somehow she managed to muster her inner strength and, with a morbid curiosity, to take another look outside.

  Slowly, pushing some clothes aside, she peered through the crack in the door. She squinted hard. She saw the bed.

  The duvet was ruffled from the struggle and she could see that the pillows had been thrown to the floor.

  Lowering her eyes, she caught sight of her friend's hand, lifeless and pale, reaching out from behind the bed. A pool of blood slowly seeped across the wooden floor.

  Then she heard the footsteps.

  She imagined each frightened breath she took would give her away as fear crept over her body like cold bony fingers on her skin.

  Pressing her lips tightly together, she held her breath as someone approached the bedroom door and turned the handle.

CHAPTER 81

Father Manuela stirred in the corner of the derelict building.

His body had gone numb down one side from sitting on the dusty concrete floor. He tried his best to stretch out, despite his hands being bound together.

There was no point in trying to call for help – they'd made sure of that by securing his mouth shut with duct tape that had been pulled tightly around the whole circumference of his head.

His wrists ached and he tried his best to flex his hands and fingers out against his bonds, all the while looking at his kidnappers nervously.

He sneaked a look around the room, wondering where he was and how long he had been there since they'd taken him from his home by force, knocking him unconscious in the process.

He judged by the ache in his head that he'd been struck on his left temple. He looked down at his shirt and saw dried specks of blood.

God, please hear my prayer.

He looked around the large room, past the graffiti and drug paraphernalia etched across the walls and floors, desperate for an escape route. His eyes stopped when he caught sight of Michael, staring at him.

'Don't even think about it, old man. There's only one way out for you and it's not through a fucking door.'

His voice sounded dry, his face was unshaven and his eyes were red-rimmed with tiredness.

Their eyes remained locked on each other until Amelia entered the room and Manuela shifted his gaze to her hands. She was carrying rosary beads and a sharp piece of metal that looked like a scalpel. She placed the items down on the table in front of Michael and looked over towards Manuela.

'Do you think they've worked it all out yet?'

'They'll be on the way to the Manor by now, if they're not there already. Claire won't miss what's staring her in the face.'

Amelia grinned. 'She missed you though.'

He looked up at her, his face set in a taut stare. 'The signs were there,' he said, looking away. 'With her feelings for me…she just didn't want to see them.'

***

As Claire pulled into the driveway, Mrs Lawrence was already at the door arguing with officers.

Claire was first out of the car and when Lawrence caught sight of her she pushed herself out of the doorway, waving her arms in the air.

She pointed a bony finger at Claire as she approached. 'I keep telling your officers to leave Father Manuela alone. We don't need you here.'

As Lawrence stepped in front of her, Claire raised her hands and forcefully shoved her to one side.

'Where's Father Manuela?'

She could hear Lawrence shouting out idle threats at her as she entered the Manor and headed towards the back of the house, calling out for Manuela.

'He won't want to see you,' Lawrence bellowed close to Claire's ear, making her wince.

She turned on her heels and stared the woman hard in the face.

'I think he might when he knows his life is in danger.' She watched Lawrence's face fall. 'Where is he?'

Several seconds passed until Lawrence finally spoke.

'He was in the Rose Garden last time I saw him.'

***

Manuela was nowhere to be seen, as Claire had predicted.

She scanned the area of the Rose Garden in an instant. Spotting the blood spatter across the bench where she'd sat with Manuela mere days ago, she closed her eyes tight.

Mrs Lawrence gasped when she saw the blood and began ranting at Jane about Manuela, until Claire lost her patience.

'Mrs Lawrence!' The lady froze. 'Do yourself a favour and shut up. If you want to help Manuela you must tell me everything that's happened in the last few hours. His life will depend on it.'

***

Mrs Lawrence had told Claire all she knew in the space of five minutes, which was basically nothing of worth.

Claire had ordered officers to search the grounds and Manor, with others already on a house-to-house and a search of the area within a five-mile radius.

She had no idea where they could have taken Manuela or if he was even still alive. All she had were her instincts, and they were guiding her to the rose bushes in front of her.

What revelation lies within the beauty of a rose?

'I need a spade.'

Stefan took the initiative and retrieved one from the potting shed, racing back towards her. She grabbed it from him and forced it into the dirt and began digging.

'What the hell are you doing? You can't do that.'

'Stefan, please have Mrs Lawrence escorted back inside the Manor,' Claire said over her shoulder.

'You must be mad, woman,' Lawrence shouted at her as Stefan gently took hold of her shoulders. 'Just what are you hoping to find?' she said, pushing at Stefan, catching him off guard with her strength.

Claire ignored her and continued to dig fast, clearing just over a foot of soft soil, sending it cascading onto the grass around her.

As she paused for a breath, wiping her forehead with the back of her hand, she caught sight of something poking out of the ground.

It looked like cloth.

She threw the spade to one side, got on her hands and knees, and clawed the earth with her fingers, drawing confused looks from those around her.

It wasn't until she'd uncovered a large dirty sack weighted down with rocks that Stefan took notice. He sat down beside her and helped her haul it from the earth, out onto the grass.

The sack had been tied at one end with thick but worn rope, and it wasn't until Claire had managed to prize the rope apart that they caught the smell.

They looked at each other.

Claire pulled away the last bit of rope and slowly opened the sack.

'What is it?' Mrs Lawrence was watching when she caught sight of their faces. 'What have you got there?'

Claire looked at Stefan, and wished she'd acted sooner on her hunches. She pulled herself up from the ground, making no attempt to dust off the earth which now clung to her trousers, and looked Lawrence hard in the face.

'Do you remember the missing person case of Rebecca Turner, who attended here, Mrs Lawrence?'

Lawrence paused. She nodded. 'Yes. It was a terrible time for us all.'

Claire continued to stare at her before looking back at the sack.

'Well, she's no longer missing.'

Lawrence looked at her, confused, but before she could speak, Claire answered her unspoken question.

'We will need to confirm but I'm certain this is the disassembled body of Rebecca Turner…what's left of her.'

CHAPTER 82

Manuela was frozen with fear as he stared at the scalpel blade gleaming inches from his face.

Amelia smiled at his reaction.

'There's a problem I'm facing, Father…perhaps you can help me?' She saw his eyelids snap shut dreading what was to come. 'Or perhaps you can't,' she added. 'Either way I can assure you of one thing… I'll enjoy what's to come. After all, it's been a hell of a long time coming.'

She lowered the scalpel and slid the blade just underneath his shirt, and sliced it open from navel to throat with force.

Manuela groaned beneath his gag, his eyes giving away his constant fear. He looked down to check it was only his shirt she'd cut open and was relieved to find his skin untouched.

She leaned in closer so his eyes could not avoid hers, and he felt the blade lightly touch his skin. He prepared himself for the pain that was to come.

He shut his eyes tight and Amelia laughed.

'I see my actions are predictable, Father!' She removed the blade and he opened his eyes a little.

'You see, this is my problem…do I do you like the rest, which, although convenient, offers no real element of surprise and I end up walking the books of history as just another signature killer, or,' she paused, looking down hard into his eyes, 'do I take my time turning your withered feeble body into a pretty work of art?'

'Rebecca always did enjoy art lessons, my love,' Michael said.

Manuela felt his bladder fail him, his mind overwhelmed with fear of the unknown.

The smell of urine wafted upward to Amelia's nose and she recoiled.

'Where's your dignity, Father?'

Manuela saw Michael appear over him with the metal pole in his hands. He swallowed hard, just as it was swung high above his face.

Michael saw him cower and allowed himself a smile.

He remembered a time when he was at the Manor, forced into the basement by the same man whose life was now at his mercy.

He remembered the rats crawling over his skin in the dark. He remembered the smell, earthy and damp.

He'd cried for hours until his throat was raw.

His crime? Questioning the contradictions between the Old and New Testament of the Bible.

He'd wondered if Christ Himself would've condoned that punishment.

Michael's gaze returned to Manuela, who closed his eyes, preparing himself for the moment when cold metal would bite at his pale delicate skin.

There'd be no redemption for this soul.

2009

The main part of the Chapel was still smouldering the next morning.

Manuela sat in his study, staring out at the building, and although the damage had been limited, the rage was seething just beneath the surface of his otherwise cool exterior.

He'd told the firemen and police all he knew – which was close to nothing. He had an idea who had started the fire last night, although he had no real proof, but he was determined to find it by any means necessary.

He had called a meeting with Wainwright and Hawthorne, due to take place after he had called all those with children due in today, telling them the Manor would be closed until tomorrow.

He'd listened to but promptly forgot all the best wishes received from parents and guardians when he told them the news.

All that mattered was finding those responsible.

The cruelty swept over him as he thought about a suitable punishment – after all, what would the police actually do if they caught whoever it was?

Community service no doubt, he thought scornfully, as if the very idea left a bad taste in his mouth.

His thoughts were disturbed by Mrs Lawrence knocking at his door. She informed him that Wainwright and Hawthorne were here, and he told her to send them up.

When the men were sitting in his study, refreshments in hand, he stood and paced the room, hands clasped tightly behind his back.

'You think it was her, don't you? Amelia?' said Wainwright without emotion.

Manuela stopped in his tracks and nodded. 'It would be a reasonable assumption.'

Father Hawthorne sat upright in his chair and cast a worried look at both men.

'You can't go around making accusations based on your assumptions, Jeremy,' he said, not bothering to hide the appalled tone of his voice. 'Just tell the police what you know to be true. It's in their hands now.'

Hawthorne went to speak again but changed his mind when Manuela turned his icy gaze towards him.

***

Manuela tried to open his eyes but the lids felt heavy. He knew he was drifting in and out of consciousness and he was remembering the past that he'd tried so hard to erase from his memory.

He remembered the conversations that'd passed and wished now he'd listened to his dear friend David.

It was too late for that now.

He remembered the days he'd spent planning to make Amelia admit to starting the fire.

He had convinced himself God was on his side.

If only Rebecca had stayed away that day…

***

'It was me, Father.'

Manuela had been glued to the spot by the sound of her words – unexpected, and if it wasn't for the fact he knew he was awake and lucid, he could easily have mistaken her words for a dream.

He looked down at the girl seated before him and rage began to grow as he listened to her words.

'*It wasn't Amelia, Father. I planned it, I started it. It had nothing to do with her. If you must punish me, I'll accept that for what I did, but you must know I will tell your secrets. I'll tell everyone what you did to Amelia.*'

Manuela shut his eyes as he listened to her voice betray him. He heard her say how she would report their cruelty to Amelia over the years and how she'd remained silent because of her fear.

But Rebecca Turner was no longer a scared, frightened little girl. She had seen enough.

'*I'll tell them everything…*'

The final sentence echoed through his head as a mere distant voice until she repeated the words louder and more defiantly than ever.

Manuela opened his eyes and looked into hers.

He saw her determination and he knew that even if he kept her secret, she would not be keeping his.

He watched as she turned towards the stairs.

He felt the anger boil up inside him.

Any rational thought he may have had left his body. He felt as if his soul had left him and the man who edged closer to her from behind as she took her final steps had no control.

He saw his own hands reach out in front of him, lunge forward and make contact with her back.

One push was all it took.

He watched as her legs fell out from underneath her, her hands grabbing at nothing but air.

She seemed to turn her body easily as she fell and he saw the fear in her eyes right before her body hit the first stair with such force, he almost heard the wind knocked out of her.

Even as she continued to fall, rebounding off each stair with force, he felt little emotion.

Even when he heard the sound of her head crack against a stair corner, he didn't weep or wince.

When her body was finally stationary at the bottom of the winding staircase, he made no attempt to rush to her aid.

Instead he stood still, watching to see if she was still breathing...and, after a few seconds, he heard her draw breath.

CHAPTER 83

Manuela awoke to a white-hot pain along his torso.

His eyes flew open and he screamed through the gag. He looked down, saw the burn and the smell was so sickly, he vomited.

He heard laughter and saw Amelia beside him, waving a cigarette lighter in her hand.

'We can't have you sleeping, Father.'

Manuela started to choke, his face turning red. Amelia reluctantly pulled the gag from his mouth and he spat what was left of his stomach contents onto the floor.

He drew in a few deep breaths then tried to move.

Rope cut into his body with each movement and he realised he was bound and stretched on a cold metal table in another part of the derelict building to where he'd been before he was knocked unconscious.

He twisted his head around.

Amelia was staring hard into his eyes and Michael was nowhere to be seen.

'Please…let me go.'

Amelia edged towards him, flicking the lighter on and off, bringing the flame closer to his face each time she flicked the switch.

'You can't escape the fire, Father. God was watching you that day.' She brought the flame close to his right eye and he snapped it shut. 'And *Rebecca* is watching you now. Can you feel her spirit, restless, in limbo...?'

The sheer heat from the flame made him feel like his eyes might boil inside his skull.

Then she lowered the flame and he heard her voice as clear as day, her mouth next to his ear.

'*I* was watching you that day...all of you.'

She waited until Manuela opened his eyes again, his face a mixture of confusion and fear. She could read the questions that were racing through his mind and she grinned.

'Did you think you'd sent *everyone* home that day?' Manuela tried to speak but his voice failed him. 'You think you had control. You thought it would be so easy blaming me, making me suffer. You thought you had it all worked out.'

'I know it wasn't you who started the fire.' Manuela's voice was barely audible.

'You don't know anything, old man,' said Michael.

Manuela's head swung to one side and he saw Michael standing to the far side of the room next to another table, with a large cloth covering the top.

'It was you,' Manuela whispered.

Michael looked to Amelia and they both started to laugh.

'He still can't work it out. He can't see it.' Michael let his laughter die as he slowly pulled at the tablecloth. 'Redemption,' he said, eyeing Manuela with such intensity that he was forced to look away. 'Redemption, and atonement. Isn't that what you preach about? Do you think they'll be a chance for you to save the fate of your soul when the time comes, Father?'

The statement hung in the air and the cloth fell to the ground. Manuela could now see the glimmer of metal objects that had previously been hidden, and knew what they were for.

They were meant for his wretched body.

He wished his heart would give out. He wished he would die of fright.

Anything would be better than what they had in store for him. His options were running out, his chance of rescue slim. His only chance was to bide some time – keep them talking.

'Rebecca told me. She started the fire,' he managed, his voice weak. 'I couldn't let her go unpunished.'

'Rebecca was protecting me, you stupid fuck!'

Manuela felt the hot spray of spittle from Amelia's mouth against his face and turned his head away, but she grabbed a fistful of his hair and twisted his face towards hers.

'She wouldn't let me stop her. She wanted to help me and spare me a lashing and look what good it did her. You pushed her, watched her fall. You could've helped her… She was still alive when she hit the bottom!'

Manuela groaned in anguish upon hearing the words spilling from her mouth. Amelia showed no signs of letting up, her face now bright red, eyes wide with pure rage.

'I was so scared, I hid in the wardrobe in your room. Do you know how many long nights I've cried myself to sleep wishing I'd done more instead of being frozen with fear at what you'd done?'

He began shaking his head, trying to block out her words. His face was screwed up, his eyes shut. His mind was willing him to be somewhere else and wake up from this nightmare.

'I saw you carry her body into your room. I saw Wainwright help you. It was all done so casually. So *normal*, like you'd done it before.'

'No, Amelia. It wasn't like that.'

'I saw you!' she screamed into his face. 'I went to help her after you left the room, but then you came back with Hawthorne. I wanted to leap out and save her, but I was so frightened of what you'd do to me if I was found, a witness to her murder, but I'm not frightened any more, Father. God spoke to me and His will shall be done.'

Manuela saw the scalpel in her hand just as she plunged it into his side with such force, he felt like her hand had penetrated his entire abdominal cavity.

Letting out another scream, his world returned to darkness once more.

***

'*She's not dead!*'

The voice of David Hawthorne rang in the ears of both the other men, as they watched him cower over her body.

The blood from her head wound was now seeping into the floor, and time felt like it had sped up, allowing no room for anyone to think clearly.

'*Get away from the body, David,*' *Wainwright said, roughly pulling Hawthorne from her body and onto the bed.*

Hawthorne began to struggle.

'*She's still alive! There might be a chance to save her if we act now. Let me call an ambulance, the police…*'

'*And tell them what?*' *said Manuela, a dark look in his eyes.* '*Tell them that she fell by herself?*' *He looked down at the blood coming from Rebecca's head.* '*She will say I pushed her.*'

'*And we have already moved the body – no, this will raise too many questions,*' *said Wainwright.*

Hawthorne looked aghast at their words. '*What do you mean by "body"? She's still alive, damn you!*'

Manuela and Wainwright exchanged a look.

They seemed to agree to something which remained unspoken.

Hawthorne watched as Manuela went to a chest of drawers and removed something buried underneath his folded clothes.

A dagger, almost ritualistic in design, was revealed to both men before he stooped over and grabbed a mass of Rebecca's hair at the back of her head.

Hawthorne, realising Manuela's intentions, cried out in protest but was held down on the bed by Wainwright, whose hands gripped him with an iron force.

Hawthorne cried out for them to stop, but Manuela looked to Wainwright as if seeking his permission.

'If you're going to do it, do it quickly, man!'

Manuela looked down at Rebecca's face and she slowly opened her eyes. They bored into his.

Her confusion turned into terror when Manuela forced her head back and she saw the blade.

She tried to scream, but only a light croaking sound escaped her lips.

Her eyes widened as he lowered the blade to her throat, and her hands flew up to push his arms away but to little avail – she was far too weak.

With one slow deep movement, Manuela cut through her skin, and looked away as blood poured from the wound as he severed her carotid artery.

All Manuela could hear was Hawthorne's cries of anguish, and the subtle gurgling sounds as Rebecca tried to cry out.

Seconds passed and soon she was still.

Wainwright released his grip on Hawthorne.

He scrambled across the bed and fell, hitting the floor hard as he tried to reach her body.

He soon felt Manuela force him back.

'Stay away from the body.'

From within the wardrobe, Amelia had bit back tears, and found she couldn't move, even if she'd wanted to.

There was no way she could reveal her hiding place now. For all they knew, she hadn't been at the Manor for hours, and that was what she needed them to keep believing.

She listened as they argued about what to do, and inwardly cursed each man.

She heard Hawthorne give in and agree to keep their secret, and they forced him to clean up the mess in the bedroom while Rebecca was disposed of.

She heard them remove the body and carry it down the stairs and into the basement.

She had stayed in the wardrobe for hours after her friend's death, before daring to make her escape.

She had snuck to the bottom of the stairs and all she could smell was the stench of cleaning agents, which had made her gag.

Satisfied she could make it unseen, she'd bolted for the main doors, and ran down the driveway with such speed that her muscles burned and her legs almost gave way under the strain.

As soon as she'd made it to the main road, she knew she had to find Stevie.

***

As darkness was falling, they worked in the twilight.

Hawthorne had dug away the dirt and made the grave, but it was Manuela who had calculated how and where to bury her.

He and Wainwright had pulled apart her frail body into easier pieces, all wrapped up in black bin bags. Then the bags were placed into a cloth sack.

Hawthorne sat on the nearby bench and sobbed as they began to bury her.

He watched as Manuela planted rose bushes he'd retrieved from the potter's shed that he'd bought a few days beforehand.

Hawthorne couldn't believe the man who he'd called a friend over many years seemed to have changed into a man who could quite easily have done this before.

In the space of a few hours that night, Manuela had given them the story they would tell when she was reported missing and the police came knocking.

He even gave them the story they were to tell Mrs Lawrence in the weeks Rebecca would have a community looking for her and appealing for help.

He had planned for everything, with no remorse or worry for his soul.

This was no more a man of God than the Devil himself, and Hawthorne knew that someday he too would pay the ultimate price for the dark deeds done on this day.

CHAPTER 84

'Time's running out fast and I'm drawing a blank.'

Claire shut her eyes and ran her hands through her hair. She looked back at Stefan, who was standing mere feet from her. 'Where the hell are they?' she said, turning her back on him.

They were back inside the Manor, alone by the staircase. Teams of SOCOs were doing a full search of the Manor and gardens, and Claire had decided to take a break to try and think.

'Let's look at what we've got,' said Stefan at length. 'Michael – or Stephen – whatever we'll call him, hasn't taken Manuela to his place. Officers are already there searching for any leads. You know him better than anyone, Claire. If you were him, where would you take Manuela?'

Claire looked back over her shoulder.

'But that's just it, Fletch, I don't know him better than anyone, do I? None of us could've known. He's had plenty of time to practise this whole charade all these years, faking official documents and probably paying people off to get himself placed exactly where he needed to be.'

She turned around to face him and he saw the hurt fixed upon her face. 'The bastard shared my bed and all the time he was this…this monster. What I thought I knew was a lie. He built up a wall and I barely scratched the fucking surface.'

'You don't need to share that with me, Guv, it's your private life,' Stefan said, feeling uncomfortable.

Claire shook her head. 'Don't say that, we both know I'll be questioned over this. There'll be a review and I'll be asked why I didn't know, how I could put my job on the line and mix business with pleasure. Why I failed to spot the warning signs. Why I compromised a case…list goes on.'

Stefan edged closer.

'Look, none of us had any idea. They can't blame you for this. Michael had us all fooled. He and Williams have been planning this for years.'

'And look at how many people have died because of them. All of this because I failed and couldn't see what was staring me in the face every day.'

There remained an uncomfortable silence, until Stefan cleared his throat.

'Is there anything, no matter how irrelevant it might seem, that you can remember which he may have slipped up on? Was there anywhere significant you and Michael talked about, maybe from his childhood?'

Claire let out a mock laugh. 'When I think about it, we hardly ever talked. All we seemed to do was fuck.'

Stefan recoiled at her words.

'Sorry.' She avoided his eyes. 'I mean he never talked about his past much. In the end I gave up asking, and this was before we ended up in each other's beds.'

'You were married, so you can't have been seeing each other in public places around here,' Stefan said, treading this ground carefully when he saw the pain in her face. 'Where did you go?'

Claire paused, feeling uneasy talking about this to Stefan.

She'd never told anyone about her affair, despite the fact people were suspicious, or talked much about her divorce.

This was unknown ground she was treading and she wasn't sure just how much she could trust Stefan to keep it to himself.

'Hotels mainly.' She caught the look on Stefan's face before he could hide it. 'Oh God, that sounds so seedy.' Her face flushed red and she looked away from him.

'I'm not here to judge.'

'I'm uncomfortable with this, I'll be honest.'

'This isn't about you, Claire.'

The remark was unexpected and his bluntness caught her off guard. She turned to him and glowered.

'You can look at me like that all you want, I don't care. What I *do* care about is the people who've been sucked into this, the families who've had to deal with what's left behind.'

'Careful, Fletcher.'

'I'm not scared of you. I'm here to do a job and right now I'm asking you to remember because so far we've got no leads as to where they've taken Manuela. For all we know he's dead already.'

Claire was about to speak when she saw Matthews coming towards them. His face looked pained.

'We've found Harper.'

Claire pushed Stefan aside. 'Where?'

'In some bushes off the main drive. He's alive but he's taken a bloody good whack to the head.'

'Has he said anything?' asked Stefan.

Matthews shook his head. 'He's unconscious.'

Stefan looked back at Claire. 'You've got to remember something. Time is running out.'

She sucked in a deep breath. She closed her eyes and tried to put everything else to the back of her mind and force herself to relive every moment she'd shared with Michael.

At the moment when it all seemed futile, something clicked into place and she remembered something.

'God, that's a long shot,' she said to herself.

'You remembered something,' Stefan said, his eyes narrowing.

Claire shook her head. 'I don't know. Maybe. I don't even know why I just thought of it.'

'Well, that's better than what we've got so far,' Stefan said, pulling her by the arm. 'We've not got much time.'

CHAPTER 85

'You're sure about this address?' Stefan looked at her, confused.

Claire was driving her car just above the speed limit, dodging traffic expertly.

She nodded.

'It'd make sense. Michael talked about it a few times before we…' She cut herself off and started again. 'He said it was his refuge when he was a kid, that's all he'd say. My guess is this is where he'd sleep rough after he left the Jenkins house.'

'How'd you know the address?'

There was a long pause.

'He took me there…'

Stefan frowned. 'A derelict office building?'

He glanced at her and saw the red flush across her cheeks. He looked ahead and didn't seek an answer from her. He felt as awkward as she did.

'It was exciting at the time and I guess that's what I needed,' she answered at length.

Stefan made no further comment, and as they drove across to the other side of Haverbridge, up to the industrial area, he hoped they were not too late.

Father Manuela had a lot to answer for, that much was certain, but their job right now was to prevent another horrific murder.

***

Michael pulled away a large slice of skin in his hands and waved it in front of Manuela's face.

Manuela was barely conscious but knew all too well what he saw before him.

His head leaned to one side and vomit spewed from his mouth, over his shoulder and onto the floor.

Michael stepped back, pulling a face. He turned to Amelia, who was smearing Manuela's blood over her hands.

'You want to take over? He's been sick again.'

She turned to look at him then at Manuela.

'Let him choke on it.'

She walked over to the table and ran her fingers over the instruments for torture. She played with each item, picking it up, watching Manuela's response. She picked up a claw hammer and looked down at his knee caps, then back to his face.

'No, please...' Manuela said his voice barely audible.

Something in Michael snapped and what he was looking at became all too much. He shook his head, walked towards her and pulled the hammer from her hands.

'Stop toying,' he said, slamming the hammer back down on the table. He picked up a familiar-looking object and passed it to her. 'Finish it.'

She looked down at the dagger and remembered the day it had taken Rebecca's life.

She felt the blade between her fingers but stopped when she heard a car on the gravel outside.

They both looked out from the smashed window beside them, the wind coming through and casting Amelia's hair around her face.

'They've found us.' Her eyes returned to his. 'If it comes to it…I'm not afraid to die.'

Michael smiled and kissed her forehead.

'It won't come to that. I promise you.'

CHAPTER 86

As Claire drove onto the forecourt, Stefan looked up at the derelict office block. The five-storey building had been abandoned for as long as he could remember and it wasn't likely to be renovated and occupied any time soon.

The many windows were nearly all smashed, and shards of glass flashed across the forecourt under the glare of the sun. Graffiti tags snaked their way over the brickwork and continued around the far corner leading to an underground car park.

The glass panels in the large entrance doors were shattered, but Stefan could still make out the piles of leaflets, old newspapers and empty food cartons scattered beyond into the reception hall.

The thought that Claire had been inside this cavernous monstrosity with Michael made him more than uncomfortable.

Places like this were usually used by squatters and junkies or where people conducted their 'business' and less than savoury deeds. It reminded Stefan of a building he'd once seen in Budapest. It'd had the same effect on him then that he was experiencing now.

A sense of dread.

'You can't think they've brought Manuela here? They can't guarantee they wouldn't be disturbed. This is a junkie hotspot,' Stefan said, turning to face her. 'Plus, I don't see any vehicle.'

'It's the best we've got so far.' Claire undid her seatbelt. She got out of the car and looked at each window on every floor. 'This isn't the only entrance.' She pointed off to the right. 'That leads around to the underground car park.'

Stefan walked up to the concrete ramp that led down into the belly of the building and frowned.

Sunlight couldn't penetrate through concrete and the lights that would've illuminated the way into the darkness were either smashed or missing their bulbs. He looked back at Claire. 'I don't like this.'

She was soon beside him, following his line of vision. 'I've got a torch in the car.'

'You could drive the car down there with the headlights on.'

'I'm not taking my car down there. If they're there, I don't want to cause them any panic and push them to kill Manuela. On foot is more subtle and less likely to alarm them.'

'He might be dead already.'

Claire grew angry. 'And they *might* not even be here.' She paused, staring hard into his eyes. 'Don't you think I know that?' She turned on her heels, not waiting for a response. 'We go in quietly.'

Stefan watched her as she fetched the torch. She flicked the switch and shone the beam down the slope.

'You going first?' he said.

Claire shot him a sideways glance and then gazed back into the black mouth that threatened to swallow them whole.

She took a few steps ahead of him, and raised the torch. It barely penetrated five feet in front of her. She swallowed hard and tried to keep her breathing steady.

Her lips twitched. 'You know what they say, Fletch?' she said, handing him the torch. 'Ladies first.'

***

Amelia stared down the barrel of Michael's gun.

She was sitting on the floor and holding it up to her right eye, with little emotion in her face.

She pressed it against her cheek and circled it lightly across her face, closing her eyes and concentrating on the feel of the metal against her skin. She brought it up to her right temple and her eyes flicked open.

Michael was standing next to her, staring down at the gun.

She glanced across towards Manuela who was still tied to the table. He seemed to have given way to unconsciousness again.

She looked at Michael when he crouched beside her. She let his hands move the hand holding the gun until it was under her chin, pointing up towards her brain.

'This way's better,' he said.

Her eyes brimmed with tears.

'But not yet,' he said, slowly easing the gun from her clenched fingers. He checked the safety was on before pushing it into the waistband of his trousers.

'What are we going to do?' Amelia said, sniffing back tears. 'I didn't want to rush this...*his* punishment.'

Michael looked at Manuela. The man was still. He got up and checked Manuela's pulse.

He felt a faint beat under his fingertips.

He went back to the window and gingerly peered down onto the forecourt. 'They're heading towards the underground car park.'

'They'll see the van.'

Michael shook his head. 'She won't know if the van's ours.'

'She's smart,' Amelia spat as she got up from the floor. 'What brought her here in the first place, huh?'

Michael avoided her eyes.

'How did she know about this place?' When he refused to answer, she shoved him hard. 'You told her…you brought her here before, didn't you?'

Michael dismissed her with a wave of his arm. 'She knows we'll be armed. She won't risk coming in here without any backup and advice from a tactical advisor.' He gripped her forcefully by the shoulders. 'This is our siege, Amelia. It can work to our advantage.'

She looked at him hard in the eyes and her voice was deadly serious. 'Or you could just kill her.'

His eyes narrowed. 'What?'

'You could just go down there and kill them both before they can call anyone.' She watched his face carefully. 'Or can't you do it?'

His eyes snapped back to hers. 'I can do anything… I've proven that.'

'I don't think you can put a bullet in her head.' When he didn't respond, she edged closer to him. 'She means too much to you, doesn't she?'

'No.'

'Everything you promised me wouldn't happen when you were with her is happening now. You care about her.'

'I care about justice.'

Amelia pulled the gun from his waistband and shoved it against his chest. 'Then prove it.'

CHAPTER 87

The beam of light illuminated two bright eyes.

Something was startled and scurried away, disappearing behind one of the concrete columns with a shriek that startled Claire.

She reached out in the dark and grabbed Stefan's arm.

'It was just a rat,' he said, swinging the torch around, illuminating the gap between them. 'You OK?'

She didn't answer.

Stefan shone the torch ahead of him.

What little daylight there was coming from the ramp they'd descended into the car park seemed even further away than he'd first thought. They'd walked as silently as they could, heading further into the cavernous space than either felt comfortable with.

'This torch is shit,' Stefan said, swinging it along the floor in a wide arc.

A concrete pillar came into view, peeling old white paint. They walked a little further and broken glass fragments made a popping sound under their feet with each step.

'And it reeks of piss down here.'

'Shut up. Give it to me,' Claire said, snatching the torch from him and illuminating the ground in front of them. The faded lines from a parking bay and a crushed takeaway box came into view. 'We shouldn't stray too far from the entrance.'

Stefan sighed. 'I'm already uncomfortable with this.'

'We need to find Manuela.'

'Without our eyes, going in blind? We don't know how many square feet we've got left to search for a vehicle that might not be here.'

The beam of light stopped.

Claire had stopped moving.

'You see that?' she said.

She felt Stefan come close beside her. He saw the dark spots of blood reflect back at him under the light.

'It's fresh.'

Claire slowly raised the torch and the back of a dark-blue van came into view, like it'd been creeping up on them in the darkness. She instinctively took a step back. 'The blood came from there,' she whispered.

'Where's it lead to?'

Claire shone the torch around slowly, her heart in her mouth, wary of what she might find. The blood led away from the van, and left an arc of droplets away from where they stood.

'Somebody's been dragged along here.'

They took a few steps forward, and the light soon reflected back at them off the steel doors of a lift.

Claire shone the torch off to the left, then the right, and saw a door leading to a stairwell to take them back to the surface.

'We need to check the van. Maybe Manuela—'

CRACK.

The sound cut Stefan off and seemed to engulf the space around them like a bomb had gone off, blasting in their ears.

The column next to Stefan was hit by something hard and he felt a fine mist of concrete against his face.

There was just enough time for Stefan to push Claire to the ground as another shot rang out and ricocheted off the lift doors.

Hitting the ground hard, Claire instinctively switched off the torch.

They can fucking see us!

'Smart move, guys.'

Claire froze at those words spoken in the dark.

Michael...

***

The torch light had been like a homing beacon for Michael when he'd crept through the door from the second stairwell on the other side of the car park.

They'd no idea he was there and he'd allowed himself a short while to gather his thoughts in the dark until they discovered the van.

He could think straight when Amelia wasn't there to feed the dark within him, to stoke the fire of revenge in his soul.

The first shot was only meant to be a warning shot. If it'd hit Stefan...too bad.

The second shot was aiming for Claire.

And who said I couldn't put a bullet in her?

***

There was an eerie silence. Claire tried to control her breathing, paranoid that each breath would allow Michael to home in on her and take her down.

She pressed her cheek firmly to the ground, feeling the rough surface scratch her skin. She couldn't even see her hand in front of her face. She listened hard but heard no footsteps.

Where's Stefan?

She didn't think he'd been hit but fear gripped her when she heard no signs of life from him. She stretched out her hand, clawing at the ground expecting to touch him, lying close to her.

He wasn't there.

Her eyes swivelled to one side. She saw the faint rectangle of light that managed to penetrate down the entrance ramp. It was about forty-five feet away.

Something suddenly gripped her arm.

She felt a hand clamp down on her mouth before she could make a sound.

'It's Stefan…'

He felt a shudder of relief run through her body. His mouth was close to her ear, his voice just above a whisper. 'He's waiting for us to move… You still got your phone?'

'There's no signal down here and he'll see the light if I unlock the screen. I'm not giving that bastard a target.'

'We've got to get to an exit.'

'We don't know what's waiting for us up the stairwell and we've got no weapons. We have to leave the way we came in,' she said in his ear. 'He can't shoot what he can't see.'

'He'll hear us if we run.'

Claire gripped the torch in one hand and held her BlackBerry in the other. She had to think, and fast.

They heard footsteps, faint but slowly getting closer, heading in their direction.

'I'm going to put the phone on the floor…take off your shoes, they make too much noise. Then get ready to move towards the entrance.' She felt Stefan rise up into a squatting position and carefully remove his shoes. 'Pray this works.'

She slipped off her own shoes, sucked in a deep breath and focused ahead.

Then she unlocked the screen.

CHAPTER 88

The display glowed bright, like a star in the night sky, right before the sound of another gunshot echoed around them. The light disappeared in fragments of plastic as the phone was obliterated.

Michael had taken the bait but it'd bought them only a fraction of the time they needed.

They moved fast, their feet barely making a sound on the concrete. Claire's hand was clasped in Stefan's. They had to stick together. If one lost their way, there was no going back for the other, not without a firearms team.

Then they heard it.

Heavy footfalls, coming out of the darkness, heading in their direction.

More shots rang out at random, zipping past them wide but it was enough to make them break out into a sprint.

As they neared the ramp leading up to the daylight ahead, Michael could see their silhouettes.

Another shot was fired and Claire felt a dead weight drag her down.

Stefan was hit.

Looking down at him, she had split seconds to decide what to do. His hand was still wrapped around hers. His eyes were closed, but she saw the rise and fall of his chest.

Then she felt Michael's body slam into hers.

Somehow she managed to stay on her feet and swung the torch around and made contact with the side of his head.

It didn't slow his reactions.

He pushed the gun into the middle of her forehead.

'Don't move.'

Claire's eyes shot to Stefan as he stirred on the floor, his eyes opening slowly.

Michael followed her gaze. 'It's not fatal, only a flesh wound,' he said, pressing the gun harder into her head. 'Feel like pleading for your life?'

CHAPTER 89

Amelia was untying Manuela from the table when she heard the sound of footsteps coming up the stairs.

Picking up the claw hammer, she edged closer to the door. When she saw Claire appear in the doorway, hands raised above her head, she felt her stomach tighten.

Then Michael appeared behind her, gun pointed at the back of her head, with his other hand dragging Stefan beside him.

'Get in there, against the far wall,' he said, shoving Stefan to the floor. He forcefully pushed the gun into the back of Claire's head. 'You too.'

Amelia watched as Stefan shuffled past her, one hand holding his shoulder, blood leaking through his fingers. He was followed by Claire.

As they stood against the wall at the back of the room, Stefan stared at Manuela sprawled out on the table ahead.

'What're you doing?' Amelia said. 'Why aren't they dead?'

Michael pushed past her and pulled Manuela to his feet, dragging him towards the door. 'Right now, they're worth more to us alive.'

Amelia shook her head. 'We don't need *both* of them.' Exchanging glances with Claire, Amelia still found herself looking away first.

Claire felt a cold shiver run through her body and beads of sweat formed along her hairline. She felt Stefan move closer to her. She gazed down at his free hand.

She saw his mobile.

She understood immediately.

Keep him talking.

'You need us, Michael.'

Both Michael and Amelia turned to face her.

'We don't need *you*,' Amelia said, pointing her finger with force. Claire kept her eyes on Michael's.

'You need us both if you're going to make it out of this whole thing alive, and you know it.'

His face looked pained as he let Manuela slump to the floor, turning to face her head on. '*This* is not what I wanted. I hoped you wouldn't remember this place.'

Stefan's face was neutral as his free hand worked the buttons of his mobile, hand turned, obscured behind the top of his thigh.

He closed his eyes, memorising the position of each button.

Claire shook her head. 'This isn't the way, Stephen…'

His lips hinted at a smile. 'You finally figured it out. There was a point when I thought I'd have to send you another letter.'

'Michael…you can't—'

'So it's back to *Michael* now?'

'What would you rather I call you?' She saw Amelia visibly stiffen at her words.

There was a long pause.

Michael smiled. 'I guess you can call me Stephen. Finally, the real me. Not what you expected when you first invited me into your bed.'

Stefan pressed a few more buttons and when he was ready to send, he opened his eyes.

Amelia was staring straight back at him. Her eyes shot down to his hand.

'He's got something,' she said, grabbing his hand, twisting it and pulling the phone from his fingers.

Stefan smirked.

Panic growing in her belly, Amelia looked down at the screen.

Sending...

Her eyes shot back to his. The phone beeped.

Sent.

Letting out a cry of rage she struck him hard across the face. Stefan's head swung to the side, flecks of blood spattering the wall from his split lip.

She read the sent message then grabbed the gun from Michael.

***

Matthews was standing in the gardens of the Manor when his phone beeped in his pocket.

He'd been waiting for a call from Claire about Hatton Court, the abandoned office complex, to see what the next plan of action was. 'About time,' he said, looking at the mobile screen.

1 New Msg – DI Fletcher.

It took Matthews less than a minute to realise what was happening after he'd read the text.

He dialled Hertfordshire Constabulary HQ and waited. When he was put through to the specialist firearms officer, he was blunt when he spoke.

'We're going to need some ARVs and a tactical advisor immediately.'

CHAPTER 90

Michael held up Stefan's phone in front of his eyes, dropped it to the floor and stamped on it. 'You'll regret that,' he hissed, his face close to Stefan's.

Amelia pushed the gun against his forehead. 'How much time do we have?'

Stefan grinned, revealing his blood-stained teeth. 'Not long enough.'

Michael lowered Amelia's hand. 'Not yet.' His eyes crossed to Claire. 'We've got to move them higher up.'

***

Manuela's blood was oozing from his wounds and he babbled aimlessly as Michael hauled him up to the fourth floor. Amelia followed behind Claire and Stefan, gun aimed at their backs.

Michael pushed Manuela into the corner of a small room, which had no furniture, save for another office desk and old power cables.

Manuela was slumped upright, one hand clasping at a gaping wound at his side. He was drifting in and out of consciousness with the pain and his blood pressure was starting to fall dangerously low.

When Claire and Stefan were sat on the other side of the room, Michael took hold of Amelia's arm, pulling her to him.

'We must make our stand here.'

She stared at him and nodded. He pulled her closer and kissed her hard on the lips before handing her the dagger that had been used to take Rebecca's life. 'When the time comes, make it count, no matter what comes into the building.'

'Where are you going?'

'I'll be outside on the landing. I need time to think.'

'We can get away if we leave now. We have the van.'

'We can't move Manuela again. He's lost too much blood. He'd be dead before we made it out of the city.'

CHAPTER 91

Michael sat on the top of the stairs, his head resting in his hands. A fierce headache was creeping across his forehead from his temple where Claire had struck him with the torch.

He tried to think straight.

He'd often thought long and hard about having to kill Claire if it came to it and many a time he'd feared he wouldn't be able to. Any feelings he held for her amounted to nothing if it came down to the last resort.

The moment when he'd pushed the gun against her forehead and looked into her eyes, he'd seen her fear.

It had made him feel powerful.

He sat there, trying to immerse himself back into the moment and relive the feeling, and time slipped past in a blur.

Then he heard Amelia screaming for him.

Racing back into the room, he saw Amelia by the window. Claire and Stefan were where he'd left them and Manuela appeared to be unconscious again.

He ran to Amelia when he heard the sirens.

Below them, pulling into the forecourt, were several Armed Response Vehicles crewed by Authorised Firearms Officers highly trained for hostage rescues and major incidents.

Michael felt his stomach roll.

He grabbed Amelia forcefully by the arm. 'Take him to the roof,' he said, kicking Manuela in the leg. 'Get up!'

Manuela groaned in pain as he was pulled to his feet. Amelia took his full weight as he draped his arm across her shoulders.

'He's too heavy.'

Michael gripped her chin, forcing her look at him. 'You stay strong. You have to do this…you *can* do this.' Amelia's eyes misted over as reality hit her.

They might not be coming out of this together.

Her eyes stared at Claire. 'You kill her. Don't let her walk out of this.'

Michael leaned forward and kissed her. 'Remember Rebecca… Make it count.'

He helped them out of the door and waited until Amelia had climbed the first flight of stairs to the fifth floor before turning back into the room, staring at Claire.

She took a step back.

'You,' he said. 'Come here.'

***

Specialist Firearms Officer Brendan Warren shook his head at Christoph Adler as he spoke.

'The risk's too great. We've got two officers up there with a civilian held hostage. We can't delay this. We need a plan and fast.'

Adler was a Tactical Advisor with over fifteen years' experience and he was not about to be harassed into making any rash decisions under pressure from anyone. He distanced himself from Warren as he spoke.

'We need to think this through. I need plans of the building. I need to see the exits.'

'We don't have time for that.'

Both men turned to stare at another AFO who had come up to them, his voice serious.

His face showed his hesitation, uncertainty gripping his body. 'We've got movement up on the fourth floor.

CHAPTER 92

Michael shoved Claire's body forward, leaning her torso right out of the broken window, its sharp edges digging into her stomach. He gripped the back of her shirt, as he leaned against her back.

When he saw officers looking up, he raised the gun, aiming it down on Claire's head.

'I'll shoot her, you hear me?' he shouted down. He felt Claire stiffen. 'Make any attempt to enter the building and I'll fucking shoot her, I swear to God.'

***

Amelia jumped as she heard gunfire but her eyes never left Manuela's.

They were sitting just feet from the door that led to the roof, sprawled on the floor, breathless. Amelia's strength was waning. She pulled at the dagger and stared at the blade.

Manuela's eyes felt so heavy he could barely follow her movements.

In a few moments, he knew, the pain in this life would be over, and he was preparing himself to start a new kind of torment on the other side. This was what he deserved.

This was now his fate and now he longed for it.

***

Claire felt like her eardrums were bursting as Michael fired at the officers below. Then, before she could open her eyes to see if anyone had been hit, he pulled her back from the window with such force, she went crashing down onto the floor.

She pressed the palms of her hands against her ears, her teeth gritted with the pain.

'How many more people have to die, Michael?' she said, as Stefan crawled towards her.

'You stay where you are!' Michael said, pointing the gun at him. When Stefan was back against the wall, he reloaded the gun.

'They were warning shots,' he said, crouching down to Claire's eye level. 'Don't you think I know how these things work, how they usually play out?'

'We can negotiate.'

'I've got a senior officer held hostage…as long as they know I'm serious about killing you all, they won't make any rash decisions. They'll be too busy trying to work out the best way to take me and Amelia down with the minimum threat to life possible.'

'Let Manuela go,' she said, pushing herself back. 'He's suffered like you wanted. If we can get him to hospital now, there may be a chance to save him.'

'Before his heart gives out?' Michael laughed and shook his head. 'No can do. Do you know what he did to poor little Rebecca?'

'The investigation will be reopened. Let us bring her killer to justice the right way.'

Michael acted like he didn't hear her. 'He cut her throat so deep, the blade sliced through every piece of tissue, every muscle, right down to the bone.'

Claire shook her head. 'None of this will bring her back.'

'He nearly took off her head!'

'You don't care about Rebecca Turner!' she screamed in his face. 'This has never really been about her, has it? This was just what pushed Amelia over the edge.'

Michael looked away, gritted his teeth.

'I'm right, aren't I?' His silence only confirmed it. 'Christ...' she said, shaking her head in disbelief. 'Why, Michael? None of this was worth it.'

He pressed the barrel of the gun into her temple. 'All my life I've been shoved from foster home to foster home, nobody giving a fuck about me,' he said, saliva misting her face. 'I had my fair share of physical and mental abuse at the hands of people who should've been there to protect me.

'I felt like dying. I nearly succeeded once. One day I swallowed a load of pills and enough alcohol to put me in a fucking coma but I was saved, and I came to live with Mark Jenkins and everything changed.'

Claire swallowed hard. 'Amelia...' she said.

He nodded. 'The only constant in my life, the one who kept me grounded, and even then I couldn't stop what was happening to her. Do you know how old she was when Manuela raped her?'

Claire slowly closed her eyes, not wanting to hear any more, but he shook her, and pressed the gun harder against her head. 'It only stopped when she reached fifteen. He only ever liked them *really* young.'

'You could've told someone. You could've—'

'Could've *stopped* it?' he said, cutting her off. 'You think anyone would've believed someone like me, like *us*, over them? The saints of the fucking community?'

'This won't help you or Amelia. If she's who you really care about, then you need to end this now.'

'Spare me the mind-fucking games. It won't work on me. You forget, I've trained and prepared for this day since I was sixteen…and I've got plenty of time to decide how and when you both die too,' he said, glancing at Stefan. 'So,' he said, 'any last requests?'

Claire stared back into his eyes, seeing their true colour for the first time since he'd stepped into her life.

The ice-blue irises rivalled her own in intensity like none she'd ever seen before.

'Are you ready to die?' he pressed.

'Don't…'

'Come on, Claire, I thought you liked the bad-boy type,' he mocked.

She glanced towards Stefan, then back to Michael. He was barely recognisable to her now. 'I don't believe I was nothing to you,' she said.

He paused. 'You were a distraction, a means to an end.'

'That's bullshit, and you know it.'

He grinned then. 'OK,' he said. 'OK, I'll admit, there was part of me that wanted to confess everything… What is it they say about lying? Keep it as close to the truth as possible? I did mean a lot of what I said. What we had, whatever it was, did mean something, as fucked up as it was, but…' He trailed off. '*We* never did have a future together. Even if I wanted it.'

Claire leaned her face in closer to his. 'I don't believe you want to hurt me.'

Michael paused, mulling over her words, studying her face, remembering back to the day he first met her. Then his resolve hardened.

'What I feel towards you is nothing compared to Amelia. When she hurts, *I* hurt.'

'Michael…*please*…'

'You played with fire and now you've been burnt.' He leaned in closer. 'Nothing you can say or do will stop us.'

'Even if means life behind bars?'

He regarded her for a few seconds.

'You know what they do to policemen in jail.' Her face pulled into a look of defiance. 'You wouldn't last five minutes.'

His eyes grew angry and narrowed into thin slits.

Without warning, Claire brought her forehead forward with all her strength and struck him hard across the bridge of his nose.

There was a sickening crack as blood exploded across his face. He bellowed in pain, instinctively grabbing his nose. He dropped the gun, which skidded across the floor.

Stefan seized his chance, and ignoring the pain in his body, he reached for the gun.

***

It'd taken most of her strength to haul Manuela those last few feet, but she was now closer than ever to her goal.

Amelia pushed her way through the metal door and dumped Manuela in the middle of the roof.

Her arms ached and her breath caught in her throat. She doubled over, hands resting against her thighs.

After taking several deep breaths, she stumbled towards the edge of the building and dared a look over the top. The wind nearly caught her off balance.

Realising it wouldn't take much to take her off the top, she cautiously stepped back a few paces.

***

Michael's fist made contact with Claire's jaw, sending her sprawling across the floor just as Stefan grabbed the gun.

But Michael was too quick.

He kicked the gun from Stefan's hand and stamped on his wounded shoulder, sending Stefan's nerves into overdrive as pain shot through his body.

'That was stupid,' Michael said, looking back at Claire, gesturing towards Stefan. 'And you'd choose *this* as a partner over me?'

He laughed, eyes turning back to Stefan, just as pain shot through the back of his knee.

Stefan's boot struck him with such force that Michael's legs buckled instantly. Stefan launched himself forward, ignoring the crippling pain in his shoulder, and pinned Michael down.

Claire pushed herself to her feet.

She stared at Stefan.

'Go!' he said. 'Stop Amelia!'

CHAPTER 93

Amelia hauled Manuela up on his feet when she heard the footfalls ascending the stairwell to the roof. She raised the dagger to his throat as the door was kicked open.

Her eyes instantly met Claire's.

She backed away, closer to the edge of the roof. Manuela was slumped to one side, her body struggling to hold his weight.

Claire stepped forward slowly. 'It's over, Amelia. You need to stop this. Let me get Manuela to a hospital.'

'It's not over until I spill every last drop of his blood right here across the concrete.'

'You know I can't and won't let you do that, Amelia. The place is surrounded…and we have Michael.'

'My Stevie?'

Her hand moved away from Manuela's throat. Her eyes misted with tears as the gravity of Claire's words hit home.

After a few seconds, her face changed into a look of defiance. She tightened her grip around Manuela's body. 'I don't believe you, bitch. Stevie would *never* let himself be taken. Not alive. We made a pact.'

Claire saw a window of opportunity and took it. She edged closer. 'He didn't put up much of a fight when DI Fletcher handcuffed him.'

Amelia glared at her.

'Or maybe he was just in too much pain to care once I'd shattered his nose.'

'Stay back!'

Claire froze before slowly circling her way out onto the rooftop.

The sound of gunfire startled them both.

Claire tried to remain focused on Amelia. She prayed the gunshots were from the AFOs and all this would soon be over.

Manuela suddenly jerked, crying out in despair, before slipping into unconsciousness again. Amelia began to waver under his weight and Claire knew she was growing tired.

Several more shots rang out and this time Claire heard a scream before there fell an eerie silence and the wind seemed to disappear at the same moment.

She risked a glance towards the door to the roof.

'Looks like things aren't going to your plan, Chief Inspector.' The expression on Claire's face grew tense. 'You think someone like *you* can make a difference? You'll not stop us… Stevie's under my control, not yours.'

Claire heard the door behind her swing open, the hinges whining under the strain.

Amelia smiled as Michael emerged, covered in both his own drying blood and spatter marks, fresh red in colour. His eyes fixed upon Claire and he raised a gun.

The one he'd just used to beat Stefan with.

Claire's world seemed to be crashing down around her.

'Shoot her!'

Amelia's words were barely audible above a roar of wind, which whipped around them with force.

Michael swallowed hard, trying to keep his hand steady. He aimed the gun at the point between Claire's eyes.

But he hesitated.

And Claire saw it in his eyes.

'You know we can stop this here. I can help you if you come quietly,' she said, trying to keep her voice steady.

'Just fucking shoot her. What the hell are you waiting for?'

Michael glanced at Amelia and then back to Claire, who shook her head.

'You're better than this. Let me help you.'

'Don't listen to her, Stevie. She doesn't know us, how Rebecca suffered, or anything about what we have.'

Claire saw her angle and seized her chance. 'You know I never had you as being the follower, Diego. Even with me, you always rebelled.'

'Don't listen to her, Stevie, she's fucking with your head!'

Claire edged closer towards him. 'She really does call all the shots, doesn't she?'

He remained silent, his jaw fixed and set like stone.

'Put the gun down now and we can talk, before armed officers enter this building. They'll shoot to kill if mine or Manuela's life is at immediate risk. You know that… This is your last chance.'

'No, Claire,' Michael said, 'it's yours. Nobody will be shooting anyone if you're already dead.' He moved closer to her. 'There's no way Manuela is walking away from this and I will kill you if you stand in my way.'

Frantically searching the space around her, for something, *anything*, to arm herself with, Claire felt desperation taking hold when she saw there was nothing.

Michael looked at Manuela on the floor, curled up into the foetal position.

Pathetic…

'Amelia…kill him. Do it slowly.'

She smiled and looked at Claire. 'With pleasure.'

She lifted the dagger again.

'Amelia, don't. This won't bring Rebecca back,' Claire said, the strain unmistakeable in her voice.

Amelia raised the dagger and brought it down into Manuela's chest with force. Claire screamed out and charged towards them.

Michael fired the gun and the bullet whizzed past her head, and she threw herself towards the floor, rolling as she hit the concrete.

She landed in front of Manuela. His eyes were now wide, silently pleading with her. The dagger had missed his heart, but he didn't have much time left. If he fell unconscious again, it would be a darkness he'd never recover from.

Claire looked up, her eyes locking with Amelia's as she launched herself forward, the dagger raised.

The next few seconds seemed to pass in slow motion for Claire, as she instinctively threw her body into Amelia's, twisted her arm around and buried the dagger into her thigh, driving the blade through to the hilt. She felt a mist of blood spray her face.

Claire heard Michael scream out Amelia's name as he ran towards her, his arms outstretched.

Amelia staggered back, pulling the dagger out in one fluid motion and let the blade drop through her fingers.

She stumbled back towards the edge of the roof.

Michael reached for her, pulling her against him.

Amelia turned her face from his, eyes gazing over the edge. She felt the sadness grip her, as it had done many times before, only this time was different. This time she only saw one end.

And she didn't fear it.

She could take Manuela's life. She didn't care what happened to her afterwards so long as her Stevie was with her.

Life was nothing if she didn't have him.

She looked back into his eyes.

'Stay with me.'

Her words were choked as they escaped her lips. Michael's eyes narrowed as he followed her gaze over his shoulder towards Claire. 'I won't lose you to her... As long as you're here, she's won.'

Claire backed away from them, her bones aching under the strain as she tried to push herself up from the floor.

Michael looked back at Amelia when he felt her fingers bite into the skin at his waist. 'I don't understand,' he said.

'I told you I wanted you forever...' She blinked hard, the pain in her thigh unbearable. She almost dropped to the floor, but his arms held her tighter.

'I *am* yours forever,' he said.

Amelia shook her head. 'There's only ever been one way out of this.'

'We can negotiate our way out, buy ourselves some time to make a break for it,' he said. He gripped her arms tighter. 'We're not done yet.' He looked back towards Claire. 'She's our ticket out of here.'

Claire saw the gun still clasped in his hand. If she tried to run, she knew she wouldn't stand a chance.

Amelia pulled Michael closer to her, her arms gripping him by the waist. Her chin rested against his shoulder, her eyes closed. She leaned up and kissed his cheek.

Then her eyes opened and she looked straight at Claire.

Claire realised what was about to happen, the feeling hitting her full force like she'd been punched in the stomach.

'Amelia, no!' she screamed, her body lurching forward.

Grasping Michael tight against her, Amelia stepped off the edge.

CHAPTER 94

SFO Brendan Warren saw the blood splattered over the wall and feared the worst. He and a team of AFOs had stormed the building after they heard the second lot of gunfire after Michael had shot at officers on the ground.

He feared the worst when he caught sight of Stefan lying on the ground ahead of him.

He felt his heart sink.

He pushed his fingers against Stefan's neck and waited.

He breathed a sigh of relief when he felt a steady pulse beat beneath his fingers. He searched for any other gunshot wounds other than to Stefan's shoulder but found none.

He looked up and saw bullet holes in the walls ahead of him that appeared to have been fired at random.

He carefully pushed Stefan's head to one side. It was then he saw the huge gash to his right temple where Michael had beaten him with the gun.

***

Looking down over the edge of the roof, Claire saw they lay as they had fallen.

Amelia's eyes were open, in a lifeless cold stare. Her hair was now a darker shade of red, matted in her own blood.

Michael was lying on top of her, head hung forward over her shoulder, blood leaking from his forehead.

Claire was glad she couldn't see his face.

She knew the shape of his mouth, his face and colour of his skin wouldn't look like the man she'd once known.

Her vision clouded.

Everything that was happening around her didn't feel real any more. She felt like she was walking in a nightmare of her own creation.

A nightmare she tried frantically to wake from.

CHAPTER 95

Five weeks later

Stefan poked his head around Claire's office door, which she had propped open to let some air circulate. When he saw his presence had gone unnoticed, he gently coughed. Claire looked up, startled at first, but then her face softened.

'Come in, Fletch. Have a seat.' Stefan sat and gave half a smile. 'What can I do for you?'

'Just came to see if there were any developments, and ask how you were. It's my first day back and I feel like a mushroom…kept in the dark and fed on shit.'

She nodded but didn't smile.

Her eyes were dull and all the life seemed to have been sucked from her. 'Well,' she said, anger in her voice, 'after reading the investigation into Rebecca's disappearance, it's looking like a complete botched job. Failings on all counts and the press are going to have a field day.'

'Shit.'

'Yep, and it'll be hitting the fan soon,' she said, leaning back in her chair. 'DI Benedict was in charge of Rebecca's disappearance at the time… We've got a whole load of evidence that was overlooked, statements that didn't add up and now Rebecca's parents are calling for an inquiry.

'Jane and Harper are liaising with Norfolk's CID department into identifying the body washed ashore in Cromer.'

Stefan nodded. 'Anybody's guess who that was.'

'Probably someone who wouldn't be missed. Then there's the Jenkins family. Mark at least knew of some of the cruelty aimed at Amelia and Stephen whilst under Manuela's care. He's been charged.'

'Yeah, I read that.' He ran his hands through his hair and exhaled as he digested her words. 'Any news on a date for Manuela's trial?'

'Due to be announced shortly is all I've been told. Depending on his health, of course. Despite his injuries, the old dog's got a lot of strength left in him… He will pay for what he's done, Fletch. There'll be no easy way out for him.'

Stefan nodded but remained silent, casting his mind back to Manuela's wounds. Not many would have survived the trauma. Somehow he did.

Some might call that divine intervention.

There remained a long pause before Stefan braved the subject he knew she'd be expecting.

'And how are you coping?'

She didn't look up but shrugged her shoulders.

'As well as can be expected, I guess. I even get to have private counselling sessions… I convinced the panel I was ready to return to work.'

She picked up her cup of water and drained it. Then she stared out of her window.

'*Are* you ready?' She avoided his eyes and didn't offer any response. 'You did all you could, Claire.'

'Did I?' she said immediately, as if she'd predicted his words before he'd even thought them. 'Maybe I didn't, Fletch. Maybe I could've reasoned with him more, talked him round. Maybe tried harder.'

'I think he was beyond reasoning by then. He would've killed you and he shot me, not to mention beat me unconscious.'

She paused and processed his words.

'Suicide was never an option for him. He didn't want to die. He had choices but Amelia took that away from him.' A shiver ran through her body. 'I keep…I keep seeing him fall. I keep hearing him hit the ground.'

Stefan leaned across and tried to catch her eye but she refused to look at him.

'You can't forget what he did, Claire. No matter how much you try and justify his actions.' He let his words hang for a moment. 'And you can't forget about what he did to poor Chloe.'

'I haven't!' She swung around in her chair. 'I was going to visit her today.'

Stefan frowned. 'She's still in hospital.'

'I know.'

'But you hate hospitals.'

'For her, I'll make the exception.' She pushed herself out of her chair. 'I was told she woke up yesterday. First time since he…' She broke off as she felt a lump in her throat.

This side of Claire Winters was unknown to most people.

Rude, feisty, cold and arrogant were understood, even if they weren't accepted by many, but this new-found sense of empathy was treading on new territory.

Stefan had been trying his best to stick by her over the last few weeks since she'd watched Amelia take Michael's – *Stevie's* – life.

It hadn't been easy.

'It's OK, Claire…to grieve I mean.'

Once Claire heard his words, it was as if someone had flicked a switch and she seemed to shake off her self-pity.

'Oh, fuck off, Fletch.' She sniffed and gave him a smile. 'I'm not quite ready for that yet.'

Stefan smiled and shook his head. 'Maybe not yet, but it's nice to see you're not completely dead inside as everybody thinks.'

'Yeah, I'm everybody's walking contradiction.' She didn't wait for him to answer. 'I'll be gone for a few hours. You think you can hold the fort for a while until I get back?'

'Is that a promotion I hear coming?'

Claire looked at him as she slung her bag over her shoulder. 'Don't push your luck,' she said as she walked past him.

It was only after she'd left the incident room that she found herself smiling genuinely for the first time in weeks.

CHAPTER 96

Chloe's eyes opened, squinting under the fluorescent hospital lights. She glanced at the blinds blocking out the sunshine from the window to her left and wished she had enough strength to get out of bed and pull them.

She'd known darkness for far too long these past weeks.

She was about to reach for the red call button when she heard footsteps approaching.

The handle on the door moved and then the door opened.

Chloe's eyes widened, not with fear, but sheer surprise as Claire Winters walked through the door. She thought there was some hint of a smile on her face but she couldn't be sure.

Claire hovered in the doorway.

'Can I come in? I wasn't sure if you would be up for visitors or not.'

Chloe grimaced. 'Did you bring grapes?'

'Erm…should I have?'

Chloe waved her hand for her to close the door. 'God, no. I *hate* grapes. Joe brought me some earlier, and I haven't the heart to tell him.'

'Your boss Joe?'

'Yeah. He's been coming to see me the whole time I was out. Kinda nice of him, huh?'

Claire nodded, even though deep down she thought the loathsome man was one of the last people she'd want to see. Then she realised that Chloe quite literally had no one else.

She pulled up a chair from the corner and sat down beside the bed but said nothing.

Chloe looked at her with her head cocked to one side and after a minute had passed she laughed.

'Usually when people visit they talk.'

Claire raised her eyes from the floor and smiled. 'Sorry. I'm just not used to this.'

'Yeah, I can tell… Is this a social call or police business?'

'Social.' Chloe waited for her to elaborate. 'I felt I should come, considering what happened with Mich—' She broke off mid-sentence. 'I mean Stephen.'

Chloe looked down at her hands and picked at her nails.

'You weren't to know,' she said at length. 'But it means a lot that you came.'

Just at that moment they were startled by the door swinging open and Joe Carter walked into the room. His face looked angry, especially when he clapped eyes on Claire.

'You!' he said, pointing a finger at her. 'I knew it was you when the nurse described Chloe's new visitor. Why are you here? Haven't you caused enough heartache? Chloe could've died, but I don't suppose that even mattered to you, did it? You lot are all the same.'

Claire stood up and raised her hands to calm him. 'I'm here as a friend.'

Carter sneered at her.

'You left her at the mercy of that head case. You need to get out before I throw you out.'

'No, Joe, it's OK. I want her to stay. Please, just come see me later,' Chloe said.

Carter sucked in a few deep breaths and went to speak again, but saw the look on Chloe's face. Looking back at Claire, he nodded reluctantly.

'I want you gone within the next half hour.'

For once, Claire decided to let him have the final word.

Carter leaned in to Chloe and kissed her on the forehead. 'She gives you any trouble, just use the call button,' he said, handing it to her.

Chloe rolled her eyes but took it regardless. After he had left she turned to Claire, throwing the call button on the bed.

'Sorry about that.'

Claire sat back down again and stared at her sad eyes. 'Why is he suddenly all over you? I got the impression you loathed him.'

Chloe shrugged hard and stared at the window.

'I guess I just need somebody. That's why I had been accepting his dinner dates. You know, when I saw Father Wainwright in that restaurant? That was our second date.'

She smiled to herself, and then looked at the blinds. 'Can you open those for me, please? I'm longing to see the sun.'

Claire obliged and they both squinted as the sunlight filled the room. Afterwards Claire returned to her seat.

'How would you feel if I organised some help for you?'

Chloe looked away from her and thought for a moment. 'What kind of help? Counselling, I take it?'

'Yes.'

'No, thanks.'

'Why not?'

'Because I don't need that kind of help,' she said, staring at Claire. She reached for Claire's hand and held it tight. 'I just need a friend.' Claire was taken aback but found herself holding her hand in return.

'If that's what you need, and I can help, I will,' she said, her voice genuine. 'Who knows, maybe I'll benefit from it too.'

'Do you think I could do something else with my life, Chief Inspector? That'd be pretty much a miracle in itself.'

Claire smiled. 'Call me Claire. And you shouldn't talk like that. I can help you get out of the stripping, if that's what you truly want?'

Chloe nodded and smiled back at her. A resounding unspoken yes in a silent room.

Claire paused, went to speak again, but found it hard to say the words.

'What is it?' Chloe said.

Claire shifted in her seat. 'How close did you get to Amelia?' Chloe avoided her eyes. 'You don't have to tell me now.'

'It's painful to talk about,' Chloe said. 'Guess I should just accept the fact that I did love her...*once*.'

'You got in the way of her and Stephen, didn't you?'

Chloe nodded. 'I was drawn to her, like everyone else.' She sighed. 'She chose him over me, though, which was for the best, I see that now. Our relationship was toxic, but I loved her.' She smiled sadly to herself. 'Stupid of me.'

'You were young. She had a hold on you.'

Chloe nodded, fighting back tears. She used the back of her hand to wipe them away, while the other hand clasped the locket around her neck. Something Claire had begun to notice she did when stressed.

'My father,' Chloe said, suddenly. 'What will happen to him?'

'He's not going to avoid a prison sentence, if that's what you mean.'

Chloe lowered her eyes. 'Good. I hope he and Manuela suffer and rot for what they did.'

'Your father didn't murder anyone, Chloe.'

'No, but he knew things that he kept quiet. After all these years, I've realised that what he did, how he treated Amelia and Stephen, was wrong. Maybe I could've done more. Maybe they wouldn't have ended up like they did. Guess I'll never know now.'

Claire shrugged.

'You think they were born to be like that, don't you?'

Claire was a little taken aback by her statement.

'It can be difficult for those left behind to try and get their head around something like this. I've seen enough crimes to know who was a product of their environment and who was born to do evil things.' Claire left her seat and stood by the window.

Chloe shut her eyes. 'I think about what my parents knew, about what they might have concealed. I can't forgive them. I *won't* forgive them. Whatever Amelia and Stephen became, my parents were part of that.'

'There's no chance of reconciliation, then?'

'Not a chance.'

'Not even with your mother?'

Chloe took a moment to think. Deep down she did still love her mother, but whenever she felt the urge to pick up the phone and hear her voice, she made herself remember why her life had turned out the way it had so far.

She shook her head.

'I can't forgive her. Too much has passed between us.' Claire nodded and looked back out of the window, her arms folded tightly. 'If it were your mother, would you?'

Claire smiled.

'Oh, my mother is far worse.' She walked closer to the bed, her face serious again. 'Only you can be the judge of your own decisions, Chloe. Make sure you're cutting her off for the right reasons.'

CHAPTER 97

Four months later

Claire pulled her car up to the small quaint house and turned to her passenger.

'There you go. Same time next week?'

Chloe Jenkins pulled her bag from the back seat and got out of the car. 'Yeah, sure thing. You know, I think the college course is working. All I want to do is try out all the recipes.'

Claire smiled and looked over the top of her sunglasses.

'The next Nigella in the making. I'll expect an invite to your first dinner party.'

Chloe smiled and Claire waited until she let herself into her new home before driving off.

***

Chloe watched her drive away, and stood by the window, peeking out through the slats in the blinds until the car was out of sight.

Then the mask slipped.

She sighed to herself, and longed to leave this place. It'd been four months now since everything came to its ugly conclusion. She opened the drawer to the sideboard beside her and stared down at the money she'd been withdrawing in lumps from her bank account over the last few months.

Soon she'd be away from this place. Free to start again where nobody knew her name or her past.

She reached for the locket around her neck, undid the clasp, and held it in the palm of her hand. She traced a finger over the front of the oval-shaped design before popping the catch that held it closed.

A spiral of red hair fell into her hand, and Chloe coiled it around her fingers and smiled. Instinctively she turned her wrist and looked down at her tattoo. She still remembered the day she'd got it. It had been the day Amelia had walked out of her family home.

She traced the curves of the design with the finger of her other hand.

To anyone else it was a meaningless design, something almost tribal, insignificant. At certain angles that would be true.

To Chloe, all she had to do was bring her hand up, bending her arm at the elbow, wrist towards her face and the image of the 'A' would give her the strength she needed.

Chloe closed her eyes and remembered the day she'd started the fire in the Chapel. The image was always so vivid that she could still smell the smoke, hear the crackle of the flames as it tore through the building, destroying everything in its path.

After the flames, the memory was the same.

Amelia's call after she'd broken out of Stokebrook.

It was an image that still cut Chloe deeply. Amelia had it all worked out, and Chloe tagged along for the ride.

Chloe shut the locket, squeezed it hard in her hand until it hurt.

She let it fall to the floor, and she kicked it under the sofa. In her other hand she clasped the lock of Amelia's hair.

She took it to the kitchen and ignited the gas hob on the cooker. She took a deep breath, held it until she thought her lungs might burst, before expelling the breath, and dropping the lock into the flames.

She watched it curl and disintegrate to nothing, the smell of burning hair, sickly and sweet, filling the kitchen.

It had taken every ounce of her strength to block out the past. This was her only way forward.

She shuddered at the memory of the young woman they'd found, sleeping rough on the Cromer streets. She was perfect, with her fair complexion, slight build, with long flowing red hair, greasy and hanging in limp tendrils across her face, hiding the sadness of her eyes, the light having long since left them.

Plied with alcohol and drugs, she'd put up no resistance when they'd both smothered her with the woman's own grotty pillow, one of her only processions.

After they'd changed the woman's clothes, Chloe had flinched when they'd dropped her body into the sea, the darkness of the rough water swallowing her whole, the strong current dragging her out along with the other discarded rubbish.

Chloe had told herself she'd done this woman, whoever she was, a great service, ending her misery once and for all.

Even after this, all she'd risked for her, Amelia had still raced back into Stephen's arms.

From that day on, Chloe distanced herself from their memory for the most part.

She'd got away with her secrets intact.

Amelia and Stephen were now gone.

Very soon, Chloe would be too.

***

Claire was tapping out a beat on the steering wheel, in time to the bassline of the song playing out on the radio. For the first time in weeks she felt content. Happy, even.

As she was about to take the turning towards Hexton she changed her mind. She drove through Haverbridge and on to Harwood Park Crematorium in Stevenage.

She parked the car and glanced at her phone. There was one new text message from a number she didn't recognise.

I hope one day you'll see it in your heart to visit me.

Claire stared at the words, confused at first, then realised there was only one person it could be from.

Her father.

She wondered how he could've got her new number, then realised it must have been the new carers that'd passed it on when Claire had updated her contact details with them, weeks after Manuela was arrested.

She held the phone in her palm, thumb hovering between *reply* and *delete*.

She took a deep breath and held it. When she released it again she hit the *delete* button.

She pocketed the phone and headed towards the row of plaques she had visited frequently over the last few months.

She counted along each one until she came to the one she used to dread seeing.

She reached her fingers forward and traced the lines, twists and curls of the inscription.

In loving memory of Michael Diego.

That was all Claire could bring herself to write when she'd dealt with the aftermath of his death.

Michael had no living relatives that could be traced, not even his real mother. Claire couldn't bear to see him laid to rest in a pauper's grave, despite what he'd done.

She'd deliberately not used his real name; she simply couldn't bring herself to. In her eyes he was still her colleague, once her friend and lover, and that was how she would remember him, despite everything.

She stood there deep in thought, and was only disturbed by the sudden wind which picked up around her.

She looked towards the trees that surrounded the perimeter and pulled her cardigan tightly around her. She squinted at the line of trees when she thought she saw a blaze of red hair behind them.

Amelia's red hair.

After watching for several minutes she thought back to the nightmares she'd suffered with for many a night, deprived of sleep for the first few months since Amelia had taken Michael's life.

She remembered a quote she'd once read by George Eliot.

Our dead are never dead to us, until we have forgotten them.

Claire took a slow walk back to her car, and committed herself to finally accepting Michael's death. Accepting, but never forgetting, she took comfort in the fact that in time the pain would ease.

As she sat in her car and stared out towards the trees, the red hair she thought she'd seen faded to black in her mind – Amelia forgotten, damned in her own personal Hell, without her Guardian.

Where she belonged.

Still reeling from *For All Our Sins*? Keep reading
for an extract from *The Principle of Evil*, book two
in T.M.E. Walsh's addictive DCI Claire
Winters series…

PART ONE

Present Day

5th November

'Don't run… don't run from me.'

There, deep in the wood, she hears the voice again. The same voice that had haunted her, followed her desperately. Relentlessly for months.

'Don't run, wait for me. I can offer you so much more if you'd only let me.'

But she cannot stop. She cannot learn to walk through this world again, not while the fear has a hold of her body, heart and soul.

She runs down the track through the trees. She cannot place the voice, nor tell if it's male or female. It rings like a cacophony of sounds in her head.

She risks a glance down at her feet. They are bare once again, deep in the snow. The forest floor beneath the ice scratches at her skin, and she leaves drops of blood in her wake.

She panics.

Someone will follow her home, chasing the scarlet trail left behind. But where is home? She cannot find it. Ahead, there is nothing but forest.

The mist circles the trees around her, the same as every time she sees them.

This world is stripped. Void of colour. Void of time.

Her heart pounds in her chest, but she can never understand who or what she runs from. Inside, the only thing that is always certain, is the fear. It relentlessly courses through her veins.

She sees the clearing ahead. She wants to turn the other way. She has been here time and time before, but never understands why. A force is driving her forward, which she cannot control. She runs as if the hounds of hell were at her heels.

She reaches the clearing… stops.

The voice is there, behind her.

She turns; ready to confront whatever it is that hunts her...

It's Him.

As she feared it would be; a ghost from the past.

She's almost afraid to look into his eyes, but when she does, she sees there is nothing there but darkness. Hollow pits where brilliant eyes once shone.

He reaches out, and before she can stop him, his hand grabs her hair, ripping clumps out by the roots.

Then fingers are at her chest. They tear through icy flesh, nails scratching against bone, against ribs, hungry for her heart.

As she cries out, his mouth opens in a silent scream, blood pouring out from within.

CHAPTER 1

Detective Chief Inspector Claire Winters bolted upright,
eyes snapping open.

She was shrouded in darkness and it took her several
seconds to realise where she was as her eyes adjusted to
her surroundings.

Her head was spinning but soon the shadows stopped
moving and became solid shapes, pieces of furniture she
soon began to recognise in her living room.

Her hands grabbed at her chest, which was slick
with sweat despite the chill of the room. A sigh of relief
shuddered through her body when she realised her skin,
flesh and bone were still intact.

She pushed back the stray strands of blonde hair from
her face, and then held her head in her hands. Night terrors
had become part of her, almost feeling as physical as
something she wore, but it was no badge of honour.

That one had been one of the worst she'd had in the last
year. Usually they followed the same familiar pattern, but
with subtle differences.

She sucked in a deep breath, held it until her chest ached.

Despite knowing who it was she ran from by the end
of each frantic nightmare, this was the first time she'd
actually seen Him – or at least some twisted version
of Him.

Her hands slid down her face, wiping back tears that had begun to fall. Ice-blue coloured eyes glassed over as she eventually let the tears fall freely, staining the pale flesh of her cheeks.

A loud bang outside made her jump, bolting off the sofa, stumbling over the blanket that had fallen at her feet. A series of smaller hissing sounds then followed, erupting in a series of loud bangs, and bright lights flashed behind the curtains that she had drawn earlier.

She hugged her arms tightly around her torso and shivered. She wore a rough knit jumper, its coarseness scratching at her skin, with skinny jeans that were slack at the waist and had begun to bag at the knees. She'd lost a stone in weight in the last year, but she refused to buy new clothes.

She was startled by the cracking sound as sparks seemed to dance across the roof of her house, raining down in a night so cold it stole your breath away.

She pulled back the curtain of the nearest window and saw the bright coloured fragments scatter in the sky.

Fireworks had been let off from the house somewhere across the road, at the bottom of the drive.

She released the breath she hadn't realised she had been holding. She caught her reflection in the cold glass. Dark circles rimmed her eyes, and what little lines she did have across her forehead had deepened.

She imagined she saw Him beside her, staring at their reflections. His eyes, seen moments before in the nightmare, still black pits.

Hollow.

That summed up how she felt.

She looked at Him, then squeezed her eyes shut. 'Go away,' she said. When she opened them again, she felt the fog in her mind begin to clear a little. 'It's just a nightmare,' she said in the darkness.

After several moments passed she went back to the sofa and felt for her phone, her head feeling thick, disorientated. She unlocked the screen and checked the time.

18:36.

She had less than an hour before she was due to be at the annual firework display in Haverbridge. She contemplated not going, and pulled up the last text message she had sent, about to send her excuses.

She flicked on the light, and looked around the room, phone clutched in a sweaty palm. The house looked as it had done a few hours ago when she'd decided to just rest her eyes.

The night terrors took their toll on her. Rarely a week went past without being woken by them. Grabbing a short sleep here and there when she could had been her way of coping with it for many months now.

She knew it couldn't go on like this, but no way would she ask for help.

This was something she had to overcome on her own… and she would, in her own time.

*

She headed up the stairs and put on clean clothes, dumping the sweat drenched ones in the laundry basket, before heading to the bathroom.

She stared at her reflection in the mirror of the medicine cabinet.

Her skin had taken on a grey tinge of late and her frame appeared gaunt. Others had noticed, made comments. She lowered her eyes, casting a critical eye over her stomach when she lifted her jumper.

For someone who had once taken so much pride in her appearance, even she knew her standards had slipped a little.

She could hear her colleagues' comments in her head, whispering their concerns when they thought she couldn't hear them.

The self-pity crept in briefly, before it was pushed aside by the resilience she was known for. Soft, kind eyes became hard once again, a steely glare cast at her reflection in the mirror.

Fuck them, she thought.

She splashed cold water on her cheeks, determined she would leave the house and at least appear to be social.

This is not me, she told herself inwardly. I am in control.

Minutes later she was sitting in her car, engine running, heaters clearing the fog from the windows, tapping out a text.

You twisted my arm. On my way.

She pressed send before she could change her mind, put the phone in her pocket, and headed down the drive, mindful of the ice on the ground that twinkled in the brightness of the headlights.

She headed out of Hexton, and on towards Haverbridge, taking the scenic route, passing another sleepy village before the road cut through open fields.

She sucked in deep breaths when her mind started to clog with the familiar uneasiness of before. When she breathed, she could see the faintness of her breath expelled like puffs of smoke from between parched lips.

She turned the heating up a little more and tried to relax her body. Tight muscles soon began to relax into the seat. She felt the ache in her jaw and realised she'd been clenching her teeth together. She swallowed hard, focusing on the stillness of the country road, where frosty skeletal trees and bushes hugged it from both sides.

This year autumn appeared to have bypassed the UK entirely, and winter seemed to have taken the Hertfordshire town of Haverbridge, where she worked, into its relentless clutches much earlier than anticipated.

The large town had a population just short of 100,000 people and was situated some thirty miles from London. Haverbridge had grown over the years, becoming a commuters' paradise for those who worked in the capital but didn't want the bright lights of the colourful city in their backyard at home time. They wanted to say goodnight and really mean it.

Haverbridge was beautiful, yet ugly in so many ways – not dissimilar to other towns and cities up and down the UK – but Haverbridge had a different side to it. It was exceptionally beautiful in the darker months. What made it so striking, you couldn't easily describe; it just was.

The summer sun had long disappeared and the threat of early snowfall was a very real one.

For Claire, it was bad news. It made her fall easily into an abyss of self-loathing and bitterness, something she was prone to. The cold haunted her like a restless spirit and the chill was not good for her bones.

She glanced at the clock on the dash. She'd be a little late, but she knew Stefan would understand. She took the road leading to the motorway, and as she travelled at a steady 60mph, she looked at the road ahead, bright lights and traffic rushing past, through eyes that didn't quite feel like her own.

ONE DAY EARLIER

The man glanced around the car park and stifled a yawn as he looked down at his watch. He snuggled down further in the driver's seat; his thick padded coat was warm and inviting. He was sleepy and wished he could close his eyes.

The body in the boot – it's now or never.

His car was the only one there, almost hidden in the darkness. The cold air hit his face when he emerged from the car. It caught him unawares and he gasped instinctively, clasping his hands tightly together, rubbing them for warmth.

When he stood in front of the boot, his hand hovered over it as if he had second thoughts about what he was about to do, as if the final act were any worse than what came before it.

The light inside the boot cast a dull light on what was inside. He looked down at the black bin liners, wrapped crudely around the majority of the body. Only the bottom half of the legs were left uncovered.

The once soft skin now looked waxy. He thought back to when those legs had kicked out at him, before he'd secured them together.

Shame, really.

This one had had such spirit.

His hands reached in and grabbed cold limbs. He began to haul the body carefully out onto the frozen ground.

CHAPTER 2

5th November

There was a huge whizz followed by a violent crack in the night sky as the firework exploded high above their heads.

Claire jumped, instinctively closing the gap between herself and Detective Inspector Stefan Fletcher. He glanced down at her, his tall thin frame buried in an oversized padded coat against the cold. He saw her tense, and ease herself a step or two away from his personal space.

He smiled inwardly.

Aloof and sometimes proud, with walls built so high that they could rarely be penetrated. These were Claire's bad points, but she wore the traits with pride, giving off the impression that nothing could faze her.

Stefan knew different though.

After a high-profile case the previous year, Claire had put Haverbridge back on the map. Not always for the right reasons, but in Claire's case, any publicity had turned out to be fairly good publicity. She'd become one of Haverbridge CID's best, and had ridden out the storm, forging some close allies amongst her team, and Stefan was one of those people.

Despite Claire's misgivings about herself, she was extremely good at her job, and respected. No one would've been justified in calling her incompetent, or an easy target.

But Stefan had seen the signs, seen the cracks appear since that investigation. It had exhausted her, changed her forever in some ways.

The murdered priest case – how could anyone come back from that completely unscathed?

More fireworks whizzed skywards, drawing appreciation from the assembled mass around them. Stefan watched Claire from the corner of his eye. Whilst she looked to the heavens with everyone else, he saw the glassy look of her eyes. She was there in body but the mind was elsewhere.

'The kids would've loved this,' he said, his blue eyes scrutinising every twitch in her face when she heard him speak.

She glanced at him, gave a weak smile.

Stefan would normally take his kids to Haverbridge Lake's annual firework display, but his ex had changed her plans and he was expected to fall in line. He felt sad at not seeing his children but, surprisingly, he was very glad to have Claire's company.

In the past, Claire had had a few detective sergeants as her subordinates. Most hadn't lived up to her expectations but Stefan had been different. Having watched him come into his own, and making DI in recent years, she'd relished the chance to work alongside him permanently, where possible, as an equal, despite the difference in rank.

'They wouldn't have liked the cold, Fletch' she said, at length. 'The kids I mean.'

Stefan shook his head. 'Kids are tougher than they look.'

He saw her bite her lip. Claire didn't have children, or was ever likely to. Sometimes he felt like he was walking on eggshells in the last year. He didn't know what might upset her, so topics of conversation sometimes felt stilted.

Claire had her vulnerabilities as much as the next person. She had closed the gap between them earlier, something she'd never admit to if he called her out on it.

He'd noticed her weight loss, although he'd never say so. Her face had become more chiseled, cheek bones sharp.

Those ice-blue eyes looked permanently sad.

Stefan pushed his hands deeper into his pockets, trying to draw the life back into them. The night air was bone-chilling and the breath of the eager crowd hung in the air like thick white smoke.

He breathed in deeply; the air was heavy with the smell of bonfire smoke and fast food. He followed the line of people surrounding the huge lake and caught sight of the fast food stands. His stomach growled.

'Do you want anything to eat?'

Claire was rubbing her gloved hands together for warmth and her breath cast out in clouds around her face. She shook her head.

'Mind if I?'

Claire either didn't hear him or was too cold to answer. He shrugged and pushed his way through the crowd.

When he returned, hotdog in hand, Claire saw he looked troubled.

'What's wrong?'

Stefan gave half a shrug as he bit into his hotdog. 'I wanted to talk about DS Crest.'

Claire waved her hand, dismissing the very mention of his name. 'Not while I'm enjoying myself.'

'He speaks highly of you too.'

'Look, I really don't need this right now.' Her voice turned hard. 'I couldn't care less what that Armani-wearing-metrosexual-walking-cliché thinks of me.' She turned to face him.

Detective Sergeant Elias Crest was a new addition to her team.

The last man Detective Superintendent Clifton Donahue had placed under Claire's watchful eye had lasted barely six months. Claire had hoped DS Crest would be different, but they hadn't exactly hit it off.

Elias had transferred from Merseyside after spending five years in Liverpool South's CID team. There were official reasons given for the transfer, but the real reason wasn't quite so clear cut.

Claire knew that more than anyone.

A steeliness had returned to her voice. 'I take it by you mentioning him, he's been kicking off?'

'He's found a few things out about you from your reputation alone. He thinks you hate him.'

'He's close... Hate is such a terrible word. He knows where the door is and it's open any time, day or night, if he wants to walk...'

Stefan nodded to himself, taking in her words. Then his eyes met hers. He saw the seriousness in her face.

'I'm sure it's nothing,' he said. 'Just wanted you to know he's not happy.'

'Boo-fucking-hoo.' Stefan rolled his eyes and she leaned in closer to him. 'I'm not going to apologise for who I am, Fletch. I have to be hard and when arrogant screw-ups like him are sent my way, they need to learn to toe the line.'

Stefan narrowed his eyes. 'Screw-ups?'

She fell silent.

'Is it something to do with why he was transferred? 'Cos you do realise not everybody is buying into the close-to-family excuse.'

She kept her face neutral.

Stefan shrugged. 'People talk, that's all I'm saying.'

'It's nothing, Fletch, forget I said anything.' She felt the weight of his stare but avoided his eyes. 'So,' she said, trying to deflect attention away from Crest, 'what happened to that girl you were dating? Doesn't she like fireworks?'

Stefan grimaced. 'Leigh couldn't make it. I think she's about to chuck me anyway.'

'Really?'

Stefan gave a mock laugh. 'Don't pretend to care.'

'You're questioning my sincerity?'

'Personally, I always thought that divorce of yours left you dead inside.'

She gave half a smile. 'Touché, Stefan.'

'Oh, first name for once. I'm flattered. Did I touch a nerve?'

'Simon didn't cut it enough as a husband to even come close to touching a nerve, Fletcher.'

Stefan glanced at her. 'I heard DCI Forester is dating again.'

Claire raised an eyebrow and sniffed with indifference. 'You shouldn't listen to gossip.' She knew he was talking in jest and on the surface she grinned, but inside she felt a little sad.

Claire had been married to DCI Simon Forester for three years. He served at Welwyn Garden City police station, some eight miles from Haverbridge. They'd met at a charity ball, and after a brief engagement, they'd married too quickly without really knowing anything about each other.

The relationship had turned sour after the first year and the pressure of their jobs helped drive a wedge between them, and they became more friends than lovers.

When Claire had risked an affair with another man, they became even less than that and it was Claire who filed for divorce, and immediately reverted back to her maiden name.

Surprisingly, despite feeling little for Simon, she felt the twinge of jealousy. It wasn't as if her love life was flourishing. Her dedication to her job didn't allow much time for a personal life, but she hated the thought there could be anyone else in her ex's life. Certainly not someone who could compare to her anyway.

As more fireworks erupted overhead, Claire pushed Stefan towards the edge of the lake, until they stood just feet from the edge of the frozen water.

He shoved the rest of his hotdog into his mouth and grinned. 'You're aware you're supposed to be playing the part of the submissive Leigh, aren't you?'

'Submissive? You're well shot of her, Fletch, by the sounds of it.'

'When I spend my working days with you, I need dominant like a hole in the head.'

'It's less crowded here, stop moaning,' Claire said. Then she saw Stefan's eye was trained on something else off to their left.

'You see that?' he said.

ACKNOWLEDGEMENTS

Thank you to the team at Carina UK, especially my editor, Clio Cornish. You have contributed so much to help shape this novel to be the best it possibly could be. Thank you for championing the DCI Claire Winters series from the start.

Thank you to all the other authors from the Carina UK family. What a talented and supportive bunch you are!

Further thanks must go to my Mum and Dad, for everything they have done and continue to do, to support me and my writing. To my husband, Daniel, for supporting our little family, allowing me to write full time.

And finally, thanks to my good friend, and literary guardian angel, Willow Thomas. You've been there since the first draft. Your unwavering support and sense of humour have kept me going, and for all you have done for me, I will be eternally grateful.